The Shards of the Conduit

Book 1 of Eiden Ascendant

S.N. Yusuf

Edited by Gina Kammer & Bryan Thomas Schmidt

Paperback ISBN: 978-1-0695458-0-0
Ebook ISBN: 978-10695458-1-7
Publisher: Sarah Yusuf
First Edition

This is a work of fiction. Names, characters, places, and incidents are the product of the author's imagination or are used fictitiously. Any resemblance to actual persons, living or dead, or actual events is purely coincidental.

Cover design by Miblart.com
Maps and interior art by Sarah Yusuf

None of us are free, until all of us are free.

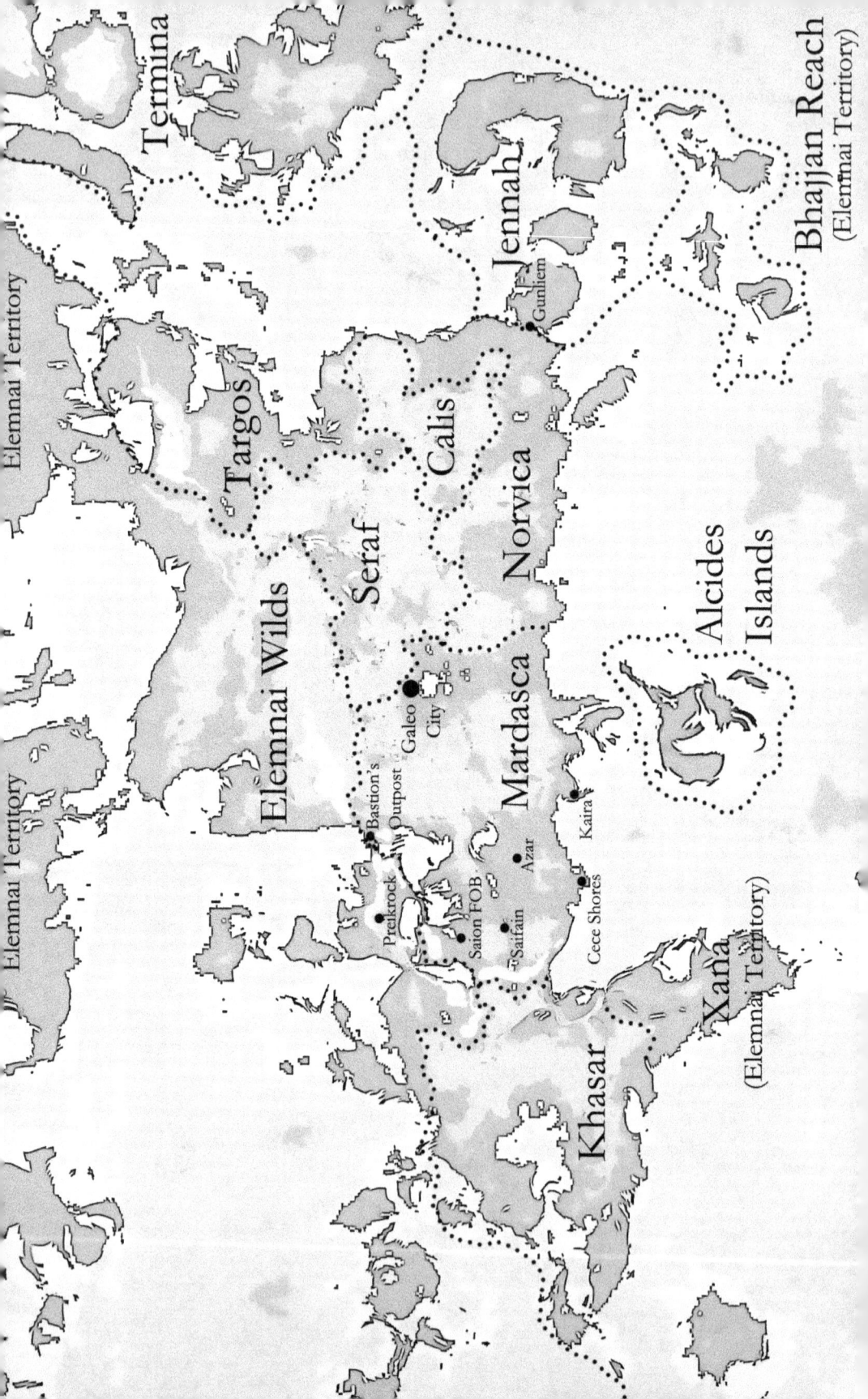

CHAPTER 1

SPECTER

Malek always knew this job would get him killed. Despite that harrowing thought, he always managed to survive. He knew how to balance risk and action and had become adept at making calculated decisions at the snap of a finger. This time felt different. It was the first time in years that Malek found himself completely incapable of calming his nerves. His eyes dropped to the floor, and he swallowed hard to soothe his parched throat. He plucked at his fitted tactical uniform, which clung too tightly to his skin. The armor and gear bore down heavily, suffocating him. Everything was off, as though a decade of successful assignments couldn't prepare him for what was coming. For once, Malek didn't think that he could do this.

Don't lose your head.

Gripping his rifle, Malek rested the barrel against his chest and shoulder as he leaned forward in his seat. His posture stiffened into an arch, and ran a thousand scenarios through his mind. Not one of them alleviated the tension. Loose wires and canvas loops swayed within the dimly lit cabin as turbulence shook the Revenant, their military personnel transport and his one-way ticket into the unknown.

One of the panels flickered, sending a flash over Malek's corneas. Just like that, he was back under the blinding fluorescents. Tufts of hair that faded from black to white fell into his lap as the razor buzzed across his scalp, exposing fresh skin to the cold, sterile air. Wires bit into his temples, his chest, and his arms. *It will only hurt for a moment—the damage won't last long.* That haunting voice drowned in the hum of machines, only for it all to fade into the steady drone of the air transport. Breathing hard, Malek lifted his eyes, relieved that his team's faces were all drawn to the abused metal floor. But... seeing them would have been validating. Though if he had his own doubts, there wouldn't be any point in looking to the others.

A faint red glow emanating from the panels overhead cast very little light over the two dozen men and women sharing this humid, claustrophobic space. Despite the compact hold, Malek couldn't shake his isolation, until an abrupt jab into his ribs from the soldier next to him buried the thought. Malek shoved the elbow away with a nudge of his arm.

"Come on, Specter. Now you're making me nervous." Jace's gruff voice was low enough to be masked by the hum of the Revenant's engine.

Malek knew things were serious when his best friend addressed him by his call sign. "We have *every* reason to be slagging ourselves."

Jace scoffed, pulling down his black face mask that shielded the lower half of his tan face, revealing a wide, wry smile over his unshaven skin. "Yeah. But, unlike some people, I actually gotta fear for my life." Jace laughed.

Malek hated it when he said things like that. "...I don't know what you're talking about. A Fireborne could easily zero me out."

"We'll see about that." After a moment, Jace leaned forward and spoke, "Damn... A Fireborne. Ever seen one before?"

Fireborne. Masters of ignition and manipulation of heat and fire, and one of the four ruthless tribes of the sapient Elemnai. To Malek, they were just the *other* slag species infringing on his and every other human's survival on their shared world of Eiden. As far as he knew, they would rather incinerate the human race, if not for the long-standing armistice muzzling their thirst for blood—according to the Alliance, anyway.

Malek still couldn't wrap his head around it being here in the first place. Why infiltrate and murder innocent people in a random lab? What was worth the risk of showing their faces after 200 years of peace, only to compromise it?

"No. No one has." Malek shook his head. "Not for a long time." *That* was the terrifying fact that knotted his insides. What on Eiden were they walking into? Malek always needed to know what was coming. He needed to know so that he could survive, and not just in the physical sense. There was always more at stake for him compared to the others. He wished they knew that. The clang of heavy boots over the metal flooring broke his train of thought before he could spiral again.

A figure emerged from the front of the cabin, stepping between the dual rows of soldiers seated across the benches at the aircraft's rear. Malek fixated on Commander Rhodes's menacing frown. It was grimmer than usual.

"Valiant Squad," Commander Rhodes bellowed, seizing everyone's undivided attention. He gripped a canvas loop that slung from the ceiling of the craft as it jolted. An increase in pressure pushed against Malek's cranium. The adrenaline kick-started his system, knowing a dip in altitude meant the drop zone was approaching. "Change of plans, grunts. Facility's in worse shape than stated in the initial reports. Jennai STG made contact—"

"Jennai STG?" Malek whispered to Jace.

"Special Task Group. Like us. An Operational Detachment," Jace replied quickly, refocusing on their commander.

"—and all comms are dead. Last check-in reported mass casualties among the facility's personnel. JSTG went full force, so we're changing our tactics for a more subtle entrance. We're doing four splits. Once inside, stick close to your six-man team and recon sections as assigned. ASFOM will attempt to re-establish power to the grid so we can access surveillance cameras and get a mark on the Fireborne. Once the location of the Fireborne has been determined, you will report on its status and fall back. The objective will pivot to provide security while Search and Rescue extracts survivors. If contact is made, be aware that support cannot immediately assist. We are under orders to lock down the facility, and anyone in between the exits and the Fireborne, officers included." Commander Rhodes narrowed his eyes on Malek, a hardened expression on his weathered face.

Malek dropped his chin to hide the roll of his eyes, grasping the subtext. It was a friendly reminder not to stray from orders...again. He couldn't help it. Malek never trusted his commander's leadership, not even after a decade of assignments together. Rhodes never kept these things close to the chest, never taking a chance where sheer victory was just one high-risk maneuver away. Could Malek do any better? A weapons officer like him still had some rungs to climb, but truthfully, he wasn't even sure if he was cut out for leadership. He was always one slag situation away from losing his head—repeating the mantra just to keep it together was hardly a worthy quality for a captain.

"So, try your best not to make contact. Barbecue is not on the menu today." Rhodes turned away from the group and faced an aide, who presented him with a datapad. Its ghostly light trembled across the commander's face as the craft wavered, and Malek caught the grimace through the datapad's transparent face.

"First split, Captain Anthem with Vale, Specter, Jace, Killem, and Nook, jump first, head for the labs located in the east wing on the first, second, and third floors of the north R&D building. Next split: Captain Helio with Gax, Junkie—"

Jace elbowed Malek again. "Rhodes wants me to flatline with you. He knows that the Fireborne is in those labs. Not that you'll die anyway."

"Slag, stow it, already. The joke is old." The banter earned Malek and Jace a scowl from their commander, and the two shut up.

After a moment, Malek suppressed a groan when Jace dared to say another word. "I'll quit calling you Specter when you finally take a hit that knocks you out of the game...for longer than a day."

Malek exhaled sharply. He was already struggling to keep calm and could've gone without another reminder about the *history* behind his call sign.

An even, high-pitched voice filled the cabin from the inlaid speakers hidden overhead. "GT-12 Wraith, Revenant inbound. Ten seconds to DZ-one insertion. Eyes up."

The Revenant jolted again, causing some ambient lights to rattle and blink in and out of existence. Malek gripped his rifle, anticipating the upcoming maneuver. The hull continued to vibrate, and pressed his feet into the floor to prevent himself from falling forward. The engine hissed as the aircraft tilted.

"Facility specs are on your portables. You have your orders, now—"

The Revenant leveled, and the wind screamed in Malek's ears as the rear gate slid open, and the platform descended. His heart lurched as he and the other two dozen members of Valiant Squad rose to their feet, readying for deployment.

"Welcome to Gunliem, grunts! North R&D is up first. First split, move it!" Commander Rhodes bellowed, and six members of Valiant Squad—including Malek—charged out across the lowered platform. His knees absorbed the impact of the hard landing when he dropped onto the concrete rooftop below.

Malek glanced at their transport as it roared toward the other research facilities marked by the same sleek, oblong-shaped buildings of black glass and brilliant steel, buried in banks of a lush rainforest, copies of the one on which he stood. It left him feeling vulnerable. Breaking the squad into four splits didn't make sense to Malek. They were weaker apart. All twenty-four should've landed here, especially given what happened to the JSTG. He forced himself to stay on task. They needed to find the damned thing and get out.

Malek hustled along with his teammates as they approached a large steel door at the opposite end of the roof. He narrowed his eyes, rushing past Anthem, who gestured at him to get into the building. The forceful slam shook him as Anthem closed the door and pursued him into the darkness. Ever the diligent leader, Malek thought. Anthem never allowed her team to fall out of line but commanded her team with integrity, which he had never seen in Rhodes. Malek always appreciated that about her.

He caught a glimpse of his teammates' eyes when the stairwell lit up with the eerie glow from the portables strapped to their arms. They glanced at one another anxiously. It sent a shiver down Malek's spine. The chill of that cold, sterile room etched memories of darkness and solitude into him, forcing him to draw a sharp breath he didn't intend to take. The power was out, that's all it was. Again, he was thankful that no one saw his reaction.

"All right, boys," Anthem spoke in a hushed voice, as the rest drew near her. "Divert your comms to my channel. We break up into teams of two and begin the search on each floor. We'll keep the chatter to a minimum, but I want regular updates. Check in every ten."

Malek was the last to power up the armored touchscreen on his portable. The sight of the building's floor plan filled his view. He had briefly studied the contrasting white lines over a black backdrop while on the transport but hadn't deciphered the extent of the intertwining corridors until now. There were too many blind spots.

"We'll head through the floor access points at the east end of the building, which is directly below us. Each pair will take a floor per the commander's orders," Anthem continued. "Scout the loop and get to the east stairwells. If we don't find anything, we'll call it in and confirm the search for the basement. For now, just focus on our current assignment. Let's move out."

Malek followed as each soldier fell into place behind Anthem, carefully descending the narrow concrete stairs in single file, their mounted flashlights piercing the shadows in their path. The air stung with fumes of charred metals and glass, and something far more haunting: the unmistakable smell of burning flesh.

A faint hum rumbled in the distance, and a scraping sound spiked Malek's heart rate. His flashlight streamed across a collapsed stairwell, next to a large metallic set of double doors, with a large "3" imprinted in black across its face. He swallowed hard when he saw they couldn't travel any further. Shattered and blackened concrete steps abruptly ended the path ahead, destroyed so completely that Malek's light could barely make out the outlines of split rubble several floors below.

"Elevators," Anthem said, turning about and motioning for Malek to go. He understood immediately—take point and clear the corridor, while the others got to work setting up the rappelling devices. Leveling their weapons, Malek and Jace pressed against the door. Swiftly and silently, the two darted across the open corridors, their eyes in line with the optics mounted over the top of their rifles.

Malek blinked at the flashing yellow lights spinning incessantly every few meters along the hallway ceiling. The facility's emergency generators were operational, at least. Though it was better than being in the darkness, this new environment left him more on edge, with his muscles stiffening from the tension. What were probably porcelain floors, with lustrous walls and expansive glass windows spanning the length of the hall, were now smeared with dust, scorch marks, and blood. A first glance confirmed no movement. Malek gritted his teeth and steeled his nerves.

Malek gestured for Jace to take the corridor across the set of tall, stainless-steel doors marking the entrance of the first elevator, while he continued down this path. He only traversed several meters before he could hear the others carefully exit the stairwell, knowing through their shuffling and hushed vernacular that they had already begun opening the shaft. The clink of rappel devices echoed in the stark quiet of the lab corridors, but Malek focused ahead. His heart hammered in his chest as he inched forward, away from his team. He expected to find a few dead bodies, but this... *this* was bad. Malek's stomach dropped when he looked beyond the first set of glass windows.

Between the smoldering heaps of embers and ash, Malek spotted glassware scattered across granite workbenches, with charred and mangled equipment collapsed over walkways. He raised himself slowly, scanning the room with muscles straining to keep his movements slow and still.

Sweat beaded on Malek's brow as he locked onto the blackened skeletal remains of two victims in the corner. One had an arm over the other, as if shielding the colleague. Pretty admirable, all things considered... It might have even done some good. Malek marveled at the exposed meat on the colleague's trunk as it glistened under the sharp light. He cursed inwardly with a mix of awe at the Fireborne's power and disgust. Searching the room, he found more corpses with a growing knot in his core. The two-hundred-year peace agreement between the Elemnai and humans was as good as gone. This deepened his anxiety, adding to the sickening weight in his stomach. The longer the Fireborne prowled and murdered, the stronger and more brutal the Alliance's vengeance would be on the Elemnai... as a whole. Even a grunt like him, a special forces officer, knew it would be disastrous for both sides. They needed to find her *now*.

A clang from an object falling in the distance caused Malek's chest to tighten, painfully tugging at his ribs. Adrenaline surged through his flexed limbs as he whipped around. Nook jumped back from the elevator and approached again, this time slowly, directing his gaze up into the shaft and down again. He shook his head, and Anthem gestured for Malek and Jace to return.

"We have a problem," Anthem said in a low voice as the two approached. "The rafters up top are unstable. We have to take it slow. Nook and Killem will remain up on this floor. You two take the second floor, and Vale and I will take the first floor. Jace, you're up."

"Of course, I am." Jace muttered curses, tilted his head side to side, and rolled his shoulders. Malek knew this also meant that he was next. He couldn't shake the images of the labs, and the blackened remains that had been targeted to near perfection, maintaining the sterile whiteness of the floors and walls. He watched as Jace approached the rappel cables latched onto the ledge of the elevator opening, while the others hooked him in place. Anthem was staring at him, dissecting his expression with her eyes alone.

"I counted five bodies in this lab right here," he murmured, nodding toward the room next to the elevator. "How many rooms are on this floor?"

"At least a dozen. No survivors, I take it?" Anthem replied.

"I don't think they had a chance." Malek thought of the pair of colleagues, and that bit of charred flesh still clinging to its ribcage. He swallowed. Then he put on a wry smirk and scoffed. "It's been awhile since anyone went up against a Fireborne. I think these guys, including the JSTG, forgot what they were capable of."

"Wait...Are *you* telling *me* to be careful?" Anthem replied coyly, and Malek chuckled.

"I know I can be stupid sometimes—"

"All the time."

"Most of the time," Malek allowed. "But even I wouldn't push it on this one. The commander is right. If the fires are still burning, we need to leave. We can't fight her."

Anthem's cheeks rose under her mask. "I'm glad you're finally growing up, kiddo."

Their exchange got cut short by Vale. "Specter, Jace needs assistance opening the door."

With a nod from Anthem, Malek took a deep breath and proceeded to the elevator shaft. He swung his rifle over his back as the others quickly applied the harnesses to his suit. He had done this before, many times, but there was always a moment as he swung himself over the gaping darkness that his heart lodged in his throat and his skin tingled in anticipation. Jace's portable device, emitting a soft glow, acted like a beacon in the pitch-blackness below his feet. It took another deep breath before Malek finally released the tension in his jaw. He began his descent carefully at first. Then, once he was used to maneuvering, he urged himself to rappel at a much steadier pace. Hanging by a single wire in a narrow shaft didn't exactly grant him any meaningful escape routes. He reached Jace within moments, finding him with a pry bar provided to him by Nook. Jace had already wedged one end between the elevator doors.

"Help me pull this open," Jace grunted. "Grab it."

Malek adjusted his position to bring himself closer, striving to get a footing. He pushed his back against the threshold, allowing him to get a firmer grasp on the doors. This had better work.

"On three," Jace said, glancing at Malek. "One, two—"

Alarm klaxons blared momentarily before cutting out into silence, and Malek's stomach lurched from the shock. As the power came back on throughout the facility, a path of lights flared up the shaft. The elevator doors slammed open, causing Jace to drop the pry bar as he recoiled. "Slag!" he hissed, steadying himself.

Malek sucked in a breath to temper the adrenaline coursing through his system. When he saw the bar land several meters below, he sighed in relief. "It's fine. Let's get you unhooked."

Malek guided his friend, inwardly repeating the same mantra: *Don't lose your head. Everything's fine. Don't lose your head.* Jace swayed and landed on both feet at the edge of the second-floor threshold. Still suspended in the air, Malek begged his hands to stop trembling as he unfastened Jace from the rappel line. The receiver in his helmet crackled, and he heard Anthem's smooth voice chime through.

"You boys all right?"

Jace tapped his portable. "Yeah. Door's open. Going in."

The screech of metal grinding on metal seized Malek's attention. Time started to crawl, and each creak in the compromised metal became an ominous howl that rode over his thoughts. He looked up into the shaft, where he spotted several steel rafters beginning to bend. Small pieces of twisted metal tumbled toward him.

"Specter! Jace!" Anthem exclaimed, her voice abrasive through the receiver. "The rafters are coming down. Get onto the second floor, *now*!"

Panic swarmed over him. Malek snapped off the last carabiner locking Jace to the rappel line, his heart pounding hard in his ears. Jace heaved as he leaped out of the elevator shaft, landing on the lip of the second floor. The rafters screeched again, and a mass of rebar and steel dropped. They scraped by Malek, knocking him into an uncontrolled swivel.

"For frag's sake..." he muttered, desperately trying to unhook his own harness. He caught sight of Jace flailing his arm to seize him. Holding his breath, Malek swayed in the opposite direction, dread bubbling up inside with each failure to reach safety. Malek looked up at the splitting metal rafters. A larger and sharper piece cleaved through the elevator cable as it tumbled down the narrow shaft, grinding against the stone walls with an ear-piercing scrape.

Malek abandoned his harness, gripped the belay device, and released. His stomach jumped into his chest as he blindingly plummeted further into the darkness. Within a few horrifying seconds, he had a split second to slow his stop before he approached the end of his rope. He collapsed onto the roof of the elevator unit below with an onerous slam. That definitely lodged his stomach back where it belonged. He could hear the pieces of the rafters quickly coming down, their inertia only slowed by the shallow walls. Malek gasped for air, felt for a latch, and seized it. Bits of stone rained around him. A moment of absolute dread clawed at his chest. He threw open the hatch and dove into the elevator, as the debris came crashing overhead with a deafening boom.

Malek breathed hard, turning onto his side. His eyes trailed toward the open hatch, now completely blocked by several inches of concrete and steel. An echo of tumbling pebbles or remnants of the fallen structures rapped against the blockade. With another exhale of relief, he glanced at his surroundings. That was close.

Since the power had been restored, the elevator itself was lit by a fluorescent white glow, emanating from a pair of sconces on either side of the walls. To his surprise, the interior remained undamaged. He was safe—for now.

Malek's receiver crackled once again, and he adjusted his helmet to listen.

"Specter? Specter, do you copy? Slag!" Anthem cried.

He reached over and pressed a button on his portable. "Yeah, I copy." Malek rose to his feet and dusted himself off. "I'm inside the elevator."

"Slag, you're hard to kill."

"So I've been told. I've got good news, and bad news…and maybe some lukewarm news."

"Let's start with the bad news."

"The bad news is that my way back up is blocked, and we know that the stairs are inaccessible, which means I'm going to have to cross this floor either way."

"What floor are you on?"

"Basement." Malek's eyes scanned the digital face of the panel above the doors. "The good news is that I can search this floor, while I'm looking for an exit. The lukewarm news is all that noise probably gave the Fireborne the heads up I'm here."

"How is that lukewarm news?"

"Fulfills the mission objective. We need to get eyes on her."

"Right… Take it slow, and whatever you do, do not engage if you make contact. Updates every five from you."

"Copy that. And uh… make sure Jace has some company. He's definitely slagging himself by now."

"Frag you too, Specter," Jace sneered over the receiver.

"Over and out." Malek smiled to himself and leveled his rifle. He shook the adrenaline from his arms to slacken his muscles, and his heart slowed to a steady beat. He appreciated the moment of calm, for what he imagined would be a storm ahead. Malek reached over to the panel with iridescent backlighting and touched a button. The doors slid open with a haunting chime. *Find her, survive, and get the frag out.*

CHAPTER 2

SURVIVOR

The fluorescent bulbs were like needles in his eyes, giving Malek a headache with their incessant blinking. He wasn't sure if things were better now that the lights were back on. The damage on this floor looked undeniably worse. Coupled with the pronounced stench of burned flesh and something else...chemicals, Malek couldn't shake the unsettling feeling snaking up his spine. It was definitely the wrong place to scout alone. With his luck, he wondered if he would waltz into the Fireborne around the next bend. He swallowed hard, clearing the next corner with a sigh of relief, and kept his arms painfully steady, one finger on the trigger.

Could bullets even kill a Fireborne? Memories of secondary school crept from the recesses of his mind. Conventional weapons used in the last war, at least the primitive models from two hundred years ago, hadn't been effective against the Elemnai. Every kid between Mardasca and Termina grew up hearing terrifying stories of bullets bouncing off their unnatural skin or melting upon impact. Reverse engineering ancient tech to create nuclear ammunition made damn sure that the war ended in favor of the human race. An example had to be made only once before the Elemnai accepted that they were outgunned. That massacre was definitely one for the textbooks.

But the stories of the military's vast superiority over the Elemnai felt like an exaggerated lie. The Elemnai were supposed to be the things of nightmares, always one step away from completely annihilating human civilization. The increase in

16

reverse-engineered tech attempts successfully neutered the Elemnai to the point that the world seemed to have forgotten why they'd ever been afraid in the first place. *These* people, here in the lab, had been victims of their own ignorance. To be fair, Malek had never thought he would face an Elemnai either, let alone one that could wreak this much havoc.

"All good here. But lots of casualties." Malek tapped his portable, cautious not to raise his voice louder than the ambient noise.

"Understood," Anthem replied in a low tone. "We're finding more bodies up here. Any fresh signs of the Fireborne?"

"None so far."

At this point, he had passed several rooms, each one as charred as the last, littered with more skeletal remains and molten equipment. Malek was headed toward the next room when he heard the distinct hum of a low voice. His heart jolted, sending waves of shock through his system. A murmur broke through the buzz of snapped power cords emitting sparks and the distant rapping of an air duct system. He paused in his steps, listening again. The voice seemed much closer than before. Someone must be alive.

Malek's blood froze in his veins. A walking corpse limped slowly out of a lab several meters ahead. The half-incinerated man's white coat, burned to brown and black, swayed with each wavering step. He collapsed against the opposite wall of the corridor, his breaths quick and shallow. It was hard to suppress a cringe when the man rested his back against the surface, showing blackened arms trembling and reduced to bone and sinew.

Malek swallowed and carefully paced over, darting his eyes between his surroundings and back to the man. He kneeled in front of him. Malek guessed he had a few moments, at best. Most of the man's body was nothing more than charred limbs where ash met broken blood vessels, and peeling skin melded with the fabric of his clothes.

"Hey," Malek pulled down his mask, drawing the man's attention.

The man took a labored breath and moaned, and then his bulging eyes fixed desperately on Malek, who stifled a shudder when he held the man's agonized gaze.

"It's alright, I'm with the ASF. I'm gonna get you out of here, but I need to know where the Fireborne—"

With what little intact flesh remained on his hands, the man clawed at Malek's armored vest. Malek instinctively jerked away, despite knowing that the man couldn't possibly harm him.

"No..." The man hissed between ragged breaths. "Get the shard... And run."

"Shard? What shard?"

The man tore his grip from Malek with a gasp and attempted to reach for something in the pocket of his slacks. Malek's heart sank as the man released an agonized moan, watching the charred hand writhing under the task. Gently touching the man's shoulder to put him at ease, Malek searched the pocket instead, finding a small rectangular device. It was a miracle that it hadn't been damaged in the Fireborne's attack as he studied the bland, polished surface. Malek noticed a crease. He removed the small cap from the remaining unit clasped in his palm with his thumb and forefinger. It was some kind of interface device but not one that he was familiar with.

"Vault... Specimen Lab...here..." The man weakly gestured to his belt loop, where Malek saw a black fob mounted on a clip. His breath quickened momentarily, and Malek's heart jumped when he heard the familiar rattle escape those peeling lips.

"Stay with me! Sir!"

After a forceful exhale, the man never drew another breath despite his mouth remaining agape. Moments, just like Malek thought. Commander Rhodes would probably scold him later for not ignoring him and staying on task. Malek flattened his lips at the thought of *that* kind of slag reprimand and unclipped the fob. Curious, he lifted his eyes to the lab coat and searched the front lapel. A metal rectangle clung to the fabric, now blackened. Malek rubbed his thumb across its surface and read the name 'Dr. M. Costa'.

"Dr. Costa, you're going to be a hero. Ah, mace," he whispered, feeling the regret morph into guilt. Malek tapped his portable. *New plan: find her, get the shard, survive, and get the frag out.* "Anthem, do you copy?"

The comms crackled before his captain's voice broke through. "Copy. What happened?"

"I've got a Dr. Costa here who was alive long enough to tell me what the Fireborne is after. I have a chance to retrieve it."

"Negative, you'll do nothing until we get there."

"How long?"

"Nook and Killem ran into survivors. Vale, Jace, and I need more time clearing this floor. Wait for us by the elevators at the entrance of the west building."

Malek frowned, feeling the seconds pass faster than ever. Before he could smother the words, they escaped, with more conviction than he was willing to let on, "I know where I need to go."

"Negative! You are not authorized to proceed."

"Get Vale to pass the intel up, will you?"

Anthem exhaled sharply. After a brief pause, she muttered, "Hold your position."

Malek barely had a moment to stew in his frustration before realizing he was no longer alone...for the second time. Adrenaline raged through his body, sending waves of magma flowing to his extremities.

A new voice from directly behind sent him into a momentary paralysis, "Hands where I can see them, pretty boy." The young woman spoke with a fluid accent.

Malek finally released a breath. His heart pulsated so intensely that it nearly deafened his racing thoughts. Rising to his feet and lifting his hands in the air, he twisted his neck to catch a glimpse of his captor. Malek recognized the outline of a tactical get-up before she snapped at him again.

"Weapon on the ground. Now," she snarled in a low voice. It was a good thing Malek had a knack for recognizing languages and accents—the perk of having been sent across the reaches of Eiden on past military assignments. His party trick, as he liked to call it. Once Malek understood who she was, he didn't need to panic. There was no danger here, but he needed *her* to figure that out, too. He calmly pulled the rifle by its strap anyway and gently released it onto the floor as a gesture of cooperation. While his eyes remained lowered, he watched his rifle slide away.

"You're from Jennah?" he called. Slag, what was the full name of the unit? "Jennai STG? We're on the same side."

"Who are you? What did that man say to you?" she demanded, cutting him off.

Malek carefully turned around, studying the soldier standing in front of him. She leveled her rifle at his head. He didn't flinch, but she staunchly maintained her aim. If he could exude enough calmness, maybe she'd catch on. Malek recognized her nation's colors of blue and green emblazoned on the shoulder of her charcoal-tinted military uniform, and on her helmet that looked way too big for her head. He noticed parts of her suit were scorched and torn. She must have been a survivor of the lost JSTG unit. Her lips and cheeks flushed pink against her beige skin as she breathed hard. Those eyes, though... they caught him off guard. Large, upturned hazel eyes glared at him from under the helmet, while raven hair matted in sweat clung to her small jawline.

This woman was... interesting. Who was he kidding? *Wrong place, wrong time, idiot.* He immediately dismissed *that* train of thought, before he could daydream about asking for her number. "I'm with the ASF, Alliance Special Forces," Malek spoke evenly. "We were sent here after the JSTG made contact. See?" he tilted his shoulder, enough to show the ASF insignia on the arm of his onyx military uniform, with his call-sign stitched below the abstract winged design.

"Specter, huh? Where's the rest of your squad?"

"On the upper floors. I came down the elevator shaft. Mostly by accident."

"Oh, so that was *you*! You made a great entrance. Knocked around some rubble. Got the survivors out, and the Fireborne off our tails."

"Happy to help an ally. Where's your team?"

The woman frowned and said through gritted teeth, "Gone."

"And the Fireborne?"

"Injured, but still dangerous."

After a short pause, Malek dropped his hands, but the woman didn't react. He could see that her poise was slacking. This was his chance to get her to back down. "Kei, is it?"

"I never told you my—"

"It's on your shoulder, too," Malek said flatly, and stifled a chuckle when Kei inched her body sideways to hide her arms, glaring at him. Damn it, she was cute. Malek kept smiling to break the tension. He'd always been told he had a contagious smile, on the rare occasions he genuinely did.

Kei sighed and lowered her weapon. "I'm just tired of holding this thing up...I've been dodging the Fireborne for hours."

"Hours? Slag."

"*Se*," Kei acknowledged in Jennai and winced, bending over with one hand on her knee. "I'm so hungry."

Malek jumped at the sound of Anthem's voice, "Specter, come in."

He tapped his portable. "I'm here. I'm with one of the JTSG. Name's Kei. She's alone. Her team is dead."

"She got eyes on the target?"

"Confirmed that she's still down here but didn't follow Kei. Fireborne might still be after this thing...this 'shard.' Could be what brought the Fireborne in the first place..." Malek paused and glanced at Kei, who fixed him with a skeptical look. "The shard is in the specimen lab. There's a vault, which seems only to be accessible by key...the one given to me by this Dr. Costa. We can get it before she does. I have support now. Kei and I can retrieve the item."

Anthem could be heard murmuring on the comms, but Malek assumed she was passing along the new intel. Her voice came through the receiver again, stark and crisp, "Specter, Commander Rhodes has been updated. Valiant Squad and ASF support are forming a perimeter around the complex. You are confirmed to proceed, acknowledging that you are without assistance from the squad and Primary Team. Do me a favor. Keep the updates coming every two... or ping me, at least."

"Copy that." Malek knew Commander Rhodes had only agreed because of his obvious disdain for Malek. Rhodes was probably thrilled at the thought of needing to replace him, which made Malek doubt surviving his little plan.

Jace confirmed this over the receiver. "Nice knowing you, buddy," he muttered in a low, deadpan voice.

"Jace, if I don't make it, tell your sister I said hi. Over."

"Frag you, man."

Malek turned to face Kei, whose eye twitched in searing frustration. "Were you planning on asking if I wanted to join you?"

"No. But you're going to. You know our odds will be better if we stick together. Besides, do you have anything better to do?"

Kei's eyes rounded. "*Se*! Staying alive."

"Anyway, do you know anything about a specimen lab?" He gestured to the remains of Dr. Costa. "Doc here mentioned something about it."

"Passed by it." She gripped her assault rifle and stood tensed. Her voice was tempered, somewhere between solemn and trembling. "It's... where the team..."

Malek cursed himself. He would hate retracing those steps where he lost his fellow officers. Malek reached for her arm, and she snapped from her daze. "You did what you could. And more. You're a survivor. It's a win, Kei. So come on...let's go do something stupid and try to get home."

Kei glanced from his hand on her shoulder, then back to him. The fatigue from her face lifted. She passed him his rifle and gestured for Malek to follow her. He hadn't been lying. They were in this together, whether they liked it or not. If they were going to survive, Malek needed someone to watch his back. The pair readied themselves and crept back into the darkness of the lab charred by the inferno of the Fireborne.

Malek understood how Kei had been evading the Fireborne for as long as she claimed. The cavernous basement halls morphed into a labyrinth. There were no glass windows or walls, and all the rooms had been sealed with heavy steel doors, each marked with vague descriptions over slabs of sheet metal. It left a creeping, uneasy tension swelling at the back of Malek's head. If Kei could hide this well, so could the Fireborne. It sent another shiver running down his spine.

Malek jolted when Kei seized his armored vest and pulled him back. Before he could shoot her a sharp glance, a muffled voice echoed from the depths of the intertwining corridors. Malek narrowed his eyes as far as he could see. A red-orange glow swayed against the uneven walls, like a light given off by a flame. *She* was close.

Following Kei, Malek urgently approached a dual set of doors at the mouth of a junction. They passed from a cafeteria and then through a large, commercial kitchen, slowing their steps as their boots rapped against ceramic tiled floors. Their feet peeled away after every footfall as Kei led him around a large cooking area, past several fridges, including a walk-in cooler and freezer, and beyond a large shutter gate that had been sealed closed. She pointed at it and looked at Malek with a nod. It took him a moment to understand. Judging from the interior steel cage visible between the gaps in the shutter, it must have been some kind of self-contained elevator. He knew this could be an alternate exit route. If Kei hadn't used it yet, there must have been a reason. Noise, maybe?

Malek pursued Kei as she neared another set of doors. He finally allowed himself to take in a full breath at the sight of the dismal halls devoid of that fiery glow. Kei tugged on Malek's arm, and she pointed to one of the overhead signs. His anticipation spiked as he read the words "Specimen Lab" with an arrow pointing ahead.

"Anthem," Malek murmured, touching his portable. "Fireborne is close. Will ping you. We're staying out of sight."

"Understood, Specter. ASFOM can see you through the functioning cams, but long-range communicators can't reach you. Rhodes is sending another split and will reach the basement in forty-five minutes. Do what you have to and get out."

It wasn't long before Malek forced down his shock as a dozen dead soldiers scattered throughout the main corridor filled his view. Everyone wore the same uniform as Kei, with Jennah's national colors on the STG emblem. Only theirs had melted to the flesh of their mutilated bodies. Some soldiers were lucky enough to have their faces preserved. At least their families could see them one last time, partially intact anyway, and free from the horrifying vision of their brutal murder.

Malek's eyes studied their surroundings. The assault left this area wrought with scorched surfaces and shattered stone walls where the bullets penetrated the structure. It had been a hell of a fight. It was unwarranted, but Malek felt suddenly ashamed that he and Kei stood here over the corpses of Jennah's most formidable military units, very much alive.

He watched Kei briefly scrutinize bodies as she passed them. Maybe she hoped one of them had survived, after all. Her gaze darkened with each fallen team member. She stopped at one body of an older man, whose eyes bulged from his skull, blood caked on his cheek and jaw and staining his peppered beard crimson. Malek knew who he was the moment she stopped. A gut-wrenching feeling lurched from within, forcing him to purge thoughts of dead teammates from his past. Graeme—one daring maneuver on his part made damn sure that the rest of the split survived. It had been during one of Malek's initial missions. Knowing that Rhodes probably wished it was Malek who flatlined that day, and not his second in command, cast a long shadow of guilt that followed Malek on every subsequent assignment since.

"Your commander?" Malek asked her gently, and she nodded. "How did you get away?"

"...I was knocked out for a bit. Her fire attacks, well... the blast is concussive. Woke up to find my team gone. Stupid *kutibusu*." Kei shook her head. "Let's go. Almost there."

Malek watched her move away, unable to shake the despair clawing in his chest. A single death in the special forces group was always difficult to process...but to lose a whole team? He wondered if he should have said more, stealing one last look at her commander. At this angle, Malek noticed burn marks forming a shadow of a five-fingered grip around his throat. They couldn't risk physical contact. The Fireborne's touch alone would cauterize their skin.

Soon, Malek stood side by side with Kei in front of another set of dual metal doors. He swallowed hard. It was becoming harder to temper that fear as he met with more and more examples of her fury. The sheen of the surface had been marred by what seemed like an onslaught of force and fire, denting them where the impact of her flames scorched the doors black. Relieved that the Fireborne hadn't passed through yet, Malek reached into his pocket. Dr. Costa's last words penetrated him as he swiped the fob over the panel to his right. *Vault. Specimen*

Lab. That damned thing had better be in there. A small beep chimed, and Malek cautiously opened the doors with ease.

Iridescent light flooded his vision when he entered the room, almost blinding him as it reflected off sleek, white finishings against steel workbenches. Machine-operated equipment, appearing almost alien to him, filled the space with each encircling empty glass containment units. Malek's attention went to a metal vault fixed within a tiled wall at the far end of the room, about half a meter across in each dimension. A datapad hung recessed into the wall beside it. Malek nodded to the vault, and Kei acknowledged him by raising her rifle to watch his back as they approached. Inwardly, he was impressed. She may have been foreign to the ASF, but it seemed so easy to communicate and read each other's moves.

His thoughts were violently interrupted when the air became acidic, stinging Malek's senses. A metallic burn clawed up Malek's mouth and stopped his breath short. His pulse kicked, and he cut his eyes to Kei to see if she felt it. Nothing...her eyes remained fixed on her surroundings. "Why does it taste like a battery in here?" He hadn't meant to voice his disgust out loud, but Kei responded anyway.

"Do... you lick a lot of batteries, Specter?"

Malek glared at her while a smirk played at her lips. He made a face before approaching a datapad at the end of the lab. It was functional, flashing the words "Insert Key" and "Unlock".

Malek lifted the device from his belt and glanced at Kei, who shrugged in uncertainty, keeping her rifle leveled. He removed the device cap and inserted the metal end into the port located next to the datapad. A new scribe flashed on the screen, reading "Administrator Access Granted" in green with a marquee directly below it. Blowing out a long breath, Malek slid his finger over the marquee and triggered the opening sequence. It was lucky that there wasn't a missing passcode or secondary key.

Gears whirred and locks unhinged from within the vault. A slight hiss escaped as the heavy iron door released, opening no more than a few centimeters. The anticipation tugged at every nerve in his body. It was almost unbearable. Malek reached over and spread the door wide. He was speechless, and so was Kei, for a moment.

"It looks like a piece of garbage," she finally blurted.

Malek wasn't sure whether he should laugh or groan. He thought it looked like trash, too. Within an open metal box rested an unusual, cubed structure. A motif of metallic alloy had been framed around what appeared to be fragments of oxidized metal. It was only as large as Malek's fist when he reached for it. He hesitated and then closed the box with its mysterious contents still within, trying to temper his disappointment. It weighed heavily in his grasp as he turned to Kei.

"Better be worth it," Malek grumbled. He pressed a button on his portable, then began searching his belt for a place to stow the box. "Anthem, do you copy?"

"Loud and clear. Status?" Anthem replied between breaths.

"Got the prize." Malek pulled open a compartment and searched its contents. "Where are you?"

"We're ushering a group of survivors out of the second floor. Cenk is leading another split down to you. They should be there in—"

"Specter!" Kei hissed, cutting through his focus.

Malek's eyes narrowed to the lab entrance, where the handles clicked. The hinges let out a low moan as the door inched open. Heat spilled through the widening gap, a fierce glow flooding the threshold. The temperature climbed fast, needling his cheeks until they burned.

Slag, she was here!

CHAPTER 3

SHARD

Malek pushed Kei behind the nearest workbench. He ignored her panicked protest as he stood in plain sight. The door swung open, and just as quickly, the Fireborne appeared at the threshold with radiating incandescence.

Mace, were they always this big?! The Fireborne was more monstrous than what he remembered from his old textbooks. Malek gaped at the three-meter-tall figure stalking into the room, slim and curved along the natural lines of a female form, wrapped only in tatters of black cloth that covered her chest and hips. The fabric danced with each dreadful step forward, fluttering in the heated air. An onslaught of bullets had left pinholes smeared in blood on her ashen skin. Her flesh shimmered with a light plated texture, almost like fish scales. She glided into the room with an ominous stride, her flesh glowing red along her long, nimble hands, which burned like dying embers. That would explain the melted skin on Kei's commander.

She tilted her head curiously at Malek. The gold beads clasping her black, braided locks clicked together as she did. Besides her body being a walking furnace, her Elemnai features were also given away by her short, pointed ears, thin chin, and high, angular cheekbones that were almost exaggerated. Malek's fear cemented once he saw her eyes fix directly on him, feeling his heart rage against his chest. Irises that flashed crimson, brilliant against the blackness of her sclera, were terrifyingly inhuman. In the dull light, Malek recognized ram-like ebony horns, glistening above her locks, twisting and curving back behind her ears. She imperiously stared him down, with the ravenousness of a predator homing in on its prey. This was definitely not the way Malek thought he would die.

No, dying was *not* part of the plan! *Find her, check. Get the shard, check. Survive. Get the frag out.* Come on, he had to think! Malek's eyes fixed on the Fireborne's injuries as she took one more dreadful step closer. Bullet holes...guns didn't stop her before. They needed something bigger.

Malek fiddled with the box and the compartment on his belt. The Fireborne closed in, and his adrenaline pulsed violently through his system as he saw her limbs flare into a blinding, heated light. She raised one hand, preparing to strike him down. He planted his feet, stood straight and lifted the box in his hand. This had better work.

Knees nearly buckling under his quaking relief, the Fireborne froze in her steps, and Malek's muscles slackened just enough to prepare his joints for the upcoming maneuver. It caught him off guard when her face shifted from a threatening glare to one of childish amusement. Malek finally exhaled, sweat trickling down the stubble on his jaw.

Kei hissed, "Mace! What are you doing?"

He kept his eyes on the Fireborne and stood his ground. Malek swallowed hard and presented the box with a little more purpose, stretching it out in front of him. "Come on, slaghead. Take it."

Unexpectedly, the Fireborne began speaking in a harsh language that Malek didn't recognize. Her voice was guttural, but her tone was mellow. Malek wondered whether she was impressed by his cooperation, but she probably still planned to kill him anyway. The muscles in his shoulders briefly slackened when he saw the glow dissipate from her hand, like hot steel cooling to charred grey.

Malek, without looking at Kei, whispered to her, "Get ready to run."

The Fireborne let out a sinister and low laugh that resonated off the lab's walls. The moment the Fireborne's abnormally long fingers curled around the box, Malek released it and, without hesitation, bolted away from her. He seized Kei, and the two scrambled around the benches and toward the doors, neither daring to look back.

"Why did you do that?!" Kei snapped as she and Malek ran as fast as their legs would allow, their heavy steps echoing throughout the halls. "You just gave it away!"

"Did I?" He grabbed the compartment on his belt and pulled out an object. Malek grinned when Kei's eyes widened in disbelief at the sight of the shard, and he laughed as he stowed it away.

The victory was short-lived. A thunderous vibration lanced through Malek's insides. Bits of stone trickled down from the ceiling as a boom violently shook the corridor. Malek and Kei nearly stumbled. A sharp, ear-piercing scream cut through the air as if coming from all directions. Not only was the Fireborne still alive, but she sounded... well, angry would have put it lightly.

"What was that?!" Kei panted, rounding a corner with Malek.

"Rip-charge. Teeny tiny, but packs a punch."

Kei scoffed. "We need something bigger!"

Malek's eyes trailed over to her as she skidded to a stop and dashed toward another door just as they had passed it. A slew of warning labels had been etched over a plaque along with the symbol "O_2." Kei tried the knob, and when it failed, took a step back and drove her foot into the latch. It didn't take long for Malek to realize her intention.

"Slag! That's either a good idea or a really bad one." His eyes darted down the hall from where they had come. A brilliant red and orange glow pulsed from the corridor, flashing against the walls. The screams pressed nearer, growing in pitch with every beat of Malek's racing heart.

"Let's just agree it's a great idea," Kei grunted, breaking open the door at last with the heel of her boot.

Malek shouldered his rifle, aiming at the incoming Fireborne. From the corner of his eye, he watched Kei scramble into the room and disappear.

"Stall her!" she called back.

Muttering a curse under his breath, Malek charged forward and dropped one hand to his belt. He pulled another rip-charge from its hold and activated it with a precise grip. Counting the seconds, he turned his body just as he reached the mouth of the hallway, where it intersected with the incoming firelight. He hurled the device across the floor, and it slid over a glistening surface that reflected the brilliance of the flames pouring from its depths. The Fireborne emerged from the blaze. A swirling ribbon of flame surrounded the enraged creature as she rushed toward Malek. She slithered through the hall, her hands glowing a luminous white. Half of her already terrifying face was shredded and bleeding heavily over the ridges of her hellish grimace.

Malek fired several rounds, only for them to be devoured by a wall of inferno raised by the Fireborne. She howled, throwing her hands forward, and a column of fire erupted from her palms. It flooded past Malek as he narrowly dodged the onslaught, and he aimed again, this time at the rip-charge that now found itself between him and the Fireborne. Timing it within a fraction of a second of her advance, he unleashed another barrage of bullets and struck the device.

A violent rush of pain flooded over his body as he slammed into the corner of the hallway and plummeted to the floor. He groaned and lifted his head, rising unsteadily as the blast's echo rattled his thoughts and a spine-deep ache pulled him off balance. The flames sagged enough for Malek to gauge the outcome. His eyes widened in horror.

The explosion had occurred directly below her. She, too, had stumbled back from the explosion, but had already regained her footing. The Fireborne clenched her teeth as she stood hunched over, with her hands twisted and extended. Directly in front of her, Malek watched the ribbons of flames dancing within a pressurized orb, fractured along seams where it emitted a blinding light, piercing through some kind of spherical barrier. The Fireborne kept her focus on the object before letting out a guttural cry, and the sphere died into dust and embers.

She *contained* the blast! Malek cursed in disbelief. His arsenal was now completely useless. Those haunting eyes met with his as Malek held his breath. She lifted her hand again as she took a step forward, staring down at him with the utmost rage, burning straight through the orbits of his skull. He was out of time.

Malek raced back down the corridor, barely dodging another flood of inferno that seared the walls in his wake. Kei burst into view ahead of him, shoving a trolley loaded with metal cylinders that clanged and rattled against one another as she wrestled it into the center of the hall. She was in danger. Malek's hand fell from the rifle, and he charged at Kei.

As time slowed to a crawl, the air grew deafeningly silent. A haze descended over him. Malek reached for one of the cylinders, and his fingers curled painfully around its valve. With his other hand, he clutched Kei by the back of her armored vest. He could feel the heat at his back, and the flash of brilliance surrounded him.

Then there was nothing at all. The ground beneath his feet, with each hard step, lost all pressure. The heat no longer pricked at his bare skin. Kei's hands were no longer constricting his arm. The smell and the acidic taste in the air vanished. He was utterly detached from his environment. He twisted his body just enough to witness the Fireborne lunging toward them, hands ignited and releasing another river of flames. Within an instant, everything around him went dark, and he fell into oblivion.

Slag. You did it again, didn't you?

"How did you do that?" Kei's voice was weak, resonating in the depths of his senses, like something bubbling up from the bottom of a lake. Her voice came again, much crisper, breaking the surface tension and rising above the water in his mind. "Specter?"

The half-lit hallway, Kei's trembling breath, the hum of a distant ventilation system, and the never-ending stench of burned flesh and metal all flooded his senses at once. Malek gasped and blinked several times into awareness. *Yep, you did it again. You idiot.*

"Do what?" he muttered, feeling the weight of Kei's arm over his neck. He glanced at her, realizing he was helping her walk.

"The oxygen tank. H-how you lobbed it like that... Ah!" Kei released a stifled cry and collapsed to her knees. She clutched the side of her abdomen and leg. Sweat glistened on her paling skin, but there was no heat. Malek's gaze flickered across the torn armor, shredded fabric indistinguishable from the gashes in her skin. His eyes rounded.

"Oh *mace...*" Malek couldn't bear to think about what just happened. Did *he* do this? Holding her steady, he scanned the charred hallway around them. They needed an exit, and fast. She already knew what was on his mind before he formulated a coherent sentence.

"...I'm going to slow you down. Get out of here before she finds us again." Kei swallowed, agony swelling in her eyes. "Take the shard and run."

"Don't say that, Kei. You nearly got us killed, so we're practically best friends now."

Kei either chuckled or whimpered, until Malek fastened the strap high on her leg as a mock tourniquet. He tried to ignore the grind of her teeth and the blood coursing over his own hands.

With another glance at his surroundings, Malek wrapped one arm around her and lifted. "On your feet, soldier."

"I hope you have some more stupid ideas."

"For the record, the tanks were your stupid idea." Malek hauled her deeper into his clutches. A lancet of pain struck the skin and muscles of his back, but it wasn't from holding Kei. It took him another half a second to realize that she wasn't the only one who was injured. He guessed they were *both* nearly out of time.

A cold sweat rolled over Malek's brow as he snapped his gaze down the corridor, where a guttural, grinding scream filled its void. His heart thrashed against his bruised ribs. The Fireborne was closing in again.

No...this time, *he* was going to have the edge.

Malek pushed their way into the kitchen. His eyes swept across the appliances, studying the fridges, walk-in freezer, and finally, the far back gate locked to its rail. He released a staggered breath as his senses came back in full swing. His vision danced, but the adrenaline forced down the pain enough for him to think. "I have one more idea. It's a little... weird," he said, and he heard Kei scoff. "I need to borrow your helmet."

Another cry, trembling and strained, echoed from the corridor. Malek took this as a good thing. She was getting weaker, and if he could ride that weakness, he could still make it out of here alive *and* get her to stand down. Malek tempered his racing heart with deep breaths and tapped his portable. "Locate the elevator and find us there."

"You're sure this will work?" Anthem spoke on the receiving end. "Cenk's team ETA's ten minutes."

"Tell them to hold. Can't lose anyone. Countdown from ten minutes." Malek lowered his voice. "If I'm not up, hold Cenk's team until ASFOM updates and procures arsenal. They'll need it."

Malek paused, staring down at his portable. He winced, and removed his helmet, feeling his hair and skin peel from its padding. Wiping the sweat on his forehead with his wrist, he adjusted the volume control on his helmet and opened the door to the walk-in freezer. After gingerly placing the helmet down, he carefully studied his display with a cringing grimace. He knew it wasn't one of his best ideas... but at least, it was believable.

Several bags of flour and dry goods had been tactfully arranged, so when Malek placed his and Kei's armored vests, jackets, and helmets, it could be mistaken for a pair of humans hiding in the darkness behind the wire shelves that hugged the walls. He backed away, feeling the sharp frigidity claw at his exposed skin. His breath clouded before him as he exhaled. It only needed to be believable for a second. Or three, preferably. If it worked, it would put an end to the killing. That was all that mattered.

Exiting, he slowly pushed the door closed, leaving it barely ajar. The muscles in his arm and hand twitched, and he released an involuntary groan. Blood trickled down his bare arm and over his knuckles. Another stupid idea inspired him to run his palm over the freezer door, a cooler next to it, the wall, and the wire shelves all the way to the kitchen entrance. He rattled the door handle, then slipped behind a counter out of sight.

That mental checklist flashed in Malek's mind as he swallowed the agony burning across his muscles. *Survive. Get the frag out. You're not done yet. Get this under control, or it all goes to hell.*

His heart rate spiked when the kitchen doors opened, and a figure crept into the room. Malek knew that the Fireborne was struggling by her heavy, trembling rasps between low, broken murmurs. Maybe his scheme would be convincing after all. Peering around the corner of the cabinets, Malek watched the Fireborne. Her bare feet pressed against the cold floor, slowing to a crawl as something piqued her interest. As Malek had hoped, she inched past the cooler, studying the bloodstains against the freezer door. She let out a low growl and pulled it open. Swallowing hard, Malek readied himself.

The obscure chatter from his helmet—thanks to Anthem—was enough to lock the Fireborne's attention a few seconds longer and lure her into the freezer. Slag, this had better work. It was now or never.

Malek sprinted as fast as his body would allow. The Fireborne whipped around, eyes blazing and hateful as they narrowed on Malek, just as he slammed the door closed. Banshee-like shrieks pulsed from the inside, and Malek reached for the cooler. The adrenaline coursing through his limbs invigorated him, and his muscles screamed as he pulled it down in front of the freezer door. The Fireborne continued her awful howling, and Malek stepped back, expecting her to burst from the freezer.

He waited, and she didn't. Puzzled, Malek listened carefully to the new sound emanating from inside. Was she sobbing?

"*Al-Khasari...Al-Khasari,*" she moaned between her wailings. "*Merismi Urith...nusami, Al-Khasari...nusami...*"

These words belonged to another ancient dialect. For Malek, it was one that he knew *very* well. It was his mother's language—Khasiri—rarely heard or spoken even among immigrant kids like himself.... But how on Eiden could she *know* it? His lip twitched, and for a brief moment, the disturbing nature of all this began to settle. She *really* spoke to him. If that wasn't concerning enough, it was her actual words...she said her name was Urith, and she was *begging* him to help her. What a load of slag!

34

Rage instantly devoured him. After what she did here, she was asking for *mercy*. Malek placed a closed fist against the fallen cooler, listening to her howling. In the polished stainless-steel surface of the freezer door, he caught a glimpse of the features that clued her in on his heritage, giving 'Urith' an idea of his descent. The Al-Khasari trademark—silvery white hair rooted in black fell over his dark, furrowed brows. Sweat and blood glistened over his olive skin and black stubble across his jaw. He thought about saying something cutting or brutal, just to remind her that she'd lost and she deserved to rot in there... but something tugged his core, tightening it into an anxious knot.

Malek looked at his reflection one last time, and instead of seeing his face, he stared back at another version of himself. He was younger, with a shaved head, and dark circles under his terrified eyes. A fresh set of stitches knotted over his brow. Malek blinked away the image, and his gaze traced over a thin scar that was etched in its place. He didn't need to say anything. The Fireborne was alone, and now, in the hands of the Alliance. That terrifying thought made him want to throw up.

Urith screamed again, and then her voice broke into a whimper. Malek sighed, closing his eyes momentarily to control his swimming vision. He turned away and fixated on food items that dropped from the cooler when he pushed it to the ground. A thin brown box flipped open, revealing some muffins, and for whatever reason, he remembered that Kei had said she was hungry. He was already holding one as he overrode his own logic that whispered how Kei was dangerously injured, and food likely wasn't going to make it all better. He made his way across the kitchen, blackness closing in from his periphery with each aching step.

Malek placed the muffin on a nearby countertop. He lifted the rifle that rested against the elevator gate. With enormous strain, he hammered the padlocks with the stock, suppressing his urge to whimper. He pulled off the remnants with a deep exhale, knowing that he only needed a few more seconds. Then he set down the rifle, lifting the gate with trembling arms. Its wheels creaked against the rail as it slid up. It was followed by a soft shuffle, coming from around the next bend.

Malek's blurred vision fixed on the shadow of Kei, her body slumped against the wall. Surprisingly, she was still mobile. He rushed to meet her and lifted her by her shoulders, guiding her into the elevator. Malek snatched the muffin off the counter, and punched the crude button for the topmost floor. Pain flared at the slightest motion, but his shoulders eased all the same as a long breath escaped him. It was over. They were getting the hell out.

Resting her against the rusted, caged interior, Malek knelt in front of her. "I got something for you," he said, carefully placing the muffin in her hand. "You said you were hungry?"

Kei either laughed, or it could have been a well-timed cough. Malek watched helplessly at those hazel eyes, barely open, glistening with each passing flash of the emergency lighting system as they rode upward. She finally closed them. Her long, raven hair wetted against her paling cheeks as a tear rolled over the strands. The ebony lashes cast long shadows under her eyes, twitching as she mustered the strength to speak. "*Se.* Starving." Her fingers briefly tightened around the muffin.

Vertigo washed over Malek when he finally slumped down next to Kei. The agony melted away, replaced by a chill. He was hardly taking in any air at all. Before a forced sleep overtook his mind, he was able to murmur, "We made a good team, Kei. Thanks for being stupid with me."

A pinch kick-started Malek's senses all at once. He opened his eyes to a pallid light that blinded him immediately. He gasped for air as he sat up, instantly noticing the smell. It smelled like, to his surprise, disinfectant, of all things. No burnt bodies...No weird metallic taste. The coldness pricked at the bare skin of his arms and torso between the gauze and bandages. He fixed his gaze on his surroundings as color and shapes formed coherent, sober details of a room. A thin blanket warmed the burning ache in his legs, while a cool steel rail on one side of him soothed the clamminess of his shoulder. On the other side, a woman stood with hands lifted in apology, he guessed. Blood trickled from a small wound above his left wrist. A slight soreness dulled into existence, firing from the nerves near the wound. Other than the fatigue in his muscles, that was actually the only pain he suffered at all.

"Whoa, scared me there," the woman said as a smile pulled at the edge of her plump lip. Malek blinked and studied the loose light pink scrubs over her stout figure. Strands of her brown hair danced at her round jawline under the gentle flow of air pushed by an overhead fan. She smiled at him and, through a Norvican accent, answered the questions gathering in Malek's mind before he could form a sentence.

"Sorry about that, love. I was removing your IV, and I'm afraid I just jolted you out of a good sleep." She approached, pressing a gauze against the injury. "You're in an Alliance mobile hospital. Just outside of Gunliem."

Malek didn't reply. He'd survived *and* gotten out. He glanced around the room. It wasn't the first time he woke up in similar circumstances, in a hospital away from home. This was probably the first time that he was relieved rather than confused, though. A taupe curtain separated him from the rest of the ward, and he watched as the folds moved against the air current. Soft voices resonated through the canvas tent, no doubt between staff and other survivors. He was safe. But... what about Kei?

He snapped out of his daze and looked back up at the woman. "Where's Kei?" His voice was gravelly against his bone-dry throat.

"Who?"

"She was with me. The Jennai soldier. Is she alive?"

"Oh, yes, her," the woman tilted her head in a particular direction. "They treated her last night, and she was flown to another facility. Her injuries were quite extensive, from what I understand."

She was alive. Malek hoped it would stay that way. He cleared his throat and addressed the woman again. "Nurse?" he asked, nodding to her ID badge that hung from her chest pocket.

"That's right." She leaned over to him, gently moving him forward as she studied his back and shoulder. "It's time to change your dressings, so I'll get the doctor to come in for a chat." She pulled away and reached for a corded, sheer white datapad at the base of his bed. As she typed, Malek rubbed his tired eyes.

"I'll be looking after you for the next few hours, love. My name is Della. Now... I'm afraid yours is a bit uncommon. Could you pronounce it?"

"Mall-lick Ruh-zah."

"Spelling is correct? M-A-L-E-K...R-E-Z-A?"

"Yeah."

"Well, good to meet you, Malek."

"How long was I out?"

"About twelve hours. You had some significant blood loss. Before we could get a transfusion, your blood pressure evened out. Quite a miracle, actually."

A miracle? Yeah, right. Malek knew exactly why, but he didn't bother to respond when Della glanced back at him.

"Back in a bit with the doctor." Della replaced the datapad. She smiled and nodded before she left.

Drawing a deep breath, Malek rested back on the angled bed, which comfortably lifted him into a partially seated position. He stared at the rotating blades of the fan. Part of him wondered if it had all been a dream. It was so incredibly surreal, and terrifying, and beyond anything he had ever experienced. A knot twisted in his chest as he recalled the way the corridor filled with flames, an inferno ready to swallow him and Kei whole. Slag... he imagined what an army of them could do...

His mind unwillingly trailed to the latest blackout he suffered back in that hallway. It wasn't the first time it happened in his career, but it *was* the only time he nearly took out an Elemnai in the process. What did he do? Kei was the only one who'd seen him... but didn't Anthem say something about cameras? No... he refused to think about it.

Malek clamped his eyes shut and purged the memory. He sighed and thought of Kei again as he tried to remember her face. The harder he tried, the more it slipped away, making him wonder if it *was* all a dream.

A quick series of steps resonated from the ward, breaking his train of thought. Someone forcefully pushed the curtain at the base of his bed. Malek drew in a tight breath in alarm as he sat up, just as Jace cried in joy at the sight of him.

"You lucky bastard!" Jace lurched forward and swung one arm around Malek's neck in a strangling hold.

"Get off!" Malek pried Jace's limbs in time to glimpse another figure standing in the curtain's wake.

Anthem folded her arms, the freckles across her face rising with her grin. Her blonde, wavy hair was secured in a high bun, with some strands falling neatly around her long face and walnut-colored eyebrows. Seeing both of his closest teammates in casual, midnight-blue Alliance uniforms was oddly relieving—it meant that they were getting ready to go home.

"I'm going to allow him to cut off your air supply because you gave me a damn scare." Anthem tilted her head. "How are you?"

"Fine. What happened? I remember getting into the elevator on the way up to meet you."

The smile faded from Anthem's face. "We found you, I'd say, maybe ten minutes after our last exchange. You and your friend were bleeding out, her worse than you. Commander Rhodes wasn't too thrilled about what you did. But he came down to see you during the extraction." She leaned in closer to Malek, dropping her voice into a whisper, "He, uh... took that item you got from the vault. Handed it off right away to the AIA, I think. Whatever it was, it's scaring a lot of people." Anthem straightened up, moving aside as the nurse, Della, returned with another woman wearing a white coat.

The new visitor was also middle-aged, dark-skinned, with wiry black hair streaked with gray. Silver rectangular glasses hung low on the flat bridge of her nose, lining up with tired eyes as she tilted her head back and studied Malek with interest. Before she had a chance to speak, Malek already felt on edge. He could read from her expression that she was amused and anticipated what she was about to say.

"Well, well... an Al-Khasari. I haven't seen the likes of you since my residency in Azar. Although I'm sure you get that a lot. I myself have always been envious of those indigo eyes. The white hair, not so much. I've already got that goin' for me."

As expected. Annoying, but Malek forced a polite nod anyway.

39

"I'm Doctor Orin." The woman gestured to his bandages. "We'll discharge you once I have a look at those injuries."

Della carted a tray over to the side of the bed closest to the curtain adjacent to Malek and asked him to turn and sit on the long edge of the bed. He complied without a word and braced himself for her touch, expecting a sting. He just wanted to get this over with and leave.

Malek looked up at Anthem. "Thanks for the assist, by the way. Wouldn't have pulled it off without you."

"Don't mention it. I'm just amazed it worked. You and JSTG did really well." Anthem paused and smiled a little. "The survivors we found escaped because of her. She was really brave, getting them out on her own. Didn't think JSTG had the guts."

"Yeah." Malek tried to stifle his admiration as best he could. He wanted to say more, but noticed that the medical staff behind him were murmuring to one another in a rushed vernacular that was hard to decipher.

Panic swelled again when Dr. Orin hissed at Della. "I thought you said the lacerations were half a centimeter deep?"

"Th-they were!" Della stammered. She reached for the datapad and began scanning its face. Anthem, with a look of concern, paced over to the physician.

"Unreal." Anthem breathed. She beamed at him, but this only made Malek feel worse.

"What is it, already?" he demanded.

"You were heavily wounded when we extracted you. All of your injuries are...gone. Completely gone. Your lacerations have healed up. You just have scars," Anthem spoke in a low voice. Malek and Jace exchanged anxious looks.

"Slag, who knew your call sign didn't give you justice? You're just indestructible," Jace said, maybe in an attempt to lift the mood, which failed miserably.

"I-I'm not." Malek's gaze twitched between his friends and Dr. Orin just as she rounded the bed. "Just...good at staying alive. And kicking ass. Call it an Al-Khasari thing."

Really? Was that even a thing?

40

Anthem released a deep laugh. "I think we're going to have to change your call sign, anyway. How does 'Immortal' sound?"

Malek glared at her and then at Jace, who grinned at him. "It... sounds stupid. Really stupid."

CHAPTER 4

SPECIALIST

The overlaying chatter of students created a low hum that reverberated off the heavy wooden door on which Nikita rested her cheek. The smell of aged varnish grounded her, at least for the moment. She peered eagerly through the crack of light, observing the rows of students arranged in the upward incline of seats gathered in half circles around the bare, polished birch floor of a grand auditorium. The podium across the length of the stage seemed like such a far walk from where she stood. Any number of scenarios could take place between *this* door and *that* microphone. Nikita pictured herself tripping in her black heels and ripping the back seam of her grey pencil skirt while trying to get back up, or something equally horrifying, all of it resulting in her absolute failure to earn the respect of the young academics awaiting her arrival.

"I can't believe the bold Dr. Nikita Valerio is terrified of a few students," a light-hearted voice murmured behind her. "You can talk to an Earthborne, but not a few kids?"

Nikita hated being teased at the best of times, and she rolled her eyes. "It's not a few, Pavo. It's a hundred. Kids can be mean."

Nikita watched the professor, Dr. Hamada—a tall, thin Jennai man—begin the lecture in his usual monotone voice. He adjusted his thick-framed lenses, rolled up the sleeves of his pale, collared shirt, and directed the quieted students to the images projected on a screen at the front of the auditorium. Nikita licked her lips, ignoring the stale taste of old lipstick—the only tube she could find. Dr. Hamada was knowledgeable about the Elemnai, without a doubt, but he lacked the passion of a storyteller. This is what Nikita wanted to change. She needed to change the narrative. But to do that, she'd needed to prove herself first.

She turned to Pavo, who stood with hands over the narrow frame of his hips, smiling at her through gaunt, unshaven features. "And Earthborne *aren't* mean?"

"They can be reasoned with."

"You're insane, Kit." Pavo chuckled.

That was probably true. It was a bit out of place to feel threatened by the opinions of students. She braved worse in the past. Why was this so nerve-racking?

Pavo leaned his head beside hers as he studied the crowd. "Well, these kids pay good aurum to be at the University of Kaira. They're going to need to pay attention to you if they want to pass the midterm."

Nikita had nothing but disdain for *that* remark. Was he implying that no one actually cared about what she had to say? Given everything they went through to get this data, Pavo could at least try to support her. "Are you trying to make me feel better? Because you're terrible at it."

"Don't worry. Remember, we're in this together. Today we're splitting the lecture, so that should take the pressure off."

Nikita scoffed. Pavo clearly didn't intend to offend, but he was on a roll. Sharing the spot of "guest lecturer" with her colleague wasn't what she'd had in mind when she agreed to share the findings of her research—research that took a great deal of courage, cunning, and understanding to put together. She pushed her aggravation down into the pit of her stomach, where it condensed into a leaden ball.

Pavo's eyes widened. "Ooh! The dean is here! But who's the angry-looking guy next to him?"

Nikita spied a pair of older gentlemen at the edge of the first row of seats, speaking to one another. The first man she recognized was the Dean of Social Sciences, Dr. Edgar Nome. He was a tall, aged but lovable Norvican with round features, graying umber hair and beard, and gold-rimmed glasses over a wide nose. His brown slacks and beige tweed jacket were a clear contrast to the charcoal gray suit of the man at his side. His peppered black hair had been slicked back. Straight eyebrows furrowed over a hard look across a clean-cut face, with sharp eyes that scanned the room like a hawk. Oddly, Nikita found him both untrustworthy and weirdly magnetic, but she couldn't pinpoint why. In a room full of students and professors, this man stood out like a sore thumb. Whatever his intentions were for being here, he'd no doubt come to judge her on her first day of teaching.

A chill of anxiety went down her neck. "Ah, he's probably not important," Nikita grumbled, more as a wish than anything else. "Let's do this." She backed away from the door, and Pavo stood before her. Pulling up her datapad, she activated the front-facing camera and scanned over her appearance one last time. She straightened out her fitted pewter blazer with her free hand, and then she ran her fingers over the long, dark curls. "How do I look?"

Pavo's face appeared behind her in the datapad's transparent screen. He stared long enough for it to be uncomfortable, and Nikita wrinkled her brow while watching him stammer. "You look gorg—I mean normal. Totally normal."

Nikita deactivated the camera and turned away, hiding her cringe. She always knew Pavo wanted to be more than colleagues, more than friends, especially since their return. Honestly, she had no interest in a relationship with him or anyone. She had more important things to do. She sighed and pressed her hand on the door. "Thanks. See you in a few!"

"Oh, um... Kit?" Pavo said hastily. She looked back at him and suppressed a scowl while he cleared his throat. "I was wondering if we could...ah, go out and celebrate after. Drinks or something. I mean, it's not every day that our research gets published, and we get a whole new course dedicated to our work...in...record time, no less." He blinked again. "You know, just drinks. If you're thirsty."

Nikita offered a strained smile. What horrible timing! The thought of enduring another exhausting charade of dating was nauseating enough...but with a colleague? It made her stomach turn in ways she needed to recover from. *Immediately.* "Sure, Pavo. Make sure you invite the TAs, too!"

"Oh, I thought it could be just—"

A flat voice echoed from the auditorium, "—And now, we will have Dr. Nikita Valerio, who spearheaded the exhibition to the Elemnai Wilds. She is the first in

Eiden's recent two-hundred-year history since the end of the last human-Elemnai war to establish an amicable relationship with the Earthborne clans of the Wilds, and will be highlighting some of her findings from her research. Please welcome—"

"Okay, gotta go. Wish me luck!" Nikita waved at Pavo just before she pushed herself out the door. She heard a meek "good luck" in her wake. Nikita shook off the irritation, letting it roll away from her shoulders. A spark lit behind her ribs, quickening her heartbeat and sharpening every sense. For the first time in nearly two centuries, and in a university course, no less, she was about to share something that would question everyone's beliefs and way of life.

Nikita's heels rapped against the wooden floorboards. She briskly moved toward the podium, fixed on landing every footfall to keep from tripping. The murmurs in the crowd dipped into an eager silence, and her hands trembled when she docked her datapad into the stand. Nikita watched Dr. Hamada take a seat in the front row. He nodded at her and folded his arms. He was either annoyed or looking forward to her talk. She could never tell with him. Nikita then furtively glanced at the two gentlemen, who were poised attentively. Her mind instinctively focused on the curious man in the suit. They locked eyes. His icy blue gaze penetrated her confidence.

Nikita rolled back her shoulders to stifle a shiver, quickly booting up her presentation. Within moments, the pallid screen behind her lit up with a script and a solo image, which earned several audible gasps from the students. Nikita soon forgot about the man in the suit and remembered where she was. With an inward smile, she dimmed the lights nearest to the screen using the switches at the podium and cleared her throat.

"Good morning, everyone," she said, trying hard to keep her voice even. "Or...in the common Earthborne language of Umbar'ok... *Su'vua*. I am Dr. Valerio. I'm told that the course title is 'The Study of Elemnai Culture and History.' The title should, more accurately, read: 'The Study of Eiden's People.'" Nikita paused meaningfully, eyeing the young faces in the rows closest to her. "All people." She looked up at the photo displayed on the screen with glowing pride.

Though Nikita had seen this photo hundreds of times, it always made her feel surreal. There she was, standing next to the gargantuan figure of an Earthborne male that towered over Nikita by well over a meter and a half. His muscles bulged under chiseled ochre skin that seemed to be carved of rock. An ivory cloak draped over a single broad shoulder, which Nikita stood beneath, beaming wildly. The Earthborne's humanoid face was sharply edged yet smooth, bearing deep golden eyes under a pronounced brow ridge, and a short, twisted beard grazing his chin. The black of his hair receded behind twin massive, sharp ebony horns, sweeping back and sidelong from his forehead, splitting into several branches like the antlers of a deer. What made this photo so remarkable, despite the beautiful details, was how the Earthborne had one massive hand over Nikita's small shoulder.

Yes, she thought to herself. *That's my friend, Johar.* This was proof that the Elemnai and humans *could* be friends. Nikita's hope renewed, and she continued with more confidence.

"Our stories are so inextricably linked that it's impossible to focus on the Elemnai's story without considering our own. The mass extinction event that ended five thousand years ago ripped entire chapters from our history. We are left to contemplate only the most recent five thousand years. During that time, humans and Elemnai spent millennia constantly at war with one another for access to dwindling resources and territories. In between such times, we had times of peace, as we do now. But conflict, unfortunately, always seems to be around the corner... waiting for an opportunity to prey on our weak relationship. It makes us wonder, were we ever actually friendly? Did we ever share resources, goods, culture, or even language? For instance, the Umbar'ok word, *deka,* and Eidean word, mace, both stem from 'Decimation'." The room filled with light laughter, melting the tension in Nikita's shoulders. "If we share curse words, certainly there are other elements that we share, as well."

After a short pause, Nikita scanned the crowd. "Fireborne. Earthborne. Windborne. Oceanborne. Human. We all ask the same questions. Where did we come from? And where are we going?" Nikita cleared her throat. She caught a glimpse of the mysterious man eyeing the photo with a disturbed expression before it vanished from the screen. That pleased her. She knew she was on the right track if she could garner *that* reaction. Her eyes trailed to the small, digital clock at the upper edge of her data pad. She had a lot of information to present, but so little time to deliver.

The minutes filled with Nikita's recounting of her travels to the Wilds, where she made contact with the Earthborne tribes and exchanged gifts as an offer of peace. Over the months that passed, she and her colleague, Pavo, had been able to decipher their language, with Nikita being the first of her team to have a fully articulated conversation with the Earthborne. In this way, Nikita gained incredible insight into their past. She learned that the Earthborne had eidetic memories and passed down knowledge and history through oral traditions. She poured what she could into her journals, desperate to hold onto every detail. Before her team left, they needed one more piece of information—one final puzzle piece to tie the great mystery of Eiden. They needed physical samples. Nikita didn't realize the value of this until she was introduced to another ancient being, Astraeos.

Nikita changed the slide, revealing several photographs of a partial skeleton, black with age, resting over a pristine, white table. She admired the remains for a moment and continued.

"Astraeos was a unique specimen comprised of a fifteen-thousand-six-hundred-year-old set of fossils belonging to an Anymm, or Eiden's first people. It is a being so unique that it perceptively fell from the sky. At the time of its discovery, its value was undermined—that is, until researchers at Galeo City University extracted and sequenced the DNA that could be obtained. Within that DNA, we found the clues that pieced together the link between the Anymm, the Elemnai, and the humans."

With a brief sigh, she eyed the clock on her datapad, and her stomach sank knowing she had gone over her time limit. She glanced at Pavo, who fidgeted at the side of the stage, and she lifted her eyes to the group of utterly enthralled students. Nikita didn't have time to relay the pinnacle of her findings—the story that would have made it all worthwhile. She shouldn't have rambled so much...She should have rehearsed. It would have to wait for another time. For now, it was best to let the students reflect. "I'll hand it over to Dr. Pavo Suarez."

The hush was swiftly replaced with several low groans.

"Hopefully, I'll have another chance to share this amazing data with you. Thank you for your attention."

Pavo stepped in behind the podium at a light round of applause. A tinge of despair knotted inside of her as she walked away, datapad in hand. It was so important to her that others knew the truth—even if it meant only a single person would be inspired. She stepped off the stage, only to catch the dean's eye. His eyebrows arched, and he subtly tilted his head, which meant he needed to speak with her. Nikita wondered if her lecture was already a failure. She trailed behind the dean and the other man, hesitating at the threshold before stepping into the adjacent exit. Her heart jumped as the heavy door slid shut in their wake.

"Dr. Nome, I didn't think you'd be joining us for our first lecture." Nikita mustered a polite grin. He returned the gesture, placing one hand over her shoulder.

"It looks like the students loved it." Dr. Nome chortled heartily. "You're a captivating lecturer, Kit, and the buzz of the department. You've accomplished so much at just twenty-two years-old!"

"I'm twenty-six, sir." Nikita's cheeks burned.

"Oh. Either way, even the science guys are jealous and want a piece of this action."

The tension in her shoulders slacked. At times, Nikita appreciated the dean for his casual and jubilant nature, but she often found he struggled to get to the point of his visits. She clasped her hands tightly around her datapad and looked over at the man standing at the dean's side. He offered a nod with a courteous smile. He looked older up close and bore a distinct scar over his square jaw. Nikita couldn't place her intimidation, but it forced her to wait for the dean to speak first.

"Right," Dr. Nome began slowly, glancing from her to the man next to them. "Kit, we need to speak with you. It's rather urgent. Join us in my office."

Nikita blinked, trying to mask her growing apprehension. She replied with a little nod and followed close behind them. Her adrenaline spiked. The dean never introduced his guest.

CHAPTER 5

THREAT

C ool air from the overhead vents could hardly keep up with the rising temperature, as the afternoon sun poured in through the glass panes of the three massive windows at the far end of the room. Nikita distracted herself by watching the light spill over the bookshelves, wrapping the rows of spines and marble statuettes in a gentle, golden warmth. She was already flustered, and the heat did nothing to ease the tightness in her chest. The strange man rested against one of the ledges of those large windows, scrutinizing Nikita as she came to Nome's side. She knew she had done nothing wrong, and yet Nikita replayed the last several years in her mind, searching her memories for an oversight or mishap. She couldn't shake the feeling of being a child sent to the principal's office.

"Why am I here?" Nikita finally asked, irritated at herself when her words quivered.

"Hah, straight to the point, as always," Nome said and chuckled, but his voice also hitched. He hummed a little as he glanced between the man and Nikita. "Sir, would you like me to remain?"

The man spoke, unmoving from his position. "I'm afraid I need to speak with Dr. Valerio alone." His voice was baritone and meaningful, resonating softly across the facets of the room. The air became thick with either humidity or tension, but Nikita's mind flew to one thing—this person held sway over the dean. You could feel the authority in that tone.

49

"I'll be off then. Please ring my assistant if you need me." Nome patted Nikita on the shoulder before he departed, gingerly shutting the door behind him.

Nikita returned her eyes to the man. "Sir?"

"It's wonderful to finally meet you, Dr. Valerio. I am General Maida of the Alliance, and Head of Special Missions, Mardascan Division."

Nikita's eyebrows knitted, scanning him from head to toe. "You don't look like a general..."

"Considering the reticent nature of my visit, it would have been fairly reckless to show up in full uniform. I wanted to meet you where you would feel comfortable. The Alliance does not reach out to civilians very often, you see. It's safe to say that we require your assistance."

Straight to the point, indeed. Nikita's heart fluttered, and she felt compelled to take a seat. She slid into one of the leather upholstered wooden chairs in front of the dean's desk, hands wringing over the datapad laid across her stiff knees in anticipation. "What kind of assistance?"

"We require a very particular set of skills that you possess. You've clearly spent a lot of time with the Earthborne, for academic purposes..." He stood up, pacing over to the dean's desk, and folded his arms. "Are you familiar with the Gunliem tragedy?"

"Yes."

"Tell me what you know."

"Well...Over a year or so ago, a fire burned through a Jennai research campus in Gunliem. It trapped and killed nearly a hundred scientists and employees." Nikita shook her head. She honestly had no idea what Maida wanted to hear. "I don't remember much of it otherwise. We were on our way back from the Elemnai Wilds."

"Dr. Valerio—"

"Nikita is fine."

"Nikita, I know this is a lot to ask of you. I need to know that what I say won't leave this room. To repeat what I'm about to tell you, well..." He held her gaze, and a chill slithered down Nikita's neck. "...It would be considered treason."

A muscle in Nikita's jaw rolled, and her heartbeat quickened. If that was the truth, she immediately desired it. Her instincts screamed that there was danger in this truth, no different than what she'd hunted when she first set out to meet the Earthborne. Despite the danger, she always believed the truth would be liberating... whether in the coming decades or centuries.

After a nod in reply, Maida gestured for her datapad. "The room has already been processed, and since we've had eyes on you since your lecture, we know you're not wearing a recording device... but I will need that."

Nikita exhaled sharply and handed over her most prized possession to the general. Once ensuring it was powered down, Maida rested it on the dean's desk.

"Gunliem was a tragedy, but it was no accident. No amount of preparation could have saved those people from the attack."

"Attack?"

"A rogue Fireborne," Maida's voice dropped, and a shadow passed his expression. "The Jennai Special Task Group lost an entire section along with the hundred or so civilians to that creature."

"But...that doesn't make sense. It wasn't provoked?"

"The Fireborne had an agenda. The Alliance intervened and confirmed her intentions before overcoming the threat...but she certainly left her mark."

"And she was the only one?"

"Yes. Which is why I indicated that she was a rogue. At least, we all still hope that's the case."

With that response, Nikita stood and folded her arms. This was not only disturbing, but detrimental to her cause. She wanted to paint a better picture of the Elemnai through her research. This... this would undo it all. She slowly paced around the room to temper her panic as Maida continued.

"She was looking for something, and she nearly obtained it too, if it weren't for one of my ASF Officers and a sole surviving member of the JSTG. Based on your research, I think you have an idea of what that could be. An artifact... once lost and partially recovered."

Nikita's eyes rounded in understanding, and she nodded slowly. "...It was something that the Earthborne spoke of in their stories," she began, running her slender fingers over the small curve of her chin. "The object, or the idea, that first pitted us against one another thousands of years ago. Besides the genetic component, it was the one tie the Elemnai had with humans. The common objective that could grant one's civilization the power to thrive. Whatever it was, it's considered to be long gone... The Elemnai, or at least the Earthborne, know that." Nikita's stomach sank with dread. "Wait, you said you hope that's still the case? As in, the Fireborne might not just be a rogue? What's changed?"

Maida's eyes locked onto hers, but she stood, unflinching. "Yes, something has changed. But this is as far as our conversation goes on the matter. This is the part where you have to decide whether you'll be joining us."

Nikita scoffed. "Joining you? I'm not even sure what you want from me. How can I agree to something if you're not giving me any information?"

"Because the mission proceeds, whether you're a part of this or not," Maida replied sharply, his voice a pitch louder than perhaps he intended. Nikita recoiled and glowered at the response. She never took *that* tone well.

With an aggravated sigh, Maida placed both hands on the desk. Nikita could see him tempering himself as he clamped his eyes shut for a moment. Maybe he didn't care for *her* tone either. "There are those in this world who are looking for a reason to obliterate the Elemnai. Like you, I seek to understand them. The military has had the odd interaction with them over the last two hundred years. None of these events, however, have been this close to destroying what peace we have with the Elemnai as the events of Gunliem...and of those today." Maida lifted his gaze back onto Nikita. "That is why I am putting together a team. A small team...composed of specialists, both military and civilian. The team must identify and neutralize the Elemnai threat, if any, before this escalates. And if the Elemnai are seeking these certain items of interest, I need this team to locate them or otherwise relieve them from the Elemnai. From you, Nikita—I need you to *understand* this threat. I need you to guide us. Yes... we proceed no matter what, but if we want to avoid an all-out war, I think you are the woman for the job."

Nikita's insides now churned with apprehension. Guide them? *The Alliance?* The military behemoth that held the world in its grip—and now it wanted her help?

A faint beep chimed in the air, and Maida's hand flew under his blazer. He glanced at the screen before stifling the small device latched to his belt.

The break in focus allowed Nikita to gather her panicked thoughts. "That's a lot of...pressure."

"I don't want another war with the Elemnai. I don't see an impending victory. I see doom. Theirs...as well as ours. I hope you understand the risk here."

Nikita said nothing in response but could sense the general watching her. Maida rounded the desk until he met her at her side. "I'm leaving now. The commander of this mission arrives this evening, and I need to brief him immediately."

"So, if I do agree, he's going to be the one in charge of this team?" Nikita asked stiffly. "He decides the course of our actions?"

"Don't sound so disappointed. This is an Alliance initiative, first and foremost." Maida's eyes flickered up at her, and she smoothed her scowl. "You can trust him, but he will need your guidance. Whether he likes it, or not."

"And if he doesn't like what I have to say?"

"I believe your philosophies align fairly well. However, I regret to inform you that he *also* conversed with Elemnai. Perhaps around the same time as you."

"What!?"

"The Fireborne at Gunliem spoke to him in Khasiri."

Nikita's anger instantly morphed into curiosity, and her words softened. "So, he's an Al-Khasari?"

"Yes. Well, at least half, as far as we know." The general took a few steps toward the entrance of the office. He rested his palm over the brass handle of the heavy door and paused. "Now, isn't that another mystery? Who knew that the Elemnai *could* speak with humans, after all this time? If not through common Eidean, then why Khasiri?"

Maida glanced over his shoulder. "My aide, Derk, will be waiting at the lamppost near the roundabout by the old administrative building. By eighteen hundred hours, he will be departing, as will be your last opportunity to participate in the assignment. If you show up, you will be taken to Galeo City for processing and review weapons training... though I understand from your CV that this should all be very familiar. If you don't show up, well," Maida opened the door "We'll just have to find another specialist who is willing to meet the Elemnai once more, and uncover the *real* reason for these attacks."

Nikita's heart jumped at his words, and the door closed. They struck a chord deep in her chest. Again, she felt like a child. It was as if he knew her answer before she was willing to give it. Her inner voice screamed, *No! Join an Alliance mission?* Why would she ever do that? The Alliance was already superseding in strength and influence over the nations and heads of state that opted into its coalition. That kind of power was toxic... She had seen horrors firsthand as a child when the government seized total control over her home city of Trelle of the Alcides Islands, and terrorized her people. The lies had come after, smooth and practiced, masking atrocities committed by men not unlike General Maida, who thrived behind their polished titles. When truths stayed buried, they festered. No one learned. No one changed.

Several trajectories took shape in her mind of the events to come. If she declined the assignment, it would go on regardless. It would be nothing more than a military operation. There would be no room for debate or discovery—only violence. She thought back to her time with the Earthborne. They were formidable, but there was serenity in that strength. Nikita refused to believe they were the aggressors, but turning down the assignment could risk them to something worse. Without the truth, innocent Elemnai would bleed for the sins of a few. They didn't deserve that. Not after everything she had fought for.

Nikita's thoughts raced. Maida was right. She was the woman for the job. Her burning disdain for the Alliance had been tempered by a deeper drive to bring the humanity they so desperately lacked... the compassion the Elemnai needed. Shock subsided into silent conviction. Nikita wouldn't be swayed by the Alliance's cause, either. She immediately seized her datapad and made for the door, hoping this "Derk" would be easy to spot.

CHAPTER 6

COMMANDER

The engines of the massive aircraft slowly powered down with a deep, resonating hum rippling throughout the hangar bay. It tightened the knot in Malek's chest. Despite Valiant Squad's return to Mardascan soil from the Alcides Islands, Malek didn't feel thrilled to be home from another assignment. His operational detachment of Alliance Special Forces officers emptied from the personnel cargo, greeting the ground staff with ecstatic handshakes and accolades to one another and the air base crew. Several junior officers bounded past, and one strummed his back in celebration as he joined a few others further down the offloading line. Malek recoiled at the touch, half expecting pain to fire through the scars raked across his spine. He instinctively glared at the young recruit before returning to the mundane task of triple-checking the weapons inventory. Malek lost his train of thought, and his count, so he lowered the datapad in his clutches to his side with a groan.

"You can't blame the fresh grunts," a voice, firm but with a light inflection, spoke from behind him. "After a slag-show that was Trelle? Come on, I thought you'd at least smile, too." Anthem raised an eyebrow when Malek finally looked her way, unable to hide his disdain.

"I'll smile when I know I got the job done."

"But... you *did* get the job done."

"Forget him, Anthem," Jace blurted from somewhere nearby.

Malek lurched as another slap across the fabric of his casual, carbon black Alliance jacket nearly caused the datapad to slip from his hands. The jolt was enough to cement his prickly mood.

Jace rounded on him, and Malek's glare went ignored. "He's just sore because some Alcidian girl gave him the eyes, and *maybe* her number, and it's been a long time since he's felt the touch of a woman—"

"Jace, you know I only have eyes for your sister!" Malek cut in, and that was enough to make the man's jaw slack in alarm. It was almost too easy to disarm Jace... he fell for it every time!

"So, what's really going on?" Anthem asked and folded her arms.

Despite having mulled over the events of his last assignment for the past thirty-six hours, and having endured Rhodes' less-than-stellar command for the past six months, Malek couldn't put together a coherent thought, let alone a sentence. "I didn't realize that Rhodes could have made the call to stay in Trelle," he finally said. "Just thought there was more we could have done for the army. Or should have done. I don't know." Malek shook his head and placed the datapad on a massive ammunition container. His eyes wandered over to his commander.

Rhodes' leathery face was creased into a frown as he spoke with one of the ground staff members while another jogged up to him, gesturing toward the airbase runway.

"Reza! Reza!" Malek's attention darted toward the group of younger squad members, who were lined up together.

"Get in here!" one young man said, holding up a mobile at arm's length to take a photo.

"Dorro and the kids really look up to you." Anthem chuckled.

"By kids, you mean the grown-ass men who are the same age as this baby?" Jace jutted a thumb in Malek's direction, which Malek slapped away.

"Didn't take you for the jealous type, Jace."

"I'm not. I'm just saying that we've both been in this gig for like, what? Ten years? I think we *both* deserve that love."

Had it been ten years already? Malek could hardly believe it himself, but then again, he joined Valiant Squad at the atrociously young age of eighteen... and not really by choice, either. Among other things, this probably explained why he hated it when he had no agency. As usual, the topic always made Malek uneasy, so he tried to dismiss the remark. "And he's jealous." Malek smirked at Anthem, who nodded with a teasing grin.

"Next time, volunteer to take on an Elemnai." She regarded Jace.

"Reza!" the man known as Dorro called again amidst the laughter between him and a few other officers.

The noise got drowned out when another, much deeper and hoarse voice bellowed over the chatter of the officers mulling about the air base, bringing the room to an uneasy silence. "Lieutenant Reza! Up front!"

Malek whipped around, in unison with Jace and Anthem. He swallowed hard, his hand instinctively running over the back of his silvery white hair until its dark roots broke through. He dropped his hands immediately, hoping no one noticed his nervous habit. Rhodes sounded more aggravated than usual, and apparently, the rest of Valiant Squad also noticed, given that all eyes in the base had now turned to Malek.

"Frag me," he muttered, exchanging glances with Jace before breaking into a brisk jog.

Rhodes had made it no secret that Malek Reza had been a burden forced upon him, and he took every opportunity to shine a light on that fact, especially at Malek's expense. It was obvious even in the way Rhodes spoke to him.

"Sir?" Malek saluted Commander Rhodes with an open palm across his heart and stiffened posture. He was met with an icy stare, as if Malek was somehow intruding on an important brooding session. Malek had to suppress the urge to roll his eyes. This was just getting stupid.

"The hell you did now, Reza?" Rhodes said with a scoff and nodded his head toward the runway. "General's here for you."

"Me?"

"*You*. Get going."

It never made sense why Rhodes just didn't cut the antics. Malek had outlasted many of his peers in the rigors of Valiant Squad's physical and mental demands. Since Gunliem eighteen months ago, Malek's identity had morphed from an unwanted recruit to a highly capable and clever officer, and one of Valiant Squad's core members. Earning the respect of his team was the best way to stick it to his commander, but Rhodes should have changed by now, too. At this point, it was a waste of time to hope things would be different.

Malek's skin crawled with anticipation. He knew that dozens of eyes were fixed on him as he trekked over to the runway. He spotted the silhouette of the Galeo City skyline in the distance, shimmering against the glow of the late summer sun. The Spire was particularly luminescent even from this distance. Malek drew in the cool afternoon air and approached the man in the dark suit, the black vehicle beside him vibrating with the soft purr of its cell-powered engine.

Whenever Malek met his general, there was a mix of warmth and coldness. Maida, his mentor, had discovered Malek at sixteen years old as a non-combatant recruit. He'd rescued him—or further endangered him, depending on who you talked to—by bringing him into the Alliance Special Forces. After all, Maida always liked to push Malek beyond his limits, given their complicated history. It was another old habit Malek wished his commanding officer would break, no different from Rhodes's insistence on being a pinnacle piece of slag at all times. The pair often caught up between assignments. Meeting right after his return meant Malek was either in trouble for mouthing off again or was about to be on the receiving end of another test. He would be willing to play along, too, as long as it took him farther away from the four walls of that cold, sterile room, where he and Maida had first exchanged words nearly twelve years ago.

"Sir." He saluted as he met the general on the empty runway, palm over his chest.

Maida smiled and returned the gesture. "Let's go for a ride, Reza," he said and stepped back into the vehicle.

Well, this is weird. Malek raised an eyebrow as he rounded to the other side, only to be met by a tall, angular-faced Jennai man in a deep navy uniform who opened the door for him.

"You don't need to do that, uh...Brandt." Malek studied the name stitched on the breast of the uniform. It was slightly embarrassing that he couldn't remember the name of Maida's second aide. He had always met the first during these little catchups. "Derk got the day off?"

"On an errand," Brandt replied and nodded to Malek to enter.

"How did the assignment proceed?" General Maida asked, breaking the silence as the vehicle cruised along the runway. "Are you satisfied with the outcome?"

Malek ran the back of his hand over his forehead and tried his best to smooth over his voice. "It went well, sir," he began. "We...accomplished our objective."

"That's not what I asked."

Malek let out a long breath. "I'm not challenging Commander Rhodes' effectiveness or leadership, or ASFOM's direction... or the Primarch for that matter. Us pulling out of the joint Alcidian-Alliance Coalition was a slag move."

Maida shrugged and shook his head. "Hassentio is a warlord, and his brigade are terrorists. ASFOD Special Warfare Groups, such as yours, are not meant to bridge ties. You carry out the task given. Your only job was to apprehend Hassentio and his high command—the latter of which you were successful in completing. The Alcidian government received the help they needed, per our agreement with the state. Once the contract is up... well, we're not humanitarians. They have to sort out their house, so to speak."

"But the contract was amended and cut short. We never got Hassentio himself. Going home has left the Alcidians just as compromised as they were before. They don't even have enough bodies to keep their POWs locked up. Hassentio will just get those soldiers back, including all his little BFFs. All of our work will be for slag. The Alcidian Army is fragged and so are all the civilians in between."

"The line often gets blurry between duty and morality. Unlike Rhodes, I don't see acknowledging our failure to honor our humanitarian responsibility as a weakness." Maida paused and shifted in his seat to face Malek, leaning on arm on the car door. "I agree. It was a poor decision. I urged Primarch Usona to honor the contract to its full extent. Based on your answer, you would have done the same, given the opportunity. I also believe that if you were in Rhodes's position, you would have ensured that the Alcidians were left...in a less vulnerable position. So, do *you* think you can do better?"

Malek stared at the general. "Better?"

59

"At making the *right* decisions."

Malek's lips parted, and a fierce grip tugged at his heartstrings. "That's not my intention... I don't want to challenge Rhodes's command, like I said—"

"I'm not talking about Valiant Squad." Maida interrupted. "Malek," he said, lowering his tone to a hush.

Malek inwardly groaned, dreading when Maida shifted to the role of the father figure. Now it was time to have an honest conversation. Or at least, Maida's version of "honest."

"Do you remember the first time we met?" Maida continued.

Malek scoffed and nodded in reply. "Hard to forget when the commander of Valiant Squad of two-twelve shows up and drags you out of a Terminian torture camp."

"I didn't need to drag you out," Maida chuckled. "You dragged yourself out. And took the liberty of taking out your captors while you were at it."

Malek's insides squirmed, and a heaviness settled in his chest that made him sick. This was the one topic he wanted to bury, never to be brought up again. Finally, he muttered, "Not that I remember."

"I'm not here to talk about your blackouts. The point is, I always knew you could achieve anything... and do the impossible. Once I made General, I also knew I would need you one day, that there would be something that needed to be done, and you would be the only one I could possibly ask. Not just because of what you are—"

Mace, he said it.

"—but because you're the only one I could trust."

Malek kept his focus on the scenery beyond the window. He already hated where this was going.

"You're a rare breed, kid. You're tenacious, fearless, and brilliant. You're the only one I can depend on to get the job done."

That settled it. Maida wasn't going to let him say no. For all he knew, it was all in his head...but it was like a barrier in front and behind him. Refusing would force him into a new role, or something far worse. Malek sighed deeply, eyes skimming the sunburst clouds as ravens flew overhead. He ached for that freedom. But since he neither had wings nor anything else that would help him escape the confines of this vehicle—or circumstances—he fixated on the distant, hazy silhouette of the Spire instead. The structure towered over the city, its face glittering, but masking a deeper threat that sent a chill down Malek's neck. He kneaded it instinctively.

No...he wasn't going to let anyone decide *for* him. This had to be his choice to take on the assignment. *His* choice. Malek finally nodded, with a show of conviction. "What do you need?"

"Go home and rest. Right now. All of your new team details are uploaded to your issued datapad. Then meet me at zero-seven-hundred at my office. As soon as the briefing is over, you deploy."

"You know you're the man's lab skurr," Jace sneered as Malek clawed at his face in despair. "The way he pushes you, he's definitely running some kind of experiment..." He leaned in closer to his friend. "...To see if you'll pop." He pursed his lips together, then released an audible popping noise, which made Malek reactively groan. He was already on edge, and so far, Jace wasn't helping.

"Don't joke about that! Never joke about that!"

"Look, you're out in the field. It isn't the same thing."

Malek strained to hear Jace's voice over the honking of electric vehicles, gliding cell trams, and chatter from the nearby nightspots. Living in the heart of this urban community, Malek should have been used to it, but he found it obnoxious. Everyone was blissfully unaware of anything outside of their sphere of existence, and the dangers that so many had to face across the stretches of Eiden.

Galeo City was a bustling epicenter of the world's art, culture, business, and scientific research, and also widely known for its greatest and most distinct landmark. One of the oldest structures on Eiden, the Spire, could be seen from all corners of the city. Malek tilted his face toward the sky, feeling light raindrops against his skin. It soothed his frustration only momentarily. Of course, peeking out from behind a row of modern buildings was the Spire again—a coiled, narrow pyramid at the core of the downtown area. Its surface glistened with sheets of reflective glass as it stretched a kilometer into the sky.

The steel honeycomb lattice enveloped the repurposed tower—a skeleton that survived the Decimation 5,000 years ago. It was now a stark reminder of the past, in more ways than one. Being the local headquarters of the Alliance and Alliance R&D, harrowing memories of that building urged Malek to look back at his friend... memories of that same white room where he stared down General Maida with young, fearful eyes. He was Commander Maida back then, and he was... kind. It didn't make a difference. Malek still endured brutal solitary confinement and borderline torture for their endless pursuit of the truth. Whether Maida was part of it, he'd never really know.

Another fleeting wave of nausea lanced through him as they passed a cramped coffee stand at the edge of a crosswalk. A scrappy older man crinkled his face from behind the steel counter, tapping at a mounted datapad's holographic display to lower the volume of its wireless broadcast. A droning female's voice rolled off Alliance slogans as they painfully raked through Malek's mind: "Never again–that's why we fight. Peace Through Power. Unity Through the Alliance. The Alliance stands so humanity never falls." Malek cringed as it spewed out the same mind-rotting marketing that apparently still worked two hundred years later.

"Quit slagging yourself. You stayed alive this whole time, so just extend the courtesy to your new team as their commander." Jace said. Saying the word 'commander' terrified Malek more than he wanted to admit. He didn't feel ready for that role and had never been groomed for leadership. Why would Maida push him like this now?

"Anyway, I'm happy for you, bro," Jace finished.

"No, you're not."

"You're right. I'm jealous."

"You're really not."

"Why you gotta say that?"

"Neither of us is in this for the long run, Jace. We're just waiting to age out."

"Then why'd you say yes?"

"Because…" Malek stammered, unsure of how to put it. "I…don't want to be a proxy on something this crazy. So, I make it my own. Do things how I want to. If I come out winning, then maybe this is my way out. I'll have nothing left to show."

"Then, it's survival?"

"Yeah." Malek stared unblinking at the familiar beaten sidewalk.

"You got a bad feeling?"

"Always."

"Well, don't get your hopes up about being able to walk." Jace slowed as Malek did, standing before a slate and marble entrance to a looming living complex, its glass surface reflecting the shimmering city lights.

Malek sighed, gazing up at his home with reluctance, dreading picking up that Alliance datapad.

"Might just be digging yourself a deeper hole," Jace finished and stared at Malek with an uncharacteristically solemn look.

"I know. So… in case something happens to me—" Malek said slowly and seriously. "Tell your sister that I said hi."

Jace's eyes rounded, and he grimaced, throwing an arm around Malek's neck. It was hard not to laugh as Malek tried to break free, dodging an older couple strolling past who muttered something harsh when he nearly hooked them by accident.

"We had a spark!"

"You thought wrong, you piece of slag!" Jace tightened his vise. "You touch my baby sister, I will put that 'Immortal' business to the test."

Malek struggled breathing, and he finally tapped his hand on Jace's thick forearm. "Alright…"

Jace released him, nearly tripping Malek when he shoved him away. It made Malek laugh even harder, but he had to stifle it. Jace was getting pretty upset, and the last thing Malek wanted to do was part ways on less-than-stellar terms. "Yeah, you watch yourself, Reza."

"Ease up, it was a joke."

"Whatever." Jace glanced up at the building again, shoving his hands in his leather bomber jacket. Malek was surprised to catch a hint of regret in his friend's expression. Maybe he tried not to let on... but could Jace have been worried?

Jace was the only member of the Valiant Squad who was aware of the complicated history that had brought Malek to the ASF. Not even Anthem had the privilege of knowing why Jace, who'd joined the squad at the age of twenty-four, had lost his title as Valiant Squad's youngest recruit to an eighteen-year-old punk kid. Jace could have been like the others...intolerant, indifferent, or aggressive, but Malek had been relieved to find he had at least one ally in those initial days when it mattered most. If not for Jace, Malek would have walked a much darker path. Maybe General Maida knew that, too.

"Seriously. Watch yourself out there," Jace muttered.

Malek nodded and offered a weak smile in reassurance. They were always a good team. He wished Maida could have included him in the assignment. Not that he knew who was on his team anyway... but the fact that Jace was on stand-down and enlisted in another training session, as Malek should have been, probably gave it away that Jace wasn't coming along for the ride. "Don't miss me too much," he chided, but his expression faded when the two shook hands. Jace pulled him in for a quick embrace and a pat on the back.

"By the time you're back," Jace's voice hitched when he pulled away, "You'll be calling me Jumpmaster Jabari."

"That's so stupid—" Malek walked toward the doors of his apartment, hearing Jace cackle behind him.

"Gotta spread my wings!"

"Just remember to pack a parachute. Don't screw up on your first day."

"As long as you don't fall asleep while killing all the bad guys." Jace flinched when Malek spun around and fixed him with a deathly glare.

"Still too soon?"

"Too soon." Malek shook his head and turned away to the sound of Jace's half-assed apology.

Malek never enjoyed coming home from an assignment, particularly to *this* apartment. A citrus fragrance lingered, though Malek never kept any plants. The smell always brought up the memories of life between deployments that he chose to ignore. His mind retraced his steps, entering the apartment a long time ago, where a woman he loved would smile at him from the long sofa in the center of the living room or rush him from the kitchen for an embrace...or pull him into the bedroom with a kiss. It forced him to both relive and purge the memories of one Sidra Rayn. He kicked off his boots and sternly reminded himself that *she'd* left *him*. There was no point in thinking about it.

His eye caught the reflective face of a datapad sitting on the dark wooden coffee table, and he sighed. The sofa was cool but stiff as he pulled off his cellbike jacket and settled into it. With dread nearly cramping his hands, he lifted the datapad with a little force from its magnetic stand, where it had been asleep and charging for the last six months, and brushed off the dust. His fingers ran along the thin edge and powered it up, then he was prompted to enter his Alliance credentials. His heart raced as he tapped the brilliant orange typeface.

The transparent screen morphed into a slew of new pigments of blue and green hues, displaying the Alliance emblem. Panic took over his excitement. Malek studied the small, square holographic icons barely overlaying the screen, with several standard options to choose from, such as his profile, messages, communications, and a documents folder. He furiously tapped this icon, which opened a row of dossiers to select—the titles all printed in the same, bright orange letters. Something heavy sank into his chest when he quickly scanned the horrifyingly short list of names.

Malek frowned, and his lips parted in disbelief. Only three soldiers, a member of the Alliance Intelligence Agency, and a civilian. Maida had said the team would be small... but Malek assumed it was at least half a section. This was only the size of a split: a six-member team, including himself, and one composed of civilian, military, and intelligence personnel. Malek should've resisted the task a little harder.

What was this slag? He blew out a long breath, tapping on a memo next to the files, muttering a slew of curses before his eyes skimmed over the text.

Commander Reza,

This team will serve you well as you hunt for the Earthborne in the Juven Sands. Your discretion and expertise are critical in ensuring that casualties remain at a minimum and that Mardascan civilians are protected. Your rank will allow you to deploy the Alliance Army, though as I've stressed, you need to rely on your team to carry out this assignment first and foremost. The fewer bodies involved, the better. Brush up on your Khasiri. Locate the Al-Khasari survivor. Find the Earthborne and find the shard it's after. If you cannot reason with it, and if it cannot be contained, you must terminate the Elemnai.

Between you and Dr. Valerio, I'm confident that you will discover the truth behind this attack. Prepare for immediate deployment after the briefing.

General Maida

Malek needed to brush up on his Khasiri? His jaw tightened as the thought crept in: was his Al-Khasari heritage the only reason they'd made him commander? He could be one of the only people on Eiden who spoke it fluently, at least outside of Khasar. It didn't matter, though. Maida knew he hated his people. He'd never even considered them *his* people.

He reread the memo a few more times. It was a summary of the assignment, it seemed. *Get the intel. Find the Earthborne. Survive. Get the frag out.* A repeat of Gunliem.

Malek shook his head in frustration and opened the first dossier of the civilian. He fixated on the name Dr. Valerio and pulled up her photo. The round, tanned face of a grinning woman with dark, almond-shaped eyes, a slight nose, and full lips stared back at him from what appeared to be a faculty photo from the University of Kaira. The mess of deep umber curls around her face made her seem so naïve and young. It was hard to decide whether she'd be up for the task, and Malek's anger swelled up before he gave in to his curiosity and read her credentials.

Nikita had many admirable qualities, including mountaineering, hunting, working with small, isolated groups, and expertise in field medical care and minor surgeries. But fluency in the Earthborne Elemnai language, Umbar'ok, definitely stood out from the rest.

"*You and Dr. Valerio...discover the truth,*" he repeated to himself, reluctantly admitting Maida hadn't been lying when he said Malek would be prepared for the upcoming task. Now it made sense. They were going to have a *conversation* before they ran for their lives... because Malek had only been given three soldiers.

Having a civilian on the team posed a risk. The Alliance Special Forces were made up of members who endured intense, brutal training. Malek's old team, Valiant Squad, were warfare specialists assigned to the most critical missions. Each section, including the commander, had twenty-four members split into six roles: commanding officer, engineering officer, intelligence and operations officer, communications officer, and medical officer. Malek was the commander, and he assumed Dr. Valerio was medical. She seemed capable, but he still doubted whether she could keep a level head in combat situations. One couldn't know stuff like that from a textbook. He raked his hair and quickly scanned the next three dossiers, hoping the others' stories would be different.

To his relief, they were. Gene Anduran, an experienced officer from Norvica, had served in remote areas and was an expert in logistics, sabotage, and demolitions. The photo showed a calm, serious expression over Gene's pale, rugged face. His dark eyes were focused, with wavy chestnut hair swept over thick brows that knitted into a grave expression. Malek envied him, reading up on Gene's past assignments. This guy was a real professional. Doubt crept in, and Malek wondered why Maida didn't make Gene the commander instead. A few hours ago, Gene would have outranked him.

Bastion could have been a better leader, too, for that matter. This mysterious, single-named officer had a record longer than Malek's assignments in the ASF, working primarily through ASFOM, the Alliance Special Forces Operations Management. They communicated everything remotely to the ASFOD, or operational detachments like Valiant Squad. There was no photo attached, which Malek thought was unusual.

Then there was Vivika Kei, a newer Alliance recruit recently adopted from the Jennai Special Task—

"Wait." Malek exhaled, and his heart lurched into his throat.

Malek studied the large, upturned eyes and her long raven hair tied over her shoulder. She was looking up at someone in her photo, her face accented with a mischievous curl at the edge of her pronounced cupid bow lip. Malek cheeks grew hot, and he cleared his throat. With great anticipation, he looked at her past assignments. That's when he saw it: sole survivor of the JSTG at Gunliem.

The breath in Malek's lungs disappeared. He wanted to smile but couldn't. He rested his head against the top of the sofa and stared at the ceiling. It was *her*. He closed his eyes, desperately trying to remember the woman he met eighteen months ago, surrounded by a maelstrom of fire and drowning in the haunting screams of the Elemnai that preyed on them. He remembered the bodies, the scorched labs, and being completely alone in the dark until some plucky soldier caught him off his guard. It had thrilled him and scared him then, as it thrilled and terrified him now. Malek's thoughts trailed until they veered off the path of reality, catching himself desperately trying to back away from the walls burning in his apartment.

With a tight gasp, Malek sat straight, feeling the datapad slide off his knee with a muffled thud onto the carpeted floor. *Just a dream*, he thought with relief. He rubbed the sleep from his eyes, only to find himself sitting in the darkness of his apartment. His racing heart slowed with each calming breath. Reaching over to the datapad, he tapped it and revealed an analog clock, sparing a ghostly light to awaken his senses. It was nearly five in the morning. Malek's confusion morphed as wild determination took over. He jumped to his feet, reflecting on the names as he scrambled to get ready.

"Gene Anduran, gearhead. Bastion, comms. Dr. Valerio, medical, I hope. Vivika... well, considering you used a bunch of oxygen tanks as artillery to stall the Fireborne, I'd say weapons is a good fit for you. I can do this. We can do this." Malek stole a glance at his trembling hands. He repeated the words, "I can do this" as he turned to his bedroom, readying himself for the first day of his survival.

"Ah, slag..." he cursed, dashing back to pick up his datapad. "...What did it say about Casey Jaeger?"

CHAPTER 7
SPLIT

N ikita couldn't feel more awkward if she tried. She had no idea how to sit, no idea how to look, and no idea how to act—and certainly no idea how to keep herself from staring in awe at the Al-Khasari commander across the obsidian conference table. Nikita caught herself glancing at him again between General Maida's rushed but detailed briefing.

The general stood beside three vidscreens displaying various maps, and satellite captures that cast a ghostly light in the dimly lit room. It accentuated the white rooted-in-black hair of the olive-skinned man who studied the vidscreens with a mix of apprehension and frustration carved on his striking face. Those ethnically distinct indigo eyes remained starkly fixed on Maida. She had simply never seen an Al-Khasari in person... and as someone who studied ancient civilizations for a living, well, this was a pretty big deal. Thousands of questions ripped through her mind at once, and she zoned out in her muted excitement and curiosity. Nikita fidgeted in her seat and forced herself to look down at the steel case in front of her, given by Maida before the briefing. She sat there, convincing herself that she was fascinated with Malek Reza because of his unique heritage, and not his looks.

Get a hold of yourself, woman...

It had never occurred to her until now that she should journal about her commander... for research, of course, purely for an academic purpose. Nikita pulled the professionalism from the depths of her inner schoolgirl wonder and rested her chin over a closed fist, drawing her attention back to Maida. After reviewing the details of the attack on an Al-Khasari mining group, he was wrapping up a rousing speech about the value of this small team and the discretion it provided at this stage of the assignment. Nikita hardly knew how things operated on a normal basis but given the side glance Malek gave to the Norvican man next to him—whom Nikita understood to be Major Gene Anduran—she sensed it was out of the ordinary. The added wry smirk from the Jennai woman on Malek's other side, named Vivika Kei, also confirmed it. Nikita inwardly rolled her eyes at herself. She needed to stop staring at him.

"Bastion," Maida addressed the speaker in the middle of the conference table. "What's the current situation in Juven?" Nikita's ears perked up the minute she heard the voice of a young male. His intonation was mellow and warm, but oddly captivating.

"Good morning, everyone. The situation has cooled, but there is ongoing urgency and tension given the Earthborne's unknown whereabouts. Al-Khasari survivors are being treated at Azar General Hospital in a secure unit, guarded by the Alliance Army. Agent Jaeger confirmed that casualties have not risen since the initial attack at the mines at the border of Khasar and the Teokha Mountains. *That* number remains at twenty-one."

"And where is Agent Jaeger?" Maida pressed his hands firmly on the table. "The Alliance Intelligence Agency specifically stated that she would be at this briefing in person."

"Inbound. She has been delayed due to other grave circumstances. The attack came at an extremely unfortunate time. Whatever was unearthed at the mines garnered the attention of the Al-Khasari Kazi, their leader from what I gather. The Kazi, Nazar Siyana, was among the casualties."

"Heavens help us..." Maida shook his head.

Nikita's heart skipped a beat, and she realized the implications of the attack. The Earthborne was on the fringe of Juven and Khasar, it had blindly taken innocent lives, including the Kazi. If they failed to find the Earthborne, and if it assaulted a town in Juven, it would prompt the Alliance's full retribution. It would be an injustice to the rest of the Earthborne... especially if it were a rogue. She refused to believe otherwise. The peaceful Elemnai she studied and befriended couldn't have been responsible for the attack.

"Yes, sir," Bastion replied. "The Al-Khasari government is in turmoil, but that is not the only issue. The Al-Khasari reported to Jaeger that one member was missing from their group. Her name is Azka, a youth, it would seem. She fled the scene shortly after the attack."

"Why would she run?" Malek leaned into the speaker, his thick black eyebrows creasing into a frown.

"We believe she may possess the object of the Earthborne's desire. The Earthborne disengaged rather quickly upon Azka's escape."

"You mean another shard," Malek spoke, looking at Vivika. She appeared surprised when he did. "Like... from Gunliem?"

"Correct." Maida nodded to Nikita and sat at the head of the conference table. "Dr. Valerio, could you fill in the gaps?"

Nikita nearly slipped out of her chair and sat up straight. "Gaps?"

"As in, what is a shard," Malek addressed her stoically. "And why do the Elemnai care? What are we dealing with?"

Certainly not the friendliest way to start things off, but Nikita hardened to his undertone. She was used to asserting herself, and amidst this team of military personnel, she needed to prove her worth every minute she was here. *Here we go*, she thought. "I was one of the researchers who led an excursion into the Elemnai Wilds almost two years ago. I learned to speak their language, Umbar'ok, and as we conversed, we uncovered a few more pieces of our five-thousand-year history with them. The most relevant to us, which you'll understand in a minute, was that the initial wars between humans and the Elemnai somehow involved a certain weapon, person, or technology. What this object is or was is utterly vague, even according to Earthborne oral traditions. One of the many theories surrounding the Decimation is that it was not a natural occurrence and that this object somehow triggered the event itself."

Malek blinked slowly, and Nikita could see the impatience tightening around his eyes.

"W-We also discovered something else, in our research," Nikita pressed on. "It binds us not just to the Elemnai's history, but to their bloodlines. According to DNA analyses, the Elemnai and humans may potentially have a common heritage."

"You mean the Elemnai used to be...humans?" Gene leaned forward.

"Huge misconception, but no. It means that both Elemnai and humans branched from a common ancestor. We believe it's the Anymm—the only other sapient species on Eiden ever discovered, whose fossils are much older than anything we have found on this planet...dating fifteen thousand years before the Common Era. They were technological savants. The Al-Khasari are living in one of the richest archaeological sites in the world when it comes to anything related to the Anymm, which is another reason why we know so little about them. They have a monopoly on the most prized scientific finds in recent history...all of which were reverse-engineered to give us datapads, vidscreens, cell-powered vehicles, weapons, and sustainable homes. If we truly have a common heritage with the Elemnai, there is a potential that the Elemnai are just as aware of Anymmic artifacts, or technology, as we are and can harness the information in the relics, just as we have."

Nikita's eyebrows arched, and a giddiness elevated within her. *This* was what Nikita wanted to address in her lecture yesterday—the pinnacle findings of her research. Everything she'd worked toward culminated toward that understanding: the link between Eiden's three sapient species. She looked about the room, trying to gauge everyone's reactions. It was disappointing when she wasn't met with starry-eyed wonder, but concern... and perhaps a little disgust.

"What are you suggesting, Dr. Valerio?" Maida flexed a jaw muscle as he spoke stiffly.

"Well... After spending all night digging in the archives, trying to tie our historical understanding to the Elemnai oral traditions, I think I managed to isolate the term for said object in context. It's in allegorical mnemonics left by the Anymm. The most accurate term for this object is something along the lines of a channel, or... a conduit." Drawing a deep breath, Nikita began unclipping the case. "What it actually is, we won't know until we can piece it together ourselves. Its facets are damaged, suggesting this must be part of a much larger object."

Nikita immediately noticed the incredibly disturbed expressions on Malek and Vivika's faces when she lifted the item from the case. It was a strange, metallic motif where the alloys formed lines of a cube within a cube. She lifted it at chest height for all to see. "General Maida passed this to me before the briefing. I guess... this is the shard from Gunliem, what the Fireborne hunted for eighteen months ago. Based on Alliance research, the alloy that composes this fragment is not made of materials that we use, commercially or otherwise. It suggests that it's either extremely rare, incredibly old, or possibly an extraterrestrial alloy. Or maybe all of the above." Nikita shook her head, secretly doubting the words as they left her mouth.

To desire something so strongly, such as the shard, was an anomaly for the Elemnai. Powerful as they may have been, they were also staunchly attracted to simple lives, refuting many attempts to accept Anymm-based technology. If anything, she remembered the Earthborne turning up their noses at Nikita's datapad all those months ago. She had to resort to writing things down, much to her misery. She purged the thought and continued, "I'm not sure why it's all happening now...But since the Elemnai are rooted in Anymm ancestry, it's possible that they could have homed in on these shards. We don't really know the extent of their abilities... maybe this is something new."

General Maida leaned over the table, clasping his hands together. "...The alternative theory is that someone is colluding with the Elemnai and feeding the locations of the shards with their co-conspirators. Truthfully, as far-fetched as Dr. Valerio's theory may be, it's the one I prefer. Either way, we are in dire need of evidence. And that, Commander Reza, is where you and your team come in."

"There's a third possibility," Malek said darkly.

"That the Al-Khasari are the ones colluding with the Elemnai? No... Agent Jaeger spearheaded that investigation immediately after Gunliem. We have no evidence to suggest that possibility."

Nikita wondered why they both looked defeated. It started to make sense when she considered Malek again... maybe as an Al-Khasari living outside his homeland, he wanted a reason to deepen that rift.

Vivika was the first to speak after a moment of tense silence, "...What you're saying is that something led to the wars between humans and Elemnai. It was a weapon—maybe—and now we know that Elemnai can operate or understand Anymm tech just as we can. The conduit may be this weapon or tech, and what you're holding there," Vivika gestured to the shard. "That might be a piece of it? And you want us to find the other pieces?"

"In a manner, lieutenant." Maida nodded at her. "We now know the Elemnai are looking for ancient technology. If we know anything about Anymm tech, it is that it's powerful. R&D seem be consistent with Dr. Valerio's theory, in that this may be the key to another technological evolution. The Elemnai living as tribal communities has been our greatest asset in preventing any altercation between us and them for the past two hundred years."

"Then why can't we find them?" Malek cut in. "Or... home in on them, like you said? I thought you said humans and Elemnai both descended from the Anymm?"

"It likely comes down to genetics," Nikita replied coolly as she replaced the shard in its case, snatching up the chance to speak again. "Based on the Earth-borne samples we collected, it looks like they have a greater matching allele count with the Anymm than we do. I mean... who knows, though. It's all theoretical. It's not like we've sampled every population, Elemnai or... otherwise." Nikita's eyes glanced up at Malek's white hair, and he leaned back in his seat with a guarded look as General Maida continued.

"We all knew the day would come that the Elemnai would not tolerate our growing populations, almost bordering their lands without fear of consequence. This...conduit could just as easily be a weapon to the Elemnai as it could be anything else." Maida stood from his chair and paced over to the vidscreens. "The Elemnai are far superior to us in every way. All of us in this room have witnessed their strength. The lengths they have gone to seek the shards of the conduit are unheard of. We can only assume ill intent at the moment."

Wrong. Nikita frowned to herself and folded her arms. This could just as easily be an arms race. One thing was for sure, that the Earthborne feared humans, and how far the human race had advanced. Maybe they were looking for an ace up their sleeve... to be less vulnerable. If the situation were the opposite, Nikita wouldn't doubt that humans would kill for the chance to equalize the playing field. She had seen it as a child, between military and resistance factions, back on the Alcides Islands.

"Any idea where the girl ran off to?" Gene asked, glancing at the speaker as though addressing Bastion.

"Saifain," Malek blurted. Nikita was glad she wasn't the only one confused by his remark. The others exchanged questioning glances as she studied Malek, scrutinizing the vidscreens. She then traced his stare to a grid displayed over a geographical map of what she assumed was the site of the attack.

"Impressive, Commander," Bastion replied coolly. "You are correct. The Al-Khasari survivors indicated the same and said that she is potentially hiding in one of the downtown hotels. Apparently, Azka requested that her people find her once the Earthborne returned to its homeland in the Elemnai Wilds. How did you surmise her location?"

"A shot in the dark." Malek leveled a finger at the map. "But if I were on the run, that's where I would hide. Close enough to the Khasar border but doesn't cross into their territory. Keeps the Earthborne away from her people. It's in her favor that the city's a deathtrap."

"Yes, Commander," Bastion continued. "Saifain Police are in the midst of a heavy firefight with the drug cartels. Azka may be hiding among the gunfire to deter the Earthborne."

Maida stifled a smile as his fingers grazed his chin. She sensed the same pride he'd showed in the dean's office. "Do you have an accurate location?" he interjected.

"Not yet. Agent Jaeger was hoping to review her conversation with the commander, as he is likely more fluent in Khasiri, and can tease out more details from the interviews."

Malek didn't answer. He leaned back in his chair again, but Nikita noted the subtle roll in his eyes before anyone else did. He *really* did not care for anything related to the Al-Khasari...

"Agent Jaeger has arrived," Bastion said, his words measured but also eager. "Her transport is waiting for permission to land on the Spire's launchpad."

"Permission granted." General Maida turned to Malek, who immediately stood and rounded the other side of the conference table, opposite to him. "It's time for you all to head for Azar, and prep for the assignment at the main operating base. You'll be dropping down in Saifain's core, but you and Jaeger must identify a precise location for the infiltration based on the Al-Khasari questioning."

Nikita was uncertain whether she should stand to meet Maida, like the others did, but she nervously followed suit. Malek glanced at the officers in the room and straightened his Alliance uniform. It was more casual than others Nikita had seen. Plain white shirts swathed in black, high-collared canvas military jackets, with the ASF logo imprinted over the left breast. Carbon dual-toned cargo pants had been neatly tucked into black, matted boots with squared-toe busts, reaching up just below the knee.

Nikita pulled back her long, thick braid from over the shoulder of her olive-tinted jacket. She dusted off her fitted black pants that eased into her shin-high brown field boots as she stood up. Nikita was the only one not in uniform, leaving her feeling more of an anomaly than before. It took some effort to dismiss those childish feelings and focus back on the commander when he narrowed his eyes at the speaker.

"Bastion, notify local enforcement agencies and jurisdictions within one hundred kilometers of the Juven-Khasar border to report any sightings of any solo traveling Al-Khasari," Malek said briskly. "They are not to engage under any circumstances."

"Affirmative, Commander. Pulling sat images as we speak and reviewing police logs from Saifain and surrounding areas. Jaeger's transport will serve as the vehicle for our drop."

Malek nodded, then looked at the soldiers beside him. "Anduran and Kei—we'll need to move fast. We need support and equipment."

Gene nodded in acknowledgment. "I'll arrange with the CO onsite and prep the army for deployment."

"Stress that it's a last resort."

"Then I'd better make sure *we* are ready to meet the Earthborne head-on." Vivika grinned, folding her arms and winking at Nikita. Something about her made Nikita want to smile, too.

"I'm so glad you mentioned that, Lieutenant Kei!" Bastion chimed in with an excited tone. "I have some gifts for the team in Azar."

"Uh, Bastion," Malek narrowed his eyes at the speaker, "are... you not joining us?"

Maida cleared his throat. "Bastion only works remotely, but he will provide you with dedicated assistance from all of the ASFOM resources he can muster. Your team will make do with you four, and Agent Jaeger."

Nikita locked eyes with Malek for the briefest second. His cheek twitched, as though suppressing the urge to scowl. Had he expected Bastion to be present? Malek flattened his lips and stiffly saluted Maida in response. "Yes, sir."

A pang of regret knocked through Nikita. She liked the way Bastion spoke and couldn't help but feel curious about their missing teammate.

"One more thing, Commander. I don't have substantial intel to support this...but the local Army mentioned finding something in their search efforts." Maida glanced at Gene and Vivika. "Footprints, which were not Al-Khasari. Fresher. They were found before the army's arrival, and after the Al-Khasari had left the settlement."

Gene was the first to respond, "They weren't left by the Earthborne?"

"They were human. We just don't know what kind. It could be raiding gangs in the area or someone else. Take precautions." Maida released a deep exhale and saluted the group. "Good luck—to all of you."

"You can say it."

"I'm not going to say it."

"It's okay, Commander, it's a safe space."

Nikita watched the banter between Malek and Vivika as their crackled voices resounded through the clunky mouthpieces and headphones with cords that stretched into the low ceiling of the helicopter cabin. If not for these, it would have been utterly deafening. Nikita had never been much of a flier, and the roar of engines put her on edge like her days as a youth. It reminded her of the police helicopters of the Alcides Islands. Instead of gazing up at them in wonder as any child would have under far different circumstances, she had snuck through narrow alleyways to avoid their sights. Her insides tightened as the helicopter made a sharp turn away from the Galeo City skyline, pulled like a leaf caught in a turbulent river and dragging them to unforeseen places...dangerous places, even.

"What's so funny?" Nikita asked Gene to take her mind off the anxiety. He sat beside her. Between all the officers present, she found him the *least* intimidating... besides Bastion, of course. Gene was a close second—mature, but approachable, like an older brother or mentor. The man had a wry smile under his unshaven face, squinting when the wavy chestnut hair brushed his eyes.

"It's unconventional. The ASF never works as a team this small... Though speaking of unconventional things," he said and chuckled nervously, "we don't normally accommodate civvies, either. Commander is just trying to respect General Maida's decision, that's all, love."

"It's like Maida wanted us to operate as an intelligence team," Vivika beamed at her. "But with ASF leading the charge. So, you can say it." Her slanted eyes widened, and Vivika mouthed the words with comical exaggeration. "It's *crazy*."

Malek gave her a flat look but shifted his attention to Nikita. She threw her guard up when he did. He'd barely looked at her since they'd left Maida's office, with the same indifference she'd received as a young academic. She was willing to show him that she could bring something of value, namely, changing the team's feelings on the Elemnai. It depended entirely, however, on whether he was willing to listen.

"You think you'll be able to take orders?" he asked. "When we're in the field and under pressure, I mean?"

Nikita furrowed her brow. "Why not?"

"I've read your file. You made friends with the Earthborne. I'm willing to bet that's not motion sickness getting to you right now—it's guilt."

Nikita folded her arms indignantly, pretending Malek was wrong. "That isn't the same thing. Right now, we are gathering info to deal with a threat. We're not starting a war with the Elemnai."

"We're trying to avoid that. Our assignment is well-intentioned, but my question is, are you prepared if it goes south? Tough calls sometimes have to be made, and I need you to understand that orders are orders. Saifain is a death trap. The cartel guns don't care who they're shooting at. I can't have you going rogue on me, too... this isn't a school field trip."

"Yeah, I get it." Nikita frowned at him, trying to temper her tone. "You're in charge."

"That's not—"

"Leave the girl alone, Commander," a purring, smooth voice echoed in Nikita's headphones, and she looked up at the source with some relief. A pilot, or who she thought must be a pilot due to the tan jumpsuit, stepped between the console and Malek and Vivika. She pulled off her helmet and reached for her own headset, tugging her jaw-length, fringed copper hair behind her ears. She removed a pair of glistening aviator shades, and brilliant green eyes fixed on Nikita. The pilot smirked before glancing about the cabin. "Not her fault we have a little motley crew here." Nikita was unsure whether the woman had come to her aid or just cemented her status as the "ride-along." It was getting unnerving.

"Not leaving things to chance, that's all." Malek raised an eyebrow at the woman. "Jaeger, is it?"

"Call me Casey."

"Is that your real name?"

"Obviously not. But that's the handle." Casey tilted her head playfully and pulled out a box from the console. "Sorry for the delay in introductions. Just got off the line with Bastion and my contact with the Al-Khasari."

"You... have an agent inside?"

"No, of course not. She's my asset."

Malek didn't warm to that answer as he crossed his arms with a frown. Casey made her rounds, handing everyone something from her box.

When she reached Nikita, Casey gave her a small crescent-shaped, colorless device, with one edge of the material spiraling toward a soft, budded center. A minuscule blue light gleamed at the apex of the crescent. Curiously, Nikita eyed the detail of its smooth, pliable surface before placing it in her left ear, as everyone else had done already. Unlike the others, she fumbled, with the headset getting tangled in her curls.

"Communicators from Bastion. He will monitor your progress with these. We should be arriving in Azar within ninety minutes." Casey turned to Nikita, raising a thin eyebrow. "Does Maida really want us to take the kid?"

Nikita scoffed. "Kid? You don't look any older—"

"She's with us," Malek replied gruffly. "As our expert on befriending hostiles."

Nikita scowled at him, despising the remark. "I think *you're* more of an expert than me in this case."

Malek narrowed his eyes on her. "Whatever that means..." Nikita had a feeling he knew exactly what she meant. Was it supposed to be a secret that he'd spoken to an Elemnai in Khasiri? "I'm not the one who spent my summer vacation with the enemy."

Heat bloomed across Nikita's face, especially when Vivika and Gene started to laugh. "They're not...! Ugh!"

Casey chuckled and made her way back into the cockpit. "Let me get that recording for you, Commander. My Khasiri still needs work."

"I thought all you agents were savants in survival. Didn't you learn while on assignment?" Malek looked up at her, and she shrugged coyly before disappearing.

"They think I'm too spicy."

Nikita sank into her seat with a mix of fluster and anticipation as she ignored Malek's gaze. She wished she could have met the Al-Khasari and interviewed them herself. Now, *that* would make Pavo jealous. The cold heft of the case pressed against Nikita's leg, and she lifted it to her knees, clutching the steel surface with wonder. Malek, with some resistance from Maida, wanted to bring the shard to Azar. Nikita reluctantly knew that was the right call, too. No one knew what it was, so it was easy to hide. Who knew... maybe the Earthborne would find *them*, and Nikita could convince it to stop this madness. It was risky, but at least she and Malek saw eye to eye on that.

"They're a good group, Dr. Valerio," the same melodic voice resonated from the small receiver embedded in her ear, and a wave of calm settled over her when she realized it was Bastion.

"I don't know," she muttered. "I'm so out of place." The others were thankfully too busy discussing the upcoming drop in Saifain to hear their conversation... but something about his tone made her wonder whether Bastion was solely speaking with her through her earpiece.

"Everyone here is new to this type of assignment. But everyone also brings something of value. You'll see, in time."

CHAPTER 8
CONTACT

"**I**s that it?" Malek asked.

Casey glanced sideways at Malek, clearly annoyed with him. Malek didn't care. They needed to find Azka, and soon. Casey had spoken with a brother and sister, Arek and Asuza, who were the girl's uncle and aunt. While Casey and Asuza were discussing what might have attracted the Earthborne to their operation—though they had little to no additional information—a soft, rambling voice of a crazed Al-Khasari man had echoed in the background.

During the conversation, Arek unintentionally pointed Malek in the right direction: "Azka is obsessed with your world. She loves the restaurants and home-stays. All she talks about is eating fancy ethnic food at Hotel Paradise! That's what she reads... all propaganda!"

Hotel Paradise was at the heart of the city and was as good a place to start as any. The last thing Malek needed was to be wrong, though...especially in a hostile place like Saifain, with an Earthborne on the loose. They couldn't afford to waste a minute.

Casey lifted a pair of binoculars to her eyes, peering around the corner of a shattered sandstone building where Malek and his team remained, sheltered from the blistering sun and harsh desert winds. "Nope. It's the Paradi Hotel. Wrong place, guys. Let's go home."

"Are you always this funny?" Vivika griped from behind Malek, tilting her head forward to glare at the agent.

Malek wasn't the only one frustrated by Casey's behavior. Teamwork wasn't her strength, given her background as an AIA agent. Malek tried to stop questioning his general's agenda, but his patience was wearing thin. First, he was down a soldier, and now his agent was belligerent. If this were Valiant Squad, he would have decked his junior officer by now.

Casey tensed as she slid the binoculars back into a case on her belt. "We have to cross that obnoxiously huge road to get to it. In case you haven't noticed, there are potential sniper perches there—" She gestured south, then east. "And there. The firefight's heading this way, in case you haven't noticed that, either."

"We have." Gene grumbled, and Malek nodded in agreement. The desert would have been a far cry safer, and Malek caught himself wishing Azka never hid in Saifain. The cartel wasn't the only danger. Any police officer could shoot first and ask questions later. They couldn't just announce why they were in Saifain, either. They needed to infiltrate quietly and get out. But half the battle was getting the team to work together.

"...Maida never said anything about going into combat. I'm a little out of my element, that's all."

"A few of us are out of our element!" Nikita hissed sharply from Vivika's side.

Malek would have laughed if he wasn't in charge. Watching Nikita puff up and writhe was easily his new favorite hobby. "Calm down, all of you!" he barked. "Jaeger, any movement?"

"It seems like there is someone holed up in there." Casey glanced in the direction of the building. "Fourth floor, south end, blinking in the window, sunlight's reflecting on something small, like glass... or binoculars."

"You're sure?"

"It was blinking irregularly and moved. So, either cartel members are hiding, or this girl." Casey beamed at her commander. "Nice work, by the way."

"Thanks." Malek exhaled, beyond relieved that he'd been right about the girl's location. "Bastion, do you copy?"

"Yes, sir."

"Did you find the hotel blueprints?"

"Affirmative. The hotel has a lower basement which seems to run adjacent to a maintenance tunnel. You can access the maintenance tunnel through any manhole on your side of the street. There is one located approximately twenty-seven meters from your location, north, in an alley. If you backtrack, you can continue to use the alleys to make your way to the manhole. I've sent the location to your portables."

"Got it." Malek looked down at the rectangular screen strapped to his arm. A blinking blue light overlayed a green maze of lines and curves detailing the streets of Saifain, indicating their next move.

"Once you enter the maintenance tunnel, I will relay directions."

"Copy that. And Casey," Malek turned to her, "I could use a set of eyes outside the hotel...since we're not just worried about the cartel members, right?"

"Ah, the elusive somebodies, skulking around here like a bunch of skurrs." Casey sighed. "I'll move on ahead and find a spot outside to keep an eye on things."

"There is an exit point that would be suitable for Agent Jaeger, Commander," Bastion interjected. "I will inform you upon arrival."

Malek, though still a little sore about having one less member in the field, had begun feeling grateful for his mysterious lieutenant. So far, he seemed incredibly resourceful. Whatever they needed, he operated quickly.

Bastion's "gift" in Azar had also been a welcome surprise. Malek stifled his awe while Vivika excitedly reviewed their new equipment before they left Saifain. They received five form-fitting combat uniforms with a dark, metallic blue sheen. Surprisingly nimble, the suits hardly affected their mobility. Bastion described them as thin, hardened synthetic plates over titanium-dipped carbon nanotube fibers, built for flexibility. Malek thought this must have been new tech. Otherwise, why not outfit Valiant Squad with these?

Malek found himself equally impressed by the feel of his new uniform. The wrist-length gloves made of a dense but malleable leather stopped his perspiring hands from dropping his weapon. A tan, urban camouflage-patterned military jacket and cargo pants designed to be worn over the suit, which was almost overkill in this heat. The jackboots were black and thick, reaching up the shin with a square toe, with a matted, carbon-tinted mesh finish, which Bastion insisted rendered them weatherproof but breathable. Wherever they were headed, Bastion had covered all their bases. Still, a six-member field team would've been more ideal...Slag, a lot of things would have been more ideal.

Malek mimicked his former captain and scanned each of his teammates as he gestured for them to move toward the next objective. He glanced down at their weapons for a spot check. The equipment was familiar to Malek. Like himself, Gene and Vivika sported medium-sized sabers, small sidearms, and special operations combat assault rifles, no different than Valiant Squad's arsenal. As Nikita's gaze met his, he nodded her forward, her sidearm clasped stiffly between her palms. Malek was secretly glad that she surrendered the assault rifle. He honestly didn't trust her with it. Casey scrutinized him from head to toe as she passed Malek. For what reason, he had no idea.

Casey preferred a collection of personal weapons, including an unassembled, custom sniper rifle hidden in her pack which she opted over spare ammo or other supplies. Malek rolled his shoulders, loosening the constricting straps of the narrow black pack perched over his spine, after glimpsing at Gene's heavier-set bag as he passed. Thankfully, as the in-house demolitions expert, Malek knew that Gene stocked military-grade cell charges—much more powerful than the little rip-charge he used on the Fireborne, Urith.

Malek couldn't come to terms with one thing: the coin-sized camera fastened to the strap of their packs. Invasive as it was, Bastion justified the cameras for improved support. All devices were tied into the Alliance network, so it was easy for Bastion to track their movements and provide additional intelligence. Of course, this had Maida's fingerprints all over it. The general probably wanted a play-by-play of Malek's every move. He didn't give himself a chance to think about *those* implications...

Malek's chest tightened as they approached the manhole. Gene and Vivika lifted the cover in unison, and he became the first to lower himself into the darkness. Being the leader gave him more appreciation for Anthem. She cared for her teammates but always kept them in line. She recognized each of their talents and where she needed to support them. Malek needed to *be* her, despite those instincts berating him to push through and survive. He needed to *be more* if he wanted to be free of...all this. He couldn't have the Alliance reprimand him for failure. If they did, they would pull him back into that place... Whether this was paranoia or fact, he couldn't shake the feeling that his freedom was on the line. *Keep your game face on,* he repeated to himself. *No mistakes.*

Nikita looked surprised when he reached for her hand at the bottom of the manhole, helping her as she dropped into the darkness of the tunnel. It gnawed at him how he'd treated her, but he wanted to push... so she could push back. Everything about her screamed idealist, and idealists needed to face their antitheses head-on if they were going to survive. He helped the others as they descended one by one.

Malek turned on the flashlight of his rifle and guided them into the service channel, using the faint beacon on their portables to navigate the maze. Swiftly and silently, they stalked through the dank passage, with only their steps and trickling water echoing in its depths.

"Commander," Bastion said gently over the receiver, once they had closed in on their destination. Malek stopped in his tracks, and the others followed. "You're approaching a manhole. It should read the number 2789. Agent Jaeger may exit this route. It will take her to the street adjacent to Paradise. Unfortunately, she will have to maneuver herself from there on."

"We see it." Malek directed the light from his assault rifle to the gaping hole in the ceiling. The beam flashed over the degraded imprint at the lip of the opening.

"I can handle it from here, Bastion," Casey said coolly. In one quick maneuver, she holstered her weapons and jumped up, seizing the lower rung of the rusted metal ladder. She looked back down at Malek once she'd regained her footing. "Keep low and quiet, Commander. Stay away from the windows."

Malek nodded, his heart lurching in apprehension. "Got it. Report once you're in position." With a subtle gesture to the rest of the team, he led the others further into the darkness.

"Commander?" Vivika murmured. She stood right behind him, so her voice caught his attention immediately. The Jennai accent sent memories of that time so many months ago...creeping through the halls of that broken lab.

"Go ahead."

"Back during the briefing, you mentioned the shard from Gunliem before Dr. Valerio did."

"And?"

"That's not common information. Was that in my file?"

Malek slowed in his step as they closed in on the blue dot depicted on his portable. He paused in front of a large, concave doorway. "Sort of," he answered awkwardly. He knew where she was going with this. Honestly, he had been avoiding the topic since he'd read her dossier. Malek would be lying if he said he hadn't been looking forward to seeing Vivika Kei again. Not a day had passed since Gunliem that he hadn't tried to remember her face, and her voice. Now that it was happening, to say it was slag timing was an understatement. He was her commander. The only capacity in which he could know her was as his lieutenant.

Malek slung his rifle over his shoulder and seized the handle of the door—a large, valve-like metal wheel, riddled with rust and rot. A strained creak grated on his senses as he painstakingly forced it to turn, and before he could ask, he watched another pair of hands slide next to his. Vivika's shape filled his periphery. His cheeks grew hot, suddenly all too aware that he was wearing *a lot* of layers. He couldn't be more thankful for the tunnel's darkness.

"Then how did you know?" she asked quietly.

"...You mean you don't...?" Malek cleared his throat, and his heart wrenched at the realization. She didn't recognize him? "On three," he said. "One, two...three."

The pair grunted as the mechanism in the door released, and Malek drove his shoulder into the hatch, causing it to fly open.

"Cheers," Gene said. He took the lead as he shouldered his rifle and moved into the building. Nikita brushed past the pair at the door, and before Malek could take a step, Vivika touched his arm. Instinctively, he flinched.

"Answer my question." She fixed him with an eager stare. "Please."

"It wasn't... not directly anyway. I knew because—" Malek exhaled, his gaze trailing to the outlines of Nikita and Gene moving in the darkness. It bothered him that he thought about her so much over the last eighteen months. She didn't think about him? "I knew because I was there."

A small grin broke out over Vivika's face. "You're Specter?"

Malek chuckled. "Good to see you again, Kei."

"That helmet didn't do you justice."

Malek pushed back a smile that tugged at his lip. "Get moving, Lieutenant."

Darkness enveloped the team until Gene carefully opened another door, opposite the entrance from where they came, and scouted the room. The silhouette of dilapidated furnace and water heater systems forced Malek to keep his gaze ahead, and to hope that none of this equipment had been booby-trapped by the hotel's former... inhabitants.

Rows of wire shelves stood damaged and empty, likely raided by a citizen of Saifain. A few stray cans and empty boxes littered the corners, and a skurr twitched and bolted at the sight when the flashlights flooded the room. Not being a fan of closed, dark spaces, Malek gestured for Gene to keep moving, and they pushed into a vast yet wildly outdated commercial kitchen. Cracked amber tile work lined a wide, dual-row gallery. The stale fluorescent bulbs across the ceiling cast a weak, pallid light over steel cooking appliances dulled with a layer of fine dust. Pots and pans rested frozen in time in sinks and over gas stovetops, containing long-spoiled food reduced to hardened muck. An eerie feeling quickly took over. Vivika reminded him of why this trembled his nerves.

"Hmm, sneaking through the kitchen. This seems familiar," Vivika whispered.

"Don't remind me. I still have nightmares about freezers." Swallowing hard, Malek pressed on past a set of dual swinging doors, and into a dining hall.

"Mace," Gene muttered, staring at the scene before them. Chairs lay scattered while tables flipped onto their sides, several forming a barricade across the deep green carpet that browned where blood stained its fibers. Bullet holes splintered wood surfaces and shattered glass fixtures across the vast hall. Malek frowned at the sight. If there were bodies here, they'd already been cleared out. They were far from the fighting, but any of the cartel members could infiltrate this place, or worse, still be here. It wasn't safe. Malek needed to get everyone moving. He hoped that Azka would be the only person hiding out here.

"Bastion, you weren't joking. It's a disaster here," Gene spoke gravely, flinching as his boot crushed the fragments of ceramic that littered the floor.

"I can see that," Bastion replied, though he sounded unfazed. "Commander, once you pass the dining hall, you will arrive at a foyer, and then at the tower. The stairwell is located on the east end of the floor."

They passed through the lobby stocked with a pair of cherrywood bureaus and opposite a row of glass doors. Malek's senses remained heightened to the slightest sound. A vibration crawled up his legs, and the faint trill from the massive, over-hanging chandelier in the center of an ornate ceiling. He glimpsed shimmering crystals that glittered with the afternoon sun pouring in from the entrance. With a quick motion of his hand, he directed Gene and Vivika to proceed first toward the tower. The two of them scouted the blind spots of a wide, gilded entrance, tracing their stares upward.

"Commander, I'm receiving a transmission from Agent Jaeger," Bastion said. "I'll patch her through."

Malek had nearly forgot that Bastion hadn't set up cross-connections between the team while they were together. It had something to do with echoing feedback, as these receivers were a newer model, but Malek couldn't be bothered with the details. He paused, glancing back at Nikita. She immediately snapped her eyes ahead, forcing a neutral expression. Though she tried, he didn't miss the twitch of anxiety, which never left her gaze.

The receiver in his ear briefly crackled, and a new voice came through on the other end. "Commander," Casey began, "I'm in position. I have eyes on the fourth floor, but I'm a little more north of where I initially saw movement. Some curtains are in the way. I only have a partial view of the room."

"What else can you gauge?"

"Each floor where it intersects with the atrium. Where are you?"

"Main floor, about to head up."

Malek could feel Nikita right behind him, sighing in awe at the sight of the open-air atrium, and he didn't blame her. The courtyard in the middle was surrounded by balconies overlooking this old fountain. Malek looked up and down, dizzying himself though it was only a few stories high. Dead vines clung between the balcony spindles. Iron staircases curved downward, leading to a desolate garden below—a salute to the hotel's former glory. This place was likely controlled by the cartels. What a damn waste.

"Kei," Malek spoke. "Take point. Anduran next, and Valerio, stay close to me."

With a quick nod, both soldiers proceeded quietly, barrels lifted, and sights aligned with their gazes. Vivika was the first to round the corner and cross the beaten-tiled balcony to the open hallway.

"Commander!" Casey hissed, nearly causing Malek to jump. "I'm seeing some rooftop activity! South. About nine or ten buildings over. A dozen bodies, just can't make out their allegiance...wearing black cowls it looks like...so...could be the gangs."

"I don't like that," Bastion mused. "Commander, I'm deploying a small surveillance drone. I was hesitant to do so sooner due to the gang and police activity in the area, but I feel it is necessary at this time. Agent Jaeger has it on her person."

Malek was a bit surprised he didn't know that, then grimly wondered if it had been on purpose. "Affirmative. Go ahead. Order Franz's troops on standby and keep the updates coming."

"Funny man, that Franz...," Gene muttered, giving Malek a side glance. "'Keep my men out of harm's way,' he said. Remember that bit?"

Malek frowned. "Does he not realize he's in the army?"

"Just whinging about the ASF bossing him around." Gene shrugged, and moved ahead.

Malek let out a sharp breath and chewed on that frustrating thought. When they'd met Major Franz back at the Azarian MOB, the man almost recoiled when he'd realized that Malek was in command. It was hard to pinpoint his exact problem, but the list was long enough—Malek's age, ethnicity, or the fact that he was with the ASF. It didn't matter. When it was time for troop mobilization, Malek didn't give Franz an inch to disparage his command. Everything needed to work. "Are they approaching, Casey? At this rate, we won't be able to secure each floor."

"Yes, Commander. They're heading this way. I'll keep one eye on the hotel and see if I spot any more movement. For now, head to the fourth floor, as far south as you're able to go. Someone was in the southeast corner."

Malek followed Gene with Nikita in front, reminding her to keep close to the walls as they crossed the atrium toward the staircase on the opposite side. Malek's senses alerted him to every step echoing in the narrow space of a deep green carpeted hall lined with golden filigree wallpaper. His muscles tightened with every floor they ascended, diligently securing steel doors on each level, and ever wary of potential threats. When they reached the fourth floor, he signaled to Nikita to step back behind Gene and took the lead.

Carefully, with the sight of his rifle leveled to his gaze, he moved across the opening and darted his eyes up and down the adjacent hallway. Glancing at the portable, Malek moved southward down the narrow passage, his steps hushed across the fibrous surface. The echo of his racing heart hammered in his ears, nearly drowning Bastion's cautious words as he indicated they were approaching the southeast wing.

"Commander," Bastion continued, his tone grave and low. "Those bodies that Agent Jaeger had mentioned are approaching the hotel's perimeter. Two dozen personnel in total, half of which are congregating on surrounding rooftops. Their guises are... unusual. I cannot confirm their identities."

Malek's heart leaped, and dread sank into his chest like a stone. Still, he tempered his voice before responding. "Copy that...any chance they could be distracted?"

"We could use the drone, but it is hardly a worthy distraction. It is not equipped with any form of weaponry. I am developing a new exit strategy. Standby."

Throat tight, Malek touched the ajar ballroom door, eyes flicking to his team. Every heartbeat pounded with adrenaline. Without another word, Malek crept into the room.

The sun radiated through several long windows of the east wall. Deep red curtains woven with gold accents draped along its edges, and dual rows of ivory pillars ran the center of the room. It all felt off. Needles pricked at his skin, and an acidic taste filled his mouth.

"Anduran and Valerio, watch the doors. Kei, eyes forward," Malek growled, nodding to his team to take their positions. Their expressions darkened before each of them moved, with Kei brushing past him and sliding toward the nearest pillar. Unlike the rest of the hotel, this ballroom was strangely untouched, except for the small corner where a satchel and copper cup rested over a thin, square-patterned blanket. Malek slowly walked into the room in plain sight. A tight gasp cut through the air, and Malek darted his eyes to the opposite wall.

"Who are you?" a youthful, female voice bellowed in Khasiri, breaking the creeping silence at last.

Instantly, and with immeasurable relief, Malek lifted his hand and rifle in a show of peace, thrilled that he'd been right all along. "A friend," Malek called back in Khasiri. He tilted his head slightly, so Vivika could glimpse his calm expression. Her cheeks puffed with a slow exhale. "No harm will come to you," he said, stepping forward. "I'm here for the sake of your aunt, and your uncle... Asuza and Arek. I'm here to take you back to them."

A lock of silvery white hair draped from behind an ivory pillar, standing near the opposite end of the room, by the blanket with the satchel. Malek fixated on her.

"You talk funny...What's your name? Do I know you?"

"Likely not. I'm Commander Reza, of the Alliance. I, uh, I live in the Outer Cities."

His insides lurched when a small face peered out from around the pillar. She narrowed her deep indigo eyes on Malek as he stepped in her direction, and he stopped several feet from her. She was a lot younger than Malek thought... just a teenager. He respected her bravery but needed to bring down that defiance.

"Ah, no wonder you sound different. You're *that* man. Everyone knows about you. You spoke with my aunt and uncle?"

Yes, that man... the only Al-Khasari who lives outside of Khasar. Get over it, Malek thought, and pressed on despite the aggravating remark. "I did," he lied. "They're worried about you. They want me to bring you back to Azar. They're waiting for you there."

"Or, the Alliance, wanting to take me away and force me to divulge Al-Khasari secrets." Azka frowned, her tone spiteful and harsh. "How can I trust you?"

Slag, he should have scrapped the title. "You can't. But whether you like it or not, being here will likely get you killed. Coming with me will not. There's still an Earthborne out there."

Azka's expression twitched into a look of genuine concern.

Malek struck the root of it. "Whatever you have, the Earthborne will find it. They always do. A Fireborne I met months ago did the same, and a lot of innocent lives were lost that day."

"My people will come for me. I don't need you."

"They won't get here in time," Malek kept his voice subdued despite Bastion's warning for him to hurry. The urgency raged through his system like a fire, but he forced himself to remain calm and think. "But I'm right here, and I'll be honest. The Alliance doesn't care about you. They only care about what you're holding."

Azka stepped out from behind the pillar and snatched up the red leather satchel in the corner of the room. Dust clung to her black cloak as it drifted over the fitted white jumpsuit, and the hem frayed and beaten. Her long, silvery white hair hung messily over her thin shoulders, soiled with hints of the desert sand. Placing the satchel over her, she clung to it and approached Malek. Azka's dark eyebrows remained furrowed, squinting under the light of the adjacent window.

"So let me get this straight." Azka folded her arms. "You want what I have and don't care whether I live or die?"

"I said the Alliance doesn't care."

"But you're part of the Alliance."

"So?" Malek said, managing a weak smile.

Azka seemed caught off guard by this, and her hard expression smoothed over.

"I, of all people, know what it's like to be separated from the pack," Malek continued. "Chosen or otherwise—it's dangerous." He extended his hand with an open palm. A light crackle resounded in his ear, and he heard a voice laced with dread.

"Commander!" Casey hissed again. "I can see the insignia. You need to move it. *Now*. It's the GX Forces."

What the hell were the Terminians doing here?! Malek's pulse raced. Why did it have to be them, of *all* people? He stretched his hand a little further for the girl to seize. "Please, Azka. It's no longer safe here."

Azka stepped forward, painfully slow. She blinked in the sunlight bathing over her. Pursing her lips, she steadily approached Malek. Her fingers constricted around the strap of her bag.

"Commander! The drone just assessed the east wall! They're rappel—" Bastion cried, but his voice drowned in the uproar of gunfire and the crack of splintering glass.

Panic surged through his body as bullets whizzed past. Malek lunged forward, hurling his arm ahead. His touch barely reached the hem of the girl's cowl. Blood sputtered from her small, parted lips. Those indigo eyes widened in terror before rolling back into her head. She swayed in her step and fell to her knees. Shadows replaced the brilliant sunlight flowing through the panes. In the same, mind-numbingly prolonged moment, Malek flexed his shoulder and swung his rifle into his grasp, lifting the sight in time to fire at the dark uniformed agents outside the windows.

Vivika suddenly appeared beside him. Several rounds ripped through the air, followed by gurgled cries. The agents went immediately limp and fell from their lines.

"*Valerio*!" Malek bellowed, scooping Azka's limp body into his grasp.

"Pull her back. I'll give you cover," Vivika's voice shook.

Malek groaned, equally in strain and fury, doubling back to the ballroom entrance. Crimson dripped from the corner of Azka's mouth, and she could barely open her eyes. Malek called her name several times more just as he laid her on the floor, pleading with her in Khasiri. This was all going so horrifically wrong. This wasn't supposed to happen.

"Azka, you need to open your eyes, stay with me!" Malek begged.

Nikita was a swift blur in his periphery as she instantly studied the young girl's wound. She tossed the cloak aside, her hands running across Azka's trunk. In between rasped breaths, Malek could hear Nikita utter, "Slag, slag, slag..." until she stopped. Fear tightened around her eyes. "There isn't an exit! It's embedded in her lungs. I can't do anything for her except stop the bleeding!"

"Then do it!" Malek cried, startled when something touched his cheek.

Azka had one of her slender hands on him. Her mouth parted into a thin slit, and her Khasiri words were barely above a hush, "I...I am *madna* now... *Drashe* is yours... protect us all..."

"*Azka!*" Malek shook her as her hand slipped from his face. "*Frag*! Bastion, come in!" he growled, catching sight of Gene glancing over his tensed shoulder, studying the youth on the floor with a pained look. Malek's heart hammered in his chest, the adrenaline beating down the despair rising from his center.

"I'm here, Commander. I-I apologize! They rappelled into the building rather quickly, and it seems they were not expecting you—"

"We need an exit!" Malek said sharply, tempering his emotions as well as he could. It wasn't the time to grieve...Not just for Azka, but for himself. He was about to lose it all on the first day—his grip on the mission, on the team, on everything he so desperately tried to hold. If they failed here, or if he suffered another blackout, he knew what waited for him. It would be the end of whatever freedom he'd barely earned. He couldn't let it happen. Not again. No matter what, the team had to make it out alive.

"Get the team down and head back to the main floor. You will exit through the loading dock adjacent to the kitchen, where you will exfiltrate via the reassigned EZ. The GX Forces are mobilizing and are preparing to descend through the atrium. Your pilot is in transit." Bastion paused, just as Malek and his officers gathered around Nikita, exchanging desperate glances. "You have a clear path ahead, but only for a moment. Make the most of it, Commander."

CHAPTER 9

AGENTS

Nikita heard nothing. Blood ran cold in her veins. She stared down at Azka, vision tunneling as she watched the rise and fall of her chest become shallow and slow. The bandage she had strapped to the right side of the girl's trunk had already become stained a deep red. Nikita's mind unwillingly traced distant memories of her old neighbors. They were begging for her father to help their loved ones. She watched them lay the bodies of young men and women across her kitchen table. The crimson never came out of the wood, no matter how blistered and stiff her hands became from scrubbing its surface.

Adrenaline raged through Nikita's system, pulsating down into her nerves. It prevented her trembling hands from loosening their grip around her knees, waiting for the moment Azka's breathing would stop. Nikita couldn't bring herself out of that shock. The thrashing of her heart drowned the voices around her, but they slowly started to break through her senses. An argument was taking place. Her mind brought forth the pitches and words, and she homed in on her commander's plea.

"We are not leaving her behind," Malek spoke, standing defiantly over Azka.

"Commander," Gene pressed. "We'll be down a gun—"

Nikita mustered the words before she considered their boldness. "No," she said. The three soldiers looked at her. "Commander is right. We have to take her back to her people." Nikita rose to her feet, stifling the quiver creeping through her inflection. "I'm better with the cultural niceties than I am with a gun. I'll take Azka. Help me lift her onto my back."

Malek knelt, removing Azka's red leather satchel and donning the strap before lifting her off the ground. With her back turned, Nikita bore the weight of the young girl slumped over her shoulders, with her thin, motionless arms draping over her collar. She knew there was nothing she could do, except bring her home. The Al-Khasari, like so many cultures and people on Eiden, practiced funeral rites. She and the others could have easily turned their backs and ran for safety... but if they could do this one thing, they wouldn't forsake their already weak connection with the Al-Khasari. She would have done anything to preserve that, too. Nikita's heart wrenched as she looked down at Azka's slender hands. Vivika slid around to the front, clasping the ends of Azka's robe and fastening them tightly around Nikita's waist. At least Azka was a little better secured on her back.

"Thank you," Vivika's words were barely above a whisper. She touched Nikita on the head and looked at her intently. "I'll be right beside you."

Nikita nodded vigorously, blowing a curly strand of hair from her eyes. Vivika gently tucked it behind Nikita's ear and reassured her with a quick smile before regrouping with Malek.

Grimly, the commander moved to the doors of the ballroom. "Ready?" Malek stood at the front of the four, his rifle raised and finger on the trigger.

"Yes, sir." Gene narrowed his eyes toward the hallway.

"Always." Vivika said, her voice brimming with confidence.

Malek eyed each of his teammates, acknowledging Nikita last. "Let's move."

Nikita followed the single file of soldiers, quick in their stride, back the way they came. Though each step was as muffled as the last, Nikita could feel the drum of their march beating in her ears as they quickly reached the end of the corridor. She had yet to suffer the heft of the girl bearing down on her. So far so good. Just yesterday, she was educating young pupils and alluding to her bravery in the Wilds. The safety of her auditorium seemed like such a faraway place now. Today, she contemplated whether her fate would be no better than the girl on her back, all the while wondering if she was ever brave at all.

"What's your location?" Casey hissed through the receiver.

"Coming down," Malek spoke, but his words were barely audible.

Clearing the corners, Malek led his team back into the stairwell, with all three soldiers leveling their weapons and scanning their surroundings in all directions. A gesture from their commander prompted them to fall back in line and proceed down the stairwell. With each floor they approached, Malek signaled for Gene to mark and lock the doors as they passed. Nikita swallowed hard and focused her hearing on the corridors as she watched Gene do the same. Nothing resonated from the other side, but it brought her little comfort. They continued down each floor and conducted the same routine of scanning, listening, and moving with precision and speed that both awed and terrified Nikita. So far, she maintained pace with the others, either her determination or urgency lifting Azka's weight from her back.

At last, they reached the main floor. Malek was poised at the edge of the stairwell, just before entering the hall with the hanging gardens. "Casey," he murmured. Nikita found him unnaturally calm. "Visual?"

"Not yet. But I'm sure that'll change very quickly."

"It will," Bastion added grimly. "The drone has detected movement just above the atrium. Transport will be at the EZ in fifteen minutes. Commander, can you hold out? Should Franz's forces move in?"

"Connect me on my orders." Malek exhaled, leveling his rifle again. He glanced at his teammates, and with a quick nod, he turned the corner into the main corridor.

"*Contact!*" Casey cried, her voice stark and shrill.

Vivika pushed Nikita back into the stairwell's adjacent hallway before bolting across the marble floor to meet her commander and fellow teammate as they crouched against the detritus-ridden banisters. Each fierce cry from the enemy agents jolted Nikita's heart. She had never seen anything so bold. Nikita marveled as several agents dressed in black stealth suits rappelled from the highest floor of the atrium, launching over the barriers and diving into the cavity with compact, automatic weapons at the ready. Large, cat-eye-shaped red goggles flashed over black hoods under the sunbeams penetrating the skylights.

Nikita snapped her focus back to her team. Before the agents had a moment to steady and open fire, Nikita's three teammates stood and unleashed a barrage of bullets. Several agents screamed and slid from their lines into the lower level. Nikita cried out with each rippling blast thundering through the air.

"Check out these clowns!" Vivika shouted over the splintering marble as she and Malek crouched together.

"Those aren't just GX Forces," Gene bellowed. "These are AX agents! Terminian black ops. Their leader is somewhere nearby."

Shattered glass rained from above, and an agent screeched. She hung limply from her line, swaying. Nikita watched as her team glanced up at the windows of the atrium.

"Got one!" Casey hollered. "Move it, Commander! AX agents are mandated to debilitate and capture."

"Great," Malek snarled. He quickly opened fire in a short burst and hid again just as a bullet whizzed past him and into the floor, near the stairwell. "We need a distraction!"

Nikita yelped again, failing to stifle it when another bullet peppered the wall behind her. She wished she were braver.

"I have a solution," Bastion said hurriedly. "Major Anduran, do you see the pillars on the west side of the atrium? These are weight-bearing structures, according to the hotel blueprints. The AX agents are rappelling from the balconies directly above.

"Get the charges ready." Malek stepped beside him, Nikita assumed, to give him cover.

"Right." Gene whipped off his pack, pulling several fragments of electronics from the compartment. He began assembling small devices, no larger than his fist. Those...those were *bombs*. Was Gene seriously going to blow something up? While they were this close? Malek returned short bursts of fire, positioning himself to shield Gene. Nikita could barely think when she heard Casey whoop over the comm as another agent, perched on a banister several floors above, collapsed backward, and disappeared in the rising dust of devastated stone and marble.

"Kei, as soon as the charges blow, get Valerio and Azka moving."

"Copy that, Commander." Vivika swiftly shot another round, causing an agent to curse and retaliate.

"You good?" Malek looked at Gene, who affirmed with a determined nod. "Go!"

It was uncanny how few words were spoken, but everyone moved like clockwork. Nikita readied herself, staring wide-eyed as Malek daringly stood, instantly drawing the fire of several agents. He moved along the banister toward an adjacent column. Going the opposite way, while crouched, Gene slid against the barriers and rounded the first floor of the atrium. Malek rested his back against the pillar, flinching as the stone chipped away from another barrage of bullets.

Vivika mimicked her commander, shouting a slew of obscenities at her enemy before taking several precise shots, and hiding herself against another column closest to Nikita. From where she stood, Nikita had a direct view of her. Vivika's shoulders sharply rose and fell with every breath. She gathered herself while she waited for an opening to return fire. Nikita hardly believed it when Vivika gave her a wry smile and a wink.

She's nuts! Nikita hissed to herself. Azka's trunk swelled against her back as she sharply inhaled. Nikita strengthened her grip on the girl's legs, dropping her voice to a whisper, "I don't know if you can understand me…But I'm getting you back to your people. Please… try to hold on."

Nikita's focus returned to the firefight just as Malek and Casey exchanged rushed vernacular over the receivers—something about their enemy's position. Vivika took no part, but Nikita could tell she was paying close attention as she exchanged quick glances with her commander before aiming again, altering her target following their intel. Malek hissed a curse and cut sideways, rifle leveled at the corridor that led to the main lobby. Then he was gone, and Nikita's panic surged as Vivika pivoted her weapon to match him. Was their exit blocked? Across the atrium on this level, through the fine dust lacing the air, she spotted a figure behind the column, rushing across and taking cover behind the barrier again.

A stoic voice resonated through the receiver, breaking through the deafening roar of gunfire. "Pillar one all set," Gene rumbled. "Setting charges on pillar two. Commander, more incoming from the lobby."

"I got 'em," Vivika cut in, and Nikita fixated on her as she stepped out and took aim. Vivika unleashed on the enemy closing in from the main corridor.

"Commander, they're still coming in hot from up top, but I'm getting some heat thrown my way," Casey growled between sharp breaths.

Malek's voice broke through the receiver, "Get to the EZ, now. Anyone gets in your way, you take 'em out. Good hunting."

"Yes, sir!"

Nikita heard Malek mutter a curse, as though he were hesitating. "Bastion, get Franz's units mobilized to our location. They need to stop the influx of bodies. We're overwhelmed as it is."

"Affirmative."

Vivika pressed herself back on the pillar, dropping a clip to the floor, and pulling a new clip from the side of her belt.

As she reloaded, Gene's voice came through once more, "Coming to you, Commander."

Shrieks of agents relaying indiscernible information echoed from above as nearly a dozen more agents appeared overhead. Several bodies perched over the topmost banisters rained ordnance down into the atrium below. Vivika flinched, sliding down and turning her head away as the pillar continued to chip away from the onslaught. Bullets tore through the wall beside Nikita, splinters and debris lashing at her cheek. With Azka's weight throwing her off, she lurched backward and slammed into the corner.

"Do it now, Anduran!" Malek bellowed.

"Brace in three...two...one!"

Nikita had barely prepared herself for the deafening boom and the tremors that instantly followed. Dust clouded into her hallway, and as she gasped for air, a powerful grip took hold of the collar of her shirt and yanked her off the ground.

"Let's go, Kit!" Vivika shouted, and her grip transferred to Nikita's upper arm as she scrambled as fast as her legs would allow. Marble and debris hailed from above. A terrible cracking noise filled the noxious atmosphere. Nikita tilted her head in the direction where she had last seen Gene, watching the scene unfold before her with such ferocity that it felt surreal.

The concrete pillars opposite her were crumbling to dust, and the devastation crawled vertically. Beginning with the second floor of the atrium, the balcony above splintered...then it was the third, fourth, and the fifth—by the time Nikita bolted into the corridor leading to the main lobby, she could hear the screams of tumbling agents, followed by slabs of stone and concrete plummeting into the heart of the atrium and the desiccated garden. For the agents left behind on their rappel lines, Malek backed away from the precipice of the first balcony, his aim drawn upward and firing, while Gene took shots from his side at the stragglers that miraculously survived the fall as he bolted away from the devastation.

Nikita rushed past Malek, and for a split second, he fixed his intense, indigo eyes on her. They impressed something between assurance and fortitude that made Nikita's insides tighten, even more than they already had. Vivika hauled her ahead as she navigated their escape past several collapsed AX agents littering the foyer. Nikita counted half a dozen bodies, and a nauseating feeling overwhelmed her while Azka's body crushed against her spine. It dulled her vision, and she wavered in her stride.

Vivika held her steady and made her focus on her hazel eyes. "Eyes ahead, Kit. We're almost in the kitchen. Do you remember seeing a door? Like a big one?"

"Yeah," Nikita panted, barely able to keep up with Vivika's pace. "Back near the pantry, where we came in from."

"I'm glad one of us was paying attention."

Nikita's core shuddered again, and a faint clinking resonated nearby. As she and Vivika worked their way around a few tables strewn across the carpeted dining area, she heard the noise again. Instinctively, she craned her neck toward the chandelier above the main foyer as it trembled. The crystals swayed back and forth, winking in the light. What was that? An ominous feeling washed over her, forming a knot in her stomach. She swallowed hard and pressed forward, following Vivika behind the bar and into the kitchen.

Another swift onslaught of bullets met the women as they passed the threshold. Nikita screamed in terror, and Vivika dragged her behind a prep counter where bullets ricocheted off steel surfaces and appliances. Nikita's breath escaped as her heart thrashed against her ribcage. An unexpected cry rang out, likely an order bellowed in the Terminian language, immediately halting the suppressing fire.

Vivika looked up at Nikita, sweat beading on her furrowed brow. "*Staka*...They can't shoot in these close quarters," she hissed, swinging her rifle over her back. "Bastion, I've counted five agents in the kitchen. Blocking our path to the EZ."

"Can you hold your position?" Bastion said.

Immediately afterward, Malek's voice cut in, "Do not engage! We're coming!"

Vivika twisted herself against the cabinets and quickly peered around the edge. What was she doing? Nikita drew her eyes upwards, and Vivika followed her gaze as they both caught the shadow of another AX Agent steadily creeping toward them, adjacent to the long edge of the counter.

"Sorry, Commander," Vivika muttered. "No time." Her hand fell to the blade at her side. Nikita's eyes widened, and she grabbed her arm. Was she *actually* insane?!

"What! No!" she whispered, shaking her head wildly.

Vivika, fiercely determined, unsheathed the saber. In a single, swift gesture, she maneuvered around the corner of the prep table just in time to meet the agent approaching them. A shrill cry was followed by a loud thud, and Nikita watched the small automatic firearm slide across the decaying tile. Instinctively, Nikita scrambled ahead and seized it in her quivering hand, hardly sure of her next move. Her nerves rattled in her system, and all logical thought faded. Nikita rose to her knees under Azka's weight, witnessing the clash between Vivika and four other agents blocking their escape.

Vaulting over the collapsed agent, who clutched a leg where blood spurted from the thigh, Vivika brandished the saber and slid across the prep table. She swung herself with such velocity that as her leg came roundabout, she directly struck another agent. They never had a moment to adjust their positioning in the narrow walkway between the counter and stovetops, causing them to stumble backward upon impact. Landing on her feet on the opposite side, Vivika plunged her blade into the toppled agent, whose guttural cry echoed across the kitchen hall.

Releasing her grasp on her weapon, Vivika quickly seized the handle of a large cast iron pan off the grills, lifting it against the length of her forearm in time to bear the brunt of another attack. The agent snarled in Terminian, leaping over her fallen teammate and wielding a large meat cleaver. Nikita's ears rang with each clash as the saber struck the pan, and the agent fleetly readjusted her swing and advanced on Vivika from the left, right, and above in quick succession. With each charge, Vivika instantly countered with the pan and deflected, drawing a few steps back in a defensive motion.

Nikita's breath caught... Vivika was amazing! The fascination quickly vanished at the sight of another pair of agents. Faster than Nikita anticipated, they moved down to the other side of the prep table, leveling their rifles at Vivika. Eyes rounding in terror, Nikita's breath caught in her throat, and her limbs petrified. Her muscles tensed, bracing herself for the kickback as her finger squeezed the trigger.

The farthest AX Agent—a man—yelped, dropping his weapon and clutching his arm where his black uniform split. The woman in front of him appeared momentarily stunned, darting her attention between her injured comrade and then back at Nikita. She aimed her rifle. Nikita's blood froze in her veins. She was too weak to pull the trigger again. The woman shifted her muzzle to the figure fast approaching from the kitchen entrance.

A wet rasp tore from the AX Agent's throat, and she grappled at the steel wedged deep in her collar. Malek never hesitated. He charged forward, pushing his saber further into her while shoving her ahead, forceful enough that he lanced the man behind her, and the agents tumbled backward. Nikita finally let out a breath, thrilled at her rescue.

Malek yanked out the blade, snapping his attention to his teammate. "Seriously?! A frying pan?" he barked.

A final slew of resounding clangs was followed by a defeated moan, just as Vivika struck her assailant on the chin and temple, causing the agent to collapse.

"Hah!" Vivika smirked at him. Her humor drained from her face just as the large side door to the kitchen burst at its hinges. Several gray-uniformed GX Forces soldiers poured into the constricted space. They shouldered their rifles, aiming at Nikita and the others. Nikita shrunk, then jumped at the thunderous crack bursting at her side as Gene appeared, firing a round of suppressing shots. The soldiers quit their advance to take cover.

"Fall back!" Malek bellowed.

"Come on, love," Gene muttered urgently, guiding Nikita past the kitchen threshold and into the bar of the dining hall. Azka's body bore down on her, so much that she couldn't keep pace. It was impossible to breathe.

The tremor that rattled every inch of her exhausted limbs was enough to distract her from the dozen GX Forces and AX agents approaching from the foyer. All aimed their muzzles at Nikita and Gene when they scrambled back into the hall. The figures were but shades in the foggy backdrop as raw fear began to take formidable shape. The quake had shaken Nikita before, and now it did again. She didn't want to believe what it was. Her instincts begged her to see the signs.

Several lost their balance, while others struggled to keep their aim. Gene forced Nikita back behind the bar to take cover. Before he could defend their position, a second and far more vehement quake shook their surroundings. Nikita planted her feet and locked her legs into place to bear the brunt. The marble tile in the center of the foyer splintered, and cracks running like veins struck across the floor in jagged patterns, creeping up to the kitchen entrance. Nikita traced them with her horrified stare. That ominous feeling electrified her nerves. Her eyes locked onto Malek and Vivika just as they slid into the dining hall, stopping dead in their tracks upon seeing the dust and debris fall from the ceiling. Nikita looked back up at the chandelier. The crystals shuddered, colliding with one another with increasing frequency until they merged into a sharp trill.

A deep vibration resonated within her, and Nikita's shrill cry drowned before she could call out to Malek. "*Commander!* It's—"

CHAPTER 10

ELEMNAI

With an ear-splitting rumble, the ground at the center of the foyer collapsed inward. Nikita instinctively stepped back as a vast hole caved in, stretching several meters in all directions. It devoured a pair of AX agents, whose screams echoed into oblivion. She never tore her eyes away. All of the Terminian forces drew their aim to the gaping mouth of desert rock and sand. Just as quickly as the cavity had formed, a figure emerged from its depths, clambering to meet the surface. The foreboding sank into Nikita's stomach like a boulder.

It began with gargantuan fists erupting from the cavern, clawing the earth as they heaved the rest of the hulking figure from the abyss. Nikita's eyes widened at the sight. She marveled and cowered all at once. Twin enormous, ebony horns heralded the crown of the creature's skull, swooping back in a distinguished arc. Chaotic, sepia hair curtained across a pronounced brow ridge and glowing, auric eyes as it quickly studied the soldiers approaching. Its jaw was clenched, bearing cuspids that jutted over its upper and lower lips. With a low snarl, the Earthborne elevated itself. Its carved, pronounced muscular physique melded with sheaths of slate. Fragments of stone shot out from its back and shoulders, boasting an additional ominous defense.

The only thought, and the most disturbing detail, was the first thing that left Nikita's lips. "Why is he so big...?" She gasped, cold sweat beading on her brow as she examined the grotesque anomaly. She studied the Earthborne—a male with scant, dark leather cloth swathed over his hips, stood nearly five meters in height.

Gene darted his eyes at her and hissed, "Is this not normal?"

"No!" Nikita shook her head violently, unable to tear her gaze from the creature. "Average Earthborne are less than *half* this size!"

"Frag us." Malek tightened his grip on his rifle, taking aim and steadying himself before his teammates. "Anduran, take Azka. Valerio, behind me. Bastion—relay to Franz's team...they *do not* come within two hundred meters of this hotel. Apprehend or neutralize any Terminian forces heading in or out of the CZ."

Nikita nearly dropped Azka, passing her over to Gene. The Earthborne snarled, his voice grating in the acoustic foyer. An AX Agent at the room's far corner bellowed in Terminian, waving one of her hands and gesturing to the massive Elemnai, who was now taking notice of the agents drawing cautious steps toward him. Gunfire thundered for a few seconds before the air resounded with the uproar of screams and splitting of stone.

This was a nightmare come to life—the bedrock of children's stories of Elemnai looking to slaughter. The ape-like stance of the Earthborne, unbelievably, moved with incredible speed as it lurched forward. Its fist slid across the floor and up in a smooth arc, commanding the ground beneath its feet to rise and break through the tile floor. Walls of rock erupted like shields, forming a barricade around the Earthborne for a moment. It was long enough to bear the brunt of the bullet onslaught. Nikita's inner voice screamed, begging everyone to stop. This was no ordinary Earthborne. Fighting it would only bring death...*their* death.

A thundering crack echoed throughout the room, and Nikita flinched as it penetrated all her mind and lanced through her heart. With a powerful cry, the Earthborne swung his arms sidelong, breaking the barrier and forcing the slabs to propel with incredible velocity and precision. One by one, the Terminian forces were crushed or slammed into adjacent walls as each of the slabs of rock thrust onto their bodies. Seeing the bone burst through the seams of the human body caused Nikita to choke and gag. She had never seen so much blood and flesh spill from their hosts, even when helping her father.

For those who dodged the initial attack, the Earthborne threw one colossal hand in the air, and the floor caved beneath them. Another wave of stone collapsed over the gaps, instantly burying the victims. The twisted limbs jutting from beneath the slabs forced Nikita into petrified silence. It was impossible to fathom how quickly and brutally the Earthborne ended the Terminians…as if it must have been some sick prank.

The remaining GX Forces from the kitchen sprinted past Nikita and the team, either ignoring them or failing to notice their presence by the bar—she couldn't tell. They instantly came to the aid of their fallen comrades. While a few stole the attention of the Earthborne by firing burst rounds, others lifted bodies from under collapsed fragments of rock. The farthest AX Agent screaming orders rose to her feet after a boulder knocked her over the front desk of the foyer.

With her hood thrown back, the woman's long, blonde ponytail fell over her shattered, askew goggles. She tore off the eyewear and facemask, gritting her teeth as her sharp, pale face grimaced at the Earthborne.

Only a handful of the Terminian forces managed to obey her cry for retreat and escape, scrambling out of the debris and dashing into the atrium on her command. As for the leader, Nikita recoiled from her furious glare aimed at her before a cloud of dust swallowed up the agent. Who was this person? Was she after Azka?

Slowly, the Earthborne abandoned his attack on the fleeing party and turned his menacing regard onto those standing at the bar. Nikita's heart nearly burst from her chest as he advanced on her.

"And… you're up." Malek's grip on her arm broke her from her petrified stance and brought her to his side. She didn't have a moment to protest, nor did she have the presence of mind, either. She stood, frozen, beyond rattled to see an Earthborne kill so many, and so quickly. The Earthborne she'd devoted years to understanding dissolved under this carnage. She had no idea what to do, and no idea what to think.

Nikita shuddered at the horrifying face of the approaching Earthborne, who released a low, resonating snarl as he came within a few meters of her team. The others thankfully knew better than to aim, and they lowered their weapons. Despite the adrenaline fogging her mind, Nikita forced herself to retrace her memories for the words, plugging together syntax and grammar before her parched lips uttered the Earthborne language with feigning conviction.

"W-Wait!" she pleaded, raising her palms before her.

To her insurmountable relief, the Earthborne ceased in his advance.

It worked! "We are not your criminal—*ah*—enemy. We are not your enemy. Please."

The Earthborne scoffed, towering over her and the others. He seemed to be studying her.

"Tell us what you want," Nikita said, tempering her trembling voice. She glanced at Vivika on the other side of Malek, who covertly gave her a little thumbs up with an impassive expression. "H-how can you help me? *Ah*... sorry, how can we help you?"

"Help me?" The Earthborne grunted, his voice rumbling across the facets of the room. "You may step aside and give me the Al-Khasari. I know it has it."

"Has what?" She furtively eyed Gene, who had Azka in his clutches. He shook his head at her, breathing deeply.

"None of your concern, human. Do not speak to me thus, you who desecrates my tongue. Give me the Al-Khasari and its treasure, lest I break your body as well."

Nikita swallowed hard, eyes widening. A faint crackle in her ear forced her to suppress a flinch.

"Everyone, the transport is at the EZ," Bastion spoke delicately, as though not to disrupt the conversation.

Malek and Nikita looked at one another. She gingerly shook her head.

"Keep him talking," Malek whispered. His gaze wandered over to Gene, who cautiously reached for something on his belt. Vivika noticed this as well. As Nikita returned her focus to the Earthborne, Vivika slowly moved in behind her.

"Y-Yes...I understand," Nikita stammered in Umbar'ok, shifting in her stance. "May I ask you one question, before I oblige?"

The air reverberated with a low growl, and the hulking creature bore those brilliant golden eyes into her, clenching his jaw and baring his teeth.

110

Nikita clasped her hands together, catching sight of a brief exchange between her commander and Vivika from the corner of her eye. "How did you become... like...this? I have spent time with your kind and have never seen an Earthborne of your," Nikita paused uncomfortably, searching for the term, "amount?" She cursed herself. Pavo would be disappointed in her performance.

With a deep snarl, the Earthborne leaned in toward Nikita, speaking in a quiet tone that still quaked into her center, "The body is sick. That which it holds will be the cure, or the death of us. But you...you shall die first."

"Bastion, C-80 trigger response time?" Malek quickly whispered and received the answer almost immediately.

"Three seconds, sir. Shield your eyes, Dr. Valerio."

Nikita barely had a moment to process Malek's intention. He stepped forward, swinging his arm as something flung from his grasp. The device soared up, barely grazing the Earthborne's chin before Nikita was jerked back and painfully twisted. The periphery of her vision caught the initial microsecond of the blast that followed. A snap punched through the air, chased immediately by a brilliant, blinding light.

The Earthborne released a profound howl, shaking the floor beneath their feet. The scream was nowhere near as terrifying as the audacity of Malek's actions. Death was a step behind them. Along with the others, Nikita raced back into the kitchen.

The cries were deep, shattering the walls as they sprinted toward the extraction zone. Nikita homed in on the threats he roared in their wake. The terror forced her to move faster than she thought possible. She followed Vivika close behind, with Malek pushing her forward as Gene, leading the group, charged ahead with Azka over his shoulder. The tile cracked beneath Nikita's feet as she ran. Bits of ceramic splintered in all directions, adding fury to their desperate escape. She could barely hear Malek shouting from behind, urging them to keep moving, while her fear crippled all other senses but her sight.

At the far end of the kitchen, Casey waved from a separate entrance. The light of the desert afternoon pouring in from behind her. An ounce of hope plucked at Nikita's heart. "This way!" Casey bellowed, guiding each one into the open road and clearing. The cacophony from the Earthborne and his devastation was replaced by the thunderous whirlwind of helicopter blades, creating a vehement gust as it whipped up sand and debris hovering over a meter above the ground. They were almost there!

Malek, once behind her, had slowed his step as they passed the threshold. He whipped around, leveled his rifle, and removed Azka's satchel. "Get them aboard, and depart *now*!" he ordered Casey, shoving the bag into her hands.

Without a quip in retort, Casey bolted, first lifting Azka's body into the cabin with Gene. They reached for Nikita next, and she clambered in and collapsed to her knees. She could hardly breathe as every muscle in her body was cramped with terror and exhaustion.

Just as Gene rose to meet her, a deafening cracking noise overcame the beat of the helicopter blades. The stone split across the entrance of the hotel. Vivika and Casey stood near the landing skids, gaping with dread as the bricks collapsed, revealing the gargantuan figure of the Earthborne clawing his way out of the debris. Nikita's chest caved when the Earthborne released a deep, furious cry. The walls crumbled under his palms.

Malek drew several steps back toward the road and away from the helicopter, instantly firing his rifle and stealing the Earthborne's attention. It worked.

Nikita stared helplessly as the Earthborne flinched, approaching her commander and raising one of his massive fists. Instead of bearing down on Malek, the creature did something unexpected. The other hand curled its fingers inward, and the rock beneath Malek dipped and rolled into a wave. It shook and forced him to drop the rifle as he landed on all fours. The other monstrous hand shot forward and seized him. His fingers bound Malek's torso and arm. Nikita's hands clasped over her mouth as she witnessed the Earthborne lift and slam him into the wall with obvious indignation. Nikita watched in absolute horror.

As the dust cleared, Malek groaned, shaking his head as one free arm clutched the Earthborne's massive appendages, which constricted around him. He lifted his eyes to his team, spitting the blood from his lip. "*Get out of here!*" Malek roared, just as the Earthborne snarled at him again and carried him back into the devastated ruins of the hotel.

Without hesitation, Casey climbed up the skids and into the helicopter, pushing past Nikita and Gene and directing the orders to the pilot. "We have what we need!" Casey shouted to her. "Go!"

"Wait!" Nikita leaned over the helicopter, reaching for Vivika, who stood unmoving, staring at the gaping hole in the building. "Come on, Kei," Nikita pleaded.

Slowly, Vivika turned around, as if caught in a daze. A frown creased, and ignoring Nikita, she turned to the major. "Anduran, your saber!" she extended an open palm.

"Are you mad?" Gene barked. "Get in!"

She didn't bother answering him. With lightning reflexes, Vivika reached up and snatched the saber from Gene's belt before he could react. She brandished one blade in each hand and narrowed her eyes back on the hotel. Nikita already knew what she planned to do and had lost the strength to protest it... she didn't want the blood of another dead body on her hands.

"Bastion, get me the Earthborne's location. I'm going after the commander," Vivika said with conviction.

"Copy that, Kei."

"You can't be serious!" Gene stared at her wide-eyed.

"Yeah. I owe him one." Vivika glanced back at Nikita one final time. "You heard the commander. Go."

CHAPTER 11

RUIN

"I guess this is how I die," Malek muttered flatly, more to himself than to Bastion. His head throbbed from the impact, but trying to wrap his mind around the fact that he *was* still alive made it ache even more. The Earthborne had every opportunity to crush him to death... or bury him alive, whatever Earthborne preferred to do. Malek had a sliver of hope that luck was on his side. He tried to wiggle out his other arm from the Earthborne's unmoving vise. The creature shot him an imperious glare as they moved back into the hotel foyer. Malek didn't recoil. Though terrified at the idea of being turned into a pile of pulverized bone and meat, he was determined not to show any fear while studying the Elemnai's every move.

Bastion's voice chimed in through his earpiece, "Help is on the way, Commander. Try to stay alive for now."

"I said to keep Franz's men from the hotel!" Malek barked, his voice shaking when the Earthborne clung to the first balconies of the tower. "The last thing we need is this giant piece of slag to flatline an Alliance Army platoon!"

"I relayed your orders accordingly, sir," Bastion replied flatly. "Though, while on the subject, Franz reported in several skirmishes with fleeing AX agents. The enemy has been repressed or captured."

"Copy that," Malek groaned and examined the robust features of the Earthborne's scornful face. If Malek didn't know any better, he'd have guessed that his captor seemed… confused. The Earthborne's gaze wandered up and down the atrium, scanning every alcove and corner with a nervous intensity.

The Earthborne's cavernous voice reverberated through Malek's senses as it muttered something in Umbar'ok.

Bastion's voice cut in before Malek had a chance to try to decipher the Earthborne's meaning, "Where are you?"

"In the tower, again. I think he's lost?"

Malek's muscles ached with tension when the Earthborne fixed his golden eyes on him, glowering menacingly as that pronounced brow ridge furrowed even deeper. It was impossible to suppress his strangled scream as Malek's bones were forced inward and out of their joints. Every fiber of muscle screamed, trying to resist the constricting grasp of the Earthborne tightening around his body.

"Olo ak'ad?" The Earthborne bellowed over Malek's outcry. *"Kovkoki ad kodalo, uvik ad'ak va kavo. Va olo ak'ad?"*

"…The hell is he saying?" Malek tried to breathe when the grasp loosened. "…Tell me Valerio heard that?"

"Unfortunately, no," Bastion's voice broke between bouts of white noise. "Your receiver must have taken some damage. Cross-connections are compromised. I've already begun recording the conversation for future analysis. For now, try speaking to him in Khasiri. Did the Fireborne in Gunliem not address you in such a manner?"

Malek swallowed the pain and frowned. He'd never shared that information with anyone except Maida, mainly to avoid more nasty rumors about his heritage. The little chat with Urith, the Fireborne, was supposedly off the record. It aggravated him to ask, "You know about that?"

"Accessing information I'm not supposed to know is one of my talents. Try it."

Malek eyed the Earthborne with a mix of speculation and fury. He hated that it came to this, but spoke his ancestral language with conviction, *"Madhara huna?"*

The Earthborne responded with a stunned look, followed by a grimace.

"I don't think he understood…"

The Earthborne immediately drowned out Malek's words. His screams consisted of a single word, which he repeated over and over, growing louder with each encore. "*Kiyayn*?!" the Earthborne reiterated, darting his gaze left, right, and above.

"Did you understand that?" Bastion asked quietly.

"Yeah. He knows the Khasiri word for 'where.' Bastion, I get it now. He thinks I'm one of the Al-Khasari from the mining group. He thinks I hid the shard, and he wants to know where it is."

"I see. It certainly explains why you haven't been killed yet."

"*Yet*," Malek scoffed. He quickly glanced at his surroundings. Malek slowly lifted his hand and gestured toward the south, directly opposite from where he parted ways with his team. It ignited a thought that seeing them in the helicopter could have been his last. The reality of being killed on his first day as commander felt tangible. Malek could almost picture Jace both laughing and mourning at his funeral, and a sickening heaviness settled in his core. He would be lying if he said he wasn't devastated by how things were going. "Team departed the EZ?"

"Affirmative," Bastion replied, just as the Earthborne released a rumbling groan, heaving Malek and the rest of its massive body upward. Malek's insides lurch from the force of ascending several tower floors in seconds, with the Earthborne using the balcony and ledges as holds and footing. The sun sank toward the horizon. As he blinked away the brilliant orange glow bursting through the shattered panes. This was where AX agents descended into the garden tower. He gritted his teeth in fury. The Elemnai weren't the only ones who broke a peace agreement today.

The Earthborne swiped away bits of the windows as they passed through them and clambered up outside toward another expansive veranda made of stone tiles and glass barriers. The platform extended itself to the edge of the hotel, wrapping around the southeast corner and out of sight. It was quiet up here. Malek couldn't see any signs of the helicopter or anyone else.

Scanning the area, the Earthborne grunted and violently shook his head, as if confused. Malek didn't want to panic but had no idea what had changed. He readied himself. For what, he wasn't sure. The Earthborne released a deep growl and instantly drove both Malek and his fist into the adjacent wall, causing several fragments of the glass window to split. The pain fired through every nerve with such fury that it nearly caused him to pass out. Malek cried again, clutching the Earthborne's hand and clenching his jaw. He narrowed his eyes at his captor while Bastion's voice penetrated through the ringing sensation in his ears.

"Commander, what's your status? Where are you now?"

Malek couldn't respond before the Earthborne roared again, its language reverberating through the air and deafening Malek altogether. The Earthborne bellowed the Khasiri term for "where", stitched in with a series of other harsh, Umbar'ok words. Malek had no time to think...he could only focus on the dismal task of staying alive, as the Elemnai's agitation only intensified, along with the vise around him.

"Frag you." Malek seethed through his gasps for air, glowering defiantly at the creature. The Earthborne tightened his grip. Malek's bones crunched against one another while his breath got squeezed out of his lungs, unable to return. With all his might, he attempted to pry himself from the Earthborne's crushing grasp. Everything around him drowned out... and Malek desperately tried to stay awake. If it went black... it was over. He couldn't let that happen again.

The second the grasp slackened, air was sucked back into Malek's body. He plummeted to the ground as the Earthborne released a deafening howl.

Malek had never seen anything like it. Vivika's nimble figure leaped into sight. She released her grasp on a blade that she drove into the creature's massive forearm. The Earthborne roared in agony, swinging at her with his other hand. Lurching forward and scrambling under his legs, Vivika dashed and drove the second blade into the Earthborne's ankle, causing him to collapse to his knees. Malek swelled with joy and relief, feeling a sense of pride and disbelief rush down to his extremities...which may have actually been the blood returning to his limbs. He'd barely mustered a thank you before Vivika returned and seized his arm.

"Come on!"

Malek was jerked to the side, heading east along the veranda. They managed only a few steps before being knocked back to the ground. Stone tiles erupted and flew together to form a makeshift barrier. That blocked their escape, and in that same mind-numbingly long moment, Malek realized that the Earthborne was not ready to let him go. He narrowed his eyes at the Elemnai, who extended a hand and glowered until the gold in those inhuman eyes flickered with hate. Malek gasped. The Earthborne curled his monstrous fingers, as if commanding the brick and mortar to his will, poising for the next attack. Malek instinctively guarded Vivika as she scrambled to her feet.

A haze took over his periphery, and everything seemed so out of focus as he stared up at the Earthborne, as if challenging him. Time crawled, almost stopping entirely. All senses were drowning in a vacuum. He heard nothing and could feel nothing. Malek outstretched his hand. A crushing force, like the weight of the planet itself, bore down on them. The Earthborne's expression twisted with panic. Vivika screamed, and the Earthborne howled, both their voices disappearing into the void as debris and rubble raged past them. Darkness swallowed Malek, and he plummeted into oblivion.

Not again, you idiot...

"Commander?"

Malek's eyes twitched open. A paralyzing fear struck him, cramping every muscle in his body. He gasped for air and coughed, desperately trying to fill his lungs. The vertigo washed over him like an intense wave, adding to the tremendous weight on his body.

Unable to move his limbs, he twisted his neck in the direction of the voice and furiously took in his situation. Right on top of him was the gargantuan motionless body of the Earthborne, and Vivika was lying next to him. At least her arms were free, grasping at the rubble beneath them. She had dust caked over her hair, face, and shoulders, only sparing her moistened lips. Her eyes were tired, and her mouth quivered as she sucked in raspy breaths. She'd actually come to his rescue. He could hardly believe it.

"Are you okay?" he asked.

"*Se*...You?"

"Still wondering if we're dead."

"Unless the afterlife feels this squished, I think we're alive."

"What happened?"

"I don't know," Vivika strained between her wheezy breaths. "Maybe this *staka kutibusu* used his abilities and... ah... the floor just... gave out, I think."

A wave of dread bore down on Malek's already crushed body. He couldn't believe this had happened again. For the second time in front of Vivika, he blacked out. He wondered what Vivika *really* saw and measured his words carefully. "Yeah...Maybe the big guy had something to do with it."

The moment of silence made him feel worse. Vivika, meanwhile, squirmed to set herself free without much success. Finally, she said, "Maybe. Slag, this Earthborne is heavy..."

Malek couldn't press the issue without outing himself. Trying to think of what to do next, Malek craned his neck to understand his surroundings. Was the Earthborne even breathing? Beyond the body, Malek could make out the sky past the fractures of broken limestone. The mountains of collapsed wooden chairs suggested that they were in a storage room. He eyed the patches of rubble around them, laced with shredded rebar and split iron beams. Slag, they really would have been dead if it wasn't for him...The Earthborne had cushioned them from the impact of the rubble, and Malek sighed in relief.

Malek grunted, inching one arm out from under the creature. He managed to wiggle it out and clawed at the floor. The moment he flexed the muscle in his other arm, a furious stream of pain shot through his body like a bolt. He gave up immediately. "Slag," he winced.

"What is it?"

"Something's broken."

"Aren't we all?"

"Belay that sass, Lieutenant," Malek grunted, pressing his free arm against the ground. "On the count of three—let's try to push up. You try to get out first. Ready?"

Dust wafted from her hair as Vivika nodded. She positioned her hands.

"Alright—one, two…three!" Malek pushed himself upward as forcefully as he could. His body trembled, and he groaned in defeat before collapsing back on the floor. The Earthborne was too heavy, and his broken arm was searing with agony. This day couldn't get any more jarring. Jace would be laughing at him right now.

"Let's try again, Commander."

"Okay." Malek exhaled. "One, two, thr—"

Malek thought his heart would rip from his chest. The Earthborne jolted, thrashing violently like a wild animal. Chunks of rubble rolled off, crashing onto the floor beneath. The weight lifted, and Malek instinctively dove out of the way. Screaming a slew of curses, he and Vivika simultaneously scrambled across the floor as fast as their bodies would allow. The Earthborne released a guttural moan and collapsed back onto the ground with a quaking thud.

Malek's heart hammered against his ribs. He dared not move, not wanting to draw the attention of the Earthborne's wrath. The Elemnai craned its neck as the ebony horns scraped against the tile. With a mix of disgust and pity, Malek watched as one trembling, behemoth hand reached for the steel beam speared through its chest. It was then that he finally noticed other smaller fragments of rebar jutting from various limbs, where streams of crimson ran over the fissures of his muscles and rock plating. A faint gurgle resonated from the gaping maw, where its teeth were stained red, and a concoction of blood and drivel pooled beneath him.

"*Yai nik lodiliv'ad da'dho adholik…*" His voice resonated like a low rumbling storm. "*Tho'av khurr karr ik rokid ka'vad vo'ivado dho voukav…ad…ail uvdok-dalik…*" The final word left it along with a long, rasped exhale. The golden eyes, bloodshot and wide with anger, rolled until the irises were barely visible under the hood of its pronounced brow. Was it over?

An eerie silence followed. Malek's eyes remained fixed on the body, anticipating some movement or attack.

"Commander, come in," Bastion's voice slit through the stillness of his senses.

Malek clamped his eyes shut as a sickening shock ran its way into his center, and he could hear Vivika audibly gasp and mutter something in Jennai. Alarm morphed into embarrassment when Malek realized that she had one arm roped around him while he had one around her.

He instantly separated himself and rose to his feet. "Here, Bastion...Earthborne's terminated. We're still in the hotel."

"Are you injured? Do you know your approximate location?"

"We're fine," Malek said, and Vivika shot him a skeptical look. "Under the big outdoor balcony...somewhere in a storage room."

"Affirmative. I picked up on your chatter while speaking with the major. The drone is searching the area, and the transport is already doubling back."

"Copy that...What about the GX? Any activity?"

"None, sir. It appears they scattered. The Alliance Army wasn't able to capture any more Terminian forces alive...They are dead either by their injuries or by suicide, it seems," Bastion spoke grimly. "A small section remains at large. Major Franz and his troops are locking down the area."

Malek clenched his jaw. He would have loved to personally interrogate one of the Terminians—mostly as payback for everything that happened since his capture all those years ago. If not for that single event, Malek would have been a very different person. He'd made many difficult decisions, including accepting the current assignment, to survive every moment since then.

Bastion cleared his throat after a moment and pressed on, "The area is quiet, from what I can see. Franz will maintain security in the area. Ah, there you are. I'll direct the transport to your location since you have a clear path above."

Malek peered up through the broken ceiling, catching sight of a faint shadow breaking through the dying light. The aura unexpectedly soothed his anger. He took in the light's warmth, and the tension melted from his muscles. Even if one of the Terminians had been captured alive, it would only serve the Alliance. It wouldn't be payback—some scars were just too deep.

"Did you happen to catch what he said?" Malek asked, bringing his mind back to the assignment. "The Earthborne, I meant."

"I've been maintaining a record for evaluation for some time now. Dr. Valerio would likely want to hear this."

"One step ahead, Bastion. As usual."

"Of course, Commander."

Malek sighed deeply, exchanging glances with Vivika, who seemed anxious. "What is it?"

Vivika shook her head, returning her gaze to the Earthborne body. "It can't be left here...What if someone finds it?"

"Knowing the Alliance, I'm sure a clean-up crew will be on the way, if not already."

"Affirmative, Commander," Bastion interjected. "General Maida has already been informed of the Earthborne's defeat. He's sending in the so-called custodians, and he will remotely tune in for a debriefing this evening."

Another thought came to mind immediately after Bastion's statement. Malek held his arm closer, the muscles in his shoulders beginning to tense again as he met eyes with his lieutenant's. "Do... you know what happened to the Fireborne? After Gunliem?"

Vivika shook her head. "I thought you knew. Was she alive when they found her?"

"Probably. I doubt she froze to death."

Vivika's features darkened, becoming increasingly disturbed. Slowly, she unraveled the star-patterned scarf around her neck and shook off the dust. "She *should* have died," she finally spoke, softly but with conviction. "It would have been a mercy, rather than end up a skurr in Eubriel's lab."

Malek's heart skipped a beat—that name was uncomfortably familiar. "Who's Eubriel?"

"Dr. Han Eubriel? He's head of Alliance R&D. It was *his* lab that the Fireborne attacked. Gunliem and everything in it was his brainchild. I thought they'd briefed you better than that." Vivika's tone took a lighthearted turn as she glanced back at him, holding the scarf across her palms.

Malek shook his head but didn't respond. Truthfully, he hadn't been aware of that connection, but he knew he had heard the name somewhere else. The unease settled deeply in his chest, his reaction stealing his attention from his surroundings. Malek hardly noticed Vivika now standing inches from him, bringing her scarf under his forearm, and wrapping the cloth into a sling. His heart skipped a beat when she reached over and fastened it around his neck, her cheek grazing his. Malek's skin flushed hot, and he forced himself to look down at the scarf rather than her.

"Don't act so tough," Vivika said in a low but teasing voice. It made him blush even harder, and he hoped the dust was enough to hide it.

"Yeah... well, same to you." He gestured to her hand, which was settled over her ribcage. "Don't ignore my orders next time, Lieutenant."

Vivika's lips curled into a wry smile, and she stepped away. A familiar drum of whipping rotary blades filled the silence between them and drew their gaze. The twilight sun pouring through the collapsed ceiling got stifled as a shadow crossed the path of the rays. Before Malek could make out the shape of the helicopter, a rope ladder with steel rungs unraveled and swung to meet him. He nodded to Vivika to proceed.

"Commander, the transport has arrived." Bastion exhaled on the other end of the receiver, taking a meaningful pause. Malek already knew what he was going to say. Bastion spoke again, but his words were barely audible over the beat of the rotary blades and the aircraft's engine, "There is something you should be aware of. It's Azka, she..."

"I know. Get Casey to deliver the body back to the Al-Khasari."

"Affirmative. I'm...sorry."

CHAPTER 12
STORIES

W hile Nikita's hands rested at the nape of her neck, she drew her eyes to the low rafters and ducts crossing paths overhead. Her heart rate slowed with each deep exhale, calming the rigidity in her muscles. It seemed like a bad dream—because, like a dream, it all felt so far away. Raspy breaths from the overhead vents blew stale, artificially cooled air through the narrow corridors of the Azarian base bunkers. She and Vivika slowly ambled toward their assigned quarters, hoping to run into Gene, who apparently had procured some parcel from Bastion.

"I've got to admit," Vivika began cheerily, a contrast to her dusty, battered appearance, "I'm a little surprised you're not curled into a ball crying. You've...I mean, we've seen a lot today. You held it together while everything got a little, ah, crazy."

Nikita's mind was exhausted, but she also ached for the chance to really speak her mind. She found Vivika surprisingly warm and thought about how she'd remained with her throughout the firefight in Saifain. She decided to take the leap and open up for a change. "I'm no stranger to violence. Despite being a... what did the major call me? A civvie?"

"*Se*. Civilian." Vivika managed a weak smile. She paused, and spoke again, grimly this time. "Where?"

"Alcides Islands. I grew up there and experienced the civil war firsthand four-teen years ago."

"For real?"

"Yeah. My father was a surgeon, and my mother was a lawyer, working with the LevDyne Corporation branch in Trelle. That's where we used to live... right in the heart of the conflict. Whenever the rebels clashed with the military police, they would bring their injured to our doorsteps and beg for help. If they went to the government-controlled hospitals, the staff would be threatened into sharing the identities of those coming in with bullet wounds or burned lungs. The military would then target the rebels' families. People went missing."

Shaking her head, Nikita gathered her thoughts and moved on. She'd always tried to forget these memories, but somehow, they always found a way to creep back to remind her why she persisted at all. "My dad needed an assistant, and since my mom couldn't handle it with a newborn baby in tow, I stepped up. Seeing our kitchen turn into an operating theater was... interesting."

"Wait, you helped your father with the surgeries? How old were you?"

"I did. I was twelve. Soon, the violence became so severe that we had bodies leaving our house. Constant harassment by the military police came after. That's when my mom drew the line. She knew it was a matter of time before my baby brother and I would be orphaned, so she used her contacts at LevDyne to help us escape. We came to Mardasca as refugees when I was thirteen."

"That's amazing. Terrible, but amazing that you did that. And your parents?"

"They live in the suburbs of Kaira." Nikita smiled to herself. She was one of the lucky ones who had escaped Trelle with her family intact. A fleeting thought crossed her mind to visit them soon.

Just then, a familiar man turned the corner ahead of them, releasing an audible grunt. "Ladies, I could use some muscle." Gene balanced a large aluminum crate in his grasp over a flexed knee.

The pair instantly rushed forward, gripping the box and leading Gene back toward their assigned dorm.

"What's in here?" Nikita gritted her teeth, passing through another threshold. Her muscles whined, suffering from the extent of her exhaustion.

"Comforts of home," Bastion spoke at last. It had been some time since Nikita heard his soothing voice, and she realized that she'd missed it. "I apologize. I was preoccupied with amalgamating some of the recordings from earlier today. I also pre-emptively determined that you needed a care package... as a thank you. You did the hard part, which is clearly evident in these recordings."

Nikita pushed open a heavy steel door leading into their shared dormitory. She stepped in, holding it open as Gene and Vivika dropped the box in the middle of the room. Drawing a deep breath, Gene reached for the small utility blade on his belt and began cutting the adhesive ties. Nikita eyed the package curiously, then her new surroundings. A pair of simple, steel-framed bunk beds stood, one on each side, with lockers at the end of the small room. Each bed had sheets folded in place over the mattress, and a single fluorescent lamp lit the sterile room with a pale, dull light. At least it was sort of private, Nikita thought. It would have been too much to hope that she would be able to sleep alone.

"As you had very little time to prepare before we departed from Galeo City—and from your previous posts—I know it was all rather inconvenient for everyone to deploy the same day as the briefing," Bastion continued in his usual mellow voice. "I am certain that you will all need to adjust to local time. With some assistance, I managed to procure some of your personal items, such as clothing, data pads and mobiles, toiletries..."

The very first white fabric bag at the top of the crate had Nikita's name, neatly written across an adhesive sticker. Without hesitation, she hungrily snatched up her bag and swiftly paced over to one of the bunks in the room. She reached in for the only item she cared for: her datapad. With barely suppressed glee, she embraced the sleek, rectangular device and held it close to her chest.

"These should all last you several days, as I believe more intel and planning is required before determining our next objective."

"And here I thought we were done." Nikita slouched.

"You're never done until someone says you're done," Vivika muttered with a cynical grin. "Welcome to the Alliance."

"As for your personal devices," Bastion cut in, "I'm afraid there are some added security features. This was the compromise in order to return your items."

Nikita frowned, finding herself hesitant to access her datapad. She ran her fingers across its transparent face as the startup graphic displayed over its surface. Her eyes wandered over to her colleagues momentarily, both seeming unfazed by Bastion's words. Gene carefully removed the last of the contents, setting down three other fabric bags across a steel bench near the room's entrance, along with a smaller crate. He puffed his cheeks as he released a slow breath, running his thumb and index finger over his eyes. He'd hardly said a word since they returned to base. She thought she was the only one shaken by the day... but maybe that wasn't the case.

"I'm, ah... going to wash up," he said and stood. He began unzipping and removing the bulkier items and throwing open a narrow locker. "Lavatories are down the hall, if you're wondering."

"Noted," Vivika mumbled. The brilliant white light casting a ghostly pallor on her features shifted when she addressed Gene. "You okay, major?"

"Yeah, brilliant."

"See you in the mess hall?"

"Not likely."

Vivika's eyebrows perked, glancing at Nikita with a smile. "I'll order in for us, then."

"Don't forget to remove the cameras from your vests," Bastion added. "My lieutenants will be by in the morning to collect them and the shards. Please submit these items to Franz's security as soon as possible."

"Uh, Bastion?" Vivika said meekly. "I think my camera shattered when the Earthborne squished us..."

"Oh... That's unfortunate."

Confined quarters had become routine for Nikita, who had spent months with her research group in the Elemnai Wilds. Now that they had been through so much together, it was almost fun to warm up to her new teammates. She enjoyed their banter, once they relaxed after a shower and change of clothing into Alliance loungewear. Seated on the top bunk, Nikita typed a journal entry on her datapad with one hand while eating from a foil container with the other. Recording daily events, however mundane, was a habit she had maintained. Especially after an adrenaline-filled day like this, she refused to allow any detail to escape. She glanced down at her companions, dressed similarly and eating just as unenthusiastically. Vivika's laughter lit up the room, and it was enough to lift the dismal mood.

"I'm just saying if it were me," Vivika continued after praising Gene's quick work with the explosives, "I would have blown myself up, which I've done before. Tech work is not my strength."

"But sabers are?" Gene scoffed. "Tell me, why on Eiden did you charge after that Earthborne? It would have been like a skurr chasing you with a pair of letter openers."

Vivika snickered, twirling her noodles with her fork. "I don't know. Seemed like the right thing to do." She shrugged, tossing back her damp hair. Her words were measured. Nikita could tell she was withholding.

"Oh, just spill it already," Nikita quipped, poking her face over. "You two know each other, don't you?"

"Who?" Gene glanced between the women. "You mean you and the commander, Kei? I thought all of us were strangers."

"Well, we are! Were...!" Vivika protested, glancing up at Nikita, who arched an eyebrow. "Ah, maybe not total strangers. I owed the commander a favor."

"So you said." Nikita leaned over her bunk with interest. "Elaborate."

"He didn't leave me behind when he could have. That's all. It was, like, eighteen months ago."

"Lieutenant Kei," Bastion's voice echoed throughout their receivers. "I think it would be beneficial if the team understood the scope of your relationship with the commander... and the circumstances surrounding it. Consider it... supportive intelligence."

"So, *you* know, Bastion?" Vivika asked.

"Yes, but I know a lot of things. It is not my story to tell."

"*Okitoki,*" Vivika said, placing her tray down on her bunk. "The commander and I were in Gunliem, when the Fireborne attacked. I was the sole surviving member of the JSTG... and he was the ASF Officer who recovered the shard. Specter, his name was."

"Slag..." Gene rested his elbows on his knees. "You were the ones Maida was referring to?"

"*Se.* The commander and I saw a lot of slag that day... bodies so badly burned, they were nothing but ash and bone. It was so indiscriminate—the killing, I mean. We crossed paths, and he convinced me to help complete the objective."

Vivika brought her legs up on the bed and hugged her knees. "As we were escaping with the shard, the Fireborne charged at us... and there was an explosion. I had shrapnel in my leg. I couldn't walk, so he carried me out. I don't even think I was aware of what was happening. At some point, we removed our armor and gear. I don't even remember what he looked like. He was wearing a helmet, but once he took it off... I don't know, I guess I was just focusing on staying alive. Anyway, he could have left me and didn't. I wasn't ASF, and he had what he needed to complete his objective."

She exhaled and shrugged. "So... when the Earthborne took him away, I just needed to act. He would have done the same for us because I saw it firsthand."

Nikita drank in the story's details, both with awe and scrutiny. Now, it made sense why they'd been chosen. Something churned in Nikita's mind about the Fireborne of Vivika's story, and she took her datapad and began climbing down the bunk's ladder.

"...And how did you do it?" Gene asked quietly, looking up from the floor. "Stop the Fireborne?"

Vivika chuckled, and her brow knitted. "Trapped her in a freezer. You should ask the commander. It was his idea."

Gene let out a thin, shaky laugh. "Slag, you two deserve each other."

Vivika neutralized her smile, dropping her eyes to her feet. Nikita caught the exchange just as she sat next to Vivika. "A-anyway," she stammered. "I remember hearing something about you, major. You met an Oceanborne, *se*?"

"Right," Gene stood, straightening out his cotton shirt. "But my interaction was far more amicable."

"Really?" Nikita rounded her eyes. "What happened? What did it look like?"

"It was brief," Gene said, slipping his feet into a pair of boots. "It happened during an ocean training exercise. I was a junior ASF Officer myself. I was in the water, and a strong undercurrent dragged me below the surface. My gear was quickly waterlogged. I sank fast. I woke up on the causeway at Alecto Point in Seraf, close to the Terminian border, nearly twenty kilometers from the exercise. An Oceanborne was sitting right next to me. Just staring at me. A small thing; looked like a young boy or girl. I'm not sure. Huge eyes, scaly blue skin, dark hair. A pair of legs, too, which I honestly did not expect." He paused, looking back up at the women with a solemn expression. "I reacted rather...erratically. I must have frightened them as well, and they swam off. That was that."

Nikita studied his body language. Gene tried to stifle his discomfort, and she found his tone unusually dismissive. There must have been more to the story. "Still," Nikita said with a reassuring smile. "It sounds thrilling?"

"Enlightening, rather. I was a dead man. I was saved by an enemy. Or so I was led to believe." He released a deep exhale, turning the knob of the door. "Just need some air. Loads to process."

Nikita pursed her lips as an audible click resonated when the heavy door slid shut. She contemplated both stories with wonder. Everyone had such contrasting experiences, which prompted her to ask the one individual, and undoubtedly the most mysterious of her teammates, who had yet to divulge an iota of their past.

"Bastion?"

"Yes, Dr. Valerio?"

"Do you have anything to share?"

"With regards to...?"

"The Elemnai. Everyone here has met one before this assignment. What about you?"

"No, I cannot say I have had the pleasure of making acquaintances with anyone of interest. I'm afraid my posting does not sanction much outside interaction."

"Bastion, are you a hermit?" Vivika asked, and Nikita chuckled at the blunt comment.

Bastion sighed loudly. "You may assume that I am. Field ops would place an even greater burden on the team, so I am restricted to my desk."

Vivika flinched at those words. "Sorry…"

"No apologies needed. Though, without coincidence, I will bid you both good night. I have some work to do."

"Good night, Bastion," Nikita murmured.

"Night." Vivika appeared distraught. "You don't think I offended him, do you?"

"No, it sounds like he might be used to getting asked. It's not normal for a team member to be working remotely, is it?"

"Well, in the ASF, people like him usually coordinate with multiple ASF squads, and they are up in ASFOM, or Operational Management. We should feel special that he's working with us one-on-one."

Nikita barely heard Vivika over a sudden flash of imagery of the Earthborne in Saifain. *Special… unusual… anomaly…* She contemplated the words and gripped her fingers around her datapad, holding it close to her chest. "So… can I say something, without you judging me?" Nikita dropped her gaze.

"Judge you? Why would I judge you?"

Nikita paused, bringing her thoughts to her lips. "I really am upset about Azka… but I also can't stop thinking about how that Earthborne was so messed up. Its voice, its proportions… its size—all of it was so… disturbing." She studied Vivika's expression, searching for a hint of disgust. "That bothers me. More than anything else we saw today. Maybe I'm psycho."

Vivika continued to stare at her blankly.

"Oh no, you *do* think I'm psycho!"

After an unexpected cackle, Vivika grabbed her by the hands. "Girl, you're not psycho. Well, maybe a little. But maybe we are a *team* of psychos. It does sound like you're onto something."

"What did the Fireborne look like?"

"She was tall. Three meters, I would say. Thin, but toned. Face like... I don't know, scary? Black where it should be white in the eyes."

Nikita lifted her datapad, tapping the short edge against her chin. "The Earthborne told us stories about the other Elemnai. Interestingly, the Fireborne were always mocked for being the shortest. Not much taller than humans."

"So...being three meters tall is unusual? She would have been considered abnormal, just like the Earthborne?"

"Right."

"Why are they changing?"

"I don't know..." Gently shaking her head, Nikita's eyes trailed to the locker in the farthest corner, storing their most precious item. "I wonder if the shard has anything to do with it."

She stood, leaving her datapad on the bunk, and hurried to the locker. With anticipation, she retrieved the shard from Gunliem. She studied its square frame and symmetrical grooves and noted its unusual patterns across its six-sided face. Despite its mysterious design, it was just a large alloy motif, no bigger than a grapefruit. She gripped it, feeling its heft, and reached for the second shard in her backpack. Facing Vivika, her brows creased in uncertainty, she displayed both pieces: the pyramidal construct from Saifain and its cubed counterpart from Gunliem.

"I mean, they're just—" Vivika gestured between the pieces "—chunks of debris, it looks like. How could they do anything, let alone mutate Elemnai?"

Nikita gasped as a surge of pressure ran up her limbs, making the hairs on her arm shiver. A filament of light danced between the shards, followed by several tendrils of brilliant white plasma. An overwhelming force seized them from her grasp, rocketing the shards toward each other. The room's lamps flickered into darkness as they collided and hit the floor with a shrill scrape, emitting a blazing incandescence that flared and faded within seconds. With the return of the room's neutral glow, Nikita and Vivika glanced at one another in horror, both pressed against the bunks directly behind them.

"What the *frag* was that?!" Vivika cried.

Nikita breathed heavily, unable to regain her composure. "I," she stammered, her heart beating wildly against her chest. "I assembled the shards?"

CHAPTER 13
PURPOSE

W isps of smoke danced as Malek exhaled. He watched the strands disappear into the night sky, eyes trailing toward the stars sparkling across the inky-black vault. He flicked his cigarette, dropping ashes into a rusted coffee can on the balcony. From the main building at the Azarian main operating base, he had a good view of the dual rows of barracks across the massive facility grounds. A bit of tension lifted, but it soon crept back into his extremities. He felt disappointed in himself for taking up an old and useless coping strategy. It served no purpose, other than giving him a false sense of calm.

Malek half-heartedly listened to Major Franz's debrief droning on behind him. The man could have summarized it a lot quicker, but Malek took the ramblings as a sign of the major's anxiety. Maybe there was some regret in there, too, for how he'd treated Malek at the outset of the Saifain operation.

"The ASF custodians completed their task," Franz's voice rumbled from the doorway. "The area has been cleared. I'm pulling my forces back once your division leaves the area. All, uh, bodies from the scene have been recovered."

"We'll be out of here as soon as our debrief with the general is complete," Malek spoke dryly. "You can forward your written summary to Lieutenant Bastion right away. He'll contact you to arrange this. Dismissed." Malek nodded Franz away. He just wanted some space. When Franz didn't leave, Malek had to resist the urge to groan aloud when the major spoke again.

"…Commander, I know I was not eager to welcome your team," Franz said, quieter this time. "But I must thank you for…" He cleared his throat again. "It looked like a hell of an encounter. If you need anything else, please do not hesitate to let me know."

Actually, there was something Malek could have used right now. Since he didn't need to explain himself to a lower-ranking officer, he took the liberty of requesting it anyway. "Have the quartermaster procure a cellbike. The MKX-R, if you have any onsite."

"A cellbike? Why—" Franz stammered and cleared his throat again. "Yes, sir. The QM… should have that model, if I'm not mistaken."

Malek listened to the heavy shuffling of Franz's steps as he passed the threshold and closed the door. He blew out a long breath, then took another drag. The quiet seconds that passed allowed him to finally feel the weight of their actions and the gravity of what they had witnessed—the Terminians, the enemy of the Alliance, and an Earthborne, the enemy of mankind, facing off with an Alliance task force on Mardascan soil. Who would have guessed? It was all so complicated… and that was without trying to figure out why everyone was willing to kill for the shard.

Malek shifted his focus to the Terminians, and why they risked showing their faces. What could they have gained from this? What would they have walked away with? Who was their true target?

Malek closed his eyes, and his mind drifted toward the shards. A ghost of a near-forgotten memory surfaced, of him peering through a crack in the bedroom door of his childhood home. He was staring at something then, something out of place.

"There you are," Gene said from the doorway of the expansive balcony, causing Malek to jump. "Mind if I join you, Commander?"

Malek hadn't expected one of his team members to look for him, but he welcomed the company as he stood openly, facing his major. A single, dim lamp hung over the entrance, casting a yellow glow over the visitor, enough for Malek to make out the troubled expression on Gene's face.

"How's the arm?" Gene nodded to him as he leaned against the railing.

Malek looked at his limb, laced with a hardened, web-like cast. He remembered having to wait ages for the medical officers to fill a mesh with a liquid resin, which hardened into the cast he had now. "Still functional, anyway." Malek lifted his arm, but noticed that Gene was now eyeing the cigarette balanced between his fingers on his other hand.

"Most fizzies would give you a ribbing for that."

"*Fizzies...*" Malek raised his eyebrows. It was Norvican slang for ASF Officers, a mostly derogatory term used by army recruits. "I haven't heard that in a long time. Most fizzies haven't had days like today. Kicked the habit after I became one... but..." Malek took another drag, shaking his head. Again, this wasn't like other days.

Gene didn't say anything at first but nodded very slowly, a hint of restlessness in his tired eyes. Something about his posture or twitching hands also gave it away. Without another word, Malek pulled out another cigarette and handed it to Gene, who quickly placed it between his lips as Malek ignited it with his lighter.

Gene inhaled a little too earnestly and shuddered as he released a breath. "Cheers... My wife would kill me."

"I'll put it on my list of things not to tell your wife," Malek said wryly. "Right up there with...well, everything that happened today."

Gene laughed and, along with Malek, stared up at the night sky. Malek busied himself trying to spot the distant, unblinking orange dots in between the patterns of stars, marking the presence of their only two neighboring planets: the rocky world of Etana, and the gas giant, Enlil. He drew in another breath of noxious, calming fumes and heard Gene speak again.

"...Can't ever get used to it, eh?"

"No. You never do."

"How old do you think she was?"

"Oh... fourteen, fifteen, maybe."

"Aye. Brave girl." Gene cleared his throat, flicking the ashes from his cigarette. "...Do you have children?"

"No... I mean, not that I know of."

Gene chuckled and lowered his gaze. "It's a beautiful chaos, you know. Turns you into the biggest sap and the toughest brute all at once. I have two daughters. Lydia and Gemma. Lydia will be thirteen soon."

Malek realized that his offer for the company was more than just a casual gesture. Azka's death shook Gene, and it had struck uncomfortably close to home... well, for both of them. Either way, he had to adopt his duty as a commander: keep Gene's morale from slipping despite the weight of their grief. "The forces were against her and us. Not everyone comes out winning. You know that as much as I do."

Gene shrugged and continued staring off into the distance. Not Malek's best work... Malek went back to smoking in silence, too, and inwardly kicked himself for not paying more attention to Anthem's motivational speeches. Nausea suddenly came over him, and he ran his wrist over his brow, lowering his eyes to the ground. He barely noticed the aura surrounding him momentarily dimmed. A strange taste filled his mouth. His memories drifted back to that moment, staring into the crack of light, only this time, he watched his mother's eyes flicker up at him as she sat on the long edge of her bed. Her white hair fell to her waist, like a river of molten gold under the sun, and her young face sparked with amusement. Her old stories now haunted him.

"The Al-Khasari are dogmatic in a lot of ways." Malek stifled the sickness, hoping the talk would get his mind off it. "Everything has a greater purpose. The idea is that each one of us is responsible for doing something right in the world and leaving it better than it was. The whole idea is called *drashe*. Even kids know that they're meant to do something important in this life, and it's always for the good of humanity. It's what allows them to become *madna*, or part of the enlightened ones. It's what the Al-Khasari consider to be closest to godliness. Or maybe it's to follow the steps of the Anymm, I can't remember. Anyway, becoming *madna* means that you sacrificed. And no matter how small the act, if you could've saved one person, it would've been as if you had saved the world. Azka knew she needed to keep the shard from falling into the wrong hands. She protected her people and her family. So... she fulfilled *drashe*. Now she's *madna*. She died knowing that." Malek flicked the cigarette.

137

"That's... wow. Awfully deep for kids," Gene replied in a low murmur.

"Yeah. I was even taught that much. I don't know... maybe my mom wanted me to be a better person, or whatever."

"...Sounds like Al-Khasari children are raised far better than I was." Gene smiled at Malek, who could only respond with an awkward shrug. He'd never thought of it that way.

"Maybe. But we can still be morons. I should know. I had to kick the slag out of a few when I was a kid."

Gene laughed aloud, and so did Malek.

"... Despite how things went, we were successful, major. But we owe it to Azka to see this through, and to keep performing admirably, just as you have." Malek wondered if Gene had even heard him, or if anything he'd said made any sense. He snuffed out the cigarette, exhaled the fumes, and inched away. Might as well head to his quarters. Maida would undoubtedly be looking forward to his report...

"Thank you, Commander," Gene finally said after a moment. There was a calmness, or sincerity, in his eyes, and Malek knew that Gene meant it when he added, "And... Thank you for risking your life for us."

Malek didn't know what to do except nod, but his heart leaped again at the interruption of another's voice.

"Commander!" Malek whipped around, seeing Vivika at the entrance of the door, breathing hard with one hand still on her ribs. Malek already gauged from her expression that something was very wrong, and a haziness filled his periphery, which he forcefully stifled as adrenaline raged through his system. "You have to look at this! The shard... it's...it's misbehaving!"

It was hard for Malek to focus on what he had seen as he fended off his dizziness and agonized over the horrible acidic, metallic taste in his mouth. Eyebrows creased, he clasped a palm over his lips and his unshaven chin, pretending to be interested in the pair of shards now melded together on the floor in a single motif, while suppressing the urge to throw up. The nausea came completely out of the blue, and he resented why it had hit him like this.

"Should... we touch it?" Gene posed, kneeling beside the small structure. He glanced up at Malek. "Commander? Are you alright?"

"Huh? No, just," Malek muttered, then placed his hands over his hips and cleared his throat. "Damn it, Kei. This isn't 'misbehaving.'"

Vivika stared back at him sharply. "It *did* misbehave! Kit, tell him!"

Malek turned to her. Nikita's hand ran through her wave of curls, shaking her head as she stared at the shards. "It... flashed. Very brightly. Before getting stuck together like that. Almost like a pair of really, really strong magnets."

"But what started it?"

Nikita lifted her palms in a cupping motion, at level with her waist. "I just held them. Like this."

Malek frowned, kneeling beside the shards. With an exasperated sigh, and much protest from his team, he seized them and attempted to pry them apart. Unable to gain any margin with force, he twisted it and failed just as quickly. "Bastion?" he fumed.

"Yes, sir."

"Make it a priority to get these shards out of here. If fusing released some sort of signal, I'd expect more Elemnai might come looking for it." He looked up at Nikita. "I didn't want to believe what you said about the Elemnai tracking the shards, but our friend in Saifain might've supported your theory."

"What do you mean?"

"He asked me, in Khasiri, '*where,*' probably about these. He followed my directions for a while, but once you and the others had some distance, it was as if he knew it was gone."

"We can review the data, Dr. Valerio, but I believe the commander is correct," Bastion cut in. "The shard must be moved. Immediately. With the confirmation of the GX Forces in the area, Saion forward operating base at the Mardascan-Elemnai Territories border will serve as an acceptable meeting point for the exchange if the goal is to deter Elemnai advancement into Juven Sands. I will be sending a Paladin and its crew to collect."

139

"A Paladin?" Malek repeated, stifling a smile. "Didn't know you were such a high roller."

"Is that sarcasm? I can't tell. A Paladin will be on site within sixty minutes. It will take longer to reach Azar, but that is another suitable alternative."

"No, I need these shards moving."

"When can I expect one of your team members to be at the FOB?"

Malek took hold of the shards and stood with a grunt. Good thing he'd asked Franz for the cellbike. He'd be hitting two birds with one stone. "You'll be expecting me. And if Franz has what I asked him to procure, I'll be there in... seventy-five minutes, approximately."

Gene rose to meet him, his brow furrowed and staring intently at Malek. "Commander, you're injured. All three of us can take the shard. You've done enough."

Malek shook his head. "I appreciate it, Major. I grew up around here and know these roads better than anyone else. I can get there the fastest and know how to lose someone if I need to."

"Then take one of us with you," Vivika interjected. "Don't go alone."

Malek met her gaze and swallowed. "Uh, can't. Just room for one," he stammered.

Vivika narrowed her eyes. The more she stared, the more exposed Malek felt. He stifled the urge to knead his neck. She was completely onto him. "You got a cellbike, didn't you?" she smiled. "*Se.* Then it's settled. I'll go with the commander. There is definitely room for two."

"...Can't you ride on your own?" Malek grumbled.

Vivika lifted one shoulder with a playful tilt. "I'm uncomfortable."

"Excellent. Thank you for volunteering, Lieutenant Kei. I appreciate the commander having some company. And a cellbike is perfect as speed is of the essence," Bastion said before Malek could protest again. He figured he would only be inviting more questions if he resisted. Vivika must've already guessed why he needed to travel alone, which was a poor excuse at best. But *why* he'd asked for a cellbike was actually questionable. He couldn't admit to anyone that it was for a personal errand.

Malek had to accept Vivika's offer, whether he liked it or not. His nerves fired with dread, but he straightened his spine and put on a placid look. "Alright. I'll meet you at the QM in ten to get our gear. And bring this with you." He handed her the shard, and Vivika wavered from its heft. She scorned as he turned away. Not wanting to make this any more awkward, he left without speaking, gathering his parcel sent by Bastion on his way to his private quarters.

Malek tugged at the hem as he fastened the riding glove over the edge of his cast. Perched on the driver's seat of the cellbike, Malek caught a glimpse of a similarly dressed figure–Alliance casual uniform under an armored, black jacket–strolling toward him with a pep in her step and a sleek, dark helmet clutched under her arm. Malek picked up his own helmet and put it on, hoping to relax the forced neutral expression on his face. Against his will, his heart rate elevated as Vivika seated herself on the pillion. In the rearview mirror, he furtively studied the young woman pulling back her raven hair and fitting the helmet over her whimsical grin.

"Are we in for a scenic drive?" she asked, pulling the straps of a backpack a little tighter over her shoulders. Malek had yet to form an answer before he felt her hands wrap around his waist, and the temperature soared under his gear.

"Ah, no." He leaned forward and gripped the bike's handles, glancing back at his passenger. "Shards are secure?"

"Got 'em." She nodded to her pack. "Ready, Commander."

Malek dropped his visor and started the cellbike with a firm push of a white backlit button. He loved the sound more than anything else about it. The smooth hum from the electric engine and a blue light that peeked out from between its sleek front, side, and lower fairings thrilled Malek more than he wanted to admit. He ran a hand over the reflective, carbon-black finish of its composite body, his limbs tingling with excitement.

It was no secret that Malek thought these were fun, but they were also notorious for being a death trap in the wrong hands or the wrong situation. Cellbikes, after all, were known for their power, maneuverability, and speed. Although not designed to carry a passenger, military-grade bikes were usually equipped with a pillion seat in case the rider required support or urgent personnel transport was necessary. Malek and Jace used to take these out all the time...on separate cellbikes. He caught himself missing his best friend but thought he would honor him by letting off some steam, just like they used to.

"Bastion," Malek began.

"Yes, Commander. I can hear you loud and clear. The new earpiece fits well?"

"Affirmative. Set up cross-communication between Kei and me. We are heading out now."

"Copy that. Paladin is inbound, ETA seventy-five minutes."

"Let's see if I make it in sixty-five."

"Don't make me hurl," Vivika said, but her voice was crisp as it reverberated through his earpiece.

Malek scoffed, engaging his muscles. "Lean when I lean. And hold on."

The cellbike roared as he revved its engine. His heart slammed into his spine as it jolted into a gallop. He turned and headed past the open gates of the base, unable to contain his grin.

CHAPTER 14
PROMISES

M alek couldn't believe he hadn't thrown himself or Vivika off the cellbike. He had never driven so fast in his life—crossing 250 kilometres in a little over an hour. Now *that* was fun. The cellbike probably appeared as just a streak of blue light out on these pitch-black highways. Malek came to a halt when he reached the massive, armored gates of Saion FOB. He was met by a pair of soldiers, who were communicating with the base administrators in rushed military jargon. They confirmed his identity with a quick barrage of questions, and when the last one landed, the tightness in Malek's chest unwound and his breath slipped out in a slow, quiet release.

"Bastion, we made it," Malek alerted over the comms.

"Sixty-two minutes. Impressive, Commander," Bastion replied coolly. "My officer, Lieutenant Mose, is coming to you now."

The gates slowly creaked open, the hinges moaning with the effort. Malek and Vivika both dismounted and removed their helmets. He looked at her, and she smiled at him, equally relieved. It was impressive in itself that she didn't complain about his driving, given her quip before they left Azar. If he didn't know better, Malek thought she actually enjoyed herself, giggling every time he pushed the limits of the acceleration.

The two soldiers at the gate stopped Malek before he could cross into Saion FOB's main compound.

"You'll have to wait here," one said. "Paladin landed in the quad."

Malek looked up in wonder as the hum of the Paladin's engine emptied from the gates into the desert and filled his ears. He didn't expect his heart to race excitedly, especially after that trek between here and Azar. When it came to air transport, *this* was the way to ride. The sleek black aircraft perched on the open dusty surface, gleaming under the iridescent lamps of the surrounding shadowy buildings. A razor-edged hull framed a stout cockpit and a solid, compact fuselage. The quartet of short wings bore propellers in their center, which drew up the sand into a fog surrounding it. It was pretty fragging cool in person. There were at least two people inside, one in the pilot's seat and the other hidden in the rear cabin, and another officer who trotted up to meet him.

While the cellbike was his favorite, Malek was envious of the Paladin's precision in entering and exiting combat zones. He had never ridden in one before, but he watched enough vids. Bitterly, he thought of many times throughout his career when it would have been helpful.

"Commander," the ASF Officer saluted as he met them, placing his right hand over his heart. "Lieutenant Mose. Bastion sent us. We're here to secure the package."

"Obviously," Vivika muttered under her breath, bringing forth the pack to the officer.

A surge of dizziness made Malek's vision dance. He flinched at the sudden jolt ripping through his mind. A single panicked thought chased it: The Alliance should not have the shards. Malek reached for Vivika's hands just as she was about to hand over the prize. He didn't even realize he did it until Vivika shot him a perplexed look. Something inside him was screaming: *Don't let these go.*

A painfully awkward moment passed before Malek pushed down the dread and finally stepped back from Vivika. She hesitated as well, holding his gaze a little longer. Maybe she was looking for a cue to stop the handover completely, but Malek refused to give in. He nodded to her, knowing he couldn't afford to fail the objective or, worse, risk compromising his position. He needed to do everything right. If handing back the shards wasn't the right move, it was a decision he needed to live with. Implicating himself would be far more dangerous. The Alliance should never have a reason to send Malek back to the Spire.

"You guys work directly with Bastion?" Malek finally asked, purging the last clinging whispers of doubt.

"Yes, sir," Mose nodded and saluted again. Without another word, Mose turned and headed back to the Paladin. It was a pretty abrupt answer, considering Mose was speaking to a higher-ranking officer... but this was all too damn urgent. Malek wondered if they knew what they were collecting or why. The Paladin immediately lifted from the ground and soon disappeared into the wisps of ghostly clouds creeping across the night sky.

"You okay, Commander?" Vivika asked quietly, just as the gates groaned closed. It broke Malek from his daydream about the shards as they slowly paced back to the cellbike.

"Yeah. Not sure what came over me." Malek fitted his helmet again and took a seat.

Vivika, almost too eagerly, hopped onto the cellbike and seized him by his waist. This time, he relaxed at her touch, something he didn't expect. Stopping himself from smiling, Malek sped off from the base.

"Commander," Bastion's voice. "I'll be away from my station while I prepare for the shards' arrival. I will check in now and then to ensure you have returned to Azar. Do you require anything from me at the moment?"

"How 'bout some tunes, Bastion?" Vivika piped up.

"Pardon me?"

"I'm thinking this will be a leisurely stroll back to base," she spoke coyly.

Malek glanced back at her, slowing as he approached the intersection leading back to the main highway.

"I see. Any preferences?"

"Something upbeat. Electronic?"

"Ugh," Malek grumbled.

"Come on, Commander," Vivian teased. "Passenger gets to pick."

"That's not how–"

"Done," Bastion replied. A light beat filled their earpieces, followed by Bastion's smooth voice, "Safe travels, Commander. Lieutenant."

Malek shook his head. "Yeah. Thanks." He exhaled sharply, scanning each dismal stretch of the highway on either side of the junction. Lifting his eyes to the pale road sign ahead of him, he felt Vivika shift in her seat as he studied the text.

"Are you okay?" she asked.

"Just thinking. I'll drop you back in Azar."

"Why? Where are you going?"

"I have to run a personal errand. It won't take long, but it's a bit of a drive."

"How far?"

"From here, probably four hours straight south, if I'm a law-abiding citizen."

"What? No, you'll spend more time dropping me off first. And anyway...I don't like the idea of you driving alone. I'll go with you."

Malek blew out a heavy breath and eased back from the handles. He tilted his head at Vivika, who angled herself sideways to face him. He contemplated his next words. This was the only chance that he could get away with doing this. He wanted to take it while he could.

"No questions," he spoke firmly. "Not about where we're going or why. And you keep it to yourself."

"*Okitoki*, Commander. My lips are sealed."

This would have been a perfect first date, and Malek inwardly kicked himself every time he thought about it. Instead, he rehearsed protocol about fraternization and regulation to kill the thought. But he was almost there, and that alone made him smile. Even the environment seemed brighter. Deos revealed her full lunar face, rising to the pinnacle of the sky as time eased into the early morning hours. While the minutes passed, the smooth, upbeat music resonated from their earpieces and filled the silence between them. It was calming and elating enough to melt the tension in his muscles.

The terrain shifted from a desolate landscape to the familiar sight of high rock faces, with hints of lush vegetation clinging to their crevices. The odd palm took root with its companion ferns, flashing a brilliant green as they caught the cellbike's twin cat-eye headlamps. Malek nudged Vivika and tipped his chin toward the bend ahead. When she sucked in a startled breath, he couldn't help but laugh.

They followed the curve of the highway as it hugged the side of a cliff. Beyond the rocky landscape lay a drop, followed by an endless, sparkling seascape bathed in moonlight. The massive waves' crests formed silver lines across the shifting waters. The familiar sight filled him with warmth.

Though she kept her promise, he could feel Vivika swell with curiosity, fidgeting restlessly as she clung to him in silence. "Sea-Kee Shores?" she said aloud later as they passed a large, wooden welcoming sign with 'Cice Shores' written in cursive.

"No, it's sea-sea."

"It sounds like something out of a kids' book."

"I know. I think so, too." Malek slowed enough to turn onto a side road, charting the path ahead. Large, hanging palms hung like dark, shadowy fingers over a narrow path. The makeshift tunnel stayed lit by their presence for a short time. It could have been eerie, but Malek had made this trip several times a year, sometimes in the middle of the night. Vivika released an awed murmur, and Malek remained focused on his destination. The road opened to several paths and a vast clearing that rolled over short grassy hills. It was unmistakable where they were, and Vivika blurted it out instantly.

"A graveyard?!" she said, alarmed.

Malek recognized the familiar rows of headstones, varying in size and shape, which filled the clearings between the narrow paths. "No questions," Malek said. Their pace slowed to a crawl, and he stopped, powering down the cellbike while Vivika dismounted. He flicked the kickstand down with his toe and swung himself off in one motion. "You can wait here if you want." He removed his helmet. She did the same, and her eyebrows knitted together. "Or you can head up there." Malek gestured to one of the highest hills toward a cliff's edge. Palm trees and small, flowering bushes marked the path upward. "There's a great view. I'll be back in a few minutes."

He didn't wait for her to respond. Malek strode into a clearing, weaving his way through the maze of headstones and scanning them as he passed. Several moments into his journey, he stopped in his tracks and stooped.

Malek took in the cool air, brushing the detritus off the simple bronze plaque embedded in a stone obelisk, which rested purposefully over a patch of grass. A wild rose bush next to the stone stretched over its face, casting a web-like shadow as the brilliant moonlight glistened across plots. A sweet, comforting perfume from the pink blooms lifted his spirits, but only for a moment.

The sorrow from the day caught up to him, starting with the fatigue seeping into his limbs. Malek thought of Azka again. She was just a kid. A heaviness bore down in his chest, forcing him to kneel on the soft earth. He glanced behind him, seeing Vivika walking away from the cellbike toward the cliff, and inched closer to the headstone.

"Hi, *amma*," he murmured in Khasiri. "Sorry... I wish I didn't have to visit like this." His fingers dusted off the letters of the inscription.

Amira Reza
Ascended with her Love.
?-214 CE, Third Era of Eiden

Malek had never understood or liked the inscription, but his mom insisted on the wording before her death. He never wanted to fight about small things, especially since he had been forced away from home for two years at the height of their strife, for both of them.

At fourteen, a young, rebellious Malek had to suppress whatever personal gripes he had with his one and only parent, and act as a translator during Amira's oncologist visits in Azar. Though she never admitted it, Malek knew that separating from the Al-Khasari people had placed a grueling burden on her, affecting all facets of her life, including her health. It didn't help that Malek had acted like a slaghead most of the time. But she'd raised him with unshakeable love and insurmountable patience, and he wished he could tell her what that meant for him. If only he had figured it out years earlier. Amira had nourished his spirit and tempered his fire when needed, dealing with his anger with a firm hand and melting his sadness with her crippling bear hugs. She was his only family, and he was hers.

Her reliance on him was clear as he guided her through the complexities of her rare leukemia treatments. The realization that she wasn't a Mardascan citizen and ineligible for public healthcare nearly destroyed him. If not for their generous landlord, they would have been forced into homelessness. Malek had to make the most of this opportunity and earn money—fast.

Though his mother fiercely opposed the decision, Malek joined the Alliance Army Support Infantry at sixteen to cover her medical costs at the start of the Triad War in 212 CE. What he hoped would be a six-month non-combat tour turned into a traumatizing two-year horror, marked by capture and imprisonment by GX Forces and a vicious AIA assessment in the Spire. He never came back home the same. The ghost of his trauma, from both those ordeals and saying his final goodbye to Amira, followed Malek for the last ten years.

Malek shifted back on his heel, resting one palm on the stone when his aching muscles protested. He often retraced his steps to this place between training exercises and deployments with the ASF. This was the closest thing to coming home, and though he couldn't, the only person he wished he could see again.

"At least you can't say I didn't try, though. Kept my promise. Came back from another fight to show you I'm alive," he muttered, glancing at the hint of webbing underneath the leather military jacket. Images of Nikita bandaging Azka filled his mind. Her small corpse lying on the floor of their transport back to Azar pained him in more ways than he expected. "I met someone today who reminded me of you. Young and alone. Had a bit of an attitude. I couldn't stand the idea of leaving her behind. Wish I could have done things right…"

Malek sighed deeply, flexing the fingers of his broken arm, which only throbbed slightly from his movement. "I don't know if I can do this. It happened again. The blackout. I can't be responsible for others while this is happening… and while keeping it from Maida."

Malek closed his eyes, and that same memory resurfaced. He was peering through the crack in the door. His mother ran her thin hands over a strange box lying across her lap. He had seen her do this many times as a form of comfort. But this time was different. She sensed his presence and looked up, but it was no longer her face. It was gaunt, and she was terrified. Only the eyes were the same—the brilliant indigo eyes of the Al-Khasari, but they carried so much pain.

Malek dug deeper and reveled in his memories as a boy, when they used to laugh. In their isolation, she and Malek played the piano, competed in games, and ventured along the far reaches of Cice Shores' cliffs. He would give anything to be in those moments again.

"So, if you're not busy... doing whatever you're doing...maybe take this up the chain?" Malek lifted his eyes to the starry vault, its brightness only dampened by the solitary iron lamps dotting the cemetery's paths. "I could really use some help."

Her shape silhouetted against the pale moonlight, and facing the expansive ocean, she stood leaning on one leg with her arms folded loosely over her fitted jacket. Malek could only study her for a moment before she sensed his presence. Vivika beamed at him as he climbed the last of the uneven grass and rock ledges leading up to a narrow cliff.

"You never said we were going to the beach!" she exclaimed.

"I never said where we were going, period," Malek scoffed, coming to her side. She refocused on the lapping waves beating rhythmically against the shoreline far below. Malek missed this sound. It was one of the few comforts of home that reminded him of simpler times. Deos bathed the sands in hues of blue, while her distant little red brother, Artesh, played hide-and-seek in the shadowy stretches of midnight clouds.

Vivika blew out a long breath, "I always wanted to end up here. Live out my days by the ocean."

"Doesn't Jennah have a lot of beaches?"

"We do, but I lived inland. My *oba*, I mean my dad, owned a huge orchard... so I'm a farm girl. I grew up surrounded by fruit trees. Like, acres and acres. It was a maze. I was always getting lost somewhere in the peaches and ending up way back by the cherries. There was one lemon tree. It was my favorite. I knew where I was and how I could get home if I found the lemon tree."

"Sounds like a fun childhood."

"It was. Well... back when things *were* good, we used to spend summers at our cottage at the beach. It was on this grassy cliff, kind of like this one. I still remember this little path that went from the yard down over the dirt and rocks." Vivika instinctively traced the path with her fingers, its steepness shown in the arc of her gesture. "A thousand little steps took us right to the ocean. I loved that place. *Oba* was always helping me pick up crabs to scare my mom." Vivika's smile faded, and her posture stiffened.

Malek immediately absorbed the change in mood. "I take it that things aren't as good as they used to be?"

"My *oba* was killed at the beginning of the Triad War, before the war had even been declared, I think. Terminians were forcibly evicting the inhabitants of other farming communities, so my *oba* stepped in to help. Everyone looked up to him. He was so charismatic... He fought with our neighbors as a ragtag rebellion group and died with them. Never felt like home after that," she repeated bitterly, shaking her head. "After losing my *oba*, I always wanted to go back to the beach. Any beach...thinking I'd see him taking his usual stroll with his coffee...picking up pretty shells for me and pulling seaweed from his toes. I know it sounds crazy."

"It doesn't." Malek's hand fidgeted, but he stifled the urge to reach for her. Like Vivika, many of his most cherished memories with his mother took place along the beaches—memories of her building sandcastles with him, digging for lost treasures, and scanning the tide as he brazenly surfed his first waves. Malek sighed, folding his arms tightly. He found himself wishing that he and Vivika had met under different circumstances. As stupid as it sounded, he wanted to be more than commander and lieutenant... more than friends, even. He wanted to take her hands and tell her that he understood this agony all too well...the pain of losing a parent far too young, before being ready to face the world alone.

Vivika glanced at him and smiled, dissipating his train of thought. "I mean, would you look at that?" She gestured excitedly with an open palm to the vast ocean below her. "Beautiful, am I right? Nothing compares."

Malek held his breath for a moment, his words tugging in his throat. He secretly gazed at her profile, watching the raven hair resting on her shoulder as it danced across her neck in the salted breeze. That addicting smile lifted her high cheeks. Long lashes fanned over those large, upturned eyes that studied the seascape beyond the cliff. Even in darkness, Malek couldn't escape that allure. "No," he murmured. "Nothing at all."

He tore his eyes away the minute she turned to him and forced a neutral expression.

"This is your hometown, isn't it? Promise me you'll bring me back here?" Her brows shot up, and her eyes grew bright. "You can help me pick out a nice piece of real estate!"

"You ask a lot of questions. And...sure. *If* we survive this assignment."

"Don't be cynical, Commander. My morale depends on it."

"Right. I'll try to keep that in mind."

Vivika snickered, and then as she spoke again, her Jennai accent thickened, "Come on. We went up against *two* Elemnai and came out breathing. Of course we're going to survive this assignment. We're both *really* good at staying alive and kicking ass."

Malek laughed. Those were the exact words he used with Jace after Gunliem. "Okay, okay. You're right."

"I know I'm right. So, you good? Paid your respects?"

"Yeah. We should get going. Come on." He turned and stepped down the grassy ledges. "I know a charge station that's still open right now."

"You'd better keep your promise."

Glancing back, he caught Vivika staring at the ocean again before finally beginning her descent.

CHAPTER 15

DISTORTION

N ikita's eyes fluttered open at Bastion's gentle words, startling her from a dreamless sleep. For a fleeting second, she thought he was at the foot of her bed and shot a glance down the length of her bunk.

"Dr. Valerio?" her earpiece resonated with a calm, soothing voice.

"Oh." Nikita rubbed her eyes in disappointment as she sat up. Maybe it was a dream. Or maybe she wished he were here. She blinked through the morning blur as her eyes regained focus. The sun's morning glow from the long, narrow window near the ceiling of the compact dorm filled the room with hues of orange and pink. She glanced at it, seeing the Azarian base bathed in its brilliance. "Morning, Bastion."

"Good morning," he replied. "I hope you are well rested. The commander wishes to see you in his quarters."

"Right now?" Nikita didn't mean to sound annoyed, but a whine burrowed into her inflection.

"Yes. He is down the hall. Last door on your right."

"Okay. I'll be there in a few minutes." Nikita sighed and threw aside her sheets. Before she could guess why Malek would choose an obscenely early hour to meet, nearly six in the morning according to her datapad she spotted Vivika curled up on the bunk below her, sound asleep. She was still in a fitted white shirt tucked into dark military pants, with her boots kicked off at the base of the bed. When did they get back? Nikita hadn't even heard her come in.

Surprisingly, Gene was nowhere to be seen. His bed had already been made, and his boots were missing. Maybe he was an early riser. Nikita thought nothing more of it as she fished out her toiletries and casual clothing from her locker and pushed down the anxiety building up in the pit of her stomach. It was silly that she still had to remind herself that she wasn't in trouble and did nothing wrong.

"Here we go..." She took a breath and shuffled out of her dorm.

Nikita steeled her nerves. For a moment, she stood outside Malek's door, gathering her thoughts as she clutched her datapad. It was just like in the boardroom. She had no idea how to act. She couldn't read the commander like she could read her peers at the university. All she wanted was for him to see past her inexperience in the military and see the value she brought to this sensitive situation. She *knew* how to navigate the Earthborne. Couldn't he see her as an asset? If he were as caring as Vivika made him out to be, maybe he could. She raised her fist to knock, but paused at Bastion's voice again.

"A moment, Dr. Valerio. Allow me to confirm he has finished his debriefing with General Maida." Bastion's voice dropped and returned just as calmly within a few seconds, "You may knock."

"Wait... can you see me?"

"Yes, through the security cameras." Bastion sounded so matter-of-fact that Nikita was unsure whether he was joking. "Don't worry. This is not some sort of Alliance privilege. I simply wanted to keep an eye on the common areas in case there was any unsavory activity around the shards. Uh... please don't inform any of the Azarian MOB staff. They may dislike my intrusion."

"Oh... Sure thing." Truthfully, Nikita didn't know how to respond to that. Flustered, she knocked on the door without another word.

"It's open," Malek called.

Nikita stepped into a room twice as large as her dorm. Malek hardly looked up at her from a desk where he typed on a flat keyboard, his eyes fixed on a datapad that sent a ghostly white glow over his tired eyes.

"Uh, good morning," Nikita stammered, looking around his quarters. "Wow, you actually have a workspace." She sat on one of the mocha-colored leather armchairs in the same open space as his desk and then glanced at the single bed in the corner. Either he was already ready for the day, or he never touched it. It was perfectly made. Bastion's parcel rested at its foot.

Malek leaned back in his swivel chair and winced as he flexed his fingers on the arm embraced by a webbed resin cast. "Don't let anyone ever tell you that there are no perks in the Alliance," Malek's voice was gravelly and low. He finally turned to meet her, his face rough with exhaustion and frustration. "What was it about the Earthborne that made it look abnormal? Why do you think it looked the way it did?" Malek asked so quickly that Nikita barely had a moment to shift her focus back to their current assignment.

Nikita fidgeted in her chair and furrowed her brow. Even if Malek was tired, she didn't appreciate *that* tone. At least he could have recognized that the Earthborne was an individual... "*He*," Nikita corrected. "He looked... whatever happened to him, it made him a lot bigger... and abnormal. Let me show you."

If Malek rolled his eyes, she missed it. She scanned the contents of her datapad with a few strokes of her finger and found what she was looking for. The same photo from her first day of teaching—Johar, the Earthborne brave, standing next to her with a hand over her small shoulder. Her eyes lingered on the photo before she turned the datapad toward Malek. Darkness crossed his face as he took it in.

"This Earthborne is what's known as a 'brave.' The Earthborne have three classes: braves, divines, and wardens. Braves are the warrior class and generally have the most prowess among the three classes. They're usually the biggest, too." Nikita glanced down at the datapad. "Standing next to him, he's taller than me by about an extra meter or so. The horns are elegant, and his face is sculpted, but not exaggerated. This is normal."

Malek fixed her with a sober look. "So, the big guy at Saifain...abnormal, you said?"

"That's right." Nikita lowered both her eyes and her datapad onto her lap. She measured her following words carefully. "Vivika mentioned something interesting. She said you two were the officers at Gunliem. And you met the Fireborne. She was, what, three meters tall?"

"Right..."

"Earthborne speak otherwise of their Fireborne counterparts. Smaller. Human-like. I... can't say for sure without looking at it, but—"

"*Her*," Malek interrupted with a placid tone. "And she had a name. It was Urith."

Nikita's eyebrows arched, and her shoulders dropped. That was... unexpected, coming from *him*. Maybe he had a little more compassion than he'd let on since their briefing. But how did he know Fireborne's name? Slowly, Nikita nodded in understanding. "That's right. General Maida said you spoke with her in Khasiri."

"She spoke to *me* in Khasiri, and so did our friend in Saifain," Malek grumbled, and faced his datapad. "And anyway, if what you say is true about Fireborne, then yes. Urith and the Earthborne in Saifain were different. Mutated maybe? You didn't catch his name, did you?"

Nikita tensed, recalling her failure at Saifain to calm the Elemnai. "Uh, no. And 'mutated' is a *bit* of a strong term."

"Got a better one? Also, I'm calling the Earthborne 'Wallace' from now on."

"Wallace?"

"Yeah. If something doesn't have a name, I give it an absurdly non-threatening one."

Now *he* was being absurd. "You're *really* tired, aren't you?" Nikita asked in a low voice, narrowing her eyes at him.

"*So* tired." Malek palmed his face again before opening several windows on his datapad, including a messaging window. "Anyway, something's changed them. Made them worse. Bastion?"

"Here, sir."

"Send over those recordings. Just the last one for now."

"Yes, sir. Check your messages."

"I'll get Bastion to send you the rest, but Wallace said this right before he died. He was trying to tell us something." Malek tapped at the datapad to raise the volume and tilted the device toward her.

A deep, guttural voice breathed and groaned seconds before the words finally left their host, *"Yai nik lodiliv'ad da'dho adholik…Tho'av khurr karr ik rokid ka'vad dho vo'ivado voukav…ad'ail uvdokdalik…"* The speech played out, somewhat unclear between the slurred release and the distance from Malek.

Nikita already found herself coming to Malek's side, leaning one hand over his desk with a mix of apprehension and wonder. Her mind drew lines between the words, stringing them together to form a cohesive translation into Eidean. She needed to be sure, though. The meaning of it slowed her breathing and kick-started her adrenaline. "Again," she murmured. "Please."

Malek complied, and the Earthborne voice filled the silence between them once again.

Nikita leaned away, ruffling the curls at the crown of her head with one hand. Malek was not going to like this.

"Not exactly the most attractive language," Malek said, shaking his head. "What did he say?"

"It's a tad abrasive. It's all about delivery, and uh," Nikita's words trembled as she spoke. "*Wallace* wasn't trying to serenade you. He was pleading with you, I think. Or at least, trying to deliver a warning."

"Warning?" The fatigue quickly receded from Malek's face. "What warning?"

"He said something to the effect of, 'you need to return it to the others', which means that they have a shard in the Wilds, likely somewhere among Earthborne civilization… followed by 'they are going to kill us first, lest we do not unite the—*something*—a weapon or tool of our ancestors." A burning anxiety crawled up Nikita's arms as she folded them. "The words for weapon and tool are extremely similar. I… can't remember which is which."

"It's kind of important." A muscle rolled in Malek's jaw.

"I know that!"

"Can't you look it up?"

157

"No. Dr. Hamada hasn't completed the lexicon for the Earthborne language. There's no official dictionary or anything like that." Nikita lifted her hands in defeat. "We can't ask her directly, or she'll ask to hear the recording. And…honestly, she'll just defer to me anyway."

Malek glared at her, jaw clenched even tighter. "It's a good thing that you're here, then." His indigo eyes searched hers, and Nikita swallowed hard as she looked away.

Nikita wanted to rebuke him but didn't know what to say. She remained quiet and contemplated the Umbar'ok words again as she paced the room, hoping she had missed another less threatening clue.

"Unfortunately, Commander," Bastion cut in, "the resources for this matter through the University of Kaira library databases are very few. Though we have access to Dr. Valerio's files through the university portal, there is nothing official that can serve us."

"You understand *why* the distinction is critical, right, Bastion?" Malek said in a low, grim voice. "We can't submit this intel based on a guess. If Wallace is talking about a weapon in the works…"

"I'm aware, sir. We need to be cautious."

Nikita's insides lurched, and she spun around to face Malek. "Wait, what are you saying?"

"That there's a critical difference between the two translations, like I said." Malek folded his arms, blinking slowly as if stifling a blunt reply. "I need to know if Wallace said 'tool' or 'weapon.' I have to submit this information to the Alliance, so they know how to proceed."

"So, if it's a 'weapon,' that means the Alliance is going to march up to the Earthborne stronghold and what, pre-emptively attack?" Nikita replied hotly, hands curling into hardened fists.

Malek glared at her. "No, that's not what it means. And I hate to remind you, the Earthborne and Fireborne attacked first. *They* killed a lot of people. *They* broke the peace agreement, not us."

"Yeah, but it's obvious this is the work of a few rogues. Maida even suggested it."

"*Is* it obvious?" Malek barked. "This is the evidence we have. Two attacks, a lot of damaged property, and a hell of a lot more dead bodies. Now, we have one that was talking about returning the shard to the others they might have in their possession—to unite the pieces into a 'weapon' or a 'tool'... or *someone* is going to kill them. Doesn't exactly paint a pretty picture here, does it?"

"No, it doesn't, but it doesn't paint the *full* picture, either. We don't know what's happening on their side. They could be in the dark just as much as us. We *don't* know anything and *won't* know anything, if we attack. I'd be saying this if this was anyone else. Alcidians, Al-Khasari, Terminians... Attacking will not solve the problem. If anything, it will be worse. Maida said it himself: war would result in their doom as well as ours."

"Frag...that's my point," Malek groaned, running his finger and thumb over his dark, furrowed eyebrows. "I'm not looking for a reason to fight, Valerio. I'm trying to do the opposite. If you want to stop another war, then we're really going to need you to fill in the blanks, not dictate how to proceed. Give accurate information and accounts of what happened. That's our best shot at peace. I can guarantee their strategy will become more aggressive if the Alliance believes a weapon exists. So, again, how can we be sure of what he said?"

With a heavy sigh, Nikita slowly walked back to the armchair, picked up her datapad, and stared at it. Truthfully, there was only one real way to know. They could find the Earthborne and ask them directly. She wasn't ready for that, especially with the Alliance's penchant for violence. The next best thing flew into her thoughts and past her lips before she could consider the logistics. "My notes. My handwritten notes," she began. "They're in my condo in Kaira. Maybe there's something in there that could help."

Malek exhaled sharply. "How likely?"

"Very. Also, I might have notes on some possible leads for the shards."

"Are you sure?"

"I could have journaled about the shards without knowing what they were. Maybe we have more on this than we thought." Nikita paused, looking down. "And... maybe there's a clue about their possible aggressor. The one Wallace talked about when he said, 'they will kill us.'"

Nikita watched Malek wrestle with the idea, swiveling in his chair in an arc back and forth. He seemed to want to say something, but instead, tilted his head toward the datapad on his desk. "Maida is with the Primarch," Malek said in a low voice.

Nikita was uncertain whether that was meant for her. Would Maida disapprove of them going to Kaira? She supposed it made sense. Perhaps Maida wanted to keep the team safe, and where he could see them. Nikita thought of Bastion's comment about spying on the base. Why would it matter if they took a quick trip? Nikita's jaw tightened, eagerly waiting for Malek's next orders.

"Yes, sir, for the next several hours, it seems. His aide, Lieutenant Derk just replied to my message. But I do believe time is of the essence, and a quick trip to Kaira may be worthwhile," Bastion responded. "But this is your call, Commander. I can also arrange for someone to pick up the journals, as well."

"There are a lot," Nikita muttered.

"It's too important to wait. We'll get the intel ourselves. We need to be precise, and we need to be fast." Malek strained as he rose to his feet. Nikita wanted to reach out and help him stand, but she could have sworn he flinched at her approach. Instead, she clasped her hands together, trying desperately to stop a grin from pulling at her lips. *This* was the way to do things. "We can ask for forgiveness later. Bastion, find us a transport to Kaira. Something low-key. And... maybe send over some civilian clothes."

"Affirmative, Commander. I will keep Lieutenant Derk apprised until Maida is available. Get some rest. You will travel by bullet train to Kaira. Your itinerary and supplies will be delivered shortly."

"Thank you." Nikita exhaled and finally allowed herself to smile, but it was met with a scowl.

"Don't thank me yet. Do your job and get the accurate translation."

"O-of course," she stammered and collected herself.

"Commander?" Bastion's voice resonated in her earpiece again. "Agent Jaeger has arrived. She has... some company with her at the helipad. Please join her as soon as possible."

Malek palmed his hand over his eyes with a groan. "Mace... right now?"

"Yes, right now," Casey's tart words shot from the doorway. Nikita hadn't even heard her approach, and neither had Malek based on the alarmed look on his face. Casey leaned against the threshold with a smirk over a fresh, glowing face, still wearing her fitted tan jumpsuit. Offering only a nod to Nikita, Casey regarded Malek but spoke to him in a language that equally astounded and mesmerized her. "*Kazi Al-Khasari antazarakhai. Rahataji ehid laza.*"

"Your Khasiri needs work, Case." Malek shook his head. "*Chaenan takhasun hayah.*"

He continued to say a few more things to Casey, to which she only responded with that same, mischievous smile.

Nikita found herself immensely enthralled. For some reason, she doubted Malek would be this fluent, and she found Khasiri to be a dulcet, beautiful language... at least, based on the few words they had spoken so far. She broke the exchange down into recognizable terms but couldn't piece together anything cohesive, despite her desperation to learn—except, that is, for the two words: Al-Khasari, which she knew, and Kazi, a word she pulled from her time with the Earthborne.

"We're... going to meet the leader of the Al-Khasari? The Kazi?" she chimed in. They both glanced at her with a look suggesting they had forgotten she was still in the room. Nikita hoped they were impressed by her cleverness.

"No, *I'm* going to meet the Kazi." Malek nodded his head to the door with a stoic expression. "*You're* dismissed."

Nikita sighed in defeat. She cursed her enthusiasm before she ambled out of Malek's room, hearing Casey's teasing voice echoing from behind her, "See you around, Kit!"

Chapter 16

Asset

"Thanks for doing this, Commander," Casey murmured from his side as she and Malek marched up to the helipad opposite their bunker. He drew in the cool, morning air to calm the anxiety burning in his chest. Now he understood why Casey had been late returning to base after bringing Azka's body to her family at Azar's main hospital. While zooming off to Saion FOB, Casey had to alleviate the tensions and repair some broken trust with the Al-Khasari. Returning the body of one of their children was a grave task, and Malek wondered if he should've done it himself. Honestly, when it came to the Al-Khasari, he preferred as little contact as possible to keep himself emotionally in check. That didn't stop the leader of the Al-Khasari, the Kazi, from wanting to have a word with the commander responsible for her death.

It took every ounce of energy left in his already strained system to bury the resentment clouding his mind. He forced another calming breath before facing four people on the launch pad, standing beside a powered-down helicopter. Casey stayed beside him, almost like a guard, with arms tightly folded and stern.

Just as she was about to open her mouth to speak, a young woman with a tear-stained, olive-skinned face quickly came up to meet them. Like the rest of Al-Khasari visitors, her body was shielded in a long, dark cloak, with her arms clothed in a bright, constricted suit with a hexagon weave that shimmered under the morning light. A pinch of regret prodded at Malek, knowing Nikita would have loved to meet the Al-Khasari to chase whatever academic urges she just *had* to journal about.

The young woman nodded at Casey, as if asking permission, then fixed on Malek with the same indigo eyes that he'd been cursed with. She scrubbed her palm over her narrow cheeks.

"Commander, this is Asuza. Azka's aunt," Casey said quietly in Eidean. "She wanted to say thank you."

"Thank you?" Malek glanced between her and Asuza.

Casey shrugged and turned to Asuza, introducing Malek to her in strained Khasiri. Asuza drew in a forced breath, reeling in her emotions as best she could.

"You did us a great service, Commander Reza," Asuza murmured, her Khasiri words trembling. Malek flinched when she abruptly gripped him by the arm. "We are in your debt."

Malek pulled away and buried his fury. "You don't need to thank me. I'm sorry for your loss."

"You are letting us say farewell to our Azka. That's more than any outsider has done for us before. Though you're not *really* an outsider, I—"

Asuza clearly wanted to say more, but an older woman approached her side, placing a firm hand on her shoulder. Despair quickly won the battle, and Asuza nodded in understanding. She mumbled one last "thank you" to Malek before stepping back.

All eyes then focused on the woman facing Malek and Casey with her hands clasped behind her. The Kazi's long, white hair curled and fell alongside her weathered cheeks down to her chest, partially covered by a loosely draped ivory headscarf. Though the wrinkles in the corners of her wide eyes and lips cued her age, an unmistakable fierceness lit up those indigo eyes. Malek wouldn't have expected anything less from the leader of the Al-Khasari. What *did* surprise him was Casey's immediate reaction. She receded behind Malek, exchanging glances with the other young man and woman, dressed in a cloak and tan jumpsuit respectively, standing behind their leader. Malek filed *that* little exchange away for later.

"I do not think any one of us would have braved both the Earthborne and those who are responsible for her murder. So please, accept our gratitude. I promise you that it is earnest." She paused and slowly walked up to Malek. His skin crawled, suppressing memories from decades ago when Al-Khasari brutes threatened him as a child. He planted his heels a little firmer.

"I am the Kazia, the voice of the Al-Khasari as of today," She bowed her head. Malek's muscles relaxed. "I was second to the previous Kazi, Nazar Bahal, who perished at the Earthborne's hands. I will succeed him until the tribunal can determine a more appropriate servant for our people. I am Nur Siyana." She tilted her head to the side. "Walk with me for one moment, Commander." This time she spoke in Eidean, her accent almost imperceptible. Malek's eyebrows lifted. He hadn't expected that.

They walked in silence across the vast runways of the base. Malek ignored the curious stares and grimaces as they passed by army recruits and ground staff. They could judge all they wanted. Malek reminded himself that he was their superior officer. He shot venomous looks right back when he needed to, reminding the recruits to return to work and mind their own business.

"Thank you for bringing back the girl. I know it was treacherous to do so," Nur kept a measured tone. "We truly see you have done us a service. I understand, in the past, the Al-Khasari were not kind to you or your mother—"

"This has nothing to do with my mother," Malek snapped. Another memory flashed of Al-Khasari men stalking his mom as she came home one night from a late shift. It took three onlookers to pull Malek off the ringleader... right after Malek's fist connected with and dislocated the man's jaw.

Malek's reaction surprised him and Nur equally, and he tried to hide the twitch in his lip by looking away.

"Of course not," Nur murmured. "But nonetheless, I understand your anger toward our people. I... truly apologize."

Malek frowned. This was the last thing he wanted to discuss.

Nur continued, taking a few steps away, "We all need one other. We will always need one other. That is the strength of the Al-Khasari. Strength through harmony. We broke our promise to those who defended these traditions for over a millennia. Though some are divided on the matter, I truly think it will be impossible for our people to be whole again without you." Nur paused and looked up at Malek earnestly. "Please... come back with us to As-Tarut. You belong there."

"I'll pass."

"What would convince you?"

"Nothing."

Nur blinked, as though straining to keep composed. She flattened her lips and tilted her head. "Do you have the item taken by the girl? May I have it back?"

"You have a lot of guts coming here and asking. I'll give you that."

"Then what will you do with it?"

"What will you?" Malek countered. "Do you know what it's for?" Now Nur was silent, staring at him cautiously. "Why don't you tell me? Then maybe I'll join you and the rest of the *rayah*."

"Your mother taught you well in the Khasiri argot. With regards to the item... It is something precious to us. That is all."

Malek scoffed and glanced at nowhere in particular. "I'd advise putting a hold on all mining ops until things have settled." With that, Malek curled the fingers on his broken arm and turned away, allowing the pain to pull his mind off the terrible things he wished he *could* have said. He mildly congratulated himself for making it through that conversation without blowing up.

"That woman with you knows the way through the Usharn-Al-Riyah border. She will help you find your way back." Nur had already started back toward the helicopter without him. "We will wait for you."

"Right... You'll be waiting a long time," he muttered under his breath. When his anger finally subsided enough for him to look back at Nur, Casey and the younger pair of Al-Khasari moved past her and approached him. The few seconds of anticipation forced him to reset his thoughts and temper his frustration.

"...And here is the man of the hour!" the young woman in a tan jumpsuit matching Casey's spoke in Khasiri, her expression jovial and eager. Then it finally clicked, and Malek understood who she was.

"Never got a chance to say thanks for the assist," Malek replied in Khasiri. "That was some talent landing in Saifain. Great job on not losing your slag when the Earthborne showed up. So, what's your name?"

With a whimsical grin, she tucked a strand of silver hair between her ear and neatly-tied braid. Her face was young and eerily similar to the young man's, with the same fierceness in her gaze that he saw in Nur. "Zia Siyana. And yes, your humble pilot. I would have introduced myself sooner, but Casey-*jahni* insisted I allow you to focus on the assignment."

Malek shot Casey a sharp look, which she pretended not to see.

"Also, this is my twin, Zalmei."

"Greetings!" Zalmei chimed in. He brushed strands of white from his indigo eyes, pulling them to meet the rest of his chin-length hair. Then he adjusted a pair of round, gold-rimmed glasses that blinked in the light and perched over his sharp nose. Malek recognized the traditional Al-Khasari greeting when Zalmei touched his forehead with his index and middle fingers, and then brought his hand down swiftly, several inches from his mouth and chin in a cupping motion before allowing it to fall to his side. Malek didn't bother returning the gesture. "It is an honor to meet you, Commander Reza. Zia was just enlightening me about your exploits. I'm very impressed."

"Don't be. Again, I'm sorry about Azka."

"Her family is nonetheless deeply grateful for returning her to them. As is my mother," Zalmei paused, glancing at his sister, "Zia and I were just discussing, and perhaps with Casey's help, you *could* come for a visit one day. And the others, too, especially Dr. Valerio. She is quite the pioneer, and I would love to have tea with her one day."

Valerio would love that, too. Malek arched his eyebrows as he scrutinized the twins. The Al-Khasari never let anyone into their borders. Malek really must have done something right, if they were willing to let in Valerio. "I... I'll pass on the message."

"Good, I'll practice my Eidean in the meantime."

"My mother needs to return to As-Tarut immediately," Zia chimed back in. "Casey-*jahni*, I'll prepare to leave, but don't be too long."

"At peace, Commander." Zalmei nodded at him before clasping his hands behind his back, then swiftly walked back toward the helicopter with his sister.

Once they were alone, Malek and Casey simultaneously released a deep exhale. They glanced at one another in obvious relief before staring down the length of the base at the helicopter powering up, the sun's first rays glinting across the sleek metal skin.

"You saying goodbye, Case?" Malek said in a low voice. "We're headed to Kaira. Could use another body."

"Maida never said anything about Kaira." She raised an eyebrow at him.

"Maida doesn't know yet."

"Oh? As fun as that sounds, I can't. With the change in Al-Khasari leadership, I'm going to have to stay close and solidify my relationship with them."

Malek didn't like that answer, but he accepted it and changed the topic to something else that bothered him. "You could have just said our pilot was one of them."

"Would it have made a difference?"

"She was part of our team, and she's not Alliance. This has 'security breach' all over it."

"No point. Maida already approved it. She did her job. We all did."

Malek frowned at that remark. Maida wasn't always keen on sharing details. It left Malek wondering if there was another purpose in making him commander of this assignment. "Is this his way of...trying to collaborate with the Al-Khasari?"

"Possibly." Casey shrugged. "It's a topic he is quite passionate about. Not sure why."

"I have an idea why." Malek flattened his lips in stifled anger. He still remembered Maida's fascination when he found a sixteen-year-old Al-Khasari kid walking out of an occupied bunker after butchering his captors. "So why now?"

"I've been trying to uphold this relationship with the Al-Khasari for years. My current handle is Casey, the shady businesswoman. Started as trading partners. I bought tech from the Al-Khasiri in exchange for Mardascan goods and services, including false IDs. They knew I had connections in Mardasca, Norvica, Calis, and Seraf. The Al-Khasari have never been attacked so blatantly, especially not by an Elemnai. They got desperate, and I was the only outsider who could help...or at least one they trusted."

"Don't the Al-Khasari have a military?"

"Sure, but not nearly enough to take on an Earthborne." Casey glanced at Malek. "In terms of functional weaponry, the Alliance arms surplus I've sold to them is all they have right now. Call it fortunate or unfortunate, the Al-Khasari are talented in many ways, except when it comes to combat. They lack the means to wield their other 'defenses.'"

"Some long rusted tech?"

"They're not that threatening, to say the least. Anyway, the Al-Khasari approached me looking for help with the Earthborne and to find the one who lived in exile. They said he knew how to handle himself. Their words, not mine." Casey chuckled. "I presented the scenario to the AIA. I've never heard of you, personally, but the AIA thought the stars had aligned on this one. Guess they were quite familiar with you."

It settled on him like a stone dropped across his chest, squeezing his lungs with its weight. The AIA was *very* familiar with him. They'd had a whole year with Malek... all to themselves to do whatever they wanted after his imprisonment by the Terminians. Malek could already feel a haze surrounding him, and he tried to focus back in on Casey before the trauma could spill over into a noticeable reaction.

"Maida was all over it and said we had an Al-Khasari commander in stock. So, the plan was set. After letting the Al-Khasari know that I found you, they agreed to collaborate, provided they had one of their own and myself present on the task. So here we all are."

"Why on Eiden would the Al-Khasari ask for me..."

"They expected sympathy from you. Not from anyone else, and especially not from anyone in the Alliance. It's honestly purely coincidental that you *are* actually an ASF commander. This worked out beautifully."

Malek blinked, and impostor syndrome rushed in like a tide under Deos's pull. "I... wasn't a commander yesterday."

"You weren't?"

"No. I was just an officer."

"Ha, slag. Not bad for a grunt." Casey nudged him with her elbow, and Malek instinctively jolted. The flood lamps caught his gaze, and a flash of iridescence pulled him back to the Spire. The air left his lungs. His burning skin met with the cold floor, shattered bones in his limbs searing with agony.

Wonder if all Al-Khasari are freaks like him, that distant, rumbling voice hammered through the recesses of his mind.

Malek purged the memory with a shake of his head. Just as he was about to glare at Casey, she offered a genuine smile for the first time since they met. The edginess clawing at him slowly disappeared. "Maida made the right choice, for what it's worth. The AIA or Maida could have picked someone else. The ultimate goal was to improve relations with the Al-Khasari on a whole other level. You managed to do that, deal with the Earthborne, not to mention confirm the presence of the Terminian agents, and live to tell about it."

Malek couldn't process the compliment. Maybe the mission had been a success... but something felt off. He'd been lied to, or at the very least, kept in the dark. Even though he was supposed to be in charge, it was as if he were just playing a part in some grand design. Malek shook his head and decided to flip the conversation. "Does *she* know you're AIA?"

"Who?"

"Zia, your asset-slash-pilot." Malek glanced at Casey, who had furrowed her thin eyebrows into a disturbed expression. "I can see she's not just an asset."

"How could—?"

"Casey-*jahni*?" Malek scoffed. It had been well over a decade since he'd heard that word, but he could never forget the Khasiri term of endearment. "Dating the chief's daughter, Case? That's pretty bold."

"Aren't you observant..." Casey exhaled sharply. "I do what I have to and keep the Alliance and AIA at arm's length. The rest, Commander, is my business." She paused, and Malek could feel her icy stare settle back onto him. "Or should I be preparing to get off the grid?"

"No. I know something about keeping the Alliance at a distance, too." His mind trailed to his latest blackout, and he swallowed hard. "I get it. More than you know."

The pair exchanged glances, and Malek nodded at her.

Casey's posture relaxed, a glint of relief in her eye. A smirk played at her lip, and she drew her eyes back toward the helicopter on the base launchpad, where the Al-Khasari began to file in. Malek did the same and didn't bother to acknowledge Nur when they met eyes.

"Besides Kaira, do you have another objective coming up?" Casey asked quietly.

"Not that I know so far. But you know Maida. He has his own agenda."

"I'm glad you figured that out. Guess there are some brains under that beauty."

"Wait... what?"

"Malek," she said, quieting her voice. Maybe she was trying to speak to him as an equal, by dropping his title. It didn't bother Malek. It wasn't like he was used to it, anyway. She glanced at her surroundings, and Malek did the same, making sure no one was within earshot. "...Bringing that girl back here, I know that's not ASF training. You did us all right... People you didn't even know. I'm glad we met." Casey paused, drawing her gaze to the pair of Al-Khasari on the launchpad. "I'll send you my report through the proper channels. Stay safe in Kaira."

"Got it." Malek nodded at her, and she walked away. He was oddly relieved that he hadn't been the only one who kept secrets from the Alliance. Casey might have been more of an ally than he'd thought.

Malek stole a final glimpse at Zia running up to meet Casey before they trekked back to the helicopter. She roped one arm around Casey's shoulder before she moved around and climbed into the pilot seat, with Casey at her side. Malek was surprised that such a small gesture gave him hope. Maybe Nur was telling the truth when she spoke of the Al-Khasari being incomplete, especially while a half-breed like himself was running amok in the Outer Cities. If they could accept him after all this time, maybe Casey could be accepted too... and, just maybe, the rest of the world would follow suit. The Al-Khasari were relaxing their grip on their self-imposed isolation. Malek shook his head. He didn't know why he cared.

"Bastion," Malek mumbled, rubbing his burning eyes.

"Yes, Commander?"

"I need... just four hours of sleep. No more interruptions. *That's an order.*"

CHAPTER 17
ACADEMIC

I t was hard to tell whether Vivika was genuinely interested in their new environment, Nikita contemplated, studying the soldier with suspicion. Vivika, or V as she preferred, took in their new sights with giddiness, unlike the men who trailed further behind on their walk from the train station. Gene and Malek remained cautious of their surroundings, and Nikita found her insides churning when they insisted on eyeing every face that passed them, distrusting every stranger who glanced their way. It was ridiculous.

Nikita inwardly sighed. The thought of returning to Kaira would have otherwise excited her, but their current objective knotted her insides to the point of full-blown nausea. The idea of the Alliance using Nikita's translation to either maim or kill the Elemnai was hardly a positive one. Even if the shards proved to be an ancient tool rather than a weapon, she didn't doubt that the Alliance would still try to seize them at all costs. Her heart twisted with apprehension again at the thought. She tried to focus on being present and revel in the peace of her city.

The warm, early afternoon sun bathed the streets of Kaira, and a liveliness surrounded Nikita that was oddly alien to her. The people were vibrant, both in character and in their garb. Stringed instruments entwined with heavy urban bass drummed from a small plaza, where young people strolled past traditional Alcidian dancers, twirling between the rhythm of the guitars and the smooth steps of Kairan locals. Palms dotting the avenue swayed in a cool breeze from the ocean, its sparkling features barely visible between white sandstone buildings with terracotta rooftops. Had her home always been this beautiful? Nikita breathed in the spiced air that tickled her senses. So much had happened to her in a few short days that she'd nearly forgotten how wonderful it was to be back, regardless of what brought her here. At the same time, it was bizarre seeing life go on without her, despite what she'd endured. She hadn't quite placed an emotion on it before Gene's deep voice hummed from behind her.

"How much longer, love?"

"Right up here. Sorry, we're close to the university…It can get kind of loud."

"It looks so fun here." Vivika smiled at a passing couple enjoying ice cream cones. "Jennah could learn a thing or two from the rest of the world. First the fancy magnet train, now this. Our campus is so boring."

"*Maglev* train, Lieutenant Kei," Bastion muttered in everyone's earpiece.

"You know what I meant."

"Is?" Nikita repeated aloud. "You're… studying?"

"*Se*… well, I *did*. In botany." Vivika glanced back at her commander. Nikita caught a hint of a smile from him before Malek dropped his eyes to the ground, and Vivika grinned. "I have a thing for plants."

"I, too, have a thing for plants," Bastion chimed in their earpieces. "I'll be sure to send you some photos."

Vivika laughed. "Deal."

Nikita turned her body as she continued her pace up the sidewalk. "I didn't take you for someone who studied the sciences."

"Unlike the Alliance Army, all ASF Officers have to receive post-secondary education," Gene explained. "An undergraduate, at minimum, is mandatory. But that doesn't stop some officers from going above and beyond. The Alliance covers all expenses."

"Huh. I guess I had no idea."

Malek scoffed audibly. "Don't tell me you thought we were all hive-minded, intellectually starved army grunts."

"Actually, I—" Nikita paused mid-sentence. Though Malek was her commanding officer, she still needed him to trust her opinions and expertise on this assignment. A quip about military stereotypes was probably not the way to earn his respect. Nikita swallowed her attitude and impassively replied, "I just wasn't aware. What are your backgrounds, then?"

"I'm so glad someone asked," Bastion's mellow tone was a pitch higher than usual. Nikita gathered that Bastion was probably in need of conversation unrelated to military assignments. She wondered if he was lonely in that post of his. "Dr. Valerio, I have two master's degrees, mainly in computing sciences, but I've taken numerous courses in engineering, sciences, language arts, and humanities."

Nikita chuckled, admiring his enthusiasm...then caught herself wishing she could spend time with him, outside of the assignment. Between his mellow voice and his passion for learning, it was hard not to find him attractive. She shook her head, disappointed in herself. The stomach-churning memory of Pavo asking her on a date before her first lecture made her revisit her determination to avoid relationships. Bastion was just another colleague. "That's... really impressive," she finally said.

Clearing his throat, Gene spoke at last when Nikita looked his way, "So, Bastion being the prime example of an officer going above and beyond, I am not nearly as impressive. I studied business. Because... ah, tradition, I suppose. I'm expected to join the family company 'once I'm done shooting things,' so says my father."

"What's the family business?"

"Private research and development," Gene said with a weak smile. "Won't bore you with the details. Let's stay on task."

"Well, it's nice that we have such an eclectic group, anyway." Nikita stared up at a brick building laden with tall windows encased in pale, ornate stonework. She slowed in her step, and all eyes turned to Malek, who awkwardly avoided their gaze.

"Major's right. Stay on task," he grumbled.

"Come on, Commander." Vivika tilted her body toward him as she stopped in her tracks. "We all shared."

"It looks like we're here." Malek gestured toward the building. "Right?"

"Right." Nikita replied flatly, reaching for a pair of keys in her bag. "Don't mind the mess. I didn't get a chance to clean."

"We don't care."

"Everyone, I'm going to be signing off for a moment. I have some work I need to do," Bastion said. "Please shout my name several times if you require any assistance."

"Copy that, Bastion." When Malek indicated for Nikita to proceed, she caught a glimpse of exasperation on his face. She remembered what Vivika said about being down a man in the field. It was only now that Nikita realized that it must have been disappointing for Malek, not that anyone would argue that Bastion had not been helpful. As commander, she assumed it must have annoyed him not to be able to keep an eye on all the players on the field, especially if one member could divert their focus at the drop of a hat. Malek liked to do things a certain way, that much was clear. Nikita's mind trailed over to their objective once again, and her face darkened. *Get the notes. Translate. Give accurate information.* That was all she had to do.

Nikita led them off the elevator, which stopped at the top floor, and guided them across the hallway. "Home sweet home," she chirped.

"Ooh, penthouse!" Vivika exclaimed. "They must pay you really well, Kit."

"Not really." Nikita opened the white door to her suite. "There are two units up here, so it's a small space."

Nikita drew in the sandalwood smell of her home—her favorite scent. She led the group into the foyer past the threshold, where they were greeted by fresh, white walls and smooth, gray wood flooring. A closet with a heavy door stood across from the entrance. The small room to their right, which likely should have been an office, had been converted into a library. Rows upon rows of books stood on black shelves lining each of the walls, from the ground to the ceiling. Nikita was proud of it. Vivika whistled, the first to admire the space. Nikita had never believed this was fancy or anything, but their reactions made her question it. To her, this was just her cozy, little safe spot that she called home.

An arch marked the entrance to the next room, and the first space past the foyer was a beautiful, modern kitchen with sleek white cupboards. Black quartz countertops sparkled in the afternoon sun that poured in from the sliding glass doors at the far end of the room. She let out a long, relaxed breath as her shoulders eased, feeling as if it had been weeks since she was home... though it had only been two days. Nikita drank it all in with soothing delight. She really *was* home.

Past the far counter, a small ashen couch sat opposite to an ornate, iron fireplace with a vidscreen perched above the mantle, where Nikita would often curl up with a book and a warm cup of her favorite Alcidian tea. It was strange how nostalgic those recent memories made her feel now. Would she ever return to those moments, tucked away in her corner of the world, knowing what was happening outside her city?

Beyond that cozy living room, and perhaps the most impressive focal point in this space, was the massive, black walnut desk that had been gifted by her father when she'd earned her doctorate. Packed bookshelves stood in the far corner of the suite behind the desk, adjacent to the windows and opposite a large, glittering sunburst mirror next to the fireplace—another gift, but from her mother. She always wanted to add a bit of flair to her daughter's brooding, stoic spaces. Nikita just had to accept that, though it wasn't her style, it made her mother happy.

She found herself missing them and wondered if there was time to pop by their house for a quick hello before heading back to Azar. Given her family's history with the military, they would probably give her a hard time if they knew she was in the company of a bunch of soldiers. Nikita dismissed the idea and busied herself by clearing the papers scattered on her desk and repositioning her computer system.

"So, this is me." She glanced at the others.

"Not bad, Kit." Gene sat on the couch and stretched his arms behind his head. Nikita smiled at him as she readjusted a photo of her family perched in the corner of her workspace.

"And who is this?" Vivika leaned on her kitchen counter, peering into a large, spherical bowl of water. Nikita had nearly forgot about her housewarming gift from her younger brother.

"Oh," Nikita chuckled, studying the small, orange-colored fish swimming in its cavity. "That's Astraeos. My goldfish."

"Astraeos?" Malek blinked. "Why is that name..."

"Familiar? Because he was the first actual Anymm ever discovered," Nikita stated, trying her best to hide her criticism. "It's kind of a big deal. I mean, not only is it a big deal to find an Anymm, but its DNA helped us make the connection between humans and Elemnai."

Malek failed to acknowledge her and continued to study the details of her home with a much darker look in his eyes. Nikita couldn't place his colder-than-usual disposition when Vivika called back to Nikita and broke her train of thought.

"I'm feeding your fishy, Kit."

"Food's next to the bowl," Nikita called back. "Not sure how long we'll be here, but if anyone needs a nap, you can use my room. Now," she said, twirling in her chair to face the bookshelf directly behind her. A rush of excitement took over. "My journals are all in these bound books, with black and white covers. The oldest are in the library, and the most recent ones are here. It's... all a bit of a blur, but we are looking for any entries where I'm speaking with Manal. She's an Earthborne divine."

Malek spoke first, "Alright. I'll take the library. Kei, you're with—"

The creak of the front door followed the trembling of its handle, resonating eerily through the home. Nikita's heart jumped, and she seized the edge of the desk with a panicked grip. Before she knew it, all three officers drew their concealed sidearms and held them at the ready. Vivika, closest to the door, had gracefully leaped over the counter and crouched on its other side, while Malek and Gene pressed themselves against the fireplace. Nikita's heart lurched into her throat, and the blood ran from her extremities. Her gaze fixated on the figure passing the threshold.

CHAPTER 18
ANOMALY

"**K**it?!" Pavo cried out in disbelief as their gazes met. He scoffed and swiftly moved toward her. "What on Eiden are you doing here? I thought you were out of town to—" Pavo nearly jumped out of his pale skin at the sight of Malek and Gene, who now leaned casually against the fireplace mantle. Nikita found herself impressed with their ability to conceal their firearms and act so casually, but she refocused on Pavo right away.

"H-Hey, Pavo," Nikita finally replied, not meaning for her voice to crack. She had been hunched behind her desk and immediately rose to greet him. "I just, um, need..." Nikita glanced at Malek, who furtively gestured for her to see Pavo out.

Pavo traced her stare and then frowned. "Who are these guys?" he muttered, immediately fixating on Malek's silvery-white hair over a black fade. Nikita knew he'd recognize an Al-Khasari when he saw one...

"These are my friends." Nikita quickly placed herself between the men, one hand firmly on Pavo's arm. "Umm, this is Ray, and that's Jack. Oh, and that's Yuki. They're...from Norvica, f-from the University of Devescar. Everyone, this is my colleague, Pavo."

Pavo looked behind him, and he stepped back in alarm after seeing Vivika seated on a bar stool, twirling playfully. "I didn't even see her," he whispered.

"*Konnama*!" Vivika said in Jennai, waving furiously with both hands and a bright grin, wholeheartedly wanting to confuse Pavo further.

"Nice... to meet you," he managed, turning his attention to Malek. "I didn't know that Al-Khasari lived outside of their homeland."

"Oh, I'm not Al-Khasari," Malek interjected, this time with a false Southern Norvican accent. "I just surf a lot. Bleached hair and a killer tan come with the domain–know what I mean?" He stuck out his thumb and small finger from a closed fist and winked. Nikita would have laughed if she weren't so stressed. Gene had a little more trouble. He stifled a smile by flattening his lips and folding his arms tightly.

"A-Anyway," Nikita stammered. "Why are you here?"

"I just came to feed Astraeos," Pavo spoke softly. "I didn't think you were home, so..."

"Ah, thanks," Nikita guided him back to her foyer. "Sorry, we've got some work to do... and you know I appreciate you looking after me, but we're okay."

"We're *okay*? Kit, I've known you for years. And you're not a very good liar." He sighed deeply, staring at his feet as he slipped on his sandals. "I know you're keeping me in the dark about something. I wish you would trust me, instead of these 'friends.'"

Nikita's breath slowed with a painful tug in her ribs. It was true. She and Pavo ventured into the Wilds, studied the Earthborne, and often debated and researched for weeks, locked to each other's side. She needed his insight. Another idea popped into her mind, so she bit her lower lip and ruffled her curls again. "Actually, I do have a question for you." Nikita leaned close to him. "Remember Manal? The Divine?"

Pavo's shoulders relaxed. "How could I forget? She was so kind."

"Yes, and remember that one night when we were up until dawn? She was telling us all kinds of stories."

"Umm," Pavo tilted his head in thought. "It was in the middle of our expedition, so we had a hard time keeping up with her... so I want to say it was the end of Mador or beginning of Brunor."

Nikita had already opened her door and shoved him out. "That's such a huge help. You're the best. I'll send you a message soon, I promise. I owe you one."

"Yeah, a big one…" Pavo bristled and disappeared behind the door as she closed it. Nikita exhaled sharply, turning herself only to come face to face with Malek standing at the threshold of the kitchen.

He narrowed his indigo eyes on her, arms crossed and tense. He spoke in a low but burning voice that made Nikita shiver, "Anything else you want to spill to your boyfriend?"

Nikita pushed past him, heat blooming across her cheeks. "H-He's not my boyfriend," she snapped back, but with less conviction than she'd hoped. "And I don't see how this affects anything, other than pointing us in the right direction."

"All he has to do is mention what he saw and heard here today. If someone is looking for—"

Nikita whipped around. "Who is looking for us here?" she cried. "You are *completely* paranoid!"

"Nikita," Gene said firmly.

Hearing his voice, Nikita tempered herself and dropped into the chair behind her desk. She knew she had crossed a line with *that* tone. "Fine." She furiously pushed papers aside. Her hand shook with a mix of resentment and frustration. Without looking at her team, she studied the bookshelves behind her again. "Journals with the dates that include Mador and Brunor, 219 CE…They should be in the library. Anything that mentions Manal will be helpful. I'll know what I'm looking for when I see it. I'm going to stay here and look for something on the shards. It should be in my most recent volumes."

Nikita heard a gentle shuffling of footsteps, which disappeared once they reached the main entrance. Once she gathered herself, she pulled her hair back, trying to expel the anger from her body with the force of her breath. Everything about this assignment had so far screamed against her values. She was horrified by the death of the Al-Khasari girl, Azka. She utterly disagreed with the Alliance's approach, especially if the translation confirmed that the Earthborne described a weapon in their possession. She despised the idea that she, who'd worked so hard

180

for some semblance of a relationship with the Earthborne, might be responsible for tearing it apart.

Nikita had never intended for her skills to be used to decide whether the Earthborne as a whole should be targeted. She hated playing soldier, and she hated feeling like a child. More than anything... she just wanted to be right. The Earthborne *had* to be innocent. One rogue did not speak for all.

Finally, she turned around, and her heart leaped at the sight of the man still standing by her desk. Keeping her composure, she waited for him to speak.

"I know you are not military," Gene started in a low voice, his eyes fixed on hers. "But there is a chain of command that you need to respect. I'm not saying this for the commander's sake, who, by the way, saved your life. I'm saying this because our safety depends on it."

"I already heard this from the commander," Nikita muttered bitterly.

"Then hear it again until you understand it. You are not privy to his conversations with the general. You do not have the intel that he carries. Do not assume that because you were there, you know every facet of this operation." Gene turned away, glancing over his shoulder. "What's done is done. We are here to support you now. Tell us what you need, and we'll see to it."

A small part of her reason begged her to listen to Gene and swallow her lament. Nikita barely had a moment to process his words and form some sort of apology before they were interrupted.

Vivika slid into the room, jutting her thumb toward the library. "Hey Kit, I think we found something. We've got a bunch of journals about this Manal character. Commander thinks some of your translations, or transliterations, look like some Khasiri words."

What's done is done. Nikita repeated Gene's words in her mind and drew a deep, calming breath. She stood up and strode past Gene and Vivika, finding Malek staring down at a notebook as he slowly ambled into the foyer.

"So, what's the word in question?" he asked coldly. "I think—"

The front door handle trembled again, seizing Malek's attention. He and Nikita locked eyes for a moment. "This time, *I'm* telling your friend to beat it."

Malek didn't even have the chance to reach for the handle before the door opened again. It was as though time had slowed and nearly stopped. The blood drained from Malek's face. His eyes rounded, eyebrows creased, and his mouth parted in dread. Nikita's eyes darted to the entrance, where she watched it all unfold in frightening detail: the exact moment that a figure dressed in an all-gray military jacket stepped in from the hallway, the barrel of a shotgun leveled at Malek's chest. Before a single fiber of muscle could twitch into action, an ear-splitting boom rang out. Nikita was forced to do nothing except watch. Malek instantly flew back into the closet door, with a rain of splintered wood following suit as he collapsed face down onto the floor.

Nikita choked on a scream. Gene seized her arms with such intensity that she was nearly thrown to the floor. Pain coursed through her limbs as he dragged her back toward the desk. An onslaught of bullets punctured the walls, cupboards, and furniture in her wake. With the jolt, the sheer panic pierced her senses like shards of shattered glass. It forced Nikita out of her shock, and she found her voice. She released a horrified shriek, which drowned in the eruption of deafening gunfire.

Nikita clutched her head and crouched, and Gene swiftly led her behind the desk at the far end of the room. Her heart tore to pieces as Gene tipped it over with immense strain, creating a barricade to shield the barrage of bullets. Debris quickly filled the air with dusty remnants, suffocating Nikita. She trembled so intensely that her muscles cramped and locked.

"Are you alright?!" Gene cried out to her, one arm still shielding her from the splintering particles of the broken wood that surrounded them.

Nikita yelped again as a bullet ricocheted off her computing system lying beside the desk, shattering it into fragments of sleek metal and glass. A bullet shot through the photo of her family. Nikita shook, staring at the perfect circle surrounded by a halo of cracks directly on her father's head. Gene didn't wait for her response. He bravely drew his sidearm, quickly returning a few rounds before crouching again. If the man was scared, he certainly didn't show it.

The quick distraction allowed Vivika to scramble out of Nikita's bedroom. She must have escaped through the washroom, whose entrance was on the other side of the fireplace, and came back around through her room. Vivika dove behind the desk, cursing loudly and loading her sidearm as quickly as her hands allowed. Nikita, relieved to see her unscathed, instinctively pulled back so she could move to Gene's side.

"Bastion, come in!" Gene bellowed.

Nikita's eyes shifted to the sunburst mirror, which now bore a distinct web of cracks on its face, angled such that she could make out the distorted figures in the room. They were surrounded. A sick feeling of dread replaced the shock. There was no escape.

"Where's the commander? Is he alive?" Gene called out.

Vivika violently shook her head. "I don't know! He's down."

"*Bastion*, where the *frag* are you?"

"Anduran, what's happening?!" Bastion's voice barely resonated in their ear-pieces. "Where's Commander Reza?"

"He's been hit, but we can't see him. Eight armed assailants have us pinned in Nikita's flat. We need assistance *now*!"

"I'm doing what I can. Stand by."

Nikita flinched as a canister ricocheted off the bookshelf and fell to her feet. She already knew what it was and instinctively clamped her hands over her ears. With lightning reflexes, Vivika seized it and hurled it back over the barricade, where a sudden flash lit up the room with a thunderous bang that vibrated through Nikita's bones. She was that child again, hiding in the alley by her old house and trying to shut out the blasts of grenades in her streets. Vivika's tenacity brought Nikita back from that place, even as she was drowning in her terror. When Vivika peeked around the desk and fired a few shots, the assault focused back on her, and she retreated. Her desperate gaze met with Nikita's. As courageous as she was, they both knew their circumstances were desperate. Gene stood and returned fire, lowering back down almost immediately. The floor trembled beneath Nikita's fingers when a soldier dropped to the ground.

"Who's attacking us?" Nikita finally mustered the courage to scream. "Why are they in my home?"

"Looks like our old friends," Gene gritted his teeth. "GX Forces—definitely. Bastards!"

"City police have been notified and are on the way. General Maida has been informed, and we are dispatching Alliance agents. Can you hold out?" Bastion spoke quickly.

"Not long," Gene groaned, loading another clip. "Kei, I'm low on ammo!"

"So am I!"

Nikita pressed her back against the bookshelf. Her heart pounded heavily in her chest, and her breath caught. Another barrage of rapid-fire forced them all to cower. Nikita's eyes darted toward the fractured mirror again. In the facets, she could make out the reflection of several bodies taking turns firing and advancing on the group. Hopelessness was quickly taking hold. She never imagined this would happen. *This* was what Malek was afraid of? A wave of regret washed over her. Why did she doubt him? Fear cemented into her bones. The horror of being captured and taken away like so many of her old friends and neighbors was quickly becoming all too tangible.

Then a distant murmur and a scream echoed from the far end of the room. Gene and Vivika didn't hear, apparently, as they shouted tactics among the gunfire. Nikita looked up again, scrutinizing the images of the GX Forces in the mirror. This time, there was another figure, distant but notably separate from the soldiers in deep gray tactical gear.

Nikita convinced herself she was hallucinating. It was the only plausible explanation. Two of the agents closest to the kitchen rose into the air as though someone had been pulling them by invisible strings. The bodies were immediately and powerfully slammed into the counter with a terrible cracking sound. Then another two were lifted, and their cries of panic reverberated throughout the suite. The GX soldier closest to the desk where the team hid, whipped around, and opened fire at the figure now stepping between the airborne bodies.

Without a doubt, Nikita recognized Malek's clothing even in the hazy reflection. Her fear was quickly replaced with disbelief and wonder. Within seconds, the two airborne soldiers were flung into one another, and then into another pair with such force that all four men pelted into adjacent walls, rendering them immediately unconscious. Malek rushed up and seized the last one with his web-laced arm. The man struggled to break free and begged for mercy as he shouted "no" several times in the Terminian language.

Gene and Vivika looked at Nikita, no doubt in response to the bizarre patterns of screams and ceasefire over the last few seconds. Disregarding those questioning glances, she stood at the beat of their panicked protests. She barely had a moment to adjust to the scene before the final body of the GX soldier was hurled into the glass sliding door beside her, and he plummeted to the floor with shards raining around him. He groaned and passed out in a heap, startling Gene and Vivika, who jumped up at last.

At the center of the suite, Malek hunched, his arms hanging in front of him after throwing the soldier several feet across the room. Nikita watched the hard and abnormally quick rise and fall of his shoulders as he breathed. She nearly recoiled when his eyes of deep violet-blue flashed and narrowed on his unconscious victim. After a moment, he blinked and shook his head, as though his mind returned from a distant place. Nikita bolted around the desk and stood in front of him. What *did* he just *do*? They just stared at one another for one intense, timeless second.

Malek collapsed to his knees and hung his head. He clutched his sternum with both hands and gasped between bark-like coughs. He moaned in agony and writhed with every breath. Nikita should have run to him, checked his injuries like a real medical officer, but was unable to react or move. All she could do was stare in wonder.

"Is everyone okay? What happened?" Bastion called through the receiver, snapping Nikita from her daze.

Vivika knocked into her when she rushed past and knelt beside Malek. "Commander! Commander, are you okay?"

"How are you alive? You were blasted in the bloody chest with a shotgun," Gene held him by his shoulders, trying to get him to stand.

When Malek finally did, Nikita noticed as much as anyone that there was no wound in sight. A smear of ash spattered across the white fabric of his short-sleeved shirt under his onyx military jacket. Malek wiped the corner of his mouth where blood had dripped down his lip. "Bean bag round," he spoke abrasively, gesturing to his chest.

"Slag... we should have caught that. But at that range, you still could have died," Vivika muttered, holding him up by his arm.

Nikita quietly agreed, thinking about her time in the Alcides Islands during the civil war. Yes, he *should* have died! She had seen those injuries first-hand. Her gaze trailed to the bodies, as did Gene's.

"But, how on Eiden did you do this...?" Gene murmured, his words slow and measured.

Nikita fixed Malek with a suspicious stare, her insides fluttering with eagerness. He averted his eyes when they met with hers. He was stalling.

"Because I'm *amazing*," Malek finally spoke in a hoarse, but cavalier voice. "I'm your commander... for damn good reason... I'm really good at staying alive and kicking ass..."

Nikita's eyes widened in disbelief, searching everyone's faces for clues. *No one* questioned it. Vivika only smiled a little.

"Correct on all accounts, sir," Gene replied, but the humor never made it to his eyes.

"So... everyone is okay? All assailants are down?" Bastion asked again.

"Yes," Malek hissed, wincing as he clutched his chest. "Anduran, Kei—disarm them." His officers complied immediately, but not before exchanging a furtive glance.

How could they not notice? Nikita thought, furiously now. It wasn't until she lifted her eyes to study the array of bodies again that she finally started taking in the details of the devastation that surrounded her.

Artwork that had once decorated her walls and shelves was shredded. The walls of her home were punctured, and a thin layer of debris and dust lay across the floor. Her cabinets had been obliterated in a rain of bullets, and her counter, where Astraeos once resided, had been shattered. The books were torn apart, and her beautiful desk lay gutted. Her heart sank into the pit of her stomach as she drank in every detail of her destroyed sanctuary. Within moments, every memento of her home, every cherished furnishing, was gone. She couldn't speak, nor bring herself to show any sorrow.

A distant sound of sirens filled her ears, and soon after, Bastion's soothing voice, "Police have arrived. Remain where you are, everyone."

"No." Malek coughed again. "We're out of here. Get us a safe house, Bastion. Valerio, grab the books, and let's go. Now."

CHAPTER 19
WILDS

I t took every last ounce of strength to not give in to a full-blown panic attack. Malek knew he had suffered another blackout. This time, people had been seriously hurt or killed by his hands... and there were *witnesses*. Or so he assumed. No one on his team had mentioned anything since they'd left Nikita's home. Malek flinched, pressing his back against the cold glass panes of the balcony windows belonging to a dismal flat, overlooking the market district of Kaira's old city. It was a dusty old safehouse established by the AIA, hardly used in recent years, by the looks of it.

Vivika was quietly consolidating the remaining ammo and supplies on a dilapidated sofa in the center of the living space, dressed down to her fitted white shirt and military pants, with her red, cropped jacket draped over the cracked leather cushions. In a tall, cylindrical glass on the aged, wooden coffee table in front of her, swam Astraeos. It was a miracle that the damned fish was alive.

Nikita occupied the only other room in the apartment as she organized and reviewed whatever notes she could gather from her home, while Gene kept her company to measure her emotional state. The major had good insight into these things, Malek thought, and he was grateful for it. Part of him was also glad not to see Nikita. He still remembered her face the moment he'd come to his senses. If there was such a thing as being subjected to someone's awe, disgust, and fear

188

at the same time, that was the look he'd woken up to see. It sickened him. She knew... She *definitely* knew.

The busy market outside filled the silence in the room. Malek ran his hand over his sternum, finding it difficult to breathe between the humidity, his desperate thoughts, and, of course, the blast from the bean bag round. Thankfully, it *was* a beanbag round. He would have had a harder time explaining his survival if his chest had been literally blasted open. Not that he knew if he *could* survive that...ah, slag, maybe that'll be in store for him the *next* time he's in internment. Either way, he still should have been dead, but it was easier to credit his survival to the non-lethal round, rather than his anomalies. Malek thought about their attackers instead. There was little comfort knowing that the GX Forces could still be out there. How on Eiden did they follow them to Nikita's home...without *anyone* noticing?

"Commander, I have General Maida for you," Bastion's voice cut through his thoughts.

"Affirmative," Malek said, and he tilted his chin, motioning for Vivika to leave. She stole one last glance at him before she disappeared behind the door into Nikita's room, and he held that gaze long enough to catch sight of a deeper anxiety.

"Patching him through. I have you both on a secure line. Bastion out."

Malek's heart hammered against his chest, almost painfully.

"Commander," General Maida spoke, his voice abrasive and terse. "Explain. Now."

Malek closed his eyes. He knew the attack at Nikita's home would warrant a berating... It gave him a brief moment of clarity when he finally understood why Rhodes always railed at him for veering from orders. Things went wrong, and ultimately, Malek needed to take it on the chin.

"General, after our debriefing in Azar, before I submitted my report... I needed some clarification on Dr. Valerio's Umbar'ok translation." Malek sullenly reported the high-level overview of their timeline between Azar and Kaira, trying to steady his voice and gloss over the exact details of their fight with the GXF. Malek exhaled sharply, which sent a lancet of agony throughout his ribcage. "I take full responsibility, General. We should have stayed in Azar."

"Commander, you had no authority to leave Azar MOB, especially given the presence of Terminian agents. You risked the lives of your team, namely Dr. Valerio. This is another PR disaster in the making, and Usona is not taking this news lightly."

"I'm aware, sir."

"Despite this, I know the threat assessment changes significantly between the two versions of the translation. A dangerous decision, but your heart's in the right place. That's why I picked you, son."

The tension in Malek's shoulders melted, and he could breathe again. "Yes, sir."

"So, what did you confirm?"

"Still working on it. We were...delayed, thanks to the Terminians. The Earthborne also hinted at a possible threat. He seemed to be acting out of fear of death from an external aggressor."

"Interesting development. I suppose the aggressor could be humans, for all we know. Based on this, it seems that the Earthborne may have one or more shards in their possession."

"Affirmative."

"And the attack? How were you four able to overcome eight heavily armed soldiers?"

"...They had non-lethal rounds."

"So, the intention was to debilitate but not kill."

"I'd argue both ways."

"The GX Forces are a ruthless corp. You know this firsthand. There's something else happening. I believe they wanted to capture one of *you,* if not all of you."

"Dr. Valerio?"

"Perhaps. I'm beginning to think I was also correct in my suspicions that there is a collaborator in our ranks. I need to assess this further. In the meantime, I have sent officers to Dr. Valerio's home to curb an extensive police investigation. The assigned clean-up crew removed the GX officers and their artillery from the site. Primarch Usona does not wish for this attack to result in mass panic, and while she's so far taken my advice to avoid inciting further conflict, her patience is wearing thin. The scene will appear as a skirmish between Hassentio sympathizers and pro-democratic Alcidian nationals. As this was at Dr. Valerio's home, the unfortunate consequence will suggest that she may be associated with either extremist group–a minor issue, at best."

"Yeah…" Malek knew Nikita wouldn't consider this a "minor issue." He had better keep that piece under wraps, for now.

"Suffice it to say, the GX Forces have been tracking your movements since Saifain. Perhaps they believe you have a lead on the shards, which is why they may be hunting you. I suggest traveling more discreetly and avoiding public sites and routes where possible."

Getting off the grid… even from the Alliance. That's exactly what he needed right now to purge the questions. *Ah, mace!* Malek hated himself for what he was just about to say. He was going to risk the lives of his teammates and the only advantage they had over the Elemnai—adhering to the peace agreement. This was *his* call. It was the only way he could bear it and hide the truth. "There's one solution that fits. Dr. Valerio translated the recordings from the Earthborne in Saifain. They are holding another shard, possibly more."

"More?" Maida repeated.

"Affirmative. This is our opportunity to be on the offensive, for once. Send us into the Wilds to find the shard."

"The Wilds? Commander, if you proceed into the Wilds, the Alliance will be in direct breach of the armistice. I cannot condone that."

"The Alliance has never crossed into the Wilds? Ever?"

A heavy sigh was released on the other end of the line. Malek didn't have evidence, but he hardly believed that any credible threat from the Wilds would have been ignored for the last 200 years. He needed to play that up. Infiltrating the Wilds would be his ticket out of the Alliance's line of sight. If he could accomplish his mission without another blackout in one of the most dangerous places on Eiden, the Alliance would have to believe there was nothing more to scrutinize. That was the only way they'd let him go. If he failed, and another blackout assured his survival...well, maybe Khasar wasn't looking all that bad anymore. He could slip away, if he had to. Just like Nur said, he could join the rest of the *rayah*. Malek finally had the opportunity to get somewhere where the Alliance couldn't follow, especially since his blackouts were getting dangerously out of hand. He needed a plan in case he failed to control this again, or he would risk finding himself back in the Spire. *Find the shard. Survive. Get the frag out...any way out.*

"Commander, I caution you. If you proceed into the Elemnai Wilds to look for the shard, and fail," Maida began in a low voice, "the Alliance will denounce you and the operation. Besides this glaring fact, I personally will not risk sending in a support unit, nor offer any additional officers to assist with this assignment. Not while I have a security breach. This is a stealth operation. Bastion will continue to act as your communications officer, but you will be relying *solely* on Anduran, Kei, and Valerio. If Dr. Valerio confirms that the translation suggests the presence of a weapon, you will infiltrate and seize the shard. If the translation says otherwise, provide intel on its precise location. Return to Saion FOB upon completion of the assignment."

"Understood. What about Jaeger?"

"She will be re-assigned to you if I can gain permission from the AIA. Director Zane is more than familiar with this type of operation. If Jaeger is approved, meet up with her at Saion FOB. Bastion will arrange logistics and equipment. You will depart as soon as possible."

"Yes, sir. And General..."

"Speak freely, Commander."

"Do you... know what they're for? The shards, I mean. Does the Alliance have any idea?" Malek knew that question was out of line for his role, so he lilted his tone. "I almost died twice now for them."

Maida sighed on the other side. "Insofar as I could tell, Alliance R&D believes the shards could be the key to a new Era of Eiden, not unlike what Dr. Valerio surmised during the briefing. It would apparently propel us into a technological golden age the likes of which we have not seen... it is theorized that even spaceflight could be achieved."

"Spaceflight?" Malek tried to mask his awe. "So... it's a way to tap into an energy source?"

"I can't confirm that," Maida cleared his throat, signalling it was time to drop the topic. "...Is there anything else you wish to discuss?"

"No, sir."

"Commander," Maida began slowly, "I've already read the summary of Dr. Valerio's home. The manner in which these soldiers were killed... the damage to the property. I need to ask you. Did you black out during the attack? Is that how you were able to overcome the GX Forces?"

A nauseating wave of panic struck Malek's core. "I..." he exhaled sharply. "I...don't..." He couldn't finish his sentence.

Maida fell quiet as well.

Malek's head throbbed. He remembered the endless, brutal questions while he sat hunched in that cold, dismal interrogation room as a terrified and confused sixteen-year-old held captive by his own employer. The Alliance dissected every inch of Malek's mind—where his loyalties aligned, whether he was an agent posing as a teenager or even as discriminatory as whether Al-Khasari were even human. Then there were the tests... those horrible, *agonizing* tests.

Malek's skin crawled, his body instinctively reacting to the memory. He couldn't decide whether talking about his blackouts was as bad as the actual torture itself. Given that it was the second time this week that Malek had woken up from the havoc he'd viciously wreaked on his attackers, unconsciously cheating death or capture, he thought he'd better start getting used to talking about it again.

Maida didn't wait for his answer. The silence was enough to know the truth, Malek knew. "Complete your report before your departure. Stay safe in the Wilds. Good luck, Commander."

Maida signed off immediately with the sound of a low beep. The unbearably quiet room left Malek alone with his racing thoughts. He groaned aloud and cursed himself several times over. He drew his eyes to the ceiling and stared at the abstract patterns of the ancient wallpaper. What on Eiden was he doing?

The hinges of the bedroom door creaked, and Malek snapped his gaze at the person standing at the threshold.

"Call's over, Commander?" Gene said.

Malek nodded gently, his head still aching. "Everything okay?"

"Sort of. Kit will explain it better than I. She's asked to discuss this matter together. We may have some information to share, after all."

"Good."

"Oh, and Commander?"

"Yeah?"

"...Kit's asked if we could arrange to send the fish to her brother?" Gene shrugged. "Least we could do?"

Malek palmed his eyes and sighed.

CHAPTER 20
QUESTIONS

Malek blinked several times, trying to understand what he was seeing. Nikita had had a collection of books, which she'd snatched in the moments before they left her home. They'd now been laid open at various points of their contents, arranged in concentric circles on the dusty, hardwood floor, where she knelt. It looked borderline insane.

Nikita leveled an icy stare at him. It dug into Malek hard, and he was back to being that terrified kid again. His deepest secret was at the cusp of spilling over. She looked as if she was ready to tip it. Malek wouldn't give her a chance. He ignored those penetrating eyes and fixated on the books. "Bastion, tune in for the briefing."

"Affirmative. I'm here, Commander," Bastion replied. "Dr. Valerio, what did you discover?"

Nikita stood and shook her head in disappointment. "Hammer," she grumbled.

Malek frowned. "What?"

"Hammer. The translation reads like the word, 'hammer.' It could be both—a weapon to bludgeon your enemy or a tool for building civilizations. Wallace said, unite the shards to form the 'hammer' of our ancestors. They want to construct an old piece of Anymm technology that could serve as both a weapon *and* a tool." Nikita stood, brushing the dust from her knees. "Some of the stories that Manal shared with us talk about the Anymm as 'wardens' of the Conduit. This was where I deciphered the word we needed. She kept referring to this Conduit as a weapon or tool. To me, it sounds like that's what the Earthborne had in mind to reconstruct."

Malek thought about his words carefully. "Maida thinks that the shards could be used to spark a technological revolution. So, it checks."

"He didn't say what kind of technology?"

Malek shook his head, but Bastion chimed in, "Perhaps, if the Conduit can build or destroy civilizations, it may be a device that allows for the manipulation of a specific energy source... It could certainly achieve either of those things—advance or destroy—no different from nuclear power. Quite the riddle."

Malek inwardly smiled that he and Bastion had come to the same conclusion.

"Imagine," Bastion continued. "If this energy source were enough to break through Eiden's gravitational pull. We could literally fly to Deos, perhaps even Artesh and back."

"Okay, Bastion, now's not the time." Malek had to cut him off before that part of him, which was just as excited by the idea, could join in the enthusiasm. He'd always dreamed of going to space. It was the foundation of his mother's bedtime stories, and all too incredible to be real. But there were bigger things to worry about.

"Apologies, sir."

"We're also no further along trying to find out who this aggressor could be." Nikita frowned. "To do that, we're actually going to need to speak with the Earthborne."

If Malek hadn't been so frustrated with himself over his proposal to Maida, he probably would have laughed at the timing of her comment. "Maybe you'll get your chance. New orders. We're going to the Wilds."

Nikita's eyes rounded, chewing the corner of her lip as if suppressing an eagerness she'd been desperate to hide. It bothered Malek that she cared that much about seeing more Earthborne.

Gene, on the other hand, made his feelings more conspicuous. "Uh...*Pardon?*" he blurted.

"Maida wants us off the grid… Until he can figure out why the GXF are on our asses," Malek replied grimly. Making this seem like it was Maida's call caused his chest to tighten, and a sickening sensation rippled toward his extremities. He still couldn't believe he was willing to risk everyone else's safety for his own shot at freedom, if it came down to it. He bit back the agony and guilt and studied the faces of the three surrounding him. "Apart from Bastion, it will be just us four. Five, if the AIA lets us have Jaeger. We got a shard from Saifain. That one shard gave us a lead… but it's a lead, nothing more. This is a stealth mission. If we fail, no one is coming to help."

Malek searched their uneasy faces. He wondered if they *could* be trusted to follow him and keep performing. Facing another situation where he could expose his blackouts wasn't ideal… and if he was being honest, it scared him to think what could happen if they *all* knew. Would they still look at him the same? Being treated as a specimen by the Alliance, an outcast by the Al-Khasari, and a burden by Valiant Squad always made him question his place. Somehow, it bothered him more that he might lose their faith in him as their commander, but the guilt soon overtook it. He was dragging them into something dangerous.

"We're going to be stuck together and relying on one another in the coming days. So, if there's something you want to say, clear the air now." Malek focused on Vivika, who seemed surprised she was chosen to speak first.

She pressed her lips thoughtfully. "What we've seen in the last few days, and what we've discovered… It's so much." Vivika shook her head, and her raven hair danced over her cheeks. "Gunliem was eighteen months ago, and the Alliance still has *no idea* what the shard is or does. What if this is our chance to stop something worse from happening? And we can't sit around and hide from the GX Forces. The fact that they are on to this, and the Elemnai too, shows that we have to keep moving. I say we take this chance, and frag the backup. We can do this without a full OD." Malek had a hard time suppressing his admiration. It was as if nothing scared her.

"I disagree with Kei," Gene said in a low voice, and that snapped Malek out of his fixation. "Commander, without support, I feel like we are simply ill-prepared for this. This isn't a stroll in the park. It's the Wilds, one of the most dangerous places on Eiden. Maida is having us act like AIA agents on a heist. We will certainly be breaching our peace agreement with the Elemnai, if we proceed. Now we are on the offensive. I do not like where this places us."

"I know. And I hear you," Malek replied. Gene was right, but he had to justify his call. "We are crossing the border, which is a breach in itself, but hardly threatening. We aren't going to attack. We are only collecting intel, and we would never be able to move through the Wilds undetected with a full section. A small group will be more successful." Malek studied the journals spread across the floor. "This is the silver lining."

"And if we're caught?" Gene countered. "If it comes to one-on-one combat with an Elemnai, provided it's not mutated like the other, we can handle ourselves. But a horde? This is suicidal."

Then we can't get caught, Malek reminded himself. *Find the shard, get the frag out.* It was becoming a pattern... and a pattern, so far, that always led to confrontation. "Bastion, what about you?"

"Sir, your safety is my priority. I'm not the one out there with you, so my opinion is solely based on achieving the most positive outcome for this assignment. We have a greater chance of success simply because Dr. Valerio is here. My feelings on the matter, really, fall on her expertise."

Nikita folded her arms tightly. Malek held that gaze for a moment... well, it was more of a glower. If looks could kill, she had Malek by the knife's edge. "You're going to be our guide, Valerio. Can you handle it?"

Nikita cleared her throat and looked down at her journals. "We have to take a familiar route in... similar to the one we took for our expedition. At roughly thirty to forty kilometers per day, we have at least a three-day hike through the foothills before we reach Ashon, the ancient human city. We ditch the Alliance branding, pretend to be lost hikers or something."

"We can't pretend to be researchers?"

Malek was on the receiving end of another venomous glance before Nikita continued, "No. I could explain all the reasons why that is a terrible idea, but the short of it is that it will have a very *undesirable* ripple effect. From there, if we manage to move undetected, we have another day or more through the forest, depending on which acropolis we... target. Then we will have to find the shard and get out... without crossing paths with a single Earthborne." Nikita paused. "Bastion's right. I'm your best shot at success."

Nikita paced around the journals. "I can try to pinpoint some likely locations, which is better than blindly searching the settlements. I'm not opposed to us going in, but I worked too hard to make some semblance of a relationship with the Earthborne. It has to be done my way."

Malek was too surprised by her answer to notice the belligerent remark. Did she actually think this was the *right* thing to do?

"The GX Forces are getting dangerous. I mean, they nearly killed us in Saifain, and now they've destroyed my home." Nikita continued, "I don't believe the Elemnai as a whole can be blamed for the actions of a few, especially given the state of the Earthborne brave we faced in Saifain. Whatever they're planning can't be any more sinister than whatever the GX Forces have in store. They're the obvious enemy. The Elemnai are not. If someone should get the shard, I would rather it be us. I'd like to believe we won't leave a trail of dead bodies in our attempt to get it." She lifted her eyes onto Malek and spoke in a low, seething voice, "At least, I hope."

Malek swallowed hard, ignoring his pulse now hammering through his temple. "It's not the intention, as I've said."

"So, you've said." Nikita leaned in a little and spoke again, this time with more vitriol, "But that doesn't mean you're being *honest*."

A stark silence fell over the room. Malek's heart thrashed against his searing ribcage. The eyes of other teammates penetrated him, deepening the cracks of his composure until it took every ounce of willpower to stop himself from showing any emotion. "Kei, Anduran. Give us the room."

Malek continued to stare unflinchingly at Nikita until he heard the door shut behind him. *Enough*. She wasn't going to hold him hostage over this. Glancing back to make sure they were alone, he turned to Nikita, who was returning an intense frown. "You got something to say?" he said in a low, burning voice.

"Do *you*? I mean, you're the only one lying to everyone."

"Yeah. I lied when I said we'd need you to guide us into the Wilds. We'll get there without you. You're off the team."

"Oh, so *that's* how it is?" Nikita hissed. "While I'm on the way out, why don't I just go ahead and tell the others that their commander is secretly *abnormal*, just like those mutated Elemnai? Tell me, are *all* Al-Khasari like you?"

It was the AIA assessment all over again. In a split second, a terrible weight crushed him back into the same scared teenager. His anger quickly morphed into fear. Malek's eyes rounded, and he raised his hands to calm her. "Valerio, listen—"

"No!" She pulled away from him. "I watched what you did to those men. You lifted them with like, what, your *mind*? And then tossed them around like they were rag dolls! And that one guy? You threw him *across* the room with your bare hands."

"Valerio, just wait—"

"After being dragged into Saifain, getting Azka's body out, escaping a mutant Earthborne, and *especially* after what happened to my home, I deserve to know what you are and what we signed up for. And so does everyone else."

"*Nikita*!" Malek seized Nikita's flailing hands and held them in his own. He waited for her breath to slow, as she stared intently into his face. The dread swelled like a tide, drowning the words from reaching his lips. He watched the rise and fall of Nikita's shoulders and counted the seconds, calming his raging, deafening heartbeat. The AIA wasn't interrogating him. It was his specialist. He could talk himself out.

Malek inhaled deeply, bringing this reality to his mind and stamping out the nightmares clawing up to be set free. "I don't know," he finally said, barely above a whisper. "I don't know how I did those things. I don't remember doing any of it. I remember being shot. And I remember looking at you when I woke up." He released Nikita's hands, realizing he was still holding them, allowing them to fall to her sides. "That's all."

Nikita's frown softened and fixed him with a look of confusion and, unexpectedly, concern. "What do you mean, you can't remember?"

"I black out. It's a thing that... happens sometimes. They... I... mean, the Alliance thinks some kind of adrenaline response triggers it. I can't explain."

Nikita exhaled sharply. "I'm flat out asking you to explain it. Just try. Please."

Malek placed a hand over his neck and turned away. As he slowly paced the room, Nikita's eyes chased him. It was as though she was pulling back the layers of his shell, the longer she stared. It had been years since he openly discussed this with anyone, let alone someone he hardly knew or trusted. Jace only knew some of his history because it had always been off-limits.

"I just want to know who you are," Nikita said, but her tone had changed. It was gentle, and almost pleading. He didn't know if that was worse. "More importantly, *what* you are."

"What I am is *human*. Don't *ever* say otherwise."

"Fine, but you didn't—"

"I don't have to tell you anything else. If you want to out me to the team, then go ahead. It doesn't change anything. We still have a job to do." Malek turned and faced her with newfound conviction. He was still in command. He was going to make sure she knew that. "The only thing that's changed is your situation. I get the feeling that a part of you wants to go back. Maybe you want answers for yourself, and maybe you'll find them. You want to save the Earthborne so badly? Then kiss your chances goodbye. Don't threaten *me*. You *want* to come more than I *need* you to."

Nikita's gaze burned into him, like hot coals penetrating his eyes. She folded her arms tightly, her voice trembling, "Without me, the assignment will fail."

"It's a possibility. And if it does, the Alliance will never know the Earthborne's true intentions. They will assume they are building a weapon, and that will be the end of it. Maida's fears will come true. And you'll be complicit. So, what's it going to be?"

A muscle rolled in her jaw, and Malek caught the twitch in her lip. Her grimace contorted into a look of panic. He'd finally struck a chord in her.

"I'll drop it," she finally muttered in defeat. "Your... secret is safe with me."

"...And with me," Bastion said sheepishly.

Malek cursed aloud, and his lieutenant cut in to explain, "You never ordered me to log off."

"Read the room next time!" Malek snarled. He was going to deck Bastion if he ever saw him in person.

"I want you to answer at least one question," Nikita cut in. "How long has this been happening?"

"That's your question?" He had no clue about her motive in asking that, but he didn't see the harm in it either. Malek paused, looking down at one of his hands. The last thing he remembered, right before his very first blackout, was lying on the floor of a filthy bunker. It had been wet, with blood, water, or something else, he couldn't tell. A nearby bottle lay shattered. Malek had grabbed a fragment. He hid it so desperately with each blow from his captors. The thin scar across the creases suddenly stung, as if it were fresh.

"I was sixteen. Twelve years ago."

"That was the year two-twelve, CE?" Nikita glanced at her journals. "That... That was the same year as Ast—"

"Interview's over," Malek said firmly. "I need the room."

Nikita appeared to want to say more, but she pressed her lips and quietly walked out. Even the soft creak and click of the door as it shut was enough to send a wave of pain through Malek's skull. He exhaled sharply and rubbed his tired eyes.

"I apologize for listening in on that conversation," Bastion said quietly.

Malek only responded with cold silence. The headache was suppressing his urge to ream out his lieutenant.

"Commander, if I may... it might be worth explaining the situation to Major Anduran and Lieutenant Kei. Also, I cannot imagine the walls in the safehouse are very thick. Given the nature of your coming assignment, perhaps it would be best?"

"You don't know anything about it."

"Yes, sir, I do," Bastion said solemnly. "One more confession, Commander."

"Now what?"

"So... as I've hinted, I have a silly little hobby. I have a lot of access to Alliance servers, but when I don't, I sometimes like to... uh, explore. I actually coded my own hacking tool that grants me access to all sorts of fun and definitely dangerous things—"

"Get to the point."

"A-Anyway, when I was assigned to your team, I didn't know anything about you. In fact, I am quite familiar with many commanders, given my work with ASFOM. So, when I observed your name, I thought—why not? I'm going to see what I can find."

Malek didn't like where this was going. The fear slithered up into his spine again, and his nerves jolted from yet another panicked adrenaline rush trying to consume all his senses.

Bastion stammered a few times and hesitantly continued only after a brief silence., "I... found a lot more about you than I thought I would," he finally murmured. "Namely, your history around your accelerated healing, and the prowess you demonstrate during your blackouts. I briefly saw your history with the AIA, but I didn't explore this very thoroughly as the files were heavily encrypted." Bastion cleared his throat. "Either way, this information did not change my view of you. If anything, I... grew to appreciate you more. You have a lot more courage than most commanders. Believe me, I would know. You've saved your team twice now and braved bringing the shards yourself when you could have delegated it. Keeping your team safe has been your priority, and it shows. You take a lot of risks, and I believe it's because you know that you can handle it, consciously or otherwise. My only disappointment in all of this is that General Maida failed to introduce us sooner. I think we both could have benefited from it."

"What makes you say that?"

"I can't really say, unfortunately. One of the reasons I'm stationed at my post, I'm afraid."

Malek scoffed, slightly disturbed by the remark. He diverted his thoughts to something else Bastion had slipped. "Then you owe me a favor. Compensation for breach of privacy."

"Anything, Commander."

"The files you found on me. Could you... show me?"

"Perhaps, but copying the files may alert someone to my infiltration," Bastion said quietly. "Let me think on this."

"Sure. And thanks."

"At your service, Commander. I hope you take my advice as well. I have the utmost confidence that you'll keep them safe in the Wilds. I shall assist Dr. Valerio and arrange for your departure."

"Fine. Dismissed."

Malek exhaled as a low beep signaled that Bastion had signed off. It was all too much. The old AIA detention and interrogation haunted his thoughts, and he couldn't pull himself out. Instead, he dropped his gaze to the floor and lit a cigarette.

Chapter 21

Civilization

It was difficult to pinpoint the reason for the team's overall coldness. It had been almost three days since they'd departed from Saion FOB and four since the assault in Kaira. Emotions should have calmed by now, Nikita hoped, despite that particularly invasive moment with Malek. Distancing herself provided an opportunity to reset, anyway. Reflecting on those moments filled her with regret. She should have approached it differently... from a place of empathy and understanding, as she always did.

No, she thought. She had every right to feel upset, especially given everything that had happened. He could have handled things differently, too. Nikita tried to push aside her feelings about what had happened at home, though she quietly seethed during the lonely hours and mourned her old life in silence. She needed to refocus. The current assignment, at least, served as a decent distraction.

Crossing into the Wilds meant bringing next to nothing. They relied solely on their stamina to carry themselves across vast, rolling hills and rocky plateaus. Nikita led the way, keeping herself busy by taking in the sights of this untouched land. She basked in the beauty of the natural wonders around her and watched the darkening horizon as the forest's border gradually filled their view.

Nikita glanced back, catching sight of four other figures ambling behind her. Casey, directly in her wake, seemed to be the only one interested in talking. Like everyone else, she'd dressed in an issued field jacket, with a light, cropped-sleeved shirt tucked into olive-drab military pants. They were equipped with a hefty pack, a sidearm, and a long utility knife strapped to each member's leg with a cinched strap. Nikita cringed at the thought of Earthborne spotting them fully armed. It had been an uphill battle convincing the ASF members to leave their rifles behind, but in the end, she'd succeeded. Nikita, never wanting to be associated with the decision to appear hostile, was satisfied with just her hammer pick.

Her thoughts were interrupted by Casey's voice once again. It was clear from the beginning that Casey hadn't been thrilled to rejoin the group, and never missed an opportunity to mention it during the lulls in conversation. She was already on another rant, making Nikita wonder if bringing her would do more harm than good.

"It's just that you three are Alliance Special Forces! *Mace*, I'm so out of this game," Casey whined, slapping at an insect that landed on her arm. "And this is literally a walk in the park for Valerio. Remind me again why I was dragged out here?"

"Infiltration!" Malek barked at her from the end of the line. "Which doesn't help if you're loud. So, shut up."

Apparently, Malek was *still* in a prickly mood since Kaira. Casey groaned, "I had things I needed to do in As-Tarut. You know that, Commander."

"I needed a professional. Look, I'll drag myself to As-Tarut with you after we're done if it helps."

Casey perked at that remark. "They're going to love that. Holding it to you, Commander. I'll play nice."

"Didn't realize the commander was such a commodity," Vivika grumbled under her breath, now beside Nikita. Nikita caught the *jealous* notes...

"It doesn't *seem* like a big deal," Nikita replied in a low voice. "But being an Al-Khasari outsider really is a rare thing. Of course, his people want him back. If for anything, to keep up appearances that 'no one leaves the sands of Khasar.'"

"*Staka*." Vivika sneered. "He grew up in Mardasca. Khasar isn't his home, and he shouldn't be forced to go."

"Where is this newfound concern coming from?" Nikita wrinkled her brow. "Kei?"

The Jennai woman yanked on her pack straps and stomped ahead. Nikita could feel a presence fill the void she had left, and she turned to face the major.

"It's a bit obvious, isn't it?" Gene said with a smile that failed to meet his eyes.

"Well, maybe... but aren't there rules or something about relationships within the Alliance?"

"Yes, within the ASF. The Alliance Army does whatever they like." Gene cleared his throat. "Anyway, discussing Kei's prospects was not why I came here. Are we close to our next camp?"

"Yeah, just past that tree line." Nikita pointed to the lush, thick forest that formed a natural border against the rocky hills. The late-afternoon sun was warm, but its heat was quickly fading, allowing the persistent autumn wind to run its chilling touch over the travelers. The environment remained bright until the forest met the hills. The lush shrubbery and tall, violet-tinged bushes were a stark contrast to the immense, towering redwood trees that fortified the thicket.

"And then, to the nearest stronghold?"

"Should be another day or so. Could be more depending on our objective... as long as we're quiet, and don't get into any trouble." She and Gene exchanged glances, and both released nervous laughs. His wall of ice was starting to chip away.

"Not our brand, so it seems," Gene muttered.

Nikita shook her head with another chuckle. "That's why I'm here, too."

"But if all goes well, you won't have to use your talents." Gene patted her on the shoulder. "Thank you for keeping a level head through all this."

"It's... good to refocus on something else," she replied, inwardly thinking of Malek, and her determination to unearth *that* mystery.

"One more thing, love," Gene added. "When we rest for the night, try to remove the rest of that threading from your jacket. It's still identifiable."

Nikita had not even noticed it, and her fingers instinctively traced the remnants of the winged shield-shaped patch on her shoulder from an old Alliance logo. "Right. Will do. Thanks. Once you get to the tree line there, look at the ground. Don't go too far in. Let me know what you find."

They exchanged smiles, and Gene trotted off ahead.

Nikita glanced at Malek. He'd finally rejoined the group moments after everyone had moved on to scan the tree line directly in front of them, as she'd suggested. He was obviously moving more slowly than the others and straining to keep up in stubborn silence. She studied him with a quick, furtive glance, noticing hints of blue peeking out from under the hem of his shirt, just under his collarbone. The bruise must have been massive. He still had the webbed cast on his arm, too. Blotches of purple discolored his olive skin between the gaps in the resin. She would have felt sorry for him, but she also resented that he was withholding information from the team. Maybe there was more at work here that she couldn't see. What was really going on with him?

"You okay?" Nikita asked in a low tone, never meeting the commander's gaze. She sensed him look up at her, but he replied in an equally hushed voice.

"Are you asking about how I'm physically feeling? Or something else?"

"I'm referring to your injury. It's my job as your med officer, right?"

"Catching on. Good for you."

"We can slow down."

"No. Let's keep moving."

"It is pretty... unusual that you're even hiking in that state," Nikita noted, maybe in a pathetic attempt to lift the tension. "My cousin, when he lived on the Alcides Islands, used to take an active part in the revolution back when Hassentio first came to power. He took a rubber bullet in the leg at close range and couldn't walk for weeks."

"Takes one good shot. It'll do that to you." Malek exhaled, clutching his chest with his web-laced hand.

Nikita paused for a moment. "Is it getting worse?"

Malek didn't answer but examined the tree line. "What are we doing?"

"Here, walk this way. I want to show you something." Nikita led him away from the rest of the group.

"Is this relevant?"

Nikita sighed. "Yes, if we want safe passage into the forest."

"Just tell us what—" Malek's voice caught, and he quickly snapped his gaze to his feet, where his boot struck a protruding edge. Nikita studied his expression, witnessing the realization dawn on him.

Malek's eyes rounded in alarm, then narrowed as they traced the ground where a streak of oxidized metal lay embedded among the detritus and soil. Curiously, he kicked away some leaves while following the line of iron, just as it disappeared into a glade. Nikita grinned to herself and gestured for the others to join in. Malek turned around with his lips parted in awe.

"These," Malek exhaled, and for the first time in days, he actually smiled a little. "These are train tracks."

"Yes." Nikita beamed, coming closer to him. "You're staring at five-thousand-year-old train tracks. I know it's not relevant to the assignment, Commander. But it's relevant." Her gaze drew to the low-hanging branches, their waning greenery glowing in the sunlight that broke through the high canopy. "Ashon is one of the most well-preserved human cities in the world, aside from the Spire constructs. When borders were drawn two hundred years ago, this place was completely hidden by the Wilds. We can't study it. One of the last remnants of our lives before the Decimation is being swallowed up by the forest. Soon, there won't be anything to study."

"Bet that kills you."

"It does. I mean, it's innate to want to know where we came from. It's part of being human."

Malek's expression darkened. Her intuition begged her not to ask, but her impulses took over. "I mean, don't you ever wonder about *your* roots?"

Malek nodded icily toward the glade. "Get moving."

So much for getting back on his good side. Nikita cursed herself and gestured toward the thicket where the tracks slithered into oblivion. "Our path is here. It leads to what might have been a station, attached to the ruins of an old building. We can camp there, high above the ground. It's our safest option."

The night peaked, and the soft, blue glow of the radiant heat lamp at the center of their camp became almost blinding. Nikita rubbed her eyes and begrudgingly accepted that it was time to call it a night. She managed to journal a few more details about the ancient city in a small notebook. During her first expedition, the team had meticulously studied their surroundings. This time, she had to paint broad strokes in her journal, realizing that things had certainly deteriorated since she'd last visited Ashon five years ago. She had little time to record it. It was sad to see it fall further into obscurity, and even more depressing that so much would be lost by the time she returned...well, *if* she ever returned.

Remnants of white-brick buildings lay in heaps, entangled in shrubs and weeds. Trees and overgrowth choked any remaining stone pillars, while streams and makeshift waterfalls trickled over the foundations of a vanished civilization. Nikita couldn't believe how much the undergrowth had thickened in just five years. It was difficult to find the path to the station, which was really a standing arc of steel, rotted with rust and decay. From there, she led them to the veranda on the third floor of the adjacent building. It was alive with exotic flora and the sounds of small nesting birds. It was safer here and provided a good view of their surroundings from the edge. No one opposed staying close to the inner walls in case unwelcome eyes lurked in the forest.

The warmth of the cell-powered lamp was comforting as the cool air bit at Nikita's cheeks. She tucked herself and the notebook deeper into her sleeping bag, scanning the other oblong shapes scattered on the detritus-ridden floor. It appeared that everyone, except Malek, was asleep. He was on first watch, much to the team's protest. Nikita spotted him leaning against the wall at the edge of the veranda, looking out into the forest. She was unsure if he was doing this out of a lack of trust or something else. As the medical officer, she recognized that he clearly needed the rest, given all the injuries he'd sustained since Saifain... though honestly, she questioned whether he would even be up for another mission, as she'd hinted at earlier. How was he so resistant? The GXF soldier slamming into her glass sliding door filled her mind, as did the microseconds leading up to that moment where Malek effortlessly lifted a grown man, and hurled him with the strength of an Elemnai. Was his arm even *broken*?

Part of her was still angry—angry that he was lying to the team. If he wanted to suffer, that was *his* decision. A multitude of theories flooded her mind as she watched Deos' light catch Malek's silvery-white hair and die as it faded to black. The moonbeams bathed the treetops beyond him in a ghostly pallor, which, coupled with the wild trill of insects and night creatures, created a haunting ambiance. Nikita found it soothing, anyway, and it melted her fury. The symphony lulled her to sleep within moments.

A forceful nudge jolted Nikita out of a nightmare reliving Saifain. She had been stumbling through dust and debris as the monster Earthborne tore the ground beneath her feet until someone gripped her shoulder and shook her back to reality. Nikita blinked as shapes and colors shaped into a familiar face. Casey stared at her with a finger pressed against her lips. She nodded toward the edge of the veranda without making a sound. Nikita's heart began to race, and she followed Casey's cautious, slow steps as the pair crept toward the edge where Malek crouched.

Nikita rubbed her eyes, trying to discern what he was holding. Casey tapped him on the shoulder, and Malek snapped his gaze from the forest below up to Nikita. What on Eiden were they doing? Without any explanation, Malek removed a set of dark headphones from his head and motioned for Nikita to put them on. They were soundproof headphones, as she could tell from the weight pressing down on her skull. A thin wire trailed from them to the mysterious, cone-shaped device. Was it... a microphone? Casey took it from Malek and leaned over the edge of the veranda, pointing it downward.

As soon as she did, Nikita quickly understood what was happening. A conversation filled her garbled mind. It was Umbar'ok. She slid onto her stomach and peeked over the ledge with Casey, urging her mind to translate as quickly as possible.

"…Why did we need to come here? I hate this place. Stinks of humans."

"I am seeking a sign of his return."

Nikita spotted the two shadows of Earthborne wardens—slight figures with delicate ebony horns jutting from their crowns. They were female, and their voices sounded young. Gold beads clicked together when their braided hair swayed in synch with their steps. Thick cloaks danced as they pulled them over their shoulders while walking alongside a small herd of sternbeasts. These were bovine-like creatures with massive ivory horns and tusks curving over their stout bodies and square snouts. Nikita remembered these well, and the people who tended to them. The Earthborne wardens were night shepherds. Sternbeasts fed primarily under moonlight, when it was cool.

"You mean of Farduk? He is gone. He was warned that leaving the divine's care would deepen the sickness."

"Yes, but he was strong. Strongest among us. What hope is there for our people if he succumbed?"

Sickness? Nikita repeated in her mind. Casey traced the path of the Earthborne with her device as they trudged away from them. Thankfully, the voices remained crisp and clear. Nikita listened with such hungering eagerness that her stomach fluttered.

"The divines believe the relic of the Anymm is the source."

"Of what?"

"The sickness."

"Why does Elder Tor not be rid of it?"

"Sentimental, I wonder. That Anymm, from the Mother's stories, gifted it to him. Though, some say he is…"

Nikita's heart hammered as she clawed at the veranda's edge, desperate to hear their words. It was no use. They were too far away. She snapped the headphones off her head and turned to Casey and Malek.

"We need to follow them!" she hissed.

"Need?" Casey frowned at her. Malek looked annoyed with Casey, but he fixed his eyes on Nikita. She took it as she needed to explain anyway.

"Yes. I think they're talking about a shard."

Malek perked up and glanced at Gene and Vivika, who were still sound asleep. He exhaled and nodded, drawing his sidearm. "Casey, stay close to Valerio. Move out," he whispered.

Casey hung the headphones around her neck before whisking herself away like a cat on the prowl.

Quickly, the three of them clambered down the building, creeping into the dark forest thicket in the wake of the Earthborne wardens. Nikita's thoughts raged with a flurry of questions. It was too good a coincidence. Elder Tor, and an Anymmic artifact... Farduk, and a mysterious illness...if the relic was a shard, did the shard itself make the Earthborne sick? Had it caused him to mutate?

This was the evidence she had been waiting for. The Earthborne couldn't possibly be building a weapon if their own people were being affected. They had strength in their unity, and the bonds of the tribe were unbreakable. The Earthborne Nikita knew and studied wouldn't sacrifice their own so readily on the warpath. It never aligned with their values. The thought of proving this to Malek and, by extension, the Alliance, filled her with renewed hope. The Earthborne must be victims, too. Even so, if the Earthborne had been forced to do this... was the unknown aggressor to blame?

Nikita silently pursued Casey as they pushed past shrubs and long-leafed ferns. She was so deep in thought that she failed to realize where Casey had led them. The roar of water drowned out their steps on the undergrowth. Nikita looked to her left, and just a few feet from her lay the precipice of a cliff that dropped down into a river valley. She could hardly see the water, but she could tell it was there, far below the rocky steppes by the sound of it. Casey must have brought them here to stifle the sound of their movement. *Clever,* Nikita thought. She needed to be careful. One false move could cause her to slip.

Casey raised her fist, and Malek gripped Nikita's arm, startling her. Casey gestured for Nikita to kneel beside her and handed her the headphones again. The anticipation left her quivering, causing her to nearly drop them while settling the foam padding over her ears. Nikita peered through the swaying leaves of an imposing fern. Between the gaps of the fan-like stems, she refocused on the two Earthborne. They were in a treeless meadow surrounded by a herd of sternbeasts. Each warden sat on medium-sized boulders with their backs turned to her and Casey.

"...absurd. We have no reason to heed that nonsense," the Earthborne on the right spoke. She was older than the other, now that Nikita had a good view of her longer ebony horns.

The younger one looked at her. "Whether true or not, we cannot bury our voices and allow Elder Tor to continue down this path. Not at the expense of our people."

"We are speaking against the will of the elder, if I may remind you."

"*One* elder of the enclave! Others can be reasoned with. My cousin, Medini. She is a powerful brave in the southern tribe. Stronger than Farduk. I can ask her to speak with Elder Tor at Preikrock. If she addressed him in the presence of both the elder enclave and the divines, Elder Tor would have to abandon the Anymm's mission."

Anymm's mission? What could that mean? This was the lead they needed. The shard must be the root of this issue. And Preikrock... that sounded familiar. It was sacred ground—a massive cliff with a flat ridge at the edge of the southern border of the Wilds and Mardasca. It was far, but if they pushed themselves and left at dawn, they could reach it by nightfall tomorrow. The answers could be waiting for them. Maybe they could sneak in and out, after all.

"Wait...Did you hear that?" the older Earthborne girl stood, her hands whipping out from beneath the woolen cloak.

Nikita instinctively shrank deeper into the shadows, her heart pounding against her ribcage. She cautiously glanced at Casey, who'd also noticed the disruption, given her tense posture, and remained frozen. The sweat beading on Nikita's forehead was cold against the stillness of her tense, burning muscles. She tightened her breath, remaining shallow and quiet. She fixed her gaze back on the Earthborne. The wardens exchanged glances with one another.

An ear-piercing shriek ripped through the air. Nikita's muscles seized, and her heart lodged in her throat. The herd scattered in a thunderous stampede. The roar of a dark, cat-like creature erupted from the thicket as it leaped out of the tree line across the meadow. A pair of massive, ominous white fangs flashed in the moonlight as its sleek feline body pounced onto the massive back of a sternbeast. Nikita's breath caught, and she gripped Casey's arm.

"*Machaibir*!" the warden bellowed, her words drowning in the violent outpour of animalistic cries from the meadow.

Nikita's words cut through the hollering female Earthborne, "Death kitty! Run!"

"Frag us," Malek griped and pulled Nikita to her feet. She lurched as Malek pushed them back toward the path from where they came, the headphones ripping from her head when she and Casey bolted into the forest.

The once quiet night was now filled with wild groaning and stomping of stray sternbeasts as they fled the scene. Branches and shrubs snapped under their massive hooves. The cracking of stone echoed in the depths of the wood, where Nikita could hear the Earthborne wardens standing their ground to fight the feline predator in their midst. In the chaos, Nikita swore she also heard the Umbar'ok words, "Get the beasts out of here!"

The raucous hooves drumming against the ground drew closer. Nikita looked back despite Malek urging her forward, and her eyes widened at the sight of the first tusks breaking through the underbrush. "Watch out!" she cried, shoving Malek away just in time to dodge the first of a dozen gigantic sternbeasts storming down the path.

She breathed heavily as she recoiled into a fern, hiding beneath its fanning leaves that whipped over her head with each passing creature. The rumbling quieted, but she could still hear the Earthborne. Not daring to move, Nikita looked around. She expected to catch sight of Malek and Casey on the other side of the path, but there was nothing. Panic gripped her as she tried to gauge her surroundings. Before she could lift herself from the ground, she heard the light steps of a figure galloping across the undergrowth.

"Here! I'm pursuing them!" the young Earthborne called back to her partner.

Nikita receded even further into the ferns as she watched the bare, slender feet whisk by. She forced herself to count the seconds. Nikita couldn't stand up for fear of being seen, but the thought of being alone was just as terrifying. After an agonizing moment, and ensuring that no one else approached, creature or otherwise, Nikita scrambled across the forest floor and scanned the area.

"Commander? Casey?" she hissed. Nikita's boot struck something hard. She snapped her gaze down and recognized the microphone Casey had held. Swallowing nervously, she ran her fingers over the equipment. Where was she? Nikita traced the embossed earth, searching for footprints. The branches and leaves lay twisted and snapped, matted down against the undergrowth. Something had violently torn through here, too. This hadn't been caused by the sternbeasts or the Earthborne because it was too close to the...

Oh no... Nikita gasped, recognizing a familiar whoosh of water coursing far below her. A wave of dread consumed every thought. She followed the sound and broken foliage, then stopped dead in her tracks when the ground ended. Nikita gripped the edge of the valley and peered over, hopelessly and aggressively scouring the cliff. It was steep and dark. Nothing moved.

"Umm... Bastion?" she whispered, her voice shaking. "Come in. Bastion? Are you there?"

"Oh? Dr. Valerio?" Bastion's tired voice resounded in her earpiece. "It's the middle of the night. Is there a problem?"

"Yes, I..." Nikita shivered. May as well admit fault now and spare the scrutiny. "I lost Commander Reza and Agent Jaeger."

CHAPTER 22

RELIC

Malek awoke to a suffocating pressure in his chest. His lungs refused to draw in air, and an icy weight filled his cavity. Nausea churned within him. His core lurched, forcing him to cough, and as he did, water surged from his insides, spilling onto the rock face. Dizziness washed over him, and his body stiffened from the cold. His back arched, and his arm found its way underneath to support his weight as he coughed again, expelling more water.

Malek stared down at his arm with surprise. The webbed cast was now in fragments, and he shook off whatever pieces remained. His uniform, waterlogged and freezing, weighed heavily on his aching body and barely provided any warmth in the dawn's fresh light. He racked his brain for answers, trying to remember what had happened before he blacked out.

Blacked out? Had he passed out, or did he *really* black out? Malek traced his other arm, where he found it resting on the back of Casey's jacket. The fabric was clenched in his grip. He had been holding it for a while. She lay motionless against the rock face, her head turned away. The slow rise and fall of her back brought a wave of relief. At least she was breathing. Whatever had happened, he'd managed to get them both out of the water and onto the shore. Malek blinked, looking down at the moss-covered rocks beneath and around him, then lifted his gaze.

His sense of his surroundings returned to him all at once. Predatory birds swooped through the faint mist, their cries piercing the thick, humid air. Malek could barely hear them over the roaring river behind him, crashing against the rocky bank on which he found himself. Enough light peeked through the hills for him to see that he was in a river valley, surrounded by dizzyingly tall rocky cliffs on either side of the gorge. Did they fall from way up there?

Malek inched over to Casey and released his grip on her jacket. "Casey?" He shook her shoulder. "Hey, get up."

She moaned but didn't open her eyes. Malek knelt beside her, trying again to turn her. Then he noticed the enormous gash on her brow. Blood trickled from the wound, leaving a crimson smear on the rock.

"Slag..." Malek's heart raced, and ran his hands over his belt and back, desperately trying to recall what he had packed before leaving the camp. The harder he reached for the memories, the more they scattered, and the frustration tensed the muscles in his neck. He rolled his shoulders. Maybe he'd hit his head, too. Malek clawed the small day pack on the back of his belt, stocked with basic first aid supplies and rations, and let out a breath to expel the panic. Thanks to Bastion and his well-thought-out procurement, he knew its contents wouldn't be waterlogged.

Bastion! His fingers ran over the smooth surface of the receiver still in his ear. "Bastion, come in," Malek said, his words hoarse and quiet. "Bastion!"

"Commander!" Bastion finally broke through the comms after a few seconds of dreadful silence. "You're safe! Are you and Agent Jaeger all right?"

"Mostly. Casey's injured. Washed up on shore, not sure how far we drifted."

"You drifted farther than intended, that's for certain."

"Intended?"

"I picked up on some of your chatter after Dr. Valerio notified us of your, ah, departure."

"And?"

"It sounded as if, perhaps... you wanted to move further downstream? I believe there were a few opportunities for you to reach shore, but all were squandered."

"I don't remember that... Maybe I really did have a blackout."

"Interesting. I wonder what drew you here."

What drew him here? Malek repeated the words, and scanned the immediate area. The rocks of the riverbank eventually melded with the forest floor several feet from where they lay. The thicket thinned beside the gorge wall. It was a good place to start the hike back, anyway. "Do the receivers have GPS?"

"No, they don't, but the portables and cameras on your vests do. I'm going to attempt to get a fix on your position. Allow me to set up a cross-connection with the others. Stand by."

Malek exhaled, mentally preparing his muscles for the task ahead by flexing his arm. It definitely didn't feel broken anymore. He expected his nerves to fire, but no pain jolted through his system. Honestly, it never shocked him anymore to recover this quickly, but he could never deny that it was a gift that served him well. He slipped his arms under Casey's legs and shoulder, groaning as he rose. Every footfall was as careful and precise as the last as he tread across the slimy bank, anxious that the moisture and moss would cause him to lose his footing. Casey moaned again, barely able to open her eyes.

"...My hero," she mumbled.

Malek chuckled, tightening his grip. "Shut up. Almost on solid ground."

"Commander, were you able to connect with the others?" Bastion asked.

"Negative, Bastion." Malek lowered himself to his knees and gently placed Casey against the rock face, sitting up. She flinched and nodded to him in thanks as he reached for the pack on his belt. "I can hear you just fine."

"Strange. The earpiece must be damaged. What about Agent Jaeger?"

"Looks like it's gone," Malek glanced on either side of her head.

"I will keep trying. The others are preparing to leave camp."

Good. At least they were safe. The mission wasn't a total failure. "Uh, where are they going?" Malek removed the case from his belt and pulled out antiseptic wipes and butterfly enclosures from its contents. He ignored Casey's whining as he worked on her injury.

"Initially, to begin searching for you and Agent Jaeger. After confirming that you were both intact and that you were closer to the objective, we developed an alternative solution."

"The objective?"

"Based on the conversation she picked up last night, Dr. Valerio believes the shard may be located at Preikrock, a sacred site for Earthborne divines. While rescuing you and Agent Jaeger is urgent, the assignment also takes priority. Your GPS indicates that you are closer to Preikrock than the others. If you continue down the river for ten kilometers, you will reach the outskirts of the site. I will update the location on your portable, if it is still intact. Can you confirm?"

Malek tapped at the screen on his right forearm, bound in a thick nylon and canvas sleeve over a hard casing. It lit up by showing a green dot nestled in the black between white rippling lines of the terrain. He inwardly sighed in relief, and for once, appreciated the ruggedness of this device. "We're good."

"Closer to your objective, I will direct both teams to meet at a specific muster point. Do you have enough supplies for the run?"

"Barely." Malek glanced down at the case. The anxiety swelled in his chest. "Some rations, less than a day's worth, some first aid equipment, and a collapsible water pouch with a filter. I don't have my sidearm."

"And Agent Jaeger? Will she be able to make the trek?"

Malek held her gaze for a moment, searching for a hint of a deeper injury that he couldn't see. "Can you walk?"

"I will," Casey muttered. Malek placed the final bandage over her wound, and she swallowed. "I just need a minute."

"You have some time,' Bastion said. "The others have twenty-five kilometers to clear before reaching the objective."

"Okay, then proceed with the assignment. I'll let you know when we're ready to move out." Malek assembled the water pouch components and shook open the bladder.

"Understood, sir."

Malek met Casey's scrutinizing stare. "What is it?"

"*You* are *way* too pretty to be a grunt," she said in what sounded like was supposed to be a velvety voice. She smirked at him, and he tried to stifle a laugh.

"And *you* are obviously concussed." Malek stood and walked away.

"Just saying... if you were a woman... snatch that up fast..."

Malek didn't want to hear the rest. He shivered, glancing back at the bank, searching for a shallow spot to fill his pouch. The air warmed slightly as the sky bathed in hues of orange and yellow. The mist vanished up the gorge, like a ghost caught at dawn. It was actually pleasant. The Wilds were... different from the jungles of the Alcides Islands. It was calm, as if the chaos of the outside world could never touch this place. The trees' trunks were unnaturally massive, with their boughs reaching up like skyscrapers. Malek marveled at the natural fortress. The wildlife songs echoed through the haunting depths of the woods, and a strange sense of peace settled over him. It looked like a dangerous place for sure, but maybe it was only dangerous to those who feared it... and feared the truth. Maybe this was why the Earthborne would die to protect it.

Malek took a deep breath. It didn't hurt at all. He glanced down at his chest and peeked beneath his shirt. The bruise had vanished. He could almost hear Maida's voice urging him to revisit Alliance R&D to analyze his talent for recovery... again. The anxiety that seeded was enough to purge the thought immediately.

Malek's eyes wandered over his surroundings, and he found his mind drowning in the chorus of the forest's sounds. Out here, it was as if the Alliance never existed. He reveled in that idea for a moment longer. It was nice to let go, for once... not having to think of every outcome of his actions and inactions, worrying over how everything could end in disaster for him. He wished he could live that reality more than anything else in the world. He could almost taste that freedom here.

After filling the pouch, he made his way back to Casey with his spirits lifted, and placed the bottle next to her to begin the filtration process.

"...Can I ask you something?" Casey said in a hushed, sluggish tone.

Malek studied her demeanor. That head injury might be worse than he realized. "Go ahead."

"Why do you keep the Alliance at arm's length?"

"Why do *you*?"

"It's complicated."

Malek nodded and arched his brows. "Same. Complicated. I don't have a great history with the Alliance."

"Why don't you quit?"

"Why don't *you*?"

Casey smiled a little, then closed her eyes with a sigh. "Complicated."

"Yeah... complicated is right." Malek leaned one hand against the wall. His senses perked up. Something was off here. The stones... they looked as if they had been intentionally placed to seal a gap in the cliff face. Malek ran his fingers over the smooth patches of moss and lichen embedded in the crevices that formed a mortar. "Casey, I think I found something." He breathed.

"Lovely. Maybe that's why you insisted that we let the river take us further downstream."

He didn't have the words. Malek made a face at her scornful remark, then looked back at the wall, studying its uneven surface. The same question crept back into his mind...what drew him here?

"What did you find, Commander?" Bastion spoke up. "Describe it to me."

"There's a bunch of rocks piled up. And, well..." Malek paused, embarrassed by what he was about to say. "The kid in me is convinced this is a secret entrance."

Bastion laughed. "I can picture it well! Are you able to get any purchase on it?"

Malek grunted, pulling the first stone from its space and snapping the lichens. "Yeah, I can move the rocks." The moment the first stone fell out, a wave of anticipation sank into his core. It was somewhere between a nauseating and fluttering sensation. Something was in there.

With hardened determination, Malek pulled at the stones until they popped out one by one. He became so fixated on this that he barely noticed when a few of them fell a little too close to Casey, causing her to yelp. A rush of excitement electrified his senses as he peered into the once-dark cave, now filled with the ambient light of the outside world. It was a secret room after all. But... who on Eiden would build this? An Earthborne could have easily mounted a slab of rock, but this was placed by a human. From the looks of it, it had been made by someone who passed by here a long time ago.

Without a word, Malek scrambled over the pile of stones and into the shadows. His steps slowed, his eyes drinking in the impossible precision surrounding him. The walls formed nearly a perfect sphere—smooth, ochre rock met with a flat, dusty floor. It was... weird. How could someone carve out the walls like this?

At the center of the small room sat a square hearth shaped with various-sized carbon black stones. Malek's curiosity could hardly be contained. He knelt next to the hearth and studied the objects on either side of it. Dry tinder and thin logs had been carefully placed on one side, while the other had shards of flint. The most unusual thing, by far, was the object wrapped in an old linen cloth in the middle of the hearth.

A hypnotic whisper that he didn't recognize threaded through his mind. It seemed... familiar. He didn't understand the words. He could only guess at their meaning. His heartbeat quickened. Something urged him to pick it up.

Before he had a chance, Casey's hand whipped out from behind him and snatched the item away. "Ooh, what's this?" she purred, leaning on Malek's shoulder.

Malek sighed, clenching his jaw to stop himself from snatching it back like a child. The linen cloth fell away, something clinked against the ground. Both he and Casey stared at the strange and wonderful item that waited hidden underneath.

The object pulled at him, and Malek drew closer, his mind quieting to a strange hush. It was a long dagger, or short spear, that spanned the length of his forearm. Marked by sharp, deliberate edges, it had a precise form that hinted at something...otherworldly. Black metal gleamed indigo under the faint daylight, like staring into the depths of constellations in a clear night sky. Malek blinked, and he lost sight of it. He gently took it from Casey's grasp to feel its heft. Its double-edged blade and ridged handle were perfectly balanced and equal. It was a simple weapon, but something whispered to Malek that there was more to it than he could understand.

"Wonder who it belonged to..." Malek wrenched his attention from the dagger. He and Casey looked at one another, and a mischievous grin curled at the edge of his lip. "Finder's keepers."

"You're no fun," she grumbled and settled against the cave wall. "Maybe some old, idiot explorer lost it."

"I doubt it. The way it was left... It's like it was meant to be found." Malek meant by *him*, but couldn't say that part out loud. He could barely understand himself.

"What did you find?" Bastion asked.

"A blade, it looks like. And an old camp."

"Perhaps someone hid here from the Earthborne?"

"Who knows, but it's hardly a pressing mystery," Casey groaned, rubbing the bridge of her nose with her index finger and thumb. "Bastion, darling, ping us in an hour. Some quiet would be wonderful."

"Ah, yes, Agent Jaeger. Commander, I will reconnect in sixty minutes. The others need some guidance. Congratulations again on the discovery."

"Alright. Dismissed." Malek rested the dagger on his leg. He remembered hearing something fall from the cloth. Was there another part? Eagerly, he ran his fingers across the dusty floor and eventually found something cold and small. His stomach unexpectedly flipped. A nauseating sensation swept over him and vanished just as quickly. Swallowing hard, he held up the small, black, metallic object in the ambient light.

"Is that a ring?" Casey asked, just as Malek came and rested against the wall beside her. He held out the dark band in the palm of his hand.

"Here, propose to Zia with this." Malek laughed, and Casey shoved his hand away.

"She's got more class than that. Give me something that sparkles."

Malek slid it over his right ring finger. Something about it was familiar, even though he knew that was impossible. It was just a simple band. The disturbing image of his mother clutching the box over her lap flashed over his corneas, her terrified gaze meeting his through the crack of a door as she sat at the edge of her bed. Malek cleared his throat. He needed to put the strange sensation to rest and decided that teasing was the best way to do it. "So, Zia's really not an asset? You surprise me, Case. Didn't think spies fell in love."

"I know. That's why things with the AIA are complicated." Casey sighed and rested her head on Malek's shoulder. "Somewhere in my deep cover, I fell in love. Not just with Zia. She's beautiful, in and out. But her people, too. The AIA wants me to take advantage of my position and exploit the Al-Khasari for everything they have."

"I hate to ask this, but haven't you already been reporting in?"

"Just basics. Mostly on what they don't have. I play up the act of being on the fringe of their trust. But I've been to As-Tarut. Not just As-Tarut—all five cities of Khasar. It's hard *not* to fall in love. It's amazing that the Al-Khasari chose to advance themselves rather than build weapons and defenses. They have ancient Anymm artillery, burnt out and depleted, but they never focus on that. They'd rather build their people. That line of thought..." Casey gently shook her head "...doesn't exist anywhere else on Eiden. There's no scarcity. It's just...community. Everyone looks out for each other, even an outsider like me. There's a real connection. You know as much as I do how fragged up and divided this world can be, held together by the joint call for humanity's so-called defense against the Elemnai. All that 'never again', slag. It's nice to be somewhere where it's not about beating down the next target or exploiting what good can come from its civilians. That's the Alliance for you, though. Telling us who the enemy ought to be and forcing us to fall in line. I'd rather be a part of something beautiful. Now that I've tasted it, I don't know if I want to go back to my old life."

"Is this your pitch to get me to follow you?"

"Not at all. That deal was done." Casey looked up at him and smiled.

Slag, he'd forgotten about that, but didn't bother to argue. "Right." Malek stared at the hearth with the dagger in hand, spinning it about its axis over a finger. The blade had already cut the first layer of skin, and Malek slackened his grip. It was still sharp. "It sounds like you're buying time, waiting for the axe to come down."

"To do what?"

"Defect. Become Casey Jaeger for the rest of your life and disappear."

That was a seriously bold accusation, even for Malek. He would be lying if he said he'd never thought of doing the same... slag, he'd already been planning on it, if the mission went south. But it wasn't about him right now. He needed to know if Casey was truly an ally, or if this was a means to an end... and whether she was going to make him complicit.

225

"Your brevity is immaculate."

"Cut the slag, Casey."

"You think I would tell you any of this without doing a little digging myself?"

Malek instantly tensed as Casey embraced his arm and curled against him like a drowsy cat seeking warmth. The dichotomy of her affection and her chilling words left Malek more vexed with each passing moment, making him want to shake her off.

Casey tilted her head upward, her lips barely grazing his jaw. "I know what the Alliance did to you," her whisper was like a knife to his chest.

All the calm and peace he had felt in the woods came crashing down into a pit of darkness and fear. The memories of his internment with the AIA surged, sending waves of agony across his nerves that stung him into paralysis. Malek couldn't breathe.

"You and I both know you're not safe. I don't *think* you're coming with me. I *know* you will." She rested against his shoulder again.

He desperately wanted her to let him go but couldn't command his muscles to act.

"And I mean that with love, Mal. You and I were used. *Are* used. You deserve a better life. Now, give me a minute to rest. Then we'll leave. Don't bother starting the fire. You're hot enough."

"Shut the frag up."

"I meant body temperature. What did you think I meant?"

Casey's inflection was coy, but Malek was done with the games. A muscle rolled in his jaw while his fury burrowed deeper into his spine. He didn't respond, staring at the hearth. His thoughts immediately dissociated, drifting off with flashes of his youth, living under the torturous trials of the AIA assessments. He remembered the piercing gazes of the assessors and their relentless, calculating questions. The harsh fluorescent lights of the testing rooms flickered in his mind, and Malek swore he'd seen those same long shadows of the researchers dancing menacingly across the cavern walls. The weight of the restraints bore down on him as he'd been exposed to those horrifying trials, breaking limbs and coldly watching him reassemble himself. The metallic taste of fear filled his mouth as he struggled to keep his sanity when they deprived him of safety or sleep, hungering for him to black out again and reveal what he truly was. He tightened his fist around the dagger, trying to push the memories down with every queasy breath. They lingered like ghosts in the recesses of his mind, just beyond his grasp.

Were used. Are used. Malek repeated Casey's words in his mind, unable to shake the truth he so desperately wished was a lie. The AIA exercises had been designed to replicate the horrific and brutal conditions of his first blackout while held captive by the Terminians. He knew they wanted him to use his abilities on demand, no doubt for less than virtuous reasons.

Joining the ASF had been an initiative Malek took for himself… well, with Maida's backing. In the ASF, he could control his circumstances to some extent. He could live a life outside of internment. He *chose* this path, so then how was he being used? Every risk Malek took in his career was for freedom—to prove he was capable and that the blackouts were never significant. He could outperform them. That way, the Alliance would see no reason to keep him indefinitely. Being here was his choice. Not theirs. Casey's cynicism clouded her outlook. Malek knew how to deal with the Alliance. He wasn't being manipulated, especially not after all he suffered to make damn sure he was still in the driver's seat.

His mind drifted until he could no longer separate dreams from reality. The only thing that convinced him otherwise was the shadow in the secret room. Malek squinted his eyes… did Casey get up and stoke a fire? The hooded figure in a strange, dark tactical suit knelt at the hearth while the flames crackled in front of them. "Casey?"

The figure stiffened and slowly turned its head to Malek. He trembled at the sight. Instead of peering into a face, Malek's eyes filled with an infinite vault of stars, as if the galaxy itself were staring back at him. Dread and awe suffocated his breath.

A deep, resonating voice echoed off the walls of the small room, hammering all his senses at once, *"You have the force of the universe at your fingertips, Malek. Keep it close. I'll protect you."*

Malek jolted, causing Casey to slip from his shoulder and curse. He could finally breathe, and he focused on the hearth. No fire. It was just as he had left it. It must have been a dream, but the shock to his nerves made it so real, even though he knew it wasn't possible. His initial fear quickly transformed into something else, something he didn't expect. After a moment, his heart rate settled, and his eyes fell on the dagger. Someone *wanted* him to have it. It was like they had his back.

"Ugh, fine. I'm awake, thanks for asking," Casey grumbled.

Malek rubbed his eyes, then glanced at the dull light now filling the void between the smooth, rocky walls. The sun had risen. They needed to move if they were to meet the others in time. "How's the head?" Malek pushed himself to his feet and reached for her hand.

She took it and rose to meet him, still muttering under her breath, "Got any painkillers?"

"Nope. Valerio will. We've got ten k to go."

"You mean the girl who pushed us off the cliff is my only source of therapy?"

Malek led her out of the cave. "She didn't push *us* off. She pushed me, and I fell onto you... Then I think I tried to grab you..."

"Reprimand the civilian, Commander."

Malek chuckled and shook his head. "Get over it, Case. You're fine. It was an accident."

"You're in a weirdly pleasant mood for someone who almost died."

"Hey, 'almost dying' is like my thing. You would know that if you read my files. The key is *almost*." Ignoring Casey's glare, he looked at the cave entrance one final time.

Malek stowed away the memories of his dream, and picked up the water pouch, handing it over to Casey before making his way over the bank. He breathed in the fresh, cool air. The tranquility of his surroundings crept back into his extremities again. He wasn't bothered by Casey's words or the vision. He felt, of all things, secure... and sure of himself.

The mellowness of Bastion's words added a nice touch, "Commander, are you ready to move out?"

"Affirmative." Malek's eyes dropped to his portable. "Which way from here, Bastion?"

Chapter 23

Outlander

If Nikita had known how Vivika was going to react, she would have preferred to drag Malek's mangled body back, crushed by a sternbeast. It was enough to be racked with guilt, but the constant reminders of her mistake grated on her nerves. Nikita couldn't validate Vivika's anxiety any more than she already had, and she was fresh out of apologies.

"Are we sure they're going to be able to find us?" Vivika panted, hurdling over a massive, collapsed log riddled with moss. Without a response, Nikita glanced back at her teammate. It was getting harder to see her expression in the afternoon light. The towering trees blocked the last few rays of the sun, casting long, dark shadows over the forest thicket. This also meant that it would be much more difficult to find a safe entrance into Preikrock, causing Nikita to instinctively shiver.

She sank deeper into thought about the upcoming objective. It was lucky that they wouldn't have to venture further into the Wilds and risk encountering anyone from Nikita's previous expedition. She wasn't sure she could earn their trust again with a *new* group of strangers. The Earthborne were a cautious and stubborn people. She knew stealing the shard might be easier than asking for it. Nikita sighed, resisting the urge to consider all the reasons why Malek's approach might be the best one. It wasn't just about finding the shard, she told herself. Nikita needed more proof to save the Earthborne from the Alliance.

"Yes, yes, I've already confirmed the meeting point. Several times, Lieutenant Kei," Bastion replied briskly. "Please head up the ridge. Both parties will converge on that location, and it will provide a suitable vantage point."

"We will take the night and plan our next move, Kei. You know the commander is a survivor," Gene spoke from the back of the line, his deep voice breaking through the high-pitched songs of nesting birds overhead.

Nikita craned her neck to observe the steep hill they were about to ascend. The muscles in her legs cramped from the trek. They had hardly stopped for more than a few minutes at a time since they'd left at dawn. She envied that Vivika and Gene were in much better shape, which became obvious when they managed to maintain a rigorous pace despite Nikita's experience in the Wilds. She warred with her stamina as she scrambled up the ridge. Gene extended a hand to help her clamber over the final ledge. Her heart forced oxygen to her extremities. Wait... was Gene not behind her?

Panic struck her, and she nearly stumbled when she snapped her gaze up. Malek had taken her by the hand and heaved with a disgruntled look. "Move it, Valerio," he said gruffly. It was hard to tell if he was angry with her, so she stumbled past him as quickly as possible, sucking in one sharp breath after another.

Before she could speak, she bumped into Casey, who immediately glared at her with an open palm. "Painkillers. *Now*. You owe me."

Nikita exhaled and dropped her pack onto the grassy floor. "Sorry," she muttered. The guilt coursed through her in a river of ache and cold. As Nikita searched her pack, she caught sight of Malek lifting Vivika over the ridge. There were no clever remarks or formal salutes—it was simply an exchange of shy but genuinely warm smiles. So there really was something there... Nikita wasn't sure why that didn't improve her mood.

By the time she pulled out a pack of pills, Gene stood on the edge, jovially slapping Malek across the back with a grin. "Mace, you are hard to kill, mate," she heard Gene say with a laugh.

Her focus broke when Casey snatched the pills from her grasp, and Nikita could have sworn she growled. With another sigh, Nikita scanned the group with a mix of fatigue and apprehension. At least they were together now.

She placed her hand on a slab of stone next to her, at the precipice of the ridge. Her eyes followed the tree line as it faded toward the foothills of the rocky, amber mountains. Something tight fluttered in her chest, driving her gaze across the landscape, lingering on every contour and shadow. Where the tree line ended, Nikita recognized the terracotta domes and bell-shaped towers of the Earthborne village, nestled between the steppe and the high faces of the cliff. Preikrock was easy to spot. A flat edge jutted from the side of the mountain. Squinting, she couldn't discern a path to the residential district. Maybe it was hidden. Nikita focused beyond the cliff. That was the edge of the Teokha Mountain range, and on the other side was Mardasca—their one way back to safety.

"Is that it?" Malek appeared next to her.

Nikita glanced at his calm features. He didn't seem irritated, but as usual, she just needed to press anyway. "I'm sorry about the river... I was just trying to—"

"Let's just determine our next steps."

"It was a steep fall... after I saw it in the daylight. Did you have another—"

"Focus on the task, Valerio," Malek cut her off again, this time with a sharp look. "What's our next move?"

"You're asking me?"

"You and Casey." He nodded past Nikita. Casey had quietly moved to her other side at some point. Nikita shrank when Casey eyed her up and down with a harsh, scrutinizing look. "Both of you have the intel and expertise on how to get in and out. How do we proceed?"

Nikita nodded, mostly to herself for encouragement. *Here we go*, she thought. "A couple of things you should know. Preikrock is a sacred site, well-guarded all along the entrance. Those domes there mark the residential district."

Casey cut in, "That leaves going around the town and scaling the cliff. We need an escape if things go south. If we can get on the other side of the range, we'll be back on Mardascan soil."

"It's a bit of a hike... but I agree on the escape." Malek turned away from the others, pacing under the tree. "Bastion, let's assess a new EZ."

"Affirmative, sir," His steady voice filled Nikita's ear, and some of that tightness in her chest melted away.

"The entry plan is risky," Malek said, almost to himself.

"I think it's our best shot," Nikita spoke carefully over her next words, knowing their gravity. "Especially if there is an opening to take the shard."

"...You're on board with stealing it? Are you telling me that the shard is being used to build a weapon?"

"No, not a weapon... at least, not one being used by Earthborne." Nikita turned to Malek, chewing her bottom lip anxiously. "Those girls in Ashon were worried about a sick Earthborne who escaped the Wilds. They said he'd been exposed to the artifact of the Anymm, and somehow, they believed it was responsible for his illness. I...I have a hunch they were talking about Wallace. And *he* was telling you about the shard at Preikrock before he died."

"Are you sure?"

"No, but... what if it's true? What if the shard drove him crazy and mutated him? What if the same thing happened to Fireborne?"

"So, you're worried that if more Earthborne—more Elemnai—are mutated, there will be more attacks? Then the Alliance will have cause to mount an offense? That's why you want us to steal it?"

"Yes," Nikita hadn't realized she would say that with such conviction.

It even caught Malek off guard. She tried to ignore the cut of muscle shifting beneath his shirt as he folded his arms. He held her gaze, as if searching for a deeper motive, questioning and intimidating her all at once.

"If it's responsible for the Elemnai mutations and for the attacks on our soil, I'd rather take it," Nikita continued. "If we don't, we'll be responsible for an even worse fate. For everyone."

"Sounds like you're trying to emancipate yourself," Casey muttered.

Even if it were true, Nikita wasn't about to admit it. "I... I'm only relaying what I heard, and what I think it means. They said an Anymm gave the shard to one of the elders, which is, ah, another mystery since they're supposed to be extinct. But anyway, Elder Tor has insisted on keeping it despite everyone's concerns. We might be doing them a favor by taking it off their hands." Nikita could hardly believe the words as they left her lips. She'd reconciled with stealing the shard, but the thought of handing it over to the Alliance remained another hard pill to swallow. The shard, if it was truly mutating Elemnai, wouldn't be safer in the Alliance's clutches. Of that much Nikita was certain.

"As much as I think that reasoning is naive, it's also the original Alliance objective. Fine. We'll do it." Exhaling, Malek addressed each one of his teammates, "Casey, work on infiltration with Valerio. Kei, we will need to pack light for the climb and keep heavy equipment on the ground. Come up with a plan for a defense. Anduran and Bastion, reassess the EZ. See if there's any way we can at least get a ride out of here if we cross the range."

"Hopefully there's a pass," Gene said solemnly and walked away from the group. "Bastion, whenever you're ready."

By "work together," he'd obviously meant that Casey would come up with the strategy to ascend Preikrock, while Nikita was supposed to provide her with insight about the objective. Truthfully, Nikita could hardly give any more details. She had never been there before and only heard about it during her research. Casey finally snapped at Nikita when she ran out of intel for her to use. After a short argument, Casey sent her up the tree with the night vision binoculars. It was pointless, Nikita thought, other than to get out of her space while she plotted the logistics of the climb alone.

She balanced on a thick branch, her feet planted firmly against the rough bark that dug into her palms as Nikita steadied herself. The leaves tickled her bare arms, sending a shiver down her back. Cold descended again as the sun vanished behind the horizon. Rolling her neck to loosen her muscles, she peered through the binoculars one last time before calling it quits. It was the same as before. Green hues over an inky black backdrop replaced the earthy tones of the acropolis and the mountain. At this angle, it was impossible to see who or what was on the flat edge of the cliff, even when she zoomed in. Nothing new to report. She now wondered if Casey was just looking for a reason to stay angry.

"Stuck up there?"

Nikita peered through the branches below her, spotting Malek craning his neck to meet her gaze. She could only see his face because of an eerie green glow that emanated from the side of the tree. Nikita had been up there for a while, and since the cover of the dark had taken over, she had never noticed the unusual growth that gave off the dim light. It was some sort of fungus, forming shelves across the massive trunk. They were actually quite beautiful. Malek traced her stare and flicked one of the mushrooms.

"Just trying to get a better look from here."

"Need help getting down?"

"No, I'm good." Nikita smiled at him, and oddly, he returned the gesture. He... had a nice smile. "I wouldn't mind my jacket if you could toss it up."

"Yeah, sure—" Malek had already turned around when he abruptly froze. He pressed his back against the tree and, slowly and subtly, looked up at Nikita with a gentle shake of his head. Nikita's pulse raced as she heard several shouts from her teammates and the distinct growl of Umbar'ok. More voices pierced through the darkness. Hard shuffling pounded the earth beneath them. Nikita crouched with all her might, straining her muscles to hold herself steady, and slowed her breath. A sharp tightness seized her limbs, and a horrible, dreadful weight filled her core the moment a long, toned arm reached for Malek and snatched him out of sight.

They were caught. If she knew anything about the Earthborne, this meant the end of their assignment. They were never going to leave this place. They wouldn't be able to reach the shard. They wouldn't stop an incoming war with the Elemnai. It was over before they had the chance.

Nikita counted the seconds before the echoes of the cries and steps vanished from the environment. She was alone. Finally, allowing herself to draw deep breaths to calm her racing heart, she began the cautious descent. Her eyes scanned the camp for her team. Vivika's equipment and weapons were strewn across the ground. Gene's lamp lay on its side, its dim blue glow suffocating in the grass. The Earthborne didn't waste time taking them prisoner. At least they were alive.

"Bastion? Bastion, I'm here, still at the camp," she hissed, pressing herself against the tree.

"Dr. Valerio! Thank goodness... I heard the whole ordeal!" Bastion's voice pierced through the receiver in the stark quiet. He spoke in rapid bursts, and she could feel his fear matching her own. He was panicking just as much as she was.

"The Earthborne captured them. I-I don't think they're hurt, don't worry."

"What? Of course, I'm still worried! Can you see them?"

"No, I—wait," Nikita paused.

Something caught her eye. A small object glowed faintly on the ground. She crawled over and fingered the grass until she grasped a fleshy, luminescent crumb. It was... a mushroom? Or a part of one? Nikita snapped her eyes back at the tree. A section of the shelf had gone missing, leaving an uneven void. Her eyes rounded, and she whisked herself around the grass, spotting another crumb every few meters until she reached the slope of the hill. Nikita traced the path's trajectory. They were heading toward the stronghold. Malek was using the mushroom to mark their route.

"What is it, Dr. Valerio?"

"Just some quick thinking by the commander. He knew I wasn't taken because he saw me in the tree. He left me a trail to follow."

"P-Perhaps let's reassess for a moment? Are you planning on going after them?"

"Didn't Maida say there will be no support if we get caught? Who else is going to help them?"

"That's true, but..."

"But you think I should sit this one out?"

"No, I," Bastion cleared his throat and gathered himself. "No. I believe you are an asset. I have said that before, and I meant it. Dr. Valerio, how can I assist you?"

"This is all very dependent on me getting in... and successfully getting them out. What we need is a better exit strategy. A fast one. Can you do something?"

"It will be against General Maida's orders..."

"Come on. I won't be able to negotiate our way out." Nikita exhaled sharply and closed her eyes. She dug deeper and found her voice, "There's too much at stake here, Bastion. By being here, we are just as much at fault for breaking the peace terms as the Earthborne in Saifain. I don't want another war... not because of this. Otherwise, it's never going to end. Everything that I...that we worked for will have been for nothing."

"I know, I know... Ah, Dr. Valerio, you place me in a morally precarious position. But..." His pause lasted an eternity.

Nikita curled her hands into fists.

"Agreed." Bastion finally said. Nikita jumped in her small victory, pumping her fist. "Please locate a map. I will assign a new EZ and prep the Paladin for extraction. General Maida is going to kill me."

Nikita nodded in relief, her anxiety morphing into fierce determination. She navigated the path ahead and devised a plan in her mind. If she was careful, she could complete *two* objectives tonight.

CHAPTER 24

REVELATIONS

N ikita's toe kicked another glowing mushroom fragment from the stone road, hiding it under a wisp of dust. The rock wall of the terracotta dome cooled her perspiring skin as she pressed a shoulder firmly against it. She crouched, tensing at seeing the rows of long shadows. She came to another bend at the end of this road. It had been hours since she'd managed to trek from the foothills and down into the village. Luck was on her side, she knew. Earthborne braves and wardens had gone off scouring the surrounding hills, so the streets had emptied. Nikita was getting close to her team and refused to let her fatigue slow her down.

With the cover of darkness, it was easier to infiltrate the winding roads of the Earthborne residential district than she had anticipated, though it was hard on her body. Nikita had effectively been tiptoeing since crossing the village's boundary, which further strained her already tight calves. Searching for mushroom crumbs while balancing a heavy pack of small arms and a pair of climbing picks challenged her every footfall. She couldn't afford to make a sound. It took every fiber of her mental strength to compel herself to keep moving. But the gains were tangible. Almost there, just a bit further—she'd reassured herself hundreds of times. The thoughts screeched to a halt when she rounded the bend and finally caught sight of her targets.

Nikita traced the road to a steep slope adjacent to the cliff faces of Preikrock itself. She exhaled in relief, taking a moment to relax her muscles. An unusual groove in the mountainside carved up toward the lip of Preikrock. She pondered it briefly, but her thoughts quickly shifted back to their initial objective. At least they were close to where they wanted to be. Nikita's eyes fell on a pair of tall, lean Earthborne with ivory bottoms cinched at the waist and shins with copper-threaded belts and fasteners. Despite their toned physique, they were dwarfed by the hulking figure standing over the four apprehensive humans. He was an Earthborne brave, for sure... his ochre skin was painted with abstract lines of chalk and clay, concealed only by the dark fabric wrapped around his hips and trunk-like legs. He reminded Nikita of that photo she'd taken with her friend, Johar, the Earthborne brave from her expedition. His long, twisted black locs cascading over the ridges of his muscular back and shoulders. Gold beads glinted in the bright light of the torches held by the other two Earthborne wardens. She was too far away to hear their conversation. Nikita blended into the shadows and slithered closer until she could listen.

"...You should have alerted me before you took them," the larger Earthborne growled, his voice rumbling through the cool night air. The pair exchanged glances.

One of them stepped forward to speak, "It was only four of them. They were very close to Preikrock. Not the usual human interlopers we scare away. They had weapons."

The large one groaned, "Then why are they not restrained? Juveniles! All the more reason to call for the braves! These could be human warriors."

"Yes, Virat! That is why we did not waste any time! Look! That one is carrying something unusual." The smaller Earthborne gestured to Malek, who instinctively stepped back, his posture arching defensively. The Earthborne brave, Virat, snarled as he seized Malek by the arm. Malek cried out in protest, and Virat snatched something from his waist.

Nikita inched closer. What did Virat take?

"This," Virat said, losing his breath halfway. "This is..."

"I wonder why an Al-Khasari is mixed in with this lot," the other Earthborne warden muttered, staring down Malek with interest. Nikita knew he didn't understand Umbar'ok, but Malek's piercing glare back at the warden had been almost too well-timed. She furrowed her brows as she eyed the group. Why did the Earthborne care whether an Al-Khasari mingled with other people? Nikita recalled how Malek said Urith and Wallace both spoke Khasiri. What was the missing connection between the Elemnai and the Al-Khasari?

"Ram, take me to Elder Tor at once." Virat pointed to one of the wardens. "And you, Adem, watch these vermin until I return."

Ram sighed loudly. "It is not like you cannot—" Virat narrowed his eyes at him, and the warden shrank back. "Fine, fine." Ram led Virat to the slope, where the groove met the ground.

Nikita loved it when the Earthborne commanded the earth, making it look so much like a rhythmic dance or a sturdy martial art. The warden closed his fists and bent his knees—the trademark stance before they wielded their abilities. With an audible crunch, Ram punched with one hand while the other opened into a flat palm that rose into the air. Nikita marveled at the precise cracks in the ground, carving out a platform that rose with a swift arc of his hand. The slab traveled along the groove up the mountain's side. They disappeared from view in moments, and the other Earthborne warden, Adem, stared at the group with frustration and disinterest. Nikita knew that the Earthborne generally did not get intimidated by a handful of humans... which, given their circumstances, was probably her team's best chance at escaping.

"Oh, don't go anywhere, please." Adem curled his hand in front of him and shot it into the air. A dome of rocky spines rose over her team like a jagged birdcage. Nikita instinctively recoiled. The four of them stood with their backs to one another in the tight space. Nikita was relieved to see Adem peel away from the group and amble down a path that hugged the cliff wall. This would give her a chance to get even closer and find a way to free the others. She pulled up a mental catalog of what Bastion had advised her to pack, but her focus broke when she heard someone from the enclosure speak.

"Never thought I was going to die in a place like this." Casey sighed.

Vivika was the first to respond, "We're not dead yet. There's still hope."

"You're talking about Kit?" Gene said, but then he chuckled. "Girl is tough, but I don't think rescue ops are part of her resume."

"*Se,* true..."

Wow. Thanks, team, Nikita thought, clenching her jaw. She lowered her pack and gingerly searched its contents. She noted when she glanced up now and again that Adem was pacing around, seemingly bored, not bothered at all with their conversation. The three continued their back and forth about the possibilities of escape. It was only Malek who stayed quiet. She wondered what he was thinking about. His back was to her, and he remained fixed on the path up to Preikrock. She wasn't the only person who noticed this.

"Commander? Hatching an escape plan?" Gene asked, twisting his neck to meet his gaze.

"No. I mean... sort of. Just feel a bit off."

"What do you mean?"

"Something tells me that we needed that."

"He's talking about his little knife we found by the river," Casey grumbled. "Like it's got the power to—"

"No, it's not that," Malek cut her off. "I... I have to tell you all something."

The group glanced at one another. Even Nikita tensed at the words.

Malek hesitated before continuing, "You need to know that it was me. I was the one who suggested to Maida that we infiltrate the Wilds. I thought it was the right call."

Nikita could only gauge Vivika's troubled expression from where she stood, directly facing her. Vivika stared at the ground, while Gene exhaled sharply, shaking his head. Even at this distance, it was hard to miss Gene's flash of anger.

Casey folded her arms and turned her cheek in his direction. "So, why did you?"

"You know why, Case."

"Spell it out."

"It has to do with my second confession. Valerio already knows this part.... and maybe you do too, Kei."

"What are you talking about?" Vivika's brow furrowed, but Nikita caught the sadness in her eyes, smothered by her stiff words.

"That I can… do things. Inhuman things. I call them blackouts, because I can't control what I do. I think it happened in Gunliem… and back in Saifain, Valerio's home, and in the river. Every time I black out, I never remember what happened… The adrenaline kicks in, and that's it. I lose a piece of reality every time and hurt a lot of people. It sounds… insane. I know it does."

An uncomfortable moment of silence thickened their tension. Nikita was glad that he had finally told the truth to the team, but it didn't satisfy her. If anything, this burdened her with even more regret. She shouldn't have pushed Malek the way she did. It was out of his control. But the team… no, she had been lied to. Everyone had been lied to, and it could still cost them their lives.

"Well, you didn't hurt me," Casey finally said. "You saved me."

"And me," Vivika said, but she closed her eyes as though to gather herself, which Nikita found unusual. "In Gunliem, and in Saifain. Now it makes sense."

"… What does it have to do with this assignment?" Gene asked quietly. Nikita remembered that stark tone from her living room back in Kaira.

"Because I panicked. I wanted to get off the grid. But if I can keep taking on the high-risk slag and come out on top too, it's my key to getting the Alliance off my back. I could take back my life."

Take back his life? Was Malek… a prisoner of some kind? Nikita didn't have a moment to process the gravity of his words. A rumbling sound drew her eyes toward the slope. She recognized the same slab sliding down the rock face. Her heart jolted, and she scanned the area one more time. Adem was slowly pacing back, eyes also focusing back on the returning party. Nikita needed a plan, and she needed it soon.

"Whatever happens now, I swear I'll get you out. I promise." Malek fell quiet as Virat and Ram returned. Nikita's eyes rounded, studying the oversized white robes gathered around the hunched figure of an elderly Earthborne. His massive horns, ornate and thin, gleamed under the firelight. Sharp, golden eyes flickered as he scanned the humans with curiosity, but he fixed on one in particular.

"*Shahada?*" he rumbled in a deep, trembling voice, eyeing Malek up and down. "*Sinaal ralah arinneh, Shahada!*"

Nikita's lips parted. Part of her hardly believed that Malek spoke to the Elemnai in Khasiri. Now that she heard it in person, she couldn't fathom it. This must have been Elder Tor... the one Virat referred to and the one who might have the shard.

Malek did exactly what she hoped. He addressed the aged Earthborne in Khasiri, running a hand over the back of his neck. He was... nervous.

Upon receiving a nod from the elder, Adem dropped a portion of the cage with the pounding of his heel against the rock floor.

Go with him, Nikita urged in her mind, relieved as Malek stepped out from the makeshift prison. Malek snapped his gaze between Virat and Elder Tor, speaking in rushed Khasiri while earnestly gesturing to the others still trapped in the rocky cage. Nikita wondered whether he was trying to ensure their safety. The Earthborne nodded, and Malek stole one last glance at his team before following his captors. Their Khasiri murmurs were drowned out by the cracking of the stone reemerging from the rock face. Elder Tor led Malek away while Ram guided them back up the cliff.

"Elder Tor has some questions for the Al-Khasari," Virat addressed Adem in a stern voice, who restored the cage. "Keep an eye on the others until they have finished."

"Yes, Virat." Adem nodded, and Nikita stifled a smile when she caught him making a face at the gargantuan Earthborne's back until Virat disappeared.

It was now or never. Nikita did the only thing she knew how to do... better than anyone else on the team. She gathered herself and waited a moment to ensure Virat was out of earshot. Her voice needed to be steady. She forced her trembling nerves to calm so she could collect her courage.

"Help!" she cried in Umbar'ok, cupping her hand around her mouth. "There is another human on the ridge! She is escaping!"

Adem jerked his body around, his hands clawing at the disheveled walnut curls on his head. "What?! Did we miss one? Virat will truly grind my horns to dust!" He darted his gaze between the confused trio of humans in the cage and then back at the distant forest. After a long groan, he turned on his heel and bolted.

Nikita finally slipped from the shadows, eyes still fixated on the Earthborne warden dashing off into the night, tempering the adrenaline coursing through her system by fixating on the task. Adem was finally out of sight.

"Kit!" a voice hissed from the cage. "Kit, that was awesome!" Vivika grinned at her, gripping the rocky bars of the prison.

"You are a wonderful sight for sore eyes, love." Gene nodded at her, equally relieved.

Nikita rushed over to her and slipped off her backpack. She was shaking with anxiety and excitement all at once. Pavo would never believe what she had just done. She was about to stow away the handgun when an unexpected sound froze the blood in her veins. The soft shuffling of quick steps from behind seized her attention, and the faint muttering of Umbar'ok strangled her breath.

"...Virat will never forgive leaving my post, either—"

Nikita's eyes locked with Adem's the moment he appeared from behind one of the dome houses. For a moment, he seemed perplexed, as if he had miscounted how many humans were under his guard. Instincts assuming control over her limbs, Nikita's muscles tightened, and just like in Saifain, she braced for the kickback.

Adem's face contorted into a fierce grimace. He roared as he lunged forward. His long, carved arm snapped forward, but the earth rising to his fingertips immediately dissolved into dust when Nikita pulled the trigger. A cacophonous bang echoed through the still air. The Earthborne collapsed to the ground with a hard slam. Nikita's hands trembled, lowering the gun as a sheen of tears blurred her vision. The recoil still vibrated through her bones.

Adem clutched his chest as he curled onto his side. Crimson bloomed beneath him, dark and vivid against the dirt. His gasps tore into the silence—ragged, wet, and dying.

She stood frozen, staring at the Earthborne. She'd *hurt* him. She was supposed to *protect* him. Her breath came short. Her heartbeat thundered in her ears. Instead, she'd pulled the trigger.

The gun hung limp at her side as her voice screamed inside her skull. What had she done?

In a matter of seconds, the sharp rise and fall of Adem's shoulder slowed, and his groans died into embers. The weight of her actions crushed her heart to dust. If he wasn't dead now, he would be gone soon enough. She had crossed a line she could never uncross. There was no going back after this...

"Nikita?" Gene called her, his arm reaching for hers. The graze of his thumb against her bare skin pulled her from her trance. She blinked away the tears, studying the faces of her friends.

"Kit..." Vivika reached for her, but Nikita barely felt her gentle grip around her other arm. It was like a ghost brushing against her. "It's okay. It's going to be okay."

Was it going to be okay?

Nikita wasn't sure how many seconds passed before Casey's voice broke through the crushing silence. "I can't believe the nerdy girl came to the rescue," Casey said timidly. Nikita's bag slipped from her hands as Casey gripped it. "But thanks for making me check my biases."

Nikita blinked and exhaled sharply. She would have to face this nightmare once everyone was safe. "Don't thank me, yet." She scrubbed her face. Nikita begged herself to focus despite her wailing heart.

There was still a part two of her master plan, and they wouldn't like it. Nikita took one of the picks, and with all the rage and misery building up within her, she thrashed at the stone, giving Vivika a chance to boot it in one swift blow, shattering the structure into fragments. They repeated this several times until it created a hole large enough for the three of them to escape.

"This way." Nikita ushered them away from the scene, down the dark path that hugged the cliffside. She refused to allow herself to look back. She couldn't bear to know whether Adem's breathing had stopped.

It was almost dizzying to glimpse the several hundred-meter drop from the edge, plunging deep into the shadows of the forest below. As Nikita surveyed the wall, the others crept in her wake, wary of any shadows moving in the distance and the haunting echoes of creatures hidden in the night. Thank goodness for Deos, shining brightly even as she waned. Her light would guide Nikita's path. She dug around in her pack, looking for her *other* prized device, the GripAscender.

It was at least a hundred meters up to reach the stage of Preikrock, where Malek remained captive with Elder Tor. Nikita clipped the compact ascender to her guide line. Its cell-powered motor wasn't fancy, but it'd pull her up the cliff far quicker than muscle alone—of course, with the CO_2 grappling head there to give her a head start.

"Bastion, are you there? I have the team."

"Excellent work, Dr. Valerio," Bastion's voice came back. "Everyone, prepare the rappel line to the forest below. Traveling west at a running pace will allow you to intersect with the reassigned EZ. Paladin is inbound, forty-five minutes to arrival."

"What about the commander?" Vivika huffed as Gene frowned and clipped the safety lines in place.

Ignoring Gene's staunch silence, Nikita gripped her pick, and she lifted her gaze. The surface was riddled with protrusions and uneven stretches. She was a fast climber, and the ascender will ensure she gets there in time. She could make it.

"We're not leaving him behind. He's got a lot to answer for. And besides," Nikita drew in a deep breath, "there's something else that we need."

CHAPTER 25

PRECIPICE

M alek fought to suppress his panicked thoughts since hearing the distinct clap of gunfire moments earlier. He regained his composure when Ram glanced his way. Drawing slow, steady breaths to calm his racing heart, Malek stiffened his spine. His hands clasped behind him, his eyes shifted to the Earthborne known as Tor. Hopefully, this meant the team had escaped.

Tor stepped back and forth between the curved walls of an alcove embedded in the mountainside. He sheepishly reintroduced himself several times in Khasiri to jog Malek's memory of their last visit. Malek knew Tor had mistaken him for someone else, but unless he wanted to end up in a cage again, he needed to play along and pretend to be this "Shahada" character.

Dual rows of torchlight on stone pedestals gave more than enough light, but that didn't stop Elder Tor from meticulously scanning every bauble that brushed his bony fingers. It was painful to watch... which might have been Malek's impatience and anxiety pricking at his senses. The acidic taste in the air intensified the twisting dread knotting in his stomach. He could hardly process Tor's words as he droned on about ancient relics.

It's here. Malek scanned his surroundings, where, in the blink of an eye, he caught that same shadow of a man with the starry face appear and disappear beside him.

The Earthborne warden looked down at him with a confused expression.

Malek awkwardly turned away. "Can I have my dagger back?" he asked Elder Tor in Khasiri, tempering the hitch in his voice.

"Ah, yes. Ram, be a good lad and return the blade to our old friend." Elder Tor's face creased with a thousand wrinkles when he smiled at Malek.

Ram, the warden, hesitated and then handed back the weapon.

"I would not have recognized you if not for that blade," Tor said.

"Good thing you did then. Thanks." Malek nodded at him. "What did you need to ask me?"

"That item you left here... oh, where is it now? It has very curious properties. Quite alarming, actually. When word came of the Fireborne invading human land... ruthless, that one was... we added several, ah, security measures to ensure that the artifact would be kept safe."

Malek frowned. "...Safe?"

"From the humans... and the Keepers... Just as you asked."

What had Valerio said about the Keepers at the briefing? Slag, he wished he remembered. "Right, yes, that's obvious. But what were the added security measures?"

"We began taking turns keeping the item with one person. Randomly and frequently changing the bearer. If we had an invader, one could slip away. However, the artifact had egregious effects on some of my people. Farduk, a most dedicated brave, was the latest victim. I believe he may have attacked your people."

Wallace. He was talking about the Earthborne mutant. Valerio had been right... slag, why was she always right? "The matter has been dealt with," Malek managed, although not as convincingly as he hoped.

"Oh?"

"Yes, defeated in combat. He sought another, uh, artifact. No different than the Fireborne. Both Elemnai were abnormal. Neither survived."

Elder Tor's face darkened as he reached into his robes. Malek inwardly palmed his face when the Earthborne pulled out a shard from one of the wrappings over his chest. The shard's twisted metal glistened under the moonlight. If he could convince the Earthborne to give it to him, maybe he and his team would walk out of here in one piece.

248

"The illness...perhaps a side effect of the artifact?" Tor mused, staring into the metal fragment hexagonal motif, its surfaces gleaming under the flickering torchlight.

Malek pushed his luck a little more and added, "A sickness is spreading to your people, and the artifact may be to blame. I need to move it to another location."

Elder Tor, frail as he was, snapped to attention. "But you entrusted us! We are meant to keep this world safe from its purpose. It is well-hidden here."

"Look at what this is doing to your people. Look at what Farduk did to the Al-Khasari. Your people are not safe." Something caught Malek's eye. A small shadow appeared at the edge of Preikrock's flat surface. It was... a head? He eyed it momentarily. Someone was watching. When Elder Tor traced his stare, Malek placed himself in between and continued, "Farduk was looking for the other artifacts to assemble. He said someone was going to kill you all if you failed. The humans and the Keepers, as you said. This is *not* the mission I gave you, right? I didn't ask you to put yourselves in danger."

"Of course not. Farduk was ill. Both in mind and body. He...he was confused. It is forbidden to assemble the device of the Anymm. We all know death awaits us. You taught us that. As such, we cannot part with it. Forgive us, Shahada. The Al-Khasari lack strength in numbers. We will find some other way to hide the artifact."

Malek was lost for words, scavenging his mind for a solution while maintaining his grip on this persona. A cracking sound came from behind Ram, and before Malek could identify the newcomer, a booming voice filled the tense silence between them. His muscles instantly stiffened, and his heart hammered to the rhythm of Virat's thunderous accusations.

"Do not believe a word out of this scum, Elder!" Virat roared in Khasiri and furiously stepped up to Malek with something in hand. Virat threw it at Malek's feet. He cursed himself. Virat had presented one of their jackets—Nikita's jacket, specifically, with the remnants of an Alliance insignia threaded on the shoulder. "You may look like Shahada, but he was not a slave of the Alliance. The human is either a traitor or a liar!"

Malek stepped back, clenching his fist around the dagger. He glowered at Virat, feeling a haze begin to surround him. His senses heightened and drowned in a cascade of hyperfocus and adrenaline. It was happening again... the seconds before another blackout. His senses begged him to let go and do whatever it took to survive. No... he needed to hold it together.

Both Elder Tor and Ram looked at each other incredulously before turning back to Malek. "Is this true?" Elder Tor's voice quivered. "The Alliance has sent you?"

"I sent myself," Malek bit back. "I'm not leaving without the shard. Hand it over, or I'll *take* it. No one is safe while it's here."

"Virat, perhaps it is best to allow him—" Ram reached over and touched the Earthborne brave, who snapped his shoulder out of reach.

"No! He cannot be trusted. I do not care what he is. He is no longer our ally if he is with the Alliance."

"Open your eyes and look what it's doing to our people." Ram begged. "Several have died or malformed, and Farduk has already wreaked chaos on the Al-Khasari. Fear retribution, Virat. Remember what happened to the Windborne of Bhajjan."

"Silence!" Virat whipped around with his fingers curled into a tight fist. He swung backward, and a slab of rock rose from the floor, violently slamming into Ram and pushing him back against the wall with a heavy snap.

Malek's eyes went wide. He threw a sympathetic glance at Ram, who cowered on the floor, unable to move a muscle in the face of Virat's unquenchable anger. Malek clenched his jaw, glaring back at Virat. "You have no idea what you're dealing with."

Run, Malek. This is not your fight. Malek closed his eyes. That wasn't his voice. It was that familiar whisper. He looked down at the blade, shimmering under the moonlight. A pulling sensation lingered in his palm as if his hand had brushed invisible strings. Malek's eyes lifted to Elder Tor, and time had slowed. The aged Earthborne's face contorted with fear, wrinkling more, if that was even possible. Malek felt the pull again and fixated on the shard in the Elder's grasp. He could almost see a thread of light, disappearing the moment he blinked, stretching from his palm to the twisted metal surface.

Not without that, Malek thought, answering the stranger's voice in his mind.

Malek's hand lurched backward the instant the shard flew into his grasp. The cold metal tingled against his skin, like a surge of electricity coursing through the synapses of his nerves. Its weight bore down on his palm—a welcome check on reality. He let out a sharp breath, hardly able to piece together what he had just done. Without sparing another second, he charged toward the precipice of the cliff.

A wave of relief burst from within when Nikita emerged to meet him, lifting her upper body over the edge and reaching out one hand. "Here!"

Malek skidded to his knees and passed her the shard. "Rappel back down."

"Got it."

"Go!" Malek's heart leaped into his throat when he heard that same terrifying cracking noise. Virat pounded the earth with a powerful blow of his fist. Jagged, rocky spikes shot up, slithering to Malek at a ravenous speed, splitting the ground as the fissure approached. He waited until the last microsecond, until the attack barely met the tip of his boots, before every muscle in his limbs and core lurched his body sideways, rolling and dodging the blow as it shattered the ledge.

His mind flew to Nikita, who he hoped would manage to avoid the stone shrapnel from the attack, before a hammering vibration shivered up his legs when he rebalanced himself. Each one of Virat's steps quaked the ground as he charged forward. Malek hadn't taken into account how fast the Earthborne could move. Virat shot one arm forward before he could parry or sidestep another blow and seized Malek by his throat. If Malek had learned anything from Saifain, he wasn't about to let another Earthborne beat him into submission. He instinctively curled his body and wrapped his legs around the hulking arm, ignoring the crushing grip on his throat while he wielded his dagger and drove it into Virat's wrist. The Earthborne howled, and Malek lost all the air in his lungs when he slammed back on the ground.

Virat didn't waste any time on his advance. Fragments of jagged rock rocketed toward his hands, forming a plate of serrated knuckles. Malek rolled onto his back just in time to block a stone-plated fist about to bear down on him. His dagger instantly found its way between and into Virat's massive arm as he crossed it against the attack. A fury engulfed Virat's golden eyes as he grimaced, either in pain or in absolute frustration. But this time, Malek couldn't give him an inch. His mind fixated on the giant frame of the Earthborne.

That whisper threaded something barely discernible through his already panicked mind. *Pull him off, and run. Pull...*

Malek blinked. His peripheral vision rippled around him, and he homed in on that stranger's voice echoing in his rattled thoughts. He had no idea what it meant, but he willed it anyway. *Pull him off*, the words echoed again.

The seconds played out like a vivid hallucination. Virat lifted several inches and snapped backward like someone had yanked a rope from behind. He soared and tumbled against Ram, who had been wavering as if he wasn't sure if he should join the fight. Malek exhaled in relief, unable to grasp what had just happened. Did *he* do that?

Malek's feet were already off the ground again the moment he stood. He didn't see the column of earth erupting from beneath him, barely giving him a second to process. Malek groaned in agony as his bones crunched together, both from the impact of the stone and from hitting and rolling on the ground again. He didn't anticipate rolling as far as he did. The feeling of the cold, hard earth against his skin disappeared, replaced by a sudden weightlessness, then a stomach-turning lurch as he tumbled off the cliff.

Chapter 26

Earthrise

M alek reacted instantly. He plummeted several meters, narrowly missing Nikita as he reached for the rappel line below her. Every muscle in his hands and arms cramped, and the skin on his palm peeled under the friction of the line while the other hand gripped the dagger. Nikita screamed something at him, but Malek couldn't make it out. The agony rode over his senses, and he was still getting his bearings when she shouted at him several more times.

Regaining his focus, Malek's eyes widened as he finally understood. Nikita snapped her gaze from him and then back to the cliff's edge. Even in the darkness, Virat's towering frame was hard to miss. He stood, watching them imperiously, then raised his hands again.

"Go, Commander!" Nikita cried, and Malek's insides shot up into his chest as he and Nikita plummeted down the line as fast as their bodies would allow. Malek planted one foot on the rock wall as the line shuddered. He drew in a deep breath and looked up. His senses fired with horrifying anticipation. Virat slammed a fist into the earth with another audible crack, and immediately, spines of rock ripped toward Malek down the vertical face.

"Valerio!" he cried. "Left!"

Nikita's swift reaction shocked Malek as they both sidestepped the attack simultaneously. Virat lost a second to cursing, or at least that's what Malek assumed

253

it was. He and Nikita slid down the line even faster than he had ever attempted on a rappel line before. Virat launched another assault.

Focusing on the attack, Malek counted the seconds. "Right!" he bellowed orders up to Nikita. In unison, they dodged the next assault.

Virat screamed in frustration at the second evasion, and Malek knew that wasn't good. He stared up at Virat, then down. His breath left him as he eyed the several hundred-meter drop into the trees below. He couldn't see the others. They weren't going to make it! Malek didn't have a moment to consider their next move before it was decided for them. The tension in the line snapped, and he choked back a cry.

Malek couldn't tell if it had been the wind or Nikita's scream that deafened him as they plummeted. He focused on the treetops that were fast approaching. He managed to seize Nikita's hand.

Slow it down. Pull back. That same strange voice managed to cut through the noise and burrow into his mind.

Malek blinked, and it lasted an eternity. The air was cold, but its sharpness had dulled into a breeze. It might have lasted only a second, but it was enough. The fall hadn't ended with bone-breaking finality, but with the jarring tangle of branches catching them on the way down. Malek's body still lurched to a terrifying halt, and he groaned with every nip and slash against his skin. He tore through the bough and collapsed onto the grassy floor with a forceful thud.

The pain oozed through his body for a moment, like a splash in a puddle, before it dissipated completely. Nikita's broken cries echoed through the cracking and whipping of snapping branches overhead. Before Malek had a chance to turn over, a weight dropped onto his back, sending a wave of new pain that, too, disappeared as quickly as it spread. Nikita moaned as she rolled off, her hands wringing around the shard still in her grasp, and her eyes clamped shut.

"Oh good, you still have it," Malek quickly stood. "Good job."

"I *hate* you."

"Get up, Valerio. Where are the others?" He extended his hand and lifted her. Before she could answer, Nikita flinched and whimpered, losing her balance on one leg. Malek quickly scanned her limb as she grasped his shoulder. Blood flowed from a slash across her knee and thigh. Even in the darkness, Malek could see the dark stain blooming from the wound.

"Slag…" He stopped his hand from reaching over to apply pressure to the wound. That tone was laced with venom. Nikita *really* hated him. And honestly, he probably had it coming.

Another sound stole his attention. Malek recognized the distinct trill of the belay device sliding over a wire, and it sent a shiver up the back of his neck, filling him with both anticipation and dread. He snapped his gaze toward the steps fast approaching from the cliff. Malek didn't need to guess who it was.

"Here!" Malek called, but his voice was weak.

Within seconds, a dark figure sprang from between the trees. "Commander!" Vivika hissed. Spying Nikita's injury immediately, she panted and quickly slid a shoulder under Nikita's other arm to steady her.

Malek spotted two others emerging from the tree line. He locked eyes with Gene and Casey, their faces pale from fatigue and panic while sucking in one breath after another. "Are you two okay?" he asked, and they both nodded silently and stared at him more intently than usual. Something had changed. They feared him more than the echoing roars in Umbar'ok overhead. But it didn't matter. All that mattered was his promise: he'd get them out alive and get the shard out, no matter the cost. Their faith in him as a commander—even as a person—might be gone, but Malek would put everything he had on the line. If they were going to make it out of the Wilds, he couldn't leave a damn thing to chance.

The thunderous voices multiplied in number and pitch, causing Malek's core to tremble. Everyone followed Malek's gaze as he lifted it upward.

"Paladin inbound… ETA to EZ: fifteen minutes!" Bastion's voice pulled at Malek's attention. Malek found it strange that Bastion was also breathing sharply, and his voice seemed a little different… less clear and filled with static. "Are you almost there?!"

"No, Kit's injured," Vivika grunted.

Malek signaled for Gene to take his place and hold Nikita.

"Got you, love," Gene spoke solemnly. "Commander, we have to move fast."

"Not with her leg we won't!" Casey barked, instinctively stepping away from the tree line as the voices grew louder.

A haze surrounded him again. Like caught in a dream, he was speaking without thought as the words spilled out beyond his control. "Yes, you will." Malek narrowed his eyes at her, then at Gene and Vivika. "Get to the EZ."

"What about you?" Vivika's words, cautious and grave, rippled in his periphery.

"I'll buy you some time. Run."

"Negative!" Gene glanced at Vivika. "We can't let you do that, Commander!"

Malek didn't understand that exchange, but his heart leaped when Vivika slid out and reached for him, firmly grasping his arm with both hands.

Her desperate words cut deeply, her fingers digging into his flesh. "I'm not letting you out of my sight!" she hissed, hazel eyes wide and frenzied. "Not again!"

It probably would have sent a flutter through him if it weren't for the rising screams in Umbar'ok that filled the silence that followed. Malek scowled when no one moved, and he jerked his shoulder away. "I said *go!*"

Hurt swelled in Vivika's eyes, and she retreated to Nikita. Slag, he wished he hadn't seen that...but they were losing their window for escape, and fast.

"...Commander?" Nikita finally said as she was turned away. "Please... don't kill them."

Malek scoffed and turned his attention back to the trees and the looming cliff. It wasn't until the beat of his teammates' footsteps finally faded that he allowed himself to process those words. *Don't kill them*...he thought cynically. Not the first time he had heard that. Killing was part of the job. He'd accepted it and disconnected from it long ago. But this time, those words scared him. He'd chosen to be here and face these odds alone.

This night would decide the future of the Elemnai and the humans... and Malek stood at the epicenter of the coming quake. It came down to him and what he was about to do. But that wasn't what scared him the most. It was bittersweet to be present for what would have been another blackout. Malek had always been terrified of what he had done, not of what he could do. This was the first time he embraced it. He wasn't a kid anymore. He wasn't just a soldier, either. He was a commander. His people depended on him to survive, and slag, he owed them that much... especially Nikita, who shouldn't have been dragged into this in the first place. Withholding was no longer an option. It was time to accept that there was no going back—to embrace Malek Reza, in all his chaos.

Malek looked around for the dagger. That sensation returned. A pull, like a brush against a string, tickled the palm of his hand. He reached out as if greeting an old friend. The dagger, just like the shard moments earlier, flew into his grasp from the foliage. The blade cut through the air with a sharp sound and flashed under the moonlight with an iridescent violet hue. Malek would have been amazed by this newfound ability, but it was too surreal. Yet *he* was doing it. And this time, he reveled in being aware of it all. He repeated his old mantra in his already stretched mind—stay in control and stay focused.

The roars of the Earthborne drew near. Malek's feet planted firmly in the ground as it rumbled beneath his stance, readying for the coming assault.

The weapon knows you. It was that voice again.

Malek shook his head violently. He had enough to deal with... going psycho was the last thing he needed. The shape of a man flickered next to him. Malek watched it blink in and out of his view, like something in a glitched reality.

His heart raced as a shadowed hand slipped over his grip on the dagger. *Wield it.*

It disappeared. Adrenaline raged through his system, and his nerves sent electric shocks through his limbs. His senses became attuned to the screams, the trembling air, and the sudden cracking beneath his feet as the earth tore apart.

Malek leaped aside in time to dodge the sinkhole that took his place. His eyes narrowed at the hulking figure springing from the forest. Virat soared over him, bounding off a pillar of stone that flung his massive form into the air. Shards of rock gathered at his fist and merged into a sharpened spike. There was no time to move.

Malek flexed his arms, both hands firmly gripping the dagger that had knocked the stone askew. He had never owned such strength before. Virat came down again, sideways and overhead, with such intensity that Malek could feel the air pulse with every thrust he parried. Virat screamed, shaking Malek's insides. This guy needed to shut up!

Malek spun on his heel. The environment warped within a fraction of a second. He swiftly and forcefully landed a back-kick directly against Virat's center. The Earthborne gasped and flew back several meters, clutching his stomach and gagging for breath. Malek's jaw dropped. That was new!

No time for celebrating. A wave rippled through the air, and time slowed just enough. Malek tilted his head aside, and a stone projectile grazed his jaw. He sidestepped several more with lightning reflexes he was far from used to and knocked one aside with his dagger. The incoming quartet of Earthborne braves, towering males and agile females clad in rock armor over cloth and muscle, lunged from the tree line. Malek gripped the dagger with one hand and wiped the blood streaming down his cheek with the other.

Wield it! the voice hissed, and the dagger shuddered in his grasp.

"Frag, let me focus!" Malek cried aloud, momentarily stunning a female Earthborne with clay-red locs, pausing her assault of stone spikes. She stepped back, reaching for the ground and pulling from the earth like a weed. It morphed in her grasp, bending to her will and forming a long staff, fitted with a sharpened crescent blade at the tip that glittered in the moonlight. How was it shining? It was a mineral, not just any rock... diamond, maybe? Could the Earthborne manipulate carbon like that?

Malek's blood ran cold as she and another bearded male, who formed a similar scythe, charged forward. A third figure, a female embellished in gold, launched projectile after projectile. Malek defended himself and parried the stone spikes. Lifting the dagger to block the edge descending upon him from the red-haired female, he left himself exposed. The air left his lungs. A sharp pain radiated from his side, nearly blinding him. He resisted the urge to pull out the spike lodged just above the right edge of his hip. Malek clenched his teeth, using every ounce of strength he could muster to push back against the Earthborne. If he wavered, the blade would split him. Slag... if this kept up, then Malek might actually end up murdering these Earthborne during another blackout. Valerio would never let him hear the end of it.

Okay, okay, do your thing! Malek thought furiously. He stared into the Earthborne's amber eyes just beyond the edge of the dagger as she snarled at him.

The blade erupted in a brilliant violet light. It startled both Malek and the Earthborne, causing her to stumble back, and giving Malek a chance to evade the wild swing of her spear. When the aura faded, Malek realized it wasn't just a dagger. The same dark blade was longer, curving slightly at the tip. It was... a saber? No. Not just a saber. Malek grinned savagely and seized the handle, letting the wild pulses in his fingers guide his next move. With a click, he pried apart a blade within another blade. Two sabers!

Was it the dagger or Malek himself that triggered this? Or both? For once, he regretted ever suppressing these blackouts in the past. With his newfound strength, stamina, and the otherworldly weapons gripped in each hand, he was unstoppable. Imagine what he could have accomplished. He could have changed nearly everything in his past, if only he had known. Imagine...even the Alliance wouldn't have been able to stop him. Malek dropped into a fighter's stance, blades in each hand, angled at his sides. He could hardly contain a smile when the bearded male and gold-embellished female Earthborne exchanged fearful glances before looking to Virat. Another male brave, paler than the rest, was helping him to his feet.

"Kill him!" Virat roared. Malek was surprised he was still speaking in Khasiri... as if he wanted Malek to know the threat. "He is a *traitor* and deserves to *die*!"

The pair in front of Malek raised their weapons in defense, narrowing their fierce eyes back on him. *Round 2, it is...*

Malek was about to lunge forward when he heard Virat speak again... this time in Umbar'ok. He caught a glimpse of a massive arm in his periphery, gesturing at Malek, before turning away. Something was wrong. Virat bolted.

He was going after the others! They wouldn't reach the Paladin in time!

Malek panicked. This triggered another violent rush of adrenaline. All he could hear was his own heartbeat. Virat and the pale Earthborne brave had already disappeared from sight, meaning the others only had moments... He had no choice but to parry the incoming assault from all three Earthborne, who continued their relentless advance. The sabers clashed with every brutal impact of the blades and projectiles. They weren't holding back. Malek's muscles quivered under each powerful blow as he sidestepped, spun out, and dodged to spare his body the exhaustion and pain. He didn't have a moment to break through and save his team.

"Mace!" Malek jumped and skidded backward. He crossed the blades just in time to shatter another bolt, sending fragments of dust and pebbles across his face. Malek shook his head to clear the debris and ran his wrist over the moisture trickling down his temple. The crimson stain left on his hand ignited a wave of fury that burned through his limbs. He needed to finish this fight. *Now.*

The air around him pulsed, electrifying with threads of light as he charged forward. The red-haired female anticipated this and lunged, swinging the great scythe in his path. Malek skidded to his knees and rolled his spine backward to evade the blade, sliding directly under the Earthborne. He didn't second guess himself and slashed at her legs. An ear-piercing shriek rang out, and Malek held his breath and dashed toward the female in gold launching an onslaught of fresh stone missiles. The ground nearly cracked from the force of his run. It trembled beneath his feet, and he pushed ahead, knocking away two more stone spikes. The saber turned over in his grasp. He drove a hard fist into her chin before impaling the second blade into her thigh as he landed back on the ground.

A horrifying, violent thrust in his side threw Malek several meters from the second target. Agony coursed through him like magma, wave after wave forcing him to cry out despite the urge to stifle it. He knelt on the ground, clutching his ribcage with both sabers still in hand, searching for the third Elemnai. He watched the stone pillars sink back into the earth, starting from the source of the assault: the bearded male brave, who had one palm raised. Malek breathed heavily, finding it impossible to take in anything. It was now or never. He charged straight for the stone protrusions before they could retreat into the ground.

Malek bounded onto the final, tallest structure and leaped off with sabers in hand. He soared higher than he ever imagined he could jump, feeling as if he were lighter, with a force pushing at his heels. He revelled in the newfound strength and the sheer terror reflected in the final Earthborne's face. The scythe rose just in time to meet Malek's first strike. He used the blow as leverage and flipped over the Earthborne. It was disturbing how easy it was—like cutting through butter—bringing down the second blade directly over the limb gripping the spear. The male Earthborne howled, clutching his missing hand as blood spewed from the wound in a sickening crimson pool on the grass.

Malek drew one sharp breath after another, scanning all three defeated Earthborne braves with a stark mix of satisfaction and misery. He hated doing this... but in some unsettling way, it was familiar... like he had trained for this his entire life. Only he hadn't. He was just an ASF Officer, which was a feat in itself, but not as unworldly as single-handedly defeating three Earthborne braves.

Malek would have to bear the consequences one way or another. His mind flew to Virat and his team's safety. They were undefended. A new rush of Umbar'ok voices echoed in the distance. Malek's dread intensified, tensing every muscle along his spine.

"I don't know if you can understand me," he growled viciously in Khasiri, locking eyes with each brave, one by one, as they knelt and lay beaten and bleeding. "But if you or your people follow me, I promise it will end far worse. I don't *want* to kill you. I *will* if I have to."

Malek spun around and raced into the forest thicket. He couldn't afford to lose another second.

CHAPTER 27

WINDFALL

The ache in Nikita's leg swelled like the tide with every step. Between the harsh grip of her teammates on her trunk, the exhaustion of limping through the dark, and the relentless surge of terror, Nikita kept feeling as if her body was failing her. She whimpered, stumbling over small stones in her path that marked the edge of the forest. Never in her life had she wished so much that she had just stayed home.

"There! I see it!" Vivika exclaimed through her heavy breathing. Through a sheen of hot tears, Nikita's eyes followed the direction of Vivika's finger. Across the steppe of the rocky plateau, Nikita made out the distant shape of a black aircraft perched on the grass, while the buzz of four rotary blades filled her ears.

Nikita nearly lost her grip on the shard, and Gene clutched her hand. "Almost there, love. Come on."

"I can't." Nikita wanted to sob. The pain and fatigue were unbearable. She questioned if any of this was worth it.

"Yes, you can. We're getting you home, Kit." Gene turned to Casey, who came up beside him. "Go on, Jaeger. Prep for liftoff. We're on the way."

"Okay. Valerio, give me the shard." Casey reached for it.

Nikita hesitated for a moment, then relented. Casey raced off with the shard in hand without another word.

At first, Nikita was unsure whether it was her trembling legs or the ground shaking. The rumbling intensified. Her eyes rounding in alarm, she looked at Gene, who stared back at her. He sensed it, too. Her heart lurched so intensely, it was as though it launched itself behind her spine. Not a second later, Nikita recognized the cry in Umbar'ok before gasping in horror as the world jolted and swam in an unfocused array of colors. Her body hit the ground hard, and the agony flared across her limbs and head. With her fingers curling over the cold rock beneath her, she tilted her body to face the sky. A massive shadow filled her view, blocking out the moonlight. Despite her head swirling, she instantly knew it was Virat. Did that mean... Malek had been defeated?

"Please, stop!" Nikita cried out in Umbar'ok, flinching and raising her palm.

The figure stopped his advance and snarled under his breath. "Never met a human who spoke to us in our tongue," Virat sneered. "Give me the artifact of the Anymm, and I will consider sparing *your* life."

"You don't understand," Nikita begged, inching away from him. "I've seen what it does to your people. You're in danger!"

"And in your filthy Alliance hands, we will be safe? You mock me."

"You will die if another Earthborne attacks the humans. I promise you that." Nikita could feel the tears swell in her eyes. "We did not come here to start a war with your people. We came here to stop a war from ever happening."

Virat approached her imperiously, and Nikita cowered. She jumped when his movement jerked to a halt, and he released a shrill cry. His arms flailed wildly, reaching for something behind him. As he spun around, Nikita had to rub her eyes to realize it was Vivika, clinging to his back with a knife buried in the crevices of his muscles. Gene was at his waist, also embedding a blade between the slats of rock armor.

"Go, Kit!" Gene hollered at her, but Virat managed to seize him by the head and launch him over the next boulder. The Earthborne's other hand grabbed Vivika by the ankle and snapped her off his back.

Nikita shielded her arms in front of her just as Virat threw Vivika straight into her. They both moaned as they rolled off one another, hardly a moment to recover from the assault. Nikita's heart pulled into her throat. She clutched Vivika's arm in terror. Virat's thunderous howl shook the earth beneath her as he charged again with nothing between him and the two women.

Nikita couldn't understand it, then, when a powerful hurling force sent the Earthborne brave flying off his feet. Dust and detritus raged in the Earthborne's wake as the wind erupted and settled, all in a matter of seconds. Her curls beat against her cheek in a gentle breeze, while someone carefully lifted her to her feet.

"I've got you, Dr. Valerio," a young man said, wrapping one arm around her trunk. Nikita shook her head to regain focus. It was Bastion's voice... only, this time, it wasn't resonating from her earpiece. Nikita craned her neck to look up at her rescuer. As light and color returned to sharpened figures, Nikita stared in absolute marvel and confusion.

"B-Bastion?" she stammered. "You're... you're a..."

The man beside her, who was not a man at all, looked sheepish and anxious all at once. His ashen, flint-toned skin contrasted with angular golden eyes, betraying his human qualities. Deep slate-colored hair flailed across a sharp, young face, though it was in disarray as it tangled around six short, curved ebony horns jutting from the apex of his skull. Nikita forgot how scared she had been moments before. Now, she was speechless and hopelessly enthralled. Bastion was an *Elemnai*... an Elemnai working for the Alliance!

Nikita blinked, piecing together what had just happened. "Did you just...hit him with a blast of...*wind*?"

"Yes, I am a Windborne. I'll explain later," Bastion said, his voice as mellow as it had ever been. His long, toned arm reached for Vivika, and he also pulled her to her feet.

"Slag!" she squealed, reaching over and pinching Bastion on the cheek. "You're real? You're really real?!"

"Of course I'm real." Bastion furrowed his straight eyebrows, swatting her hand away. "No time to discuss. Lieutenant Kei, I need a gunner on the Paladin. Deter the Earthborne's advances and protect our transport. Get it in the air. Can you see to it?"

"*Se*... You got our girl?"

"I will bring her. Go!" Nikita's eyes remained fixed on his face as Bastion darted his eyes toward the ledge above them. "Major Anduran, are you hurt?"

Nikita heard the major's voice resonate several meters from her. He groaned, then cursed in such a way that his deep voice nearly cracked from the shock. "What the frag?! Is that Bastion?"

"Agent Jaeger is attempting to pilot the Paladin. Please assist her. There is no crew—it's just me."

"Understood, mate."

Nikita had no idea whether she was blushing or bleeding. Her face radiated with heat when Bastion finally looked at her. "Dr. Valerio? Where is the commander?"

"H-He," Nikita croaked. She cleared her throat and swallowed her shock. "He was behind us, trying to slow down the Earthborne."

"He's alive. The commander does not die easily," Bastion assured her. Nikita hardly had a moment to process the words when Bastion firmly gripped her just as they flew backward. It wasn't a violent lurch but a graceful leap. The crisp wind blanketed them, carrying Nikita and Bastion away from the incoming projectiles. An onslaught of spear-like missiles rained down where they had stood, shattering into the ground and sending shrapnel flying in all directions. Bastion called the wind to guide them out of harm's way, smoothly taking them further down the plateau.

Virat's roar from the peak of the hill rippled through the air around them. Nikita's dread silenced her when a dozen other Earthborne braves appeared from the forest line, charging down the slope like raging oxen. Bastion was only one Windborne... against so many.

"I need you to hang on!" he cried out.

Nikita did as she was told and hugged Bastion's middle, only now realizing how tall he was. He towered almost half a meter over her. His delicate face morphed into a fierce look of determination. Bastion raised his arm, a subtle twist of his wrist sending his will rippling outward. The winds picked up, whipping Nikita's hair against her bare skin. She gasped in horror as several Earthborne initiated a series of synchronous, steady movements with their arms, commanding the very planet to abide by their attacks.

The adrenaline forced the words back into her throat. "Bastion, look out!"

The winds violently raged in a sphere surrounding the two of them. Shards of rock raining down upon the pair shattered and deflected as they impacted the furious airstreams swirling into a protective wall.

Spears the size of marble columns missed her and Bastion as they flipped sideways. Nikita cried out in a rush of wonder. Wind currents swiftly carried them across boulders and ledges, evading the clutches of the Earthborne's onslaught. Bastion's palms pressed flat, his fingers rigid, almost resembling a staggered prayer. Nikita sensed his chest swell with a deep inhale. It seemed as though the breath of the world had been poised to defend him against the incoming spires of rock hurtling from all directions. Projectiles continued to shatter against the force of his tempest barrier.

Nikita recoiled from their outward aggravation as the Earthborne braves altered their attack, amplifying both fury and precision. Several others began hurling boulders that raced across the ground, scarred by the impact. Her grip tightened as panic took hold. Bastion thrust his hands outward, catching the boulders as they approached, creating a fierce cyclone around them. Nikita looked at him, desperate for him to prevail. He gritted his teeth, twisting his body to force the winds to spin the boulders faster, slingshotting them back toward the braves. Several Earthborne froze, stunned upon impact, while others shattered their artillery with steadfast fists and unrelenting brawn.

Her stomach lurched horribly, and Nikita jolted, realizing she was no longer holding on to Bastion. Her body tore from his, and she slammed into the ground, rolling several times before she finally managed to stop herself. The agony was unbearable, and she fought the urge to throw up. Groaning loudly, she once again tried to concentrate through a rattled mind. A sharp popping sound echoed, rippling through the wave of disorientation, followed by the unmistakable vibration and hum of an aircraft engine. For a split second, she was that little girl again, cowering in the streets of her home city and hiding from the police helicopters. Except she wasn't back in Trelle. She was in the Wilds. The aircraft...

Nikita craned her neck just as the silhouette of the Paladin roared over her. Its hull was black against an already dark sky, so the only shape she fixated on immediately was Vivika, poised at the edge of the gunner's station flanking the Paladin's open doors, illuminated by the faint interior light of the cabin. She clutched the massive, swivel-mounted machine gun, but she stopped shooting. Nikita could see she was trying to tell her something, but her head kept swimming. Vivika snapped her arm up and down with her palm to the sky, but her voice drowned in the deep thrum of the Paladin's engines.

Nikita finally clued in. *Get up...* she needed to get up. Her head throbbed as she rose onto her one intact knee, frantically looking around for her friend. The popping noise, which had now morphed into the thunderous eruption of gunfire, snapped her back to reality as she watched Vivika precisely aim at the grassy fringe, meters away from where Nikita trembled. The Earthborne closing in staggered back, and the bullets vexed their attempts at retaliation.

A swell of gratitude managed to seep through in those microseconds. Vivika purposefully missed. She could have killed them...

Nikita's heart twisted painfully. Where was Bastion? The thought of losing him sent her reeling with dread, and she scanned the shadowy plateau. The earth where they once stood had been violently torn apart, and jagged spires of rock jutted from the ground where there should have been a soft, grassy floor. They had struck her and Bastion from directly underneath.

Finally, she spotted him. Bastion crouched several meters away, on all fours with one hand against his long, toned leg. His gargoyle-like feet clawed into the earth as he attempted to stand up. Her eyes widened at the sight of his fitted black Alliance jumpsuit, which had been cut in several places. Bastion shifted his sights from Nikita to the dozen Earthborne rushing at them... and the Paladin.

"Fall back! Protect the transport!" Bastion called out, tapping one finger against his pointed ear. Nikita knew the others understood, and just as another wave of rock projectiles launched at the Earthborne's command, the Paladin gracefully swerved and peeled away from the assault. Satisfied, Bastion rose to his feet, and Nikita's heart hammered against her bruised ribs.

All those moments where she daydreamed about meeting that mysterious voice on the other end of the receiver culminated. Nikita couldn't bear to see him hurt, especially now, as he placed himself between her and the incoming braves. Her mind retraced the source of his abilities—whatever would give him the edge. Bastion seemed limitless. The air in their lungs was his arsenal. He needed to remember that.

Nikita called out to Bastion, her voice cutting through the booming war cries. "Breathe, Bastion!" she bellowed, snapping her arms out to the side and drawing them in toward her center. His desperate expression morphed into surprise. "You just have to breathe! You can beat them!"

The Earthborne stood only steps away before Bastion had a chance to react. With renewed determination etched on his face, Bastion thrust his arms forward and unleashed a concussive blast of air so powerful that a few Earthborne braves smashed against the steep rock faces and boulders surrounding them. As more advanced, Bastion spun and relentlessly shot one violent airstream after another from the palm of his hand. He was amazing! Not that this was the best time to study the differences between the Elemnai, but Bastion was nothing like his Earthborne opponents. Every movement was dynamic and elegant, smooth and robust all at once. Literally, he moved like the wind.

Raising stone barriers had not been enough to stop the fury of Bastion's attack from shattering the rock. The Earthborne were growing wary of him. Nikita inwardly cheered him on, banking on his victory at any moment. With one smooth gesture, Bastion swung his arm around and enveloped himself in a swirling tempest. Pushing his hands out to the sides, he unleashed another cyclone that sent the remaining Earthborne scattering and backing away. Nikita reached for him just as he turned to face her.

Her smile instantly vanished when Virat's gargantuan figure tore through the other braves faster than Nikita could comprehend. He charged ahead with the earth pushing him at his heels. Bastion didn't have a chance to see him. Her heart dropped like a stone into her center, wanting to warn him.

It all happened in a second. Virat's massive hand reached for Bastion's head. The moment those enormous fingers grasped him, Virat slammed Bastion into the ground with a violent crash that shattered the earth. Virat's other hand rose, and the surrounding debris formed a stone-like spear around his monstrous fist.

It was as if the world froze. All Nikita could do was scream and beg that rage-filled face to stop.

A spark of iridescence flashed over a sudden outpouring of liquid crimson. A figure rose skyward, leaping from behind Virat and silhouetting against the moon. Nikita stared up in awe.

Virat's face drained, and he released Bastion, just in time to turn and parry a dark blade coming down. Nikita choked at the sight of the slash across Virat's shoulder. It split flesh from his torso, pouring blood like a river down the ridges of his muscles. The blade shattered Virat's spear into fragments and cut across the brave's chest. Another burst of light streaked as the attacker slid under Virat and drove both blades into his calves.

It happened so fast that Nikita hardly recognized Malek until he kicked over Virat and planted one heel on the Earthborne's chest. Blood and dust had caked and smeared across Malek's bare skin, from his forehead to his arms. His indigo eyes flashed a deathly glare at Virat's horrified expression. Malek never allowed him to speak. He pressed one blade inside Virat's mouth, and Nikita watched the Earthborne swallow his agony and fury.

"Touch him again, and I'll *end* you," Malek raged between breaths. At that moment, he seemed far more terrifying than any of the Earthborne they faced tonight. Nikita's blood ran cold when he spoke again in Khasiri. Nikita knew it was the same message, but his voice sounded gritty and exacting.

Despite it, Nikita forced herself to stand and limp toward Bastion. He was already sitting up, grasping his head, and moaning softly.

"Valerio," Malek growled. "Translate for me."

"Why?" she replied, roping one arm around Bastion's waist as he stood.

"I need them *all* to understand something."

Nikita's insides twisted with hesitation, but she knew they still needed to escape, if that was what Malek intended to relay. Whatever hope she had of leaving this place untouched had been utterly dashed. Maybe she never wanted to be like the Alliance, but she still managed to destroy her chances of peaceful coexistence with the Earthborne... even though she knew, deep down, that her reasons were benign.

Nikita felt mentally defeated. After a moment, she looked to Bastion, who reassured her with a slight nod. With a deep exhale, Nikita translated his words as Malek spoke, loud enough that Virat and the few Earthborne around them could hear:

"Tell them that the fight is over. We walk out of here, with the shard. If anyone so much as throws a pebble our way, *I'm* coming back for them. The shard is not safe here. If they keep it, more monsters will come crawling out of this place, and they risk a full-scale war with the Alliance. And if that Anymm comes back looking for it, you tell them to find Malek Reza."

For the briefest second, Nikita caught Virat's eyes flicker at the name. He could only gag with Malek's blade between his teeth.

"Valerio, Bastion, get in the Paladin and get going." Malek twisted the blade slightly, causing Virat to choke on the blood dripping from the corner of his mouth.

It was over. Nikita wanted to leave this place rather than bear another second standing in her failures. She froze in her steps as Malek's last order hung in her ear. "What about you?" She turned back to face him, Bastion following her lead.

Malek staunchly kept his focus on Virat. Nikita's insides tightened. Then he glanced over his shoulder, with a sliver of despair clawing out from behind his eyes. She had seen that look before when they stood face-to-face. She remembered the tremble in his hands as they gripped hers, back in that small room in Kaira.

"Commander," Bastion said before Nikita could pull together a response, "please...return to the Paladin. I..." He exhaled, in pain or hesitance, Nikita wasn't sure. His voice dropped a pitch. "I meant what I said. We have much to discuss."

The realization hit Nikita, and her lungs emptied. "Please, don't leave. Not now." She desperately stared him down as if that alone would convince him.

After what seemed like an eternity, Malek finally nodded. "Give me a minute."

Nikita could hardly imagine explaining to the team that Malek *wanted* to be left behind, and she was grateful that Bastion had succeeded in convincing their commander. They walked side by side, both hobbling away. The drone of the

Paladin filled her ears, and Nikita stumbled as the craft gracefully swerved in front of them, hovering over a patch of grass. She could still see Vivika at the turret, aiming at the Earthborne crowded on the hill, where wardens and divines tended to wounded braves.

Bastion had fought many... but not this many. Had Malek caused all of this? An Earthborne brave paced the gap between the Elemnai and the Paladin, bellowing and narrowing his eyes from Nikita to his people. She never bothered to translate, though she caught a few words. He was relaying the same message that Malek had delivered. It was an odd feeling to have so many Earthborne eyes on her at once. She could sense the anger and fear. The air hung thick with tension, carrying whispers in Umbar'ok of invaders and traitorous Al-Khasari.

Would they know what they tried to accomplish here tonight? Would they know that they'd been spared an even worse fate by letting go of the shard? Was that not the point of all this?

"Are you all right, Dr. Valerio?" Bastion's gentle voice trembled.

"For now." Nikita broke free of her brooding and tried to smile. "You were amazing, Bastion."

"Thank you."

"You said you weren't fit for field work. Liar." Nikita exchanged glances with him, and he chuckled.

"I have corrective lenses. Does that count?"

Nikita tried to imagine Bastion wearing glasses, and it warmed her heart for a fleeting moment. They reached the flank of the Paladin, where Vivika had already abandoned her post at the gunner's station, ready to pull them in.

Bastion perked up, as if summoning the last dregs of his energy to assume his usual polite disposition. "Ah. You managed to protect the Paladin. Thank you, Lieutenant Kei."

"It was a group effort. I had some great pilots." She winked. "In you get, Bastion."

Vivika hauled them into the cabin. Nikita slumped against the seat behind the co-pilot's chair. She shivered, despite her muscles burning. Something soft fell onto her lap as Vivika pulled apart the fabric around her leg injury to get started with the med kit. Bastion knelt next to her and covered her bare arms with the blanket given to her.

"I never thought I would be so happy to see an Elemnai," Gene chuckled from the co-pilot's seat.

Bastion shifted from a swift pat on his shoulder, inadvertently knocking into Nikita. Her face flushed hot again.

"That was incredible, mate," Gene added.

"Wasn't it though?" Bastion said with a nervous laugh. "I mean, certainly... I know it was dangerous, reckless even... But that was my first time in the field. Maida is undoubtedly going to *murder* me."

"And us," Casey muttered from the pilot's seat. Nikita glanced at her, but she staunchly kept her gaze forward, shifting her focus between the Earthborne onlookers and the lines of the color flashing against the canopy's HUD. The ominous inflection in her words instantly changed the mood within the cabin. Bastion's gaze lowered. Vivika's expression darkened. Everyone fell into a dreadful silence.

"Where is the commander?" Vivika asked at last, barely above a whisper. "Is he safe?"

"Safe?" Nikita scoffed, then winced at the sharp sting of antiseptic. "Did you see what he did out there?"

"Everyone did."

Another scaffold in the tension. Nikita looked at Bastion, who seemed just as anxious. It was easy to understand why everyone looked scared. A Windborne Elemnai as an Alliance Officer was an incredible shock in its own right, yet whatever the reasons for Bastion's existence, it could be explained. But Malek? How could anyone explain that anomaly? Had he been capable of this all along? Why did he hide it?

A figure emerged at the mouth of the Paladin's open doors. Nikita looked toward the opening just as Malek stepped into the craft. She could see, despite his tired, brutal appearance, that his demeanor instantly changed when he locked eyes with everyone in the cabin. He said nothing at first. He took both sabers and inserted one into the other as if it were a routine procedure.

In a great flash of light, the dagger reappeared in his hand. Nikita stared at it, wide-eyed and speechless. Another mystery... Malek was running a list of things he needed to explain. He never bothered, unsurprisingly, and turned away, clutching one of the overhanging bars. "Casey, let's get the frag out of here," his voice was gravelly and quiet.

"Yes, sir," Casey responded, and Gene entered the cabin to allow Bastion to take his place in the cockpit.

Nikita noticed a subtle exchange between Gene and Vivika before she urged him to take her place in rolling the bandage around Nikita's leg. A deep hum from the engine shook her insides, and her stomach lurched as the craft lifted straight into the air. Her exhaustion intensified her vertigo as the craft made a sharp turn, prompting Malek to close the door with a thunderous slam. Malek's labored breaths filled the quiet. It was much more insulated in the Paladin's cabin than in their helicopter transport from Galeo City. Nikita drew her eyes up at him. He leaned against the door, clutching his side while suppressing a shaky moan. Malek's shirt and upper leg had been stained red, starkly contrasting against the dim, yet pale, lighting of the cabin.

"Commander," Nikita started, but Malek lifted single finger lifted from the dagger, motioning for her to stop. His eyes clamped shut, grasping at something on his side. Vivika spotted it first. She cursed aloud and seized several more sheets of gauze from the med kit. Nikita wanted to help. Her body refused to move an inch.

"Got it?" Malek murmured to Vivika, and she anxiously nodded in reply. "Pull. One... two... three..." Malek stifled an agonizing cry as he keeled over, while Vivika held out the foot-long spike, stained deep red. The rattle of the stone against metal rang out when Vivika dropped it.

Nikita stared at the blood spattered on the floor. Now it all made sense. She wasn't worried. The not-so-broken arm, the close-range shot in the chest...

"You recover...much faster than normal. Don't you?" she finally said. She didn't care whether Malek was ready to hear her out. "Things that would normally kill...they just don't kill *you*?"

"Go ahead and say 'normal' one more time, Valerio," Malek seethed through a wavering voice, sliding down against the door and seating himself on the ground.

"Apologies if it offends you, Commander," Gene interjected, shifting himself to kneel before him. "But Kit is right."

"I know she's right. So does the Alliance."

"They know about this?"

"Some."

"Including all that's happened tonight?"

"No."

"Why not?"

"Because he keeps the Alliance at arm's length," Casey shouted from the cockpit. "Did it ever occur to any of you that he keeps it a secret for a reason?"

Nikita honestly hadn't expected Casey to defend him so vigorously—nor had she considered that possibility. She looked over at Malek again. He rubbed his eyes while Vivika pressed gauze against his injury in brooding silence. Malek wasn't just suffering from physical agony or exhaustion... it was something deeper. His face had the same look she'd seen when she'd confronted him in Kaira. He was scared. If she ever wanted answers from him, she couldn't back him into a corner like she had last time.

Her eyes fell to the dagger in his grasp. "Nice toy."

She thought a smile curled at the edge of Malek's lip, but it was gone before she could be sure. "It is. Isn't it?"

"A rare loot, Commander." Bastion chimed from the cockpit. "Certainly not made by human hands. Perhaps the Elemnai? Or an Anymm artifact?"

"Where's this sudden Elemnai pride coming from? Slag, it's like you think you're impressive."

The tension within the Paladin crumbled, and everyone, including Casey, laughed aloud. Even Nikita found herself giggling, maybe a little too much. She was tired, for sure, and so was the team.

"I knew the whole time that he was an Elemnai." Malek's comment was met with several groans overlapping each other, including Nikita's meek protest.

"No, you didn't!" Vivika shot at Malek. "How?"

"He gave it away."

Bastion scoffed aloud, "No, he's wrong."

It all made for a much better conversation, anyway. Nikita listened in on the banter between her teammates for as long as she could. Her eyes grew heavy, and she curled into the soft fabric of her blanket. She fell asleep to the sound of an excited recounting of how a six-member team managed to escape the Earthborne horde... shard in hand, thanks to a few aces up their sleeves. Her final, despairing thought fixated on never visiting this place again, not after all that had happened. Tears rolled down her cheeks behind the veil of her blanket until she finally dreamt of walking side by side with her friend Johar, picking berries and revelling in the beauty and mystery of the Wilds.

Chapter 28

Secrets

Nikita studied Bastion with absolute marvel. Each action further enchanted her gaze, from pouring fresh mint tea into small wooden cups to the lemon-blueberry muffins on a steel tray Bastion scrambled to arrange. She never thought, in her wildest imagination, that she would be reconsidering her dating policy in the company of a Windborne Elemnai—among the rarest and most mysterious of all the Elemnai—especially while he was conducting the mundane task of serving them breakfast. Bastion caught her eye and immediately looked away, fixing his square-framed glasses over the low, straight bridge of his nose.

"Thank you." Nikita smiled, and he shyly returned the gesture. Her head screamed to get over herself.

Bastion placed the tray of treats over the glass table in his quaint kitchen of slate marble and black cupboards, instantly teasing Nikita's hunger. Gene, who sat across from Nikita, didn't appear to notice. She traced his gaze as he studied their surroundings.

The round table at which they sat rested on a smooth, rock-tiled floor next to an octagonal living space. Nikita basked in the warmth intruding from a massive window at the far end of the kitchen, overlooking the mesa's peak that towered over canyons of stone spires and sparse greenery. When Nikita watched the sunrise from that window, it punctuated the blue mineral strata of the auburn, ochre, and copper-toned range of the naturally thin, vertical peaks. It was a magnificent sight, and she was envious that Bastion called this home.

Beyond the canyon was the distant shadow of a forest, almost dismal in comparison to the valley itself. Stems of gathered lavender clung to the trundles between the rooms. Nikita drew in its soothing perfume, and it relaxed her. She massaged her leg perched on a stool, taking a sip of tea to comfort her senses. A dull ache radiated from the deep lacerations in her leg. Although nothing was broken, she needed to stay off it. She was envious of Malek's ability to heal. He would have already been on his feet.

Nikita's gaze drifted to Malek, who was now in the living room, either dozing or asleep on one of the several dark leather chaises positioned near the stairs leading to the kitchen. She was relieved when he showered off the blood (which he claimed was mostly his own) and dust, changing into casual Alliance loungewear like the rest of the team. He was back to his alluring, old self—damn it, she needed to stop looking at him like that. Malek was an anomaly. A fascination. And also, very dangerous.

Remembering the sight of him standing over Virat still shook her. He may not have killed, but that face... Nikita knew he'd wanted to. He had been extremely quiet, maybe frustratingly so, since arriving at Bastion's outpost somewhere on the fringe of the Teokha Mountains on Mardascan soil. Nikita had no idea what was going through his mind. Was it fear? Shame? Or could he be celebrating a silent victory? Until he opened his mouth, it was anyone's guess. Nikita never forgot the despair in his eyes when he was about to run. That little detail remained between her and Bastion, but the idea of him leaving absolutely pained her. More than anything, and though Nikita knew he would hate it, she wanted to reach out and assure Malek that things would work out, and that he shouldn't be afraid. But she even doubted whether that was the truth.

Taking her eyes off her commander, she lost herself in the walls of the octagonal living room, which had been lined with massive black bookcases overflowing with literature. Nikita thought she had a formidable collection, but Bastion put her little library to shame. Hundreds, if not thousands, of books lined the shelves that stretched up toward the central skylight high above. Casey paced around the slim stairs that spiraled the walls, disappearing beyond the comparatively low ceiling of the kitchen. She was suspiciously quiet, like Malek, eyeing Bastion's collection in stubborn isolation. On the far side of the room, before the twin steel doors that led to the rest of the outpost, a wall of floor-length windows framed Vivika as she enjoyed Bastion's small garden on the outside terrace.

"Sorry, I would have made something else if I had known you would...be *here*," Bastion spoke slowly.

Nikita snapped her gaze back at him. "Bastion, you saved us! If anything, we owe *you* breakfast."

Bastion chuckled. It was a much more exquisite, melodious laugh in person. "Well, if you did, it would have to be in my kitchen anyway. I don't, uh, get out much... at all, really."

"Wait," Gene finally spoke. "Are you not allowed to leave this place?"

Bastion solemnly shook his head, taking a seat between him and Nikita. "No. For obvious reasons. I don't believe the greater Alliance would approve of my existence. Or...anyone else for that matter."

Nikita bobbed her head, saddened by the remark.

"I'm just dying to know, mate," Gene said, releasing a lighthearted exhale. "How? How in the world are you an Alliance officer? Never mind that... How in the world are you even *here*, and not with the *other* Windborne?"

"No one has seen a Windborne in half a century." Bastion shrugged. "Except, well, since the pyroclastic eruption of Bhajjan Reach. When they found me."

"The Earthborne said something about the Windborne of Bhajjan," Malek said from the living room. He was awake after all.

"What did they say?" Nikita called back to him.

"I don't know the context. One of the guards said, 'fear retribution, remember what happened to the Windborne of Bhajjan.'"

"But a volcanic eruption is a natural event. What does the Alliance have to do with it?"

"Perhaps the context was misconstrued." Bastion furrowed his eyebrows. "I survived of the eruption. General Maida rescued me as a child, back when he was commander of Valiant Squad, our current commander's former squad."

"Hold on," Malek jumped in again. "Maida's career with Valiant Squad ended twelve years ago. When was the eruption?"

"Thirteen years ago. I remember this incident," Vivika's voice echoed from the sliding glass door as she stepped in from the terrace. "The smoke plumes covered our farm for weeks."

Nikita's eyes rounded at the remark. She did the math in her head. Ever so slowly, and somewhat painfully, her heart deflated into her chest. "How old are you?"

Bastion flattened his lips and sipped his tea.

"Bastion," Gene repeated sternly. "How old?"

"It is uncertain how Elemnai age overall. Some studies indicate that Elemnai may have shorter childhoods but longer, prime adulthoods, with overall life expectancy placing them—"

"Bastion!" Nikita repeated.

He looked very sheepish. "They... I mean, the Alliance, those involved in rearing me...They believed I had the demeanor and appearance of a five-year-old human child upon discovery."

And just like that, Nikita's policy on dating re-inflated. She blinked, staring at her tea. What was she thinking anyway? Her, and an Elemnai? Maybe this assignment left her with some brain trauma after all.

"That makes you roughly eighteen years old," Malek said. "Even in the army, eighteen-year-olds are never thrown into a firefight. If I were closer, I would smack you. Major Anduran, please do the honors."

Without missing a beat, Gene slapped Bastion on the back of the head.

"Ow! Why?" Bastion protested.

"Because you are a *child*," Gene's voice dropped into a stern rumble, "And had no business rescuing us in the Wilds... *alone*."

"Hey! It's not all his fault," Nikita interrupted, her tone edged with the guilt from complicating the extraction. "I begged him to help us."

"A-And I'm not a child! I have been an Alliance Officer for six years," Bastion stammered in his defense. "You know, I aged faster than human children. Like a dog. So, you should think of me as a dog, as opposed to a child."

Nikita heard Malek utter something in Khasiri and remembered how her parents would revert to Alcidian in public spaces to glamorize their curse words... which, truthfully, sounded much more dramatic in her native tongue. He must have been *very* upset.

Before she could gauge him, Vivika appeared beside her, arms firmly crossed under her chest. Nikita knew that look. Her own mother gave it to her so many times. "I love dogs," Vivika said. "Neither belong on the battlefield."

"I-I don't know why you're all angry with me. Would you rather that I did not extract you?" Bastion complained.

"*Yes!*" Casey shouted from the living room, but it was hardly in jest.

Nikita tilted her body to face her. A coldness settled between them as Casey's eyes narrowed on each member of the team. Her next words, no doubt, were tempered as best as she could manage. She had an undeniable tremble in her voice. Nikita knew she was stifling something... whether it was fear, anger, or both, she couldn't tell.

"Do you not realize what this all means?"

Nikita exchanged glances with the three others at the table. Bastion was the only one who seemed to know where Casey was going with this. His expression shifted, and his gaze dropped to his wringing hands.

"You have the floor, Jaeger." Gene leaned back in his chair.

"We just stumbled upon one of the Alliance's deepest secrets. For two hundred years, they spoon-fed us all that bull-slag, making us believe that the Elemnai and anyone outside the military complex were our enemies. Now look here... we not only have an Elemnai *working* for the Alliance, but he was also *raised* by the Alliance. Don't you get it?"

"I don't," Nikita finally rebuked. It was frustrating enough to be the only member of a six-person team *not* associated with the Alliance.

"Let me spell it out for you: *exile*," Casey hissed. "We are all about to be either shipped to some detention facility in the middle of the ocean, or if they're nice, we all get to find new gigs cut off from civilization. The fact that we *met* Bastion is going to *terrify* them. We are all capable of shattering the Alliance's image at the drop of a hat. That's power that you can't buy. And the Alliance *fears* power—in any shape it takes. They will do whatever is necessary to destroy it or wield it to their advantage." Casey leveled a finger at Bastion. "Don't be so sure they rescued you. And if they did, instead of returning you to your people, they made you one of their own."

Bastion's lips parted, and it took every ounce of Nikita's control to stop her emotions from boiling over. How could Casey say that to him?

Before Nikita had the opportunity to come to Bastion's defense, Malek's gritty voice cut in, "Enough, Casey." He groaned and sat up at last.

"What?" she seethed. "You of all people know that I'm right, Malek. Don't pretend that it's going to be any different this time."

"*Ralah samaamuhun*. Outside. Now."

She froze when Malek spoke to her in Khasiri, and it amazed Nikita how quickly that disarmed Casey's rage. Casey cursed under her breath and stormed off toward the terrace.

Nikita considered her argument... That couldn't really be their future, could it? She looked at Malek for reassurance. He clutched his side as he slowly stood, his lip twitching into a pained expression, his face tight as a muscle rolled in his jaw. "As you were." He turned away.

Nikita wasn't going to let this go that easily. "Is it true?" she blurted. A stark silence fell over the room.

Malek sighed, and before he left, he said, "Casey is an AIA agent. She always has to consider all angles... I'll talk to her."

Nikita heard the gentle slide of the door as it closed. She looked at Bastion, who staunchly kept his eyes on his tea. Without hesitating, she reached over and touched his hand.

"She doesn't know what she's talking about." Vivika forcefully pulled out the last chair and slumped down. She seized one of the muffins, picking at the blueberries and shoving them between her lips.

"Maybe not," Bastion murmured. "But it's a difficult concept to dismiss."

Nikita hated seeing him upset. She felt so protective of Bastion. Maybe it had to do with spending most of her academic career relentlessly defending the Elemnai. Maybe... it was guilt, for what happened last night. They desperately needed a change in topic, for his sake if not her own. "Who raised you?" she asked, lilting her inflection.

Bastion instantly perked up. "Well... effectively General Maida. He was like a father-figure. He would visit often and bring books from his travels. He always took the time to ask me questions and ensured I was comfortable. Dr. Margot Costa also raised me. She was my guardian and was always very honest about my situation. She provided me with whatever I wanted, if it could be acquired, and always ensured I had the most personable quartet of guards on-site, so I would not necessarily feel alone."

"Guards?" Nikita frowned, just as the dual heavy doors slammed from the living area. Her muscles tensed with a start.

"Who the...?!" a deep voice rumbled, approaching fast.

"Oh. Hey, it's Mose," Vivika muttered flatly, fixing the incoming soldier with a darkened expression. "Morning, sir. We met before."

"Bastion, why are these people here? Did you take the Paladin last night? Did General Maida give the order? Why was I not aware?" Mose rode over Vivika's words and never allowed them to answer. It seemed obvious that he was racing through his questions out of sheer panic, rather than genuine curiosity.

"Good morning, Lieutenant Mose. This is my team," Bastion replied without losing an ounce of professionalism. "An emergency extraction was necessary for the success of the mission."

"...But!" Mose choked and swallowed hard. "Slag... uh...Where is Commander Reza?"

"In the garden—" Bastion furrowed his eyebrows when Mose threw open the glass doors and bolted out, slamming them in his wake. "That can't be good..." Bastion shrunk into his seat.

"Why?" Gene frowned. "Would... I mean, does Mose report to Maida himself?"

"I certainly hope not." Bastion rose and withdrew into the kitchen, picking up a datapad he had left behind.

As he tapped away at its surface, Nikita released a deep exhale and watched him. She couldn't stop the layers of apprehension and despair from forming over him, nor could she find the words to alleviate that sense of uncertainty. She started feeling like that child again, lost in the troubles and secrets of the people around her.

Nikita watched the ripples form in her tea from the vibration of the terrace door opening and closing again. Seeing Malek had been expected, but Casey approached the group with a solemn expression. Both acknowledged Bastion with a nod to draw his attention.

No one stopped Casey from speaking first. "First thing is, I... apologize. Especially to you, Bastion," she muttered. "I was out of line. If you hadn't saved us, there's no telling whether the commander would have made it in time."

Bastion arched his eyebrows, but his words seeped relief. "Thank you, Agent Jaeger."

Casey swallowed and exchanged glances with Malek. Something was off... grave even. Nikita tried to twist a little further to gauge the pair. "The second thing is that I'm here to say goodbye."

"Goodbye?" Vivika repeated.

"Unfortunately, AIA agents are dispensable when we are compromised." Casey folded her arms and rubbed them. "I'm not taking any more chances. Whatever happens now, I'm... sure Maida can protect you. I'm not as lucky."

Gene shifted as he fought to keep his expression steady. "Do you know where you're going?"

"Yeah. But I need to get off this rock."

"A-Are you certain, Agent Jaeger?" Bastion stammered, rising to his feet and clutching the datapad.

"Very."

Bastion looked defeated. He nodded and cleared his throat, addressing the other lieutenant who stood quietly behind Malek and Casey. Mose appeared just as troubled, if not a little more than before. Nikita could hardly shake the heavy sensation growing in her chest. So far, everyone's reactions had been anything but reassuring.

Bastion commanded, "Lieutenant Mose, prepare the Paladin for departure. Agent Jaeger is to be transported—"

"No." Casey interrupted. "If you have... a vehicle. That would be best."

"Just some off-roading cellbikes," Mose rumbled, more to Bastion than to Casey.

Bastion nodded at him.

"I'll prep one for leave." Mose saluted but scrutinized the group one last time before he rushed through the pair of doors at the far end of the living room.

As she watched him storm out, Nikita nearly choked on her words. She struggled to temper the emotional wave swelling within her. None of this seemed fair, and none of it felt real.

Nikita flinched as she stood to meet Casey when she was interrupted.

"No, don't bother. It was...an honor working with each of you. I hope that our paths will cross again. More than you know."

Without waiting for a response from the others, Casey turned to Malek, who had been standing quietly behind her the whole time. They stared at each other for a moment.

"Seriously, why weren't you born a woman?" Casey finally said, walking away.

"*Kafia. Alashban* Zia." Malek rolled his eyes. He exhaled, and his expression shifted. Nikita never seemed to miss the hints of anguish welling up from behind those weary indigo eyes, yet Malek maintained a stoic demeanor despite it. "We'll talk when I'm back." He regarded the rest of the team before following Casey.

The doors closed, shuddering the tea in Nikita's cup. Her thoughts buried her in contemplation. Now she felt conflicted... maybe she should have stayed in the Wilds, maybe explained everything and avoided the fight. Perhaps Bastion wouldn't have needed to rescue them, and Malek and the team might have been spared from whatever lay ahead. The assignment was completed, and the nightmare of the Wilds was over. She needed to stop reliving those dreadful moments before she lost her mind and heart. They did everything right under the circumstances. The Alliance would be happy they got the shard, and the Earthborne would be relieved that their people would be spared from this mysterious sickness and these mutations. If the commander managed to get them to back down, they may have done everything right after all.

The goal was to prevent war, was it not? Nikita sighed deeply. But if the shard was so dangerous, what did the Alliance want with it?

Since the start of the assignment, when she'd first spoken to Maida, she'd had the feeling that as an outsider of the military, she needed to remain objective. She wouldn't allow herself to be used as a means to an end or as an asset to spread conflict. Her research with the Earthborne made her infamous in the academic community for mending bridges between Eiden's people. However, Nikita wondered if any of her actions preserved that, given what happened—or worse, whether providing the Alliance with the shards might have enabled darker motivations.

"Something on your mind, Dr. Valerio?" Bastion's words smoothly pried at her senses.

Nikita slowly turned her cup, studying the painted floral patterns on its ceramic surface without taking in an iota of detail. "Just thinking about the shards. What the Alliance gains from all this."

Vivika shifted in her seat, enough to gather everyone's attention. "You guys want to hear something fragged up?"

"Slag. Always." Gene chuckled, though Nikita could see the scowl behind those laugh lines. "I'm sure it's not half as fragged up as what we saw in the Wilds." He nodded to Bastion. "No offense to you, of course."

"None taken." Bastion shrugged and regarded Vivika. "Please proceed."

"It's about Gunliem... I hadn't really thought about it until now," Vivika said, barely above a whisper. "But the Fireborne never broke *into* that lab. We never found an entry point. We combed that building, and I know we would have seen or heard reports if she'd broken in... I mean, she wasn't exactly subtle in her attacks. She was *there*. The whole time."

"Are you *serious*?!" Nikita hissed, absorbing the gravity of that statement as it rippled through her, like a punch in the gut. "You mean she was a prisoner? And she was *already* mutated?"

Anxiety tightened around Vivika's eyes. "All I know is that she was in that lab before the call came to the JSTG. Whether she was already a mutant, we'll never know."

"Mace..." Gene exhaled, shaking his head and turning to Bastion. "Do you think there's a possibility that Alliance already knew what the shards could do to the Elemnai?"

"Or they may have discovered it." Bastion scrutinized the group, his expression darkening. "It's a bold, if not terrifying, accusation to infer that the Alliance was the root of the attack."

Nikita couldn't fathom what she was hearing. She allowed her leg to rest on the ground and leaned over the table, steepling her hands through her long, curly hair. The pain swam up her limb, pulsating into her head with throbbing fury. "Maida made me believe that it was up to us... up to me, to make sure the Elemnai didn't call for war. In the end, it was just another form of oppression. They want the Elemnai to feel weak. Maybe Casey was right. Maybe we just made the problem worse."

She buried her face in her palms. Adem's face filled her thoughts, as he lay curled and gasping for breath. She hurt, maybe even killed, an Earthborne. She was no better than the Alliance, after all. "I wish I'd stayed home. I wish I'd never accepted this assignment."

A hand gripped her left shoulder, which meant Vivika had reached over, and Nikita had to suppress the tears welling in her eyes from her touch. "We would have been worse off if you didn't join," Vivika murmured close to her ear. "Don't you see?"

"The commander may have guided us forward," Gene's voice resonated across the table, "but you showed us another way of doing things, love. We needed that perspective... more than you know."

"It was your contribution that made the assignment a true victory. You affected the commander and, in turn, stirred something within me," Bastion's soft and reassuring voice flowed over her like a warm breeze. "What you've done is beyond what words can express. It's given me the freedom to be my authentic self, behind all the roles I've assumed. If you have any doubts, know that I have none. Meeting you has been an extraordinary gift. I don't have all the answers. I... I'm scared of what's to come. But I also never felt braver."

"Brave?"

"Yes. Brave enough to be myself. Brave enough to defend you, the others, and what we accomplished. General Maida used to say something to me, oddly, that fits our situation very well."

Nikita finally calmed and scrubbed her face as she faced her friends. She found Bastion's hand, and she could feel those long fingers embrace her own. "What did he say?"

"That fear is for the brave. It means you stood there and looked fear in the eye. Only cowards look away." Bastion chuckled. "It's acceptable to feel scared."

Vivika roped an arm around hers, and Nikita basked in the warmth of her friend as she leaned her head against her own. Gene caught her eye, and he nodded at her, not the nod of a soldier's approval, but the brother's exuding pride.

Nikita had had no idea that she'd had any impact on this team. Memories etched themselves over the canvas of her mind—the shift in Casey's demeanor after Nikita's rescue, the crack in Gene's stoic façade as he laughed with her, and Vivika's relentless protection of her, just like a sister. And Malek… had she convinced him to tread a path of mercy against the Earthborne?

Maybe her impact had been trivial, but she acknowledged that she'd guided the group toward new possibilities, steering them away from the Alliance's default approach of acting first and questioning later. She'd changed her methods, too, as painful as it had been. It might take an eternity to forgive herself for what she did. At least now, she understood why it had to be done. Nikita may have saved many more Earthborne. Maybe that had been necessary to do the right thing and defy the shadows and ignorance of their past experiences.

"Well, in the spirit of facing our fears," she said, leaning into Vivika a little more, her fingers tightening around Bastion's, "I'll try to understand the world a little better the next time I try to save it. As long as we do it together."

Bastion dipped his chin and smiled. "Well said, Dr. Valerio."

CHAPTER 29

EXIGENCY

"I need you to give me a few hours before you report in. As long as you can," Casey said in a low voice.

Malek glanced between her and Mose. The lieutenant rolled a small, but bulky cellbike onto the lowest platform of the terrace, with a stiff upper lip and flushed face. Malek wanted to disappear with her. Honestly, he would miss these candid conversations with Casey. It didn't feel like saying goodbye to an asset, or a fellow soldier.

"Maida isn't going to like this, believe me," she said. "You have to leverage something to soften the blow."

"We have the shard. That should be enough."

"One would think. But there's fallout from the compromised peace agreement." Casey folded her arms and closed her eyes, as if trying to forget their circumstances. He understood that terror. It was the same reason he had felt paralyzed since they'd arrived.

"I'll take responsibility. It was my call that we ended up in the Wilds, and by extension, my call that led to Bastion having to extract us. The others should be spared from the fallout."

"No guarantees, Mal." Casey's expression changed. It was softer, but stern all at the same. "Exile might still be in everyone's cards. Are you fine with that?"

"I think I have to be. Unless we all get some bikes and bail with you."

"They will hunt you if you run. You may not have living relatives, but the others do. They'll be targeted. You don't strike me as the type who can live with that decision."

Malek dropped his eyes to the ground, shaking his head. "I can't." He'd always had a knack for finding a solution, however dangerous, to ensure his survival. But now, he couldn't see the path ahead, no matter how hard he tried...other riding to Khasar or somewhere far away, fragging over everyone else in the process.

He didn't think Casey had more to say until his heart dropped at her question. "Were you in control this time? Of your blackout." She always seemed to know more than she let on.

"Yes." Malek considered mentioning the mysterious figure that haunted his waking moments, whispering and guiding his command of these abilities. He quickly dismissed the thought. The last thing he wanted was for his team to think he might be losing his mind, too.

"Could you leverage that?"

"Not without going back into internment."

"Maybe you won't have to." Casey tilted her body to face him, placing one hand on his arm. "You said it yourself. Maybe the high-risk moves kept you safe. They give you agency."

"And what if it backfires?"

Mose's voice resonated from the lower terrace, calling for Casey. Malek shifted his gaze to the lieutenant, who signaled that it was time to say goodbye. He studied the bare frame of the cellbike, rugged and exposed without its fairings, revealing the raw mechanics underneath—tempting him. He didn't even notice Casey standing on the tips of her boots. She pecked him on the cheek, her lips brushing against his unshaven skin before she pulled away. It jolted him more than anything, like it truly was goodbye.

"Don't let them take you," she said, slipping something into his hand. Before Malek could respond, Casey whipped around and trotted down the steep stone stairs toward the last makeshift platform of Bastion's outpost. Malek stole one last glance at her before she mounted the cellbike, throwing a small rucksack of supplies over her shoulders, and snatched a pair of goggles from Mose's hand.

Malek's thoughts drowned in the roar of the cellbike's engine. It didn't take long for Casey to vanish in the whirlwind of dust as she descended the steep, winding path down the rock face. Malek wondered about the chances of seeing her again. Her friendship had been so unexpected...and he'd needed it, more than he wanted to admit.

Mose's steps disappeared beyond another set of doors at the base of the platform, and Casey's final words haunted Malek in the coming silence. *Don't let them take you.* A chill ran down his spine, and as it did, it petrified every nerve until it reached his extremities. His greatest fear was now teetering on the brink of reality. Malek only realized how long he had been staring at the wisps of sand and dust when the hum of the cellbike's engine became nothing but a mirage.

He couldn't shake the feeling of helplessness. Would Maida forgive this so easily? What would Malek be willing to do now to keep his team safe? To keep himself safe? Would he be willing to surrender everything so they could walk free? Malek's eyebrows furrowed as he stared down at the rectangular device Casey had slipped into his hand. It... looked like a mobile. He tried turning it on, but it was dead. With a sigh, Malek's eyes then traced the scar on his palm—a memento left by his imprisonment at the hands of the GX Forces.

"Thought you'd be down by now," a deep voice spoke from behind him, and Malek turned around to face Gene. If the major had been trying to smile, he did a slag job of hiding the coldness brewing underneath.

"Yeah. Just thinking."

"About our next step?"

"Among other things." Malek glanced toward the vast mountain range and the impossibly narrow paths between the vertical faces. Casey had passed completely out of sight. He took in the thin mountain air again, cooling the heavy feeling in his chest.

Gene folded his arms. "So perhaps, while we wait, are you willing to continue our conversation from the Wilds?"

The tone of that question already put him on edge. Malek closed his eyes for a moment, feeling like an imposter. He noticed that Gene had not once referred to him by his title. Maybe he had lost respect for the role, Malek thought sullenly. Or…maybe he was reading into it a little too much.

"The others are eager to hear, as well," Gene added when Malek never responded.

"I know. It's just…" Malek clutched the device firmly. It was time, whether he liked it or not. "Never mind. Let's go."

Malek's elbows leaned on the glass table in the kitchen, anxiously twirling Casey's mobile in his grasp. It was hard to ignore the eyes of his team settling on him at once.

"Here you are, Commander," Bastion's words were as careful as the act of placing the datapad in front of him. "These are the AIA files you asked me to procure. I… hope it's enough. You don't have to open it now."

Malek stared at it for a moment before he slid the datapad closer. Even though he had a good idea of its contents, he still dreaded what he was about to see. "Thank you. You didn't have to do that."

"I wanted to." Bastion brought a stool and seated himself next to him.

Malek mindlessly began opening several files. He just needed to get this over with. "It started when I was sixteen, while I was in the Support Infantry," Malek started, barely over a hush. "You know, the kids who are never supposed to see a firefight? Had a stroke of slag luck… GX soldiers attacked our outpost. Terminians took over and killed anyone who resisted. I survived. Maida was the commander of an ASF OD at the time," Malek nodded to Bastion, still not daring to look up. "Valiant Squad. Around the time he found you, probably."

"Busy year," Vivika murmured. She sat on the other side of Malek. He could feel her hands wringing under the table. This would all be a lot easier if he could hold them.

"Maida was the first to find me in that outpost," Malek continued. "He was the first person I saw when I woke up. I couldn't remember a damn thing. I was covered in blood...and every single slag Terminian in that outpost was dead. Because of me." Malek's head lowered. "Instead of going home, I was sent to an AIA facility for over a year, so the Alliance could 'figure me out.'"

Bastion shifted in his seat. "I-I read over the AIA files. All of them. And I apologize."

"You don't need to apologize," Malek grumbled, pulling up a file with the initials 'AR - 214 CE'.

"You misunderstand. I am... sorry. For what *they* did."

Malek's breath caught, and his chest tightened. He found himself unable to speak or look away from the datapad. Everyone stared at him, and he couldn't stand it. He wanted to snap the device in half and scream.

"Commander, you were not in detention all those years ago. It's plain to see what it was," Bastion spoke gently. "A-And it's important that we call it what it was. It was unlawful. It was imprisonment. It was torture."

The more Bastion spoke, the more Malek wanted to disappear. He absently continued to open random files, pretending to be a little less present, reeling in the full-on breakdown with calm, steady breaths he forced himself to take.

"The trials they put you through were not meant for training ASF officers, as they indicated in their rationale," Bastion continued. "It's clear from the contents of these files that they were trying to replicate your blackouts to see how they were triggered in the first place. Their methodologies were brutal, a-and certainly not meant for—"

"A kid?" Malek clenched his jaw, instinctively reaching for a cigarette in his pocket, and cursed himself, remembering that he had lost his pack back in the Wilds. He didn't expect Vivika to slide her hand over and intertwine her fingers with his. She'd read his mind. The warmth of her touch blanketed his nerves, bringing his system back to baseline. He stole a glance at her face, which had been drawn to the datapad. She understood protocol as well as he did. At that moment, he didn't have the strength to refuse.

"Yes. A child," Bastion repeated, then let out a long breath.

Nikita cleared her throat, and Malek dreaded the incoming question. "They were hoping you would be able to be triggered?" she asked. "So they could figure out how to make it happen on demand?"

"Yes." Malek swallowed. The memories flooded back, colliding and shattering the walls he had spent a decade fortifying in his mind. Memories of endless syringes, agonizing extractions, and noxious cocktails of drugs that aimed to elicit a physiological response, all made his skin crawl. If not those, there were the countless broken bones, sleepless nights, and... well, Malek couldn't bear to dive in deeper. He wanted to forget. "They tried to replicate the conditions and amplified them. It started with pain... which was also meant to figure out how long it took for me to heal."

He heard Gene curse under his breath as he continued, "Then the conditions would change. They would develop scenarios where I'd feel fear, anger, sorrow... joy, and calm, too. Those were considered good days."

A grim pause followed. Malek wished this would end.

"And," Nikita added softly, "they were never successful, were they? They never got you to black out?"

"Not that I know of."

"How did you leave the program?" Gene asked finally, his voice hitching.

"I wanted to go home. My mom was dying. Maida and I cut a deal to get me out, so long as I joined the ASF after she was gone."

"Then becoming an ASF Officer...?"

"Was survival. As long as I stayed with the ASF, I could avoid internment. I thought if I agreed, I could control what happened to me to an extent. For the last ten years, the blackouts haven't happened often or in obvious ways. R&D never had a reason to take me back, because I never failed as an ASF Officer, or did something... extreme."

"Like take out a horde of Earthborne?" Gene added grimly.

Malek nodded, the realization sinking in his chest like a stone. "Yeah. Exactly like that." He ran his finger and thumb over his eyes. "Mace...."

"If they knew your blackouts returned in full force, you believe that the AIA would not only detain you," Gene finished off. "But the conditions would be more extreme?"

"They were using kid gloves last time." Malek dropped his hand. "And yes. Internment... or worse."

Nikita exhaled, her eyes drawn to his datapad with a solemn expression. "What could be worse?"

"No idea," Malek muttered. Honestly, he felt ridiculous saying what was on his mind. Maida had said something ages ago, while he was held at the AIA facility. The program aimed to develop "the greatest soldier humanity had to offer, to match the Elemnai threat." Malek always thought it was stupid, some bullslag Alliance pipe dream...but maybe there had been something more that he refused to see. He thought about the shards again, and the mutants they'd created.

Something clawed at his mind, and Malek landed on the ring he'd found in the Wilds. That feeling... that nauseating, dizzying sensation that debilitated him every time he faced the shards. It was all connected somehow... Was this why he'd been picked to be in command, after all? Could the Alliance have been preparing him for a far more terrifying fate? He twisted the ring over his finger, unable to place this newfound dread.

"If that is the fear, then why have they not acted upon it?" Bastion asked after a moment of quiet, gesturing to the datapad. "Those files contain footage retrieved from Gunliem, and it was quite obvious back then that your abilities were... improving."

"Who's to say they won't? Everything is different now." Malek shook his head. "Back in the Wilds, up against the Earthborne... that wasn't a blackout. I was aware. And I...I knew what to do. And I wasn't afraid to do it. If anything, it felt—"

"Natural?"

Malek nodded. "Yeah. I was so scared of it ever happening again because of what it meant, that I never wanted to let go and embrace it. Once I did... well, you all caught the rest."

"It was amazing. Made me jealous," Vivika said. Malek looked at her, and she smiled at him, secretly curling her fingers between his. "So, what made you let go?"

"I..." Malek begged himself to stop blushing. "I guess circumstances changed."

"How so?"

Malek tried not to look at her face for so long. "I had people to protect." He cleared his throat, snuffing out the fluttering sensation. He had a sudden urge to pull his hand away and followed through with a pang of regret. He was still her commander. He had to remember his place.

"Congratulations, by the way." Bastion tilted his head at him.

"For what?"

"Mastering your abilities. As Lieutenant Kei said, you were quite impressive during the battle with the Earthborne. I regret that I could not assist you with the revelation sooner."

"I still don't have any idea what I..." Malek paused, looked up at Bastion, and then lowered his voice. Saying it quietly somehow felt like they were talking about someone else, not their personal anomalies. "Do you know what you *really* manipulate? I know it's air... or wind. But it can't be that simple?"

"Electromagnetism. That's my theory." Bastion's golden eyes drew toward the ceiling, and he leaned back in his chair with his arms folded. "I tested my abilities against all known gaseous elements in their stable states. I discovered that I am not controlling any particular molecule, such as nitrogen or oxygen, contrary to my initial assumption. I also did not seem to affect completely inert particles, which I thought was strange. But in our atmosphere, which is primarily made up of nitrogen and oxygen along with dozens of other gasses, I have no issue moving anything. Thus, this pointed me toward something known as electric wind."

"Yeah, ionic wind," Malek added, trying hard to remember his physics courses at university, which he dove into between assignments. It was one of the only things that interested him enough to force him to meet the academic criteria for the ASF. He could feel Nikita eyeing him suspiciously. Yes, Valerio, he had a brain, believe it or not. He didn't bother entertaining her curiosity, either way. "I know where you're going with this."

"Corona discharge," Bastion said. "A strong electric field rips electrons from air molecules, producing free electrons and positive ions. Those accelerated electrons slam into other molecules and create more charge in a runaway avalanche. The moving ions and electrons transfer momentum to neutral air, producing an ionic wind. Therefore, it seems I manipulate the wind, as fabled for centuries. Interestingly, it is the only thing I can manipulate."

Malek frowned, but more at himself. Bastion had clearly put a lot of thought into this. Given everything that had happened to him—from the imprisonment under the Terminians to the testing conducted during the AIA's internment—Malek had never once thought about what he'd precisely felt in those moments. He'd just been terrified of blacking out and being sent back to that cold, bright room, facing another round of needles shoved into his spine or something equally horrifying.

Malek thought about that moment on the cliff with Virat. He had willed him off. Bastion's reasoning for controlling the wind made sense, he supposed, but to flip an entire Earthborne brave with just a thought? What did Malek control? "How do you know you're doing any of this?" Malek said in that same hushed voice. If he were any louder, it would be too real.

"As in, what do I feel?" Bastion plucked the thought right out of Malek's mind. "For myself, it feels as though the air around me is an extension of a limb. I move the air no differently than raising my arm. When I wish to condense the gas particles, it's as if I am flexing a muscle, or inhaling. When I relax or expand, I'm exhaling or stretching out." He tilted his head again, those ebony horns glinting in the afternoon light. "Does that assist you?"

"Not really." Malek rose to his feet. "I need time to think. And...for what it's worth, you're all the first people I've told. About any of this. Valiant Squad has no idea. My best friend, Jace, knows some... but not everything..." Malek ran his hand over the back of his neck but caught himself, and then seized the datapad from the table instead. "I hope that clears up some of what's been going on these past few days. Sorry about your leg." He looked at Nikita. He hadn't expected to see that softened expression on her face. She looked, if anything, relieved. Maybe it all would have been easier if he had owned up to the truth from the start... exactly what she wanted from him in the first place. "And sorry... for not giving you a chance. I didn't want to hear you out, but I needed to."

"Thank you, Commander." Her lips pressed into a cautious but warm smile, which made him feel slightly lighter. "Really."

Malek glanced back at the others. "I know going to the Wilds was a slag call. I shouldn't have put you all through that." He didn't wait for their answers, quickly turning to exit the kitchen with the datapad, heading for the terrace. "I'm going to review these alone. Bastion, I'll let you know when it's time to reach Maida."

"Commander," Gene called after him.

Malek's stomach lurched, and he stifled a groan before he turned to face him. Gene was already advancing. "Thank you. I appreciate... *we* appreciate what you did for us, if that was unclear."

Malek didn't know how to answer that. He simply nodded to Gene and tried to keep moving. A firm hand gripped his shoulder, and his chest caved.

"Malek," Gene's voice tempered into a softer tone. "It was never a slag call. Through it all, you made the right choices. We might not have known each other long, but I've never trusted a commander as quickly or as fully as I trust you. You did what others couldn't—you protected us and made sure we survived despite the odds. I don't care what you are, or what the Alliance thinks you are. We've seen the real you, the one who stands with us in the thick of it and never backs down. And as long as I'm alive, I'll fight beside you, wherever your command takes us."

"Not just Anduran," Vivika said. Malek glanced back. She and Bastion had risen and stood beside Gene.

"All of us," Bastion voiced as coolly as ever.

Malek could feel his eyes burning, but he didn't dare rub them. Although Gene's hand was still on his shoulder, it wasn't enough for Malek to look back again. He had never known that kind of acceptance. And he couldn't handle it. He didn't know how. No amount of gratitude could be expressed without giving way to the mountain of emotion.

"Me too!" Nikita's light inflection rose from behind the group. "And I'm sorry I said I hate you. I really don't. You're just insufferable."

Just like that, everyone chuckled, pulling Malek from his shock.

"Shut up, Valerio. And...thank you," he finally said, nodding. "All of you," Keeping his eyes drawn to the floor, he lifted the datapad. "I... need a minute to look at these."

The terrace door closed behind him, and Malek let out a long, trembling breath. The fresh mountain breeze opened his lungs. That was close. Settling on an old wooden bench nestled between a pair of massive apple trees, Malek pulled up the datapad. It was time to find some answers. Maybe these files would hold the clue to the true nature of his abilities. The anticipation made him sick with restlessness. He had no choice but to begin sifting through the files to find out what the Alliance knew.

CHAPTER 30

DARKNESS

Hours passed like no time at all until the sun sank below the horizon. Malek rubbed his dry eyes. He had been staring at the screen, scanning each relevant file he could find. It turned out it hadn't been very much. All of it seemed obvious to him, at least—Malek had great resilience to pain and recovered faster than the average human, with some notes suggesting he might even surpass El-emnai. Report after report detailed the same pattern of observations, his healing, and his resistance to medication and other drugs. What had been the point of all those tests? Malek's stomach twisted with nausea as he tried to forget being pumped full of some kind of cocktail of drugs, especially when Maida wasn't around. More tests, they would always say. Malek never bothered to tell Maida any of this. They knew that too. He considered it his way of saying "frag you" to his assessors while they despaired, round after round of failures to make Malek use his abilities on command.

Malek's boredom finally morphed into anticipation when the subject of his genetics percolated through the reports. Finally, something new… his DNA analysis. The jargon in the report findings hardly made any sense, and it didn't help that biology had always been his weakest subject in both secondary school and university. Prying at the aged memories of droning genetics topics, one statement finally tugged at his subconscious as he read: "…the estimate would be that 98% base pairs are exactly shared between MR and sample Ast-212, the divergence due to base substitution at 1.2%, and additional 1.8% difference due to the presence of in-dels."

Ast-212.

Malek could feel the edge of Nikita's scorn as she glared at him from behind her desk in Kaira—what had she said? *Its DNA helped us make the connection between humans and Elemnai.* Malek frowned, running a hand over his head. Something slowly settled in his chest like a cascade of water, filling the cavity between his lungs. It suffocated him, and the first vision of the man with the face full of stars overtook his waking sight. It was that same fear and awe that crippled him into a daze that day in the cave, fixating on one word echoing through every synapse in his mind: Anymm.

The sound of the terrace door closing made him drop his hands. It startled him when Vivika stepped out. The memories and the noise immediately disappeared, as if it were a bad dream.

"I'm not coming to bother you," Vivika chirped with her palms raised. She had a pair of gardening shears in one hand. "Just going to harvest the tomatoes and zucchini."

Harvest? Malek watched her incredulously and in silence as she hummed a soft tune, gathering her raven hair into a high, messy bun with a tie. His dread faded, and a calmness washed over him like a river. Kneeling in front of a wild tangle of vines, Vivika clipped a few times, pulling out two long zucchinis and placing them at her feet. Next, she leaned over to a tomato plant, picking several small red ones, along with a heap of green and yellow ones.

"Why are you grabbing the unripe tomatoes?"

"Don't question the process," Vivika called back at him.

"Just help me understand."

With a grin, she picked up her vegetables and placed them on the bench between her and Malek. "The unripe ones are ready, just need some time to change their colors. Place them in the dark, and give them a few days to weeks to turn red." She beamed at him again, those large, beautiful hazel eyes gleaming under the setting sun. "Change is most often seen in darkness."

"That's a hell of an analogy."

"My *oba* used to say that to me." She said, as if measuring whether she should continue. "What they did to you... It's unforgivable. I'm also sorry you couldn't be there for your mom when you wanted to."

"Yeah. You get it."

"I do. It's not easy to admit how much I miss my *oba*. Not many people understand." Vivika looked past him. "They say that time heals all scars, but some scars never disappear. They just become who you are."

Malek leaned back, palming his eyes again as she continued, "I just want you to know that even though I never went through what you did, I understand what it means to live with those scars. It's a lonely existence. And... unless you talk about it, you would never know that the person next to you was just as alone."

Malek snapped his gaze onto her, and she also leaned back into the bench with her eyes lifted to the wind-swept leaves, arms crossed.

"I know you feel like you're in the dark. But the change will be for the better," Vivika said quietly. "I promise you."

"What makes you say that?"

"Like Anduran said. Because we're with you." She tilted her head toward him and smiled. "I'm with you."

"...And if I walk us straight to hell?"

"Then, into the abyss, we'll go. Together."

Malek would have kissed her then and there. Everything about her—those hazel eyes sparkling gold in the fading light, the smile that disarmed him with its warmth and steadied him with its quiet strength—and it wasn't just how she looked. It was what she said. Through the chaos and calm, she'd been there. And she was so damn perfect.

The rumbling of protocol resonated from the back of his mind and it left him paralyzed. All he could do was finally offer her a smile in return and a solemn nod. "Thank you," he murmured. That was stupid. What else was he supposed to say? He cleared his throat and tried to make the situation feel less awkward. "H-Hey, want to see something?" He pulled the datapad closer, and Vivika scooted next to him with an eager grin, her eyes lighting up with a childish sparkle.

"What is it?"

"Something I think you'd appreciate." Malek pulled up the file AR-214. It was an audio recording, so instead of the usual window pulling up a black-and-white feed, it was a single line with a marquee. Malek had thought about the name "AR," and his theory proved correct. It was the single iota of joy he found in all this data.

A faint crackle started the audio feed, then a voice. It was a woman's voice, speaking broken Eidean, *"Who are you?"*

"I am Commander Maida of the Alliance. Forgive my intrusion, but you and I need to speak."

"Maida..."

"You seem like you know who I am?"

"Malek speaks of you."

"Is that your mom?!" Vivika whispered, wide-eyed and excited.

Malek nodded vigorously and gestured for her to listen as Maida continued.

"Oh? Then you understand the nature of my visit."

"No... I don't understand. Where is my son?"

"He's safe. He's at an Alliance facility in Galeo City."

"Then, Commander Maida, you may leave and speak to me when my son is here."

"Unfortunately, that's the reason for my visit."

"What are you saying?"

"We cannot let Malek leave, unless you have information for us."

"Information?"

"Tell me, Amira. Who is Malek's father?"

"Malek's father is Reza. He is dead."

"I...yes, but what other information do you have? Your son's return depends on it."

"Malek's father was a gift to this world. Just like our son. Not you, the Alliance, can take that from me... or him. If you break him, he will pay in kind. If you build him, so will the world. Eiden will rise, simply because he is my son. Take that back to your boss. Tell them that Malek comes home now. Or don't. He will come back, one way or another. Choose, or he will choose for you. Now, get out of my house."

"Ow! Did you just throw a slipper at me?"

"Out!"

The recording stopped. Malek stifled a smirk, and Vivika seized Malek's arm with a hard grip. "Did... she just...throw a shoe at Maida?"

Malek exchanged looks with her. The moment he did, she exploded into a fit of laughter. For the first time since...well, he actually had no idea when, he did too. He laughed until his eyes watered, and his sides hurt.

"I didn't know your mom was such a badass!" Vivika rubbed her eyes and cheeks, with her laughter morphing into a whimper.

Malek's heart jolted, and he dropped the datapad on the bench. "Are you crying? Why? It was supposed to be funny!"

"*Se*, it was. It was!" The more she tried to talk, the more tears came. Before Malek's annoying inner voice kicked in again, his hands reached out and cupped her face.

"Take a breath, V," Malek ran a thumb over the tear rolling down her soft cheek. "What's wrong?"

"Imagine, in all this horrible slag, you found such a beautiful gift. I'm happy for you." She sniffed, dropped her palms at last, and so did Malek. She stared at him through bloodshot eyes. The sight made his heart ache. "I...I wish I could hear my *oba*'s voice one more time..."

Malek chuckled, and thankfully, so did she.

"I never thought of it like that." His face instantly grew hot, and the words tugged at his throat, but that same inner voice didn't reel him in this time. "In all this slag... I... found a lot of beautiful gifts." He held her gaze, envisioning the million other things he wished he could say.

Vivika's lips parted briefly. She scoffed at herself to break the tension. Malek turned away, equally flustered. Adding fraternization to the list of his non-compliances? Idiot. He was still going to be judged for his actions... he shouldn't drag Vivika down with him more than he already had.

"Sorry." She scrubbed her face again before standing with a sharp exhale. Vivika gathered her vegetables in her arms, but a few small tomatoes slipped from her grasp. "I'm cooking tonight, and I could use a hand. Unless you'd rather sit here and keep... looking through memories."

Malek's eyes dropped to the datapad. She wasn't wrong. These were just memories... He already knew that. Reliving the terror wasn't going to let him move forward. Just like Vivika said, it was time to look at changing his colors—to accept what happened, keep going, and live with the scars as part of himself. Malek rose to meet her. He picked up the last tomatoes that rolled around the bench and noticed a blush of red over the pale green skin. Embracing what he was also meant that he would be ready for whatever would come his way.

At least this time, he wouldn't have to face it alone.

EPILOGUE

General Maida gripped the edge of his desk, staring at the holographic comms icon floating above the datapad. Its screen emitted a ghostly pallor in the dimly lit office deep in the heart of Norvica. The Board of Generals awaited an update in the next room. Maida exhaled sharply, casting a troubled gaze at the glittering skyline, the sun scorching the glass panes stretched across towers of steel. The capital city of Devescar appeared as daunting and foreign as ever beyond the expansive windows lining his dismal room.

A faint pulse throbbed against his temple, anxiety bleeding into dread the longer he contemplated and counted the minutes. Malek should have checked in hours ago. He also knew Malek needed time. At least that much, General Madia could afford to give.

However, the longer he waited, the more impatient the Board grew. He didn't want to provoke their ire more than had already occurred. Maida's career was already on the line for allowing Malek to infiltrate the Wilds. Detrimental to the fragile peace agreement, the Board cursed—and even more so, a potential loss of an invaluable soldier.

Slag... Maida needed that update. He needed to know that Malek was alive, and he needed him back. Now.

Disposing of his hesitance, Maida tapped Bastion's name under the comms icon. A steady beep trilled in the vacuum of his office, and his chest tightened at the sound of his officer's familiar voice, "Bastion, here, sir."

"Connect me to Reza."

"Uh...he..." Bastion cleared his throat.

"Spit it out. Has the team exfiltrated the Wilds?"

Maida furrowed his brows at the change in Bastion's tone. "Yes, sir. Commander Reza has successfully...uhh, exfiltrated. The team is intact. The prize has been obtained."

A wave of relief washed over Maida, but the feeling was short-lived when it dawned on him that Bastion was uncharacteristically furtive. "Where is he?"

"Um, shall I connect you?"

"For frag's sake, yes."

"Affirmative, sir. Standby." Bastion paused for a few seconds, and as Maida expected, he relayed the usual message, "I have Commander Reza. Patching you through. Bastion out."

When the line connected at the sound of a familiar beep, Maida didn't waste time. "Commander Reza, where the hell are you?" his voice came out louder than intended, but he didn't care. This wasn't the first time Malek had bypassed protocol regarding open communication, but he'd pushed too far this time.

"With Bastion," came Malek's even reply.

Maida blinked, feeling a weight drop in his center, forcing him to lean over his desk as a breath caught in his throat. "*With*... Bastion?" he repeated, more of a demand than a question.

"Affirmative. At his outpost. And with another shard, secured from the Wilds."

The words hit Maida harder this time, and his heart skipped a beat as dread filled its chambers. Maida clamped his eyes shut, his fingers curling tighter around the desk until the blood drained from his knuckles. Malek was *with* Bastion. He repeated this in his mind while Maida's fury grew by the second. He needed to respond, but he felt voiceless for the first time in a long while. This now meant that, aside from Bastion's handpicked guards, several others, including Malek, knew that the Alliance had an Elemnai in their ranks. The Board would not tolerate this breach.

Malek's voice cut in again, "With Dr. Valerio's help, we were able to—"

"Don't say another word," Maida growled. He couldn't afford to hear more, at least not over an insecure line. Not in here. Not with ears everywhere. He needed to de-escalate the Board before Malek faced them head-on... for both their sakes. No doubt they would want to debrief Malek themselves. "I cannot discuss this with you now. This goes above me. You need to stand before the Board of Generals tomorrow evening in Devescar. Bring the shard and your team. Lieutenant Mose will transport you straight to Alliance HQ. Proceed directly to the hearings floor. I... I will send Bastion the details. I expect a full written report within the hour."

The words spilled out cold and detached, but Maida was reeling in fire and brimstone. He was gambling now, placing faith in the Board's willingness to see reason... and faith that they would overlook this breach in favor of Malek's success in obtaining another shard. The commander could be unpredictable at times, but Maida had to believe that despite the outcome, the Board would see this as a win.

But Malek, ever the wildcard, didn't leave it there. "Why didn't you tell me about him?" Malek's voice sharpened with disdain. "After everything...you couldn't trust me to know?"

The words landed with more weight than Maida cared to admit. Jaw tightening, his mind raced as he searched for the right response. Maida inwardly seethed. He'd never accepted an ounce of insubordination... not even from Malek. "I did trust you," Maida hissed. "But you went against direct orders. No assistance in the Wilds. *That* was the condition for the assignment."

Malek defiantly shot back in a tone that was not expected. "I got the job done. And I got the Earthborne to back down. That's what matters."

"Then you better hope you're getting a fragging medal. You have one hour to submit your report," Maida snapped before cutting the line with a sharp jab to the datapad.

Silence filled the room, broken only by the steady drone of the outside traffic. *Damn it, Malek...* Maida tempered his rising heartbeat by settling in his chair, firmly placing his elbows over his desk, and rubbing the ache in his temples. Despite his fury, he had to remain focused on the facts...Malek had accomplished what no one else could. He brought back two shards on this assignment alone. The Board must forgive this transgression.

A flash of dread clawed at Maida again. One of the greatest secrets in the Alliance had been leaked. The Board would tear them apart for this. All of them, most likely. But in the back of his mind, one thought relentlessly pushed forward beyond all the others: there wasn't just a berating awaiting them.

Maida pulled in the datapad, tapping open his messages and opening one in particular from his aide, Lieutenant Derk. There was no text aligned with the media, but Maida didn't need a description or context. He ran his thumb over his jaw, fixated on the distant but very discernible footage of Malek. His prized soldier stood over the gargantuan figure of an Earthborne brave, twin blades grasped in his crimson-stained hands. The view panned to reveal the dozens of other Earthborne victims scattered across the plateau before cutting out within seconds.

Not only had Bastion been exposed, but so had Malek. Once the Board knew, everything would change. Danger was closing in... on all fronts.

AFTERWORD

Dear reader,

I cannot thank you enough for reading my debut novel. Publishing this book was a long and demanding journey, but it becomes meaningful the moment it reaches a reader. Knowing that this story found its way into your hands, and that you gave it your time and attention, fills me with genuine gratitude... and maybe some tears.

This project began in the summer of 1997, which is to say—when I call it a long road, I truly mean it. What started as an idea in the mind of a little girl grew slowly, patiently, through years of change, doubt, and persistence. If you've enjoyed this story, know that in reading it, you've helped fulfill a dream that has been quietly carried for decades. And if you really enjoyed this story, please consider leaving a supportive review!

Malek, Nikita and the team will return in Books Two and Three of *Eiden Ascendant*, where their fight will deepen...not just against external threats, but against the systems that define, confine, and command them. As the cost of their actions mounts, so too does their search for something far more elusive than victory: freedom.

This is only the beginning. I hope you'll stick around as the story continues.

Sincerely,
Sarah N. Yusuf
For more art, updates, and goodies:

www.eidenascendant.ca
Instagram: @sarah.yusuf.creates

www.ingramcontent.com/pod-product-compliance
Lightning Source LLC
Chambersburg PA
CBHW071248170626
46809CB00001B/121